D0098272

BROWSING COLLECTION
14-DAY CHECKOUT
No Holds • No Renewals

The
Peach
Seed

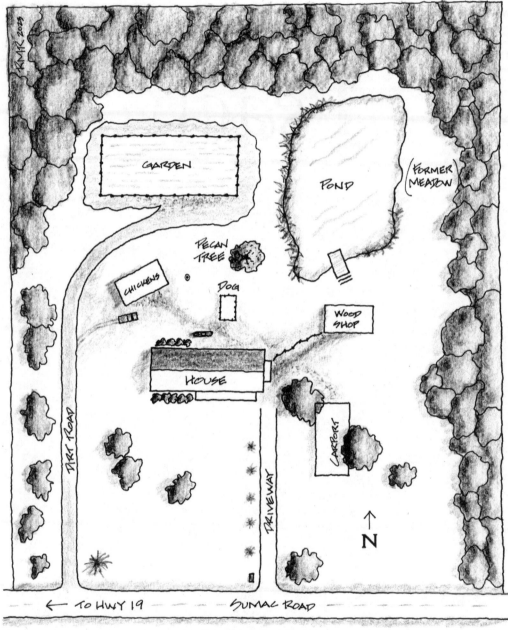

FLETCHER'S PROPERTY

The Peach Seed

~

Anita Gail Jones

Henry Holt and Company
New York

Henry Holt and Company
Publishers since 1866
120 Broadway
New York, New York 10271
www.henryholt.com

Library of Congress Cataloging-in-Publication Data is available.

ISBN: 9781250872050

Our books may be purchased in bulk for promotional, educational, or business use.
Please contact your local bookseller or the Macmillan Corporate and Premium Sales
Department at (800) 221-7945, extension 5442, or by e-mail at
MacmillanSpecialMarkets@macmillan.com.

First Edition 2023

Designed by Meryl Sussman Levavi

Printed in the United States of America

1   3   5   7   9   10   8   6   4   2

For my family ~ past, present, and future

To Silas, Irene, and Bettye
For all that you are

For me, a peach-seed monkey has become a symbol of all the promises which were made to me and the energy and care which nourished me and created me as a human being. And, more fundamentally, it is a symbol of that which is the foundation of all human personality and dignity. Each of us is redeemed from shallow and hostile life only by the sacrificial love and civility which we have gratuitously received.

~ Sam Keen, *To a Dancing God*, 1970

~

One could not be in any Southern community for long and not be confronted with the question of what a man is, should do, or become. The world in which we live is, after all, a reflection of the desires and activities of men. We are responsible for the world in which we find ourselves, if only because we are the only sentient force which can change it. What brought this question to the front of my mind, of course, was the fact that so many black men I talked to in the south in those years were—I can find no other word for them—heroic. I don't want to be misunderstood as having fallen into an easy chauvinism when I say that: but I don't see how any observer of the Southern scene in those years can have arrived at any other judgment. Their heroism was to be found less in the large things than in small ones, less in public than in private. . . . What impressed me was how they went about their daily tasks, in the teeth of the Southern terror.

~ James Baldwin, *No Name in the Street*, 1972

Act I

~

The camel driver has his plans and the camel has those of his own.

~ BERBER SAYING

1

Albany.

A southern city running on country fuel.

Divided east to west by the Flint River, this corner of southwest Georgia is graced with majestic pecan groves and wildflower carpets buffered by blue skies; a region where flip sides coalesce, modern and antebellum, old growth and new wood. A place of long, deep pain, still refusing forgiveness; and yet propelled by joys and triumphs. In many ways, even in 2012, life here was the same as it was fifty years ago: a patchwork of citizens—from farmers and businesspeople to college students—going about their days as any other, separate and unequal.

Fletcher Dukes lived a few miles south of town in a widening-in-the-road called Putney. His property has been in their family since before he was born, back when a Black man wasn't likely to own a paltry lot, let alone seven acres.

Fletcher's single-story brick house sat on three acres. A long driveway shot like a red clay ruler, straight from Sumac Road into

Fletcher's front yard. If you parked a line of cars bumper to bumper, Car #1 would touch his front porch, and Car #10, his mailbox.

His property's back section faced north and included a four-acre pine forest stretching out eastwardly in an L-shape, and wrapping around a large meadow where two rusting cars and a pickup had become fixtures. Kudzu mushroomed through windshields, and dog fennel hugged flat tires.

It was unseasonably hot for March. Engulfed by diesel fumes, Fletcher paused, his body jiggling to the old tractor's rhythm. He used a crisp, white handkerchief to wipe sweat from his neck, then swerved in a wide turn, and maneuvered around each vehicle to mow down what was left of weeds.

Tractor parked, he paused in his seat. If he closed his eyes, hot wind blowing through pines could be waves breaking on a beach somewhere. He had time for a shower before picking up his elder sister, Olga, who lived across town, for their weekly grocery run.

A little while later, Fletcher pulled his Ford Fairlane into Piggly Wiggly's parking lot, grumbling to Olga about a red Volvo wagon hitched to a U-Haul trailer and parked across three spaces.

"Now whoever this is from Michigan ought to park this rig out on the edge and leave these good spaces up front for local folk."

Olga, who was slowly losing her sight, said, "We got our handicap space no matter what."

Ordinarily she would have more to say about northern license plates, but as she adjusted to blindness, she had become more and more quiet. Her reticence continued as a pink-faced man joined them, walking toward the front doors.

"Yeah, I seen'er pull in," the man drawled, "act like she own the place."

Fletcher chuckled. "Well, I guess they don't teach 'em how to park up north."

"Whoever she is," he said to Olga, his hand cupping her elbow, "she can't be all bad: got Obama/Biden in her windshield."

As always, they started in produce, Olga pushing, with Fletcher holding both lists, out front guiding. They turned down the liquor aisle, headed for meat, poultry, fish.

Fletcher smelled her perfume first, a scent he knew well but could no longer name; a soft powdery bouquet that instantly made him think of Altovise Benson.

He and Olga walked slowly past a tall woman with short, wavy, salt-and-pepper hair and skin in shades of paper shell pecans. Her head was bowed reading a wine label, revealing smooth, clear skin at the nape of her neck—a spot women in Fletcher's life call their *kitchen*. This woman had a birthmark in her kitchen: a perfect strawberry, almost like a tattoo. This, together with her perfume and long beaded earrings, gave Fletcher reason to hurry past, his heart throbbing. He was grateful that Olga wasn't in a talkative mood.

At checkout, he watched, thinking about Michigan plates. All six of Altovise's albums were recorded in Detroit.

Olga chatted with her cashier, a former student, as Fletcher split his attention between the aisle and his sister's hand holding her ATM card.

If only he could glimpse the woman's hands, he was sure he'd see matching medicine knot tattoos beneath each wrist. Altovise was part Muscogee Creek.

She rounded the corner, pushing her cart away from him. He took a few steps back, needing to see her walk to confirm what he already knew.

"I'll be damn," he whispered, his heart lurching.

Like watching a scene in a favorite movie, he smiled at her long strides, slightly slue-foot. He was only four months older but seemed like a relic by comparison. His granddaughters would say Altovise was fierce in her crisp white oversize shirt. Denim legs vanished behind a Coke display and Fletcher flashed on walking hand in hand, her with a giant teddy bear, at Dougherty's county fair. If Olga only knew how close they both stood at that moment to their very own Altovise.

As they fastened seat belts, Olga said, "Well, that doesn't happen every day."

"What you mean?"

"Estée Lauder Youth Dew. I smelled it in the store on somebody. That's an old-timey perfume, was everywhere in the '50s and '60s, but not that much anymore."

Fletcher stared ahead at Michigan plates, which now took on a completely different meaning.

He couldn't explain why he didn't mention Altovise as he drove Olga home. Later, he would look down through the backbone of this day in search of signs he had missed, and he would recognize that red Volvo wagon as the calm before a storm called Altovise Benson—walking around his Piggly Wiggly. After fifty-two years.

❧

Before dawn, Fletcher's bedside radio hissed a song buried in static, and he woke from a shallow, restless sleep. Eyes still closed, radio off. Altovise's face played behind his lids like a beautiful song stuck in his head.

"Onethingaboutit," he said out loud, feet hitting bedroom slippers, "she ain't just here for a quick visit."

Seconds later, another song blared from the kitchen and Fletcher scuffed past the living room, reminded that he could stop by his vinyl collection and pull every one of Altovise's albums. The old spinet had sat idle in the living room since the twins, Georgia and Florida, gave up piano lessons after junior high school, leaving shining mahogany to take on life as a what-not shelf and photo gallery. In other words, a haven for Florida's feather duster. Usually, keys and springs complained silently, but now they conjured Altovise's music, and left him thinking how you have to be careful what you wish for: as he made plans to dig a pond in the meadow, he welcomed any distraction from having to get into it with his grandson, Bo D, around the junk vehicles. But Altovise Benson was not what he had in mind.

Bedroom slippers hit kitchen linoleum. Rockhudson, his liver spots speckled with gray, sat dutifully by his bowls as Fletcher started just enough grits for one.

With Minnie Riperton on the radio, hitting notes too insanely high for such an early morning hour, Fletcher pulled his last slice of cured ham from the refrigerator. Rockhudson stared him down until he filled his bowl with kibble.

Fletcher reserved these morning hours for ruminating about family problems. Whatever he could carve off before time to wash dishes, he would act on. Otherwise, he moved on until breakfast tomorrow. He tried to sift through ongoing problems with Bo D, but Altovise Benson kept cutting him off. She must be sick—that always brought people home. But she sure didn't look sick.

Ham sizzled in hot grease.

Fletcher heard that Bo D was working long hours, but what was he doing with his time off? Water splashed over hot pan drippings to make red eye gravy. He would ask Olga what her spies knew about Bo D's whereabouts. He fried an egg for himself and cracked one into Rock's dish.

After breakfast, as Fletcher dried and put away dishes, a devout Friday rose over Dougherty County, sending a golden blade of light jutting across a legal pad on his dining table. Since talking to Bo D no longer worked, he sat down to write a note.

He had first thought to send a telegram, but you can't do that anymore, and he wouldn't know how to send a text even if he owned a cell phone.

Fletcher squinted through reading glasses, yellow pad pulled closer, away from blinding glare, and took a direct action: even his chicken scratch would demand Bo D's attention:

You have ten days. At 9:00 a.m. sharp on March 30 a tow truck will remove your junk from my property.

With his note neatly folded and tucked in his shirt pocket, Fletcher stepped out into a church fan painting: lacy-green leaves sat motionless on laurels and live oaks, lit by the crystal light of spring.

He drove to Hooper Tire, where he found Bo D's 1969 Mach 1 parked away from the crowd, as usual. He slipped his note under the wiper and couldn't help but smile at his reflection bouncing up from a hard-wax finish, shimmering like black glass.

&

Ten days. Fair enough warning, but March 30 came with no word from Bo D. In spite of this, Fletcher's pond-digging project gave him plenty of tasks that mainly involved dealing with white people he didn't know, either on phone calls or in their places of business. Living on Albany's outskirts, he could have as much or as little contact with folks as he wanted, and thereby avoided gossip around town about Altovise. It was odd that Olga—who knows everybody's business—had not once mentioned her. Barbershop day was coming, and Fletcher was gearing up to punt, knowing his barber, Blue Jean, would be ready to talk about their work together in the Albany Civil Rights Movement.

Along his property's west edge, a second driveway stretched for several yards, looping around to his backyard. Fletcher was on tow truck watch, pacing along this narrow belt like an expectant father. His boots sank into springy, moist ground, crunching through pine needles, shocking green moss, and leaves. Routine sounds hovered near and far: cackling hens, a chain saw, a bobwhite's nonstop call.

Fletcher paced on. These seven acres were his blood. He had once been sure he'd spend his life on this land with Altovise. The day he chased her around his pecan grove began as his life's dream, and was a nightmare by the time he drove her home. Every inch of this land connected parts of him, and at every turn he could shave off memories to savor or regret.

He pulled his shoulders back, thinking of Altovise's perfect posture. Without a doubt, the soon-to-be-seventy warranty was up on a few of his body parts, but his barbershop buddies still envied his tall, sturdy physique that had gone soft only in places that didn't matter from afar. When his wife, Maletha, died seven years ago, he instantly became a target for her fellow churchwomen, divorced, widowed, and otherwise. This repulsed him and further validated not being a churchgoer. Family ties have always been religion enough for him. He harbored dreams and hopes for his kin and for himself, separate pockets, same pair of pants, starched and ready. As with any religion, there are tests of faith. When least expected, a dream will slip through a pocket hole—happens all too often with Bo D.

In the six years since high school graduation, Bo D's rusting vehicles—inventory from an abandoned car restoration business— had become a problem that Fletcher finally knew how to solve. In another two months, instead of a meadow, he'd have a fishing pond. But even thoughts of fried catfish from his own backyard couldn't tamp down a solid fact: what he was about to do would make a bad situation worse.

Fletcher fiddled a dried peach seed in his pocket, stepping heedfully around fire ant nests—mounds of red clay scattered like land mines through wire grass and sandy spurs. Up near the mailbox, in car spot #10, OBAMA/BIDEN 2012 signs flashed red, white, and blue. Four years ago, Fletcher had edged his property along Sumac with yard signs like a Burma-Shave campaign, and reveled in a victory he never thought he'd live to see. Olga's election night party had gone until dawn. Fletcher told Bo D the whole world was witness to a historical miracle. Now, they focused on President Obama's second term, and Fletcher had a feeling of naive hopefulness that comes with spring. If gray, hard tips of winter branches can soften under a bud's pressure, and a woman can materialize from the dust of memory, then anything is possible. Barack and Michelle can be back in the White House in November, and at any minute, Bo D's Mach 1 could pull in.

Fletcher whistled. Seconds later, Rockhudson lumbered toward him.

"Good boy." Fletcher rubbed Rock's short, bristly coat, checking for ticks. "You got a smile on your face, must've been a good walk." Both man's and dog's muscles recollected swifter days.

Fletcher uprooted young dandelions with his steel-toed boot, his mind crossed with a question Olga had asked recently:

You and Bo D are in the thick of it again, she had said, *but the question is—are you showing your teeth, your belly, or your hands?*

He was in no mood for Olga's sayings. He knew he couldn't kiss Bo D's fallen dreams up to heaven—like a piece of candy that touched the floor—so he focused on the move he could make.

Dust clouded as a well-polished, electric-green flatbed tow truck pulled in. Anthony Smith was driving. He had been Bo D's friend and former business partner, the Mach 1 being their one and only car restored to mint condition that sweltering summer after high school.

"Hey, Anthony. How you?" Fletcher approached the open window.

"Doing fine, Mr. Fletcher, you?"

"Not bad—heard you and your wife getting ready to be parents. Congratulations!"

"Yes, sir, I'm more than a little nervous, I can tell you that!"

"You'll make it. You starting out whole-footed." Fletcher raised his chin. "Not quite nine yet. Get you a cup of coffee while you wait?"

"Naw, sir, got it covered." Anthony held up his thermos and gestured toward Sumac Road. "You reckon he'll show up?"

"I expect not."

"Been a long time since I seen Bo D," Anthony said. "If he do come I bet he'll be ready to cuss me out."

"This is strictly business—between you and me." Fletcher pointed at Anthony. Then he and Rock walked back toward the house.

Months after Maletha died, the first time Fletcher opened the back door and told Rockhudson to go in, the dog backed away, whining. It took a few tries before he would set foot on the slick linoleum, skating, claws spread wide, eyes peering around.

"It's OK, boy," Fletcher urged him, "she don't mind. She told me so."

Indeed, he'd heard it many times from Maletha, *When I'm gone you can do whatever you want; bring in dogs and even chickens—and won't that be grand!*

When his pocket watch showed 9:00 A.M., Fletcher signaled Anthony, setting levers and chains into motion, cranking a '72 Chevy pickup from its weedy grave. Clanking metal swallowed up the morning stillness and bobwhite's song.

Bobbing his head to music, Fletcher washed his hands and pulled a can of biscuits from the refrigerator. Spongy, pale dough exploded with a pop. Maletha would be turning over in her grave. She taught him to make biscuits in this kitchen shortly after he built the house, as he was growing his contractor business.

He circled one of many cast-iron skillets with flat, sticky biscuit discs, misshaped by his calloused fingers. Metal scraped against metal as biscuits went into the oven.

Center stage on his kitchen table was Maletha's old punch bowl, iridescent blue, rescued from museum state in her china cabinet and given a job: holding mail and paper supplies. He and Maletha enjoyed cooking together. Their kitchen became neutral ground. Time among pots and pans was off-limits for arguing. It wasn't unusual for her to end a heated discussion by patting a nearby surface with both palms saying, "Let's table that for now. I feel like some biscuits. You?"

He had not made biscuits from scratch since she died.

Rockhudson raised his head and whined as a fake-buttery-biscuit aroma encircled them. Fletcher fished his checkbook out of the punch bowl, preparing to pay bills.

His oven timer went off and Fletcher watched through the screen door as Anthony finished loading the Chevy and pulled away.

"There you go, boy." He crumbled warm biscuits into Rock's dish, then slathered another two with butter and went cupboard fishing for a fresh bottle of sugar cane syrup.

2

~

Heavy bass vibrated a hip-hop soundtrack to Terrence "Bo D" Fowler's windshield movie: frilly green leaves sparkled in vibrant March sun. Budding pecan branches arced like fireworks and azaleas lined Highway 19 South in a magenta blaze. Bo D wore a gold chain necklace holding a tiny monkey carved from a peach seed. He rubbed the charm across his lips, tasting sweat from his morning weight-lifting session.

A handwritten note from his grandfather was a first. Fridays are his day off, his grandfather knew that, so why would he expect him to be up and out at 9:00 A.M.? Bo D had every intention of being on time, just to prove a point, but he stuck with his Thursday night routine and took an oxy before bed.

He overslept and still had to do his curls, so this called for borrowing energy from his version of a highball—a custom mix of weed, Adderall, and beer—a perfect balance to normalize things before facing his grandfather. He was proud of this personal cocktail, took years to perfect, and he had it down to a science, tweaking the drugs to match his various situations: family, work, and otherwise. He added meth when he needed more energy. Not necessary today.

Now that he was in his car with music pumping, and drugs surging, he had a quiver in the pit of his stomach. He knew he was late, but at least he was showing up. There was a time when that would get him points. His grandfather hadn't understood him in a very long time. How had they landed on opposite ends of mistrust and empty threats?

Bo D had always been interested in anything with wheels. Shortly after mastering his BMX Mongoose, he became addicted to cars. He and his grandfather were inseparable then; shade-tree mechanics, fighting gnats as Bo D stood on wooden crates learning to read engine sounds on Fletcher's '59 Ford Fairlane. Years later, they installed a new exhaust system; his grandfather was reluctant at first but ended up liking that souped-up feel.

With thoughts shifting into overdrive, Bo D switched off the music to listen to his Mach 1's deep V8 rumble. He counted north-bound cars until time to exit.

He had left behind the pampered lawns and mini mansions of Dove Cove, the mostly white development where he lived with his mother. Driving into Putney, the landscape changed to small ranch houses with spacious country yards, rickety sheds, and woodpiles.

His highball threatened to turn Bo D's stomach. Really his life turned his stomach: He was a father but not a husband. He had a job and no career. He lived in a house that was not his home.

He pulled off Sumac Road into his grandfather's long driveway, and parked in spot #1.

"Fuck that!" He smacked the steering wheel, seeing Anthony's shiny bright green tow truck.

He walked toward his grandfather's woodshop a few yards away. He kicked a pink beach ball farther into the yard before stepping inside to watch Anthony loading the '88 Impala. Sawdust and the mercy of wood summoned memories from when Bo D was three— same age as his daughter, Cricket, owner of the pink beach ball. He'd spent many hours in this cozy room, piano-stool spinning while sanding a block of wood as his grandfather built furniture or whit-tled toys and peach seed monkeys.

Anthony seemed to glance toward Bo D's Mach 1. Would his ex-friend walk over to talk? And if so, what could he possibly say?

Bo D marched toward the house, fingering his necklace. Before entering, as always, he tucked his peach seed monkey charm inside his T-shirt collar.

When he walked in, his grandfather was scrubbing cast iron and did not look up.

"Damn, G-pop." Bo D stood in the doorway. "You couldn't cut me some slack? I was on my way."

"You over an hour late." Fletcher placed the skillet on a burner to dry and glanced at Bo D. "And you forgetting something."

Bo D removed his baseball cap and slowly tucked it into his back pocket.

"Why you just up and had my stuff towed like that? That was inventory!"

"You had plenty warning," Fletcher said.

"Shoot. I thought that note was a ticket at first."

With a wadded-up paper towel, Fletcher oiled the dry, hot skillet.

"C'mon, G-pop." Bo D aimed for levity. "Even Visa gives you a grace period."

"Grace?" Fletcher said, oily towel flung into sink. "You don't know a damn thing about grace—not unless she's wearing some high heels and a miniskirt. And onethingaboutit, Visa ain't nothing but a pack of white folks that'll give you just enough rope to lynch yourself."

Anthony knocked on the screen door. Bo D turned.

"C'mon in, Anthony," Fletcher said.

"Hey, man!" Anthony smiled.

"Hey." Bo D's face was stern.

They cupped palms and moved in stiffly to bump shoulders.

Fletcher interrupted. "Thanks, Anthony. Now you remember—you promised me right of first refusal on that Chevy C10."

"It's yours, Mr. Fletcher. You want ASU blue, right?"

"That's right. Maybe they'll let me drive it in the homecoming parade."

With his highball lifting him above the moment, Bo D watched in silence as Anthony awkwardly said his goodbyes and left.

"So," Bo D whacked his baseball cap on his leg, "instead of you just giving away my inventory, Anthony and his daddy ought to be cutting you in on some profit."

"Business is business," Fletcher said, trashing the slick paper towel.

Bo D flung his cap next to the punch bowl. "And Anthony? Of all the tow truck companies in Albany, you picked his daddy's?"

"Him and his daddy full partners now," Fletcher said. "Anthony's got himself a future."

"So now you sayin I ain't got no future?"

"Don't much matter what I say." Fletcher's back was turned, wiping countertops. "It's all about what *you* gone *do*."

"Fuck it then," Bo D snapped, surprised that his grandfather let the cuss word slide.

In that slip of time before his grandfather turned, Bo D yanked his little monkey from hiding at his collar and dropped chain and monkey into papers in the punch bowl.

He put on his baseball cap, visor twisted to the back, and let the screen door slam behind him.

❧

Just after nightfall, Fletcher put away leftover meat loaf and cabbage. Spring air was still sticky with heat, like summer days when the girls were young; barefoot, jumping double Dutch and chasing fireflies, with a rotating flow of cousins.

Over time, he and the house had found a way of living without Maletha. He spreaded-up his bed every morning and tucked pajamas under a pillow. His biggest stockpot held dirty dishes in the sink under its lid until he could get to them. Now, ever present in his quiet rooms was the hidden smell of citronella sewing machine oil, and remnants of giggles and quarrels.

He had never talked about being overwhelmed in a house full of females. Wasn't exactly something a man goes around whining about. One day he called one of the daughters "son." He doesn't remember which one or why? All three girls were very young, and to them it seemed like just another nickname, something to bring them closer to Daddy. In 1981 when Georgia and Florida turned thirteen, they began emulating their fifteen-year-old sister, Mozell. Fletcher and Maletha put a quick end to all three trying to sneak out to a party in denim shorts and sawed-off T-shirts, navels out to the world, hair whipped into frenzied ponytails and tied with bandannas on top of their heads. They had one full-blown and two burgeoning obsessions with Sugar Hill Gang rap music and rooms plastered with "Girl Power" posters.

"Where you think you going?" Maletha asked the girls, headed for their seldom-used front door to meet their cousins' idling car out on Sumac Road. "Y'all live in the middle of seven acres at the end of a small airport runway. And this is your plan for sneaking out?"

Fletcher had to use all his power not to laugh.

"To your rooms," Maletha added. "Change your clothes. I'll take care of your car service."

Maletha had a way of rising above child-rearing drama, tempering their would-be stormy adolescent years. Except when she joined all three daughters' loud revolt around being called "son." Fletcher couldn't say it out loud, but he had been desperate for anything to restore the peace of bygone days when his girls thought he was their hero.

And right in the middle of their lives, covertly observing, absorbing: three mint condition peach seed monkeys lived in Maletha's jewelry box, MADE IN ITALY, with a rose inlay, still sitting on top of their chest of drawers. With each daughter's birth, Fletcher carved a monkey, ready to bestow tradition upon sons. Maletha carried Mozell high and wide (predictions say a girl), and Georgia and Florida were low. This, of course, raised his hopes. He sorted through a mountain of seeds to find two that were mixed but perfectly matched. In a more meddlesome way than Maletha, those little charms haunted him. Maletha fussed and hounded, but she also still made him laugh out loud. Though he hid it well, those three peach seed monkeys scratched at his remorse at not having boys. His answer: close jewelry box, turn key, move on.

He and Rockhudson followed sixty feet of white Christmas tree lights, draped on a line, from kitchen door to woodshop door. Their father-son tradition infuriated Maletha to no end: watching their three girls join other Dukes women on the sidelines.

"Why not carve monkeys for the boys *and* the girls?" she would say. "Stands to reason that we all want to keep the monkey off our backs."

Fletcher didn't expect her to understand. Her family didn't have a ritual that had been theirs alone since slavery.

"Tradition is tradition for a reason" was his adamant reply, to which she'd counter:

"Dukes. We're not talking about green eyes or freckles, those things are not arbitrary. Your beautiful rite of passage is precious and sacred, but it is, after all, a choice."

"Look like we just have to agree to disagree," Fletcher said.

"That's bullcrap," Maletha said. "You know as well as I do that never works."

This was one issue she never tabled. The last time she stepped over agreeing to disagree was when Fletcher had to carve a monkey for a great-nephew three months before she died. Their war of words never lost its potency, on either end, and nothing ever changed. At least not from Fletcher's point of view.

He slipped on reading glasses, radio dialed to jazz, and sorted through half-carved peach seeds stretching across a shelf, each speaking the same deep-rooted language Fletcher could not hear and yet fully understood.

He was blasting "Stormy Monday" and organizing carving tools in two old cigar boxes, separating sandpaper and cloths from awls, rat-tail files, and knives. He ran his hand along ebony wood boards waiting to be assembled into a set of bookcases Olga commissioned for a special collection of books and memorabilia she was donating to Albany State University. Her order calling for divided-light doors may prove to be too much with everything else going on in his life.

From his bed under the saw table, Rockhudson's snoring mixed with Coltrane's saxophone as Fletcher moved on to sharpening penknives and jackknives. After a few songs, a headlight beam broke through the window, sending shadows dancing on walls.

"Ourdaddy," his daughter Florida said seconds later, leaning on the doorjamb, her face a glow in Christmas tree lights.

"Hey, son," Fletcher said, quickly registering Florida's brow of concern.

"Don't you be *Hey-sonning* me like nothing's wrong—I been calling and calling you since dusk dark."

"Who's hurt?"

"Nobody. I was beginning to think *you* were." She lingered in the doorway, arms folded across chest. "I knew you were up to something, but I can guarantee you, this is like throwing kerosene on a fire." She held up Fletcher's yellow note. "Found it in Terrence's room."

"I can see why he wants to padlock his door," Fletcher said, focused on sharpening.

Miles Davis' trumpet was too mellow for the mood as Florida walked closer. Fletcher noted an essence of gin on her breath, laced with lemon and mint.

"I know you know my policy," she said, "since I learned it from you: whatever is under *my* roof is *my* business.

"Seem like everybody in this family think they know better than me what's best for my son. Just like that nickname thing—I don't want folks calling Terrence by no so-called gangsta name. Bo D. What's that suppose to even mean? Auntie Olga always telling me, *Pick a different battle, Florida, 'a rose by any other name would smell as sweet.'* I hate when she quote that Shakespeare stuff. How come she can't quote scripture like everybody else?"

"You working on making a point?"

"Point is—you don't need to be slipping him notes, Ourdaddy. Y'all need to be talking. Man-to-man."

Fletcher turned to face her. Florida crossed her arms tighter and looked away.

"You all in the Kool-Aid and don't know the flavor," he said, looking straight at her now, "but you *do* know better than to drink and drive."

"I'm fine."

"You may think that, but we can't be letting you shuttle Cricket around if you gone be driving like this." He turned, putting away cigar boxes. "I'm through talking. Present moment included."

Florida left. Fletcher repositioned peach seeds, and Rock followed him back into the house.

He passed up television in the den for his living room activity: an ongoing solo chess game. Thanks to their arthritic piano and Maletha's gold velvet French provincial furniture, this room was half museum, half man cave. Decades of family portraits populated walls and shared a large shelving unit with Fletcher's late '80s stereo system, complete with turntable, cassette, and CD decks. He had an annex stack of puzzle books and magazines, and too many bowls of peach seeds lying around. Sitting atop a table by the window, his lazy Susan chessboard waited. He made it right after Maletha died; his interpretation of traditional pieces using various scrap woods. Often during chess he listened to his vinyl collection. Altovise's six albums remained front and center: a scant one inch of vinyl real estate covering immeasurable ground. Except for Florida and her relentless cleaning, he never invited anyone in. He could hear Maletha—*use this living room, Dukes, entertain guests like folk.*

At times it seemed odd that Maletha and Altovise never met. Olga called them both *plucky*, a word Fletcher thought was still sticking to Olga after living all those years among white people in Amsterdam. But she had a point. Both women were determined.

Maletha Givens was from Tallahassee, Florida. She and Fletcher met at a mixer at Albany State a year after Altovise left. Maletha was a freshman, studying to be a teacher. Fletcher was working in construction and had dated only a few times, still on the rebound from Altovise. Olga forced him to attend the mixer. He and Maletha connected that night around many things. Not long after, rumors of Fletcher's drinking found her, although she had not yet seen him drunk. In his way of confronting things head-on, he broached the subject and she said—for the first of what would be many times—"People talk no matter what. You can't control what they say; so worry about what you can worry about. I'm with you now, and if you want to be with me, then we don't have any problems."

Maletha graduated in three years, a time they spent in a slow, intense courtship, which ended in marriage a year later.

In 1972, they were seven years in and had a six-year-old and four-year-old twins when Altovise's first album moved into the house on Sumac Road. Fletcher spoke freely about the album to ward off any discomfort for him and Maletha.

Sundays when Maletha took their girls to church, Fletcher played Altovise's albums most freely. One of her gospel blues tracks, "Same Train," became his anthem, his church. A few of Maletha's fellow church members had also worked in the Movement and knew all about Fletcher's relationship and breakup with Altovise. When Fletcher's collection grew to three albums, once again he talked to Maletha and she said, "Now Dukes. How could I, a grown woman, hold a grudge against *your memory* of a teenage Altovise Benson, on the brink of discovering who she is? What kind of woman would that make me?"

Fletcher often chose music based on which mood his family had brought out in him. Resuming his chess game, he opted for quiet, to hear himself think.

Florida was too easy on Bo D. Being young and bullheaded was like a fishing line that only goes so far before you have to reel it back in. If only he could get all these young folk to understand his methods behind what they can only see as an old man's madness.

The phone rang.

"Dukes here." Fletcher paced, phone cord trailing behind him.

"How you?" Olga said.

"Better than I've been."

"I take that to mean towing is a done deal."

"Yep. Hours ago."

"I'm sure that came as a shock to Bo D."

"Oddly enough—it did."

"Well," Olga said, "it's like my Berbers say, *the camel driver has his plans and the camel has those of its own.*"

"Heard that a time or two."

"Fletcher. You spent three years rebuilding that bridge over troubled water with Bo D. I think you just knocked it back down with one big blow."

"In that case," Fletcher said, "it's a good thing I know how to swim, so both of us won't drown."

A pause between them was never wholly quiet.

"We started spring cleaning," she said. "What day you coming to touch up my stove?"

"That's up to you. Just let me know."

Fletcher sat down at his chess table and before spinning to the black side he glanced at a bowl of peach seeds on the windowsill. He hadn't seen Bo D's monkey since his rite-of-passage ceremony—no doubt lost, stolen, or broken. He needed music after all, and chose Altovise's album #3: *Dance 'Til You Knock the Blue Do' Down.*

He set the black king upright, studying moves, his head bobbing to Altovise's raunchy vocals.

"Would you look at that." His smile bent as he moved his black queen to e4.

"Check. Mate."

3

Lift. Walk. Bend. For twelve hours straight, these three moves defined Bo D. By his shift's end as a curing press operator, he will have walked twenty-seven miles and added over nine hundred passenger steel radials to Hooper Tire's inventory. Breathing in April's tepid breeze, he joined foot traffic flowing through HOOPER SQUAD ONLY doors, saying farewell to daylight. As they passed by, he greeted coworkers in various ways: a wink for possible female hookups; polite nod to older folks from his mom's church; and fist bumps with his many dealers. On Hooper's hustling, bustling plant floor there was no shortage of resources for pills, meth, and weed.

No matter where he turned, his G-pop feud haunted him, even in the old-school track "1999" pulsing through his headphones. He turned ten that year and felt solidarity with his grandfather—being his only grandson. "1999" was on every radio, and when his mom and aunts swooned and raved about their *Purple Rain* prince, with as much preteen swagger as he could muster, Bo D said, *He ain't no cooler than you, right, G-pop?* That was the first time he used *G-pop*, which his grandfather liked and Bo D deemed his territory alone.

It didn't take long to spread to Dukes cousins far and wide. Now he welcomed twelve hours of sweaty physical labor to keep his grandfather off his mind.

Hooper offered exercise sessions before every shift. Bo D almost always dropped in because the tracks were on point and Lycra stretched over bulging breasts, thighs, and cheeks always got him going.

Later, sweat dripped from his bright orange headrag, and his tank top clung to his chest and back. His feet throbbed with heat in steel-toed boots. He couldn't imagine trying to get through his shifts without highballs. His first time around in rehab, they talked about drugs being like a lover; but what lover could you count on to show up—every single time—as various drop-dead shades of bliss? A synonym for *luscious blankness*. His standard highball started with an instant high from quality weed, leaving him a little unsteady in a magnificent way. His first few years he swallowed pills, he now chewed for fast results, and washed down with Miller Light to maintain balance. But there was one way his highballs were just like a lover: he was still chasing that first time.

He was one-third short of a full highball buzz; skipping weed was fine for work. He couldn't afford to forget things or sink into paranoia. For work Adderall or Ritalin ensured that he'd be high functioning. Oxy was for party mode. And, of course, he had to have his tracks.

Once his presses were running, his every move repeated to a hip-hop beat. He raised his chin to greet his start-up guy, who was moving on to other presses. Then Bo D shot bursts from an air hose to remove mold debris and sprayed dope solution to keep tires from sticking. Reaching the saddle truck's top shelf, he glided a warm, thirteen-pound green tire down his chest and into an oven-like mold. Walk. Bend.Lift. He was in sync with thirty-two press units—man, music, machine—kicking out baked tires with ten minutes to reload. His pay was good but not enough to support his preferred lifestyle, and his kid, and her mother. Most days he doubted that he'd ever get there. How did his mom do it? She had a lot of help from the family but it was hard raising him on her own working all those years at the brewery.

His supervisor's computer watched for cycle failures—a press open for too long equaled a write-up. This final stage turned a round concoction of melted rubber and chemicals into a tire in eleven minutes.

An ever-present haze of lube, rubber, and dust hovered, and Bo D replayed himself walking out on his grandfather's back. A man turns his back on another man for one of two reasons: he either trusts you or discounts you just that much.

That factory-caustic smell was bringing on a headache. He blew his nose, wondering, as he often did, when would $24-per-hour-plus-sweet-OT stop making up for one simple fact: he hated his job?

On trips back and forth, out of habit, he checked for his missing necklace and thought back to his thirteenth birthday ten years ago. His grandfather rented dirt bikes, transformed the meadow into a course with mud, sand, and ramps. The next day was his rite-of-passage ceremony at the Dove Cove house. He and his mom had moved in one month before. Outside was a stifling summer day, but they basked in air-conditioned comfort—a far cry from oscillating fans moving air around their Jackson Heights apartment where Bo D was born. Granmama Maletha made Bo D's favorite foods, ending with caramel cake.

He had witnessed a few ceremonies for cousins in South Georgia and heard about others as far away as Miami, D.C., Pennsylvania, and even California. His turn had finally come. Fletcher presented a pocketknife and Bo D's freshly carved monkey inside a brown suede pouch, swaddled in fresh cotton bolls. He told Bo D that every Ezekiel Dukes man was one of a kind, like the monkey he held in his hand. Bo D had stood a little taller as they shook hands, and Fletcher repeated their family catchphrase:

"This will keep the monkey off your back,
because being a man is more than a notion."

Bo D had looked forward to his ceremony since he turned seven. That year his father, Walter Fowler, left, and Fletcher became grandfather and father rolled into one. After the divorce, Bo D reasoned that being the son of a Dukes woman, as opposed to a Dukes man, made him a fallback-son who would grow to be a secondhand man. For a long time, he wanted to come right out and ask his G-pop if this were true but could never pluck up that courage, or mention this to his mother, or anyone else. All through middle school he pretended not to care. He kept his peach seed monkey hidden in a drawer. In high school his mother gave him a gold chain and pushed him to wear his monkey as a necklace, which girls adored and guys wanted. What could be better? But he never let his grandfather see him wearing it.

Every few minutes, Bo D glanced toward his inspector's station, where LaChondra worked one to two days of his rotation. She checked his line only once a shift—unfavorable odds—but her whole package was worth the wait.

Midway through his shift, she walked toward him. He kept his rhythm. Bend.Lift.Walk. She stopped a few feet away, making notes on her clipboard.

He wondered how she could write with two-inch-long fingernails. Her blond and red extensions were piled on her head in a messy knot that flopped around as she walked. A few tendrils framed her dark, baby doll face.

"Hey, Bo D," LaChondra yelled, guiding braids out of her face with a dagger-like nail.

"Hey!" He freed one ear from his headphone.

"Look like you on schedule with these."

"Nothing new."

"Right." She smiled, lowered her chin, and watched him.

He licked his lips. Lift. Walk. Bend.

"So. You coming tonight?" She made notes, stepping aside as he kept his rhythm.

"I don't know, I might be busy," he said, knowing he'd promised Auntie Olga he'd drop by after work.

He blocked her way. She slipped past, their sweat almost mingling.

"Well, you ought to come," she yelled, backing away, "'cause it *will* be lit!"

LaChondra loved to party and she also worked hard enough to buy a little house in Waycross. On nights like this, rather than drive two hours, she would sleep over with a relative in Albany. He watched her swaying hips as she walked away, knowing his languishing smile matched hers.

When his shift ended and he joined a reverse flow of foot traffic, Bo D's phone vibrated, showing an Atlanta number he had been ignoring all week. He let this call go to voice mail, too.

Later, Bo D drove through warm spring air past sidewalk letters, black spray paint spelling: *C-M-E*. This stood for Christian Methodist Episcopal. Hines Memorial, one of Albany's oldest churches, was a few blocks over. When his tires bumped over railroad tracks on North Davis, Bo D broke through an invisible portal into a different CME, where newer public housing and older homes with picket fences mingled with blight devouring much in its path, except in cases where even poverty was shrouded by small, well-kept churches and a grandeur of trees.

Families sat on porches under bare light bulbs. Each cozy scene, hanging in darkness like a stage set, seemed frozen in time, but for the make and model of cars and televisions. Bo D knew his Mustang's rumble was familiar to people on porches—hardworking parents, raising kids, making ends meet somehow. Contempt for anybody visiting Fellowship Alley showed in gestures from mothers and grandmothers, looking out, heads tilted, hands on hips. Bo D couldn't blame them. Each time he broke through the cloak, he held that same contempt for himself. He made this trip often, down a dirt lane wide enough for one car, headed for a half-abandoned duplex tucked behind overgrown weeds.

He lumbered up two porch steps, his backpack filled with a

six-pack of Miller Lite, a box of KFC hot wings, and a bag of Famous Amos cookies. A tall, slender young man held the screen door and offered a joint.

"Naw, man. I'm good," Bo D said, sliding past into a small, dim living room.

A thundering rap beat vibrated underfoot. In one corner, a couple engulfed by a big easy chair shared a joint. On the couch, two young men brandished joysticks, answering a video game's call on a huge flat screen.

From living room to small dining room, heads bobbed in unison, repeating lyrics word for word. Music and laughter rebounded off cinder block walls in the tiny kitchen, stuffy and crowded with more partiers, happy to greet Bo D bearing gifts. He pushed aside dirty paper plates, cans, and bottles to make room for his wings and cookies, then took a Rolling Rock from a dish pan filled with ice. Not his first choice, but since he wasn't buying, why be picky? He kept his six-pack hidden. He banged on the bathroom door and two voices answered, *We in here, damnit!* With no one nearby to see, he licked a middle finger and touched it to one of several little white oxy pills in his Altoids tin, then washed it down with beer.

Bo D claimed the smoking couple's chair and waited for oxy oblivion, his cares floating on thick, smoky mist, music pounding through his body. He was listless until tickled by a two-inch fingernail. LaChondra, in low-slung jeans, came into focus. Nearly a year ago, when she became an inspector at Hooper, she introduced Bo D to this party house.

Her braids now fell to her waist and a tight, cropped T-shirt revealed a gold navel ring. Like a drum majorette high-stepping backward, she beckoned Bo D. Spellbound by her kohl-lined eyes, he followed, hallway to bedroom, as pumping music drowned out potato chip bags crunching underfoot.

An unwitting wallflower, Bo D lingered as LaChondra stopped in front of a young man waiting.

"You on deck?" she yelled.

"What you want?" he asked.

"I'll take a sack." She dug into her jeans pocket.

"Loud or mid? Got some nice Kush."

Bo D, still leaning, counted red-white-and-blue stripes on his dealer's T-shirt. Voices faded. Bo D glided on and collapsed on the squeaky bed, smiling as he listened to voice mails. Tyrone Bailey had left three messages and each time his childhood friend had found a way to make Bo D laugh. *Here come de Judge, Here come de Judge, Everybody knows that he is the judge! Yo man—you need to call me back. I'm in Albany and I got news!*

He hadn't seen Tyrone in years, but his old friend's voice sounded like yesterday. What was he doing back home with an Atlanta area code? They grew up running around his G-pop's property and Auntie Olga's garden. Senior year in high school, Tyrone played Iago opposite Bo D's Othello. In random firings of his highball brain, these lines came back, word for word:

> *Haply for I am black,*
> *And have not those soft parts of conversation*
> *That chamberers have, or for I am declined*
> *Into the vale of years—yet that's not much—*
>
> *She's gone. I am abused, and my relief*
> *Must be to loathe her.*

"OK, Bold Daddy," LaChondra cooed, dangling her bag of weed and closing the door, "time for some *jubilatin*—ain't that what you call getting your buzz on?" She draped a red scarf over the floor lamp and straddled him, lifting her top over her head. "Show me what you got."

Over Snoop Dog's muffled rap, LaChondra moaned. Bo D buried his face between her breasts and she moaned again, gripping his head. The mattress creaked and Bo D was at the mercy of habit, his moves firm, direct, and mechanical. *One—two—three—four*: counting rungs on a ladder-back chair, he saw red and placed his hands on LaChondra's hips, thrusting.

Bo D played football three years in high school and excelled as quarterback—without passion—by relying on technique. Dukes family members came out in droves to watch #11. QB-1. Top of the chain. Practice after practice, play upon play, highly trained to think, and lead, and deliver a pigskin to his wide receiver's chest. As junior year ended, he took a bad hit that injured his back, and was looking for a reason to stick with football when Tyrone dared him to join a community theater production of *A Raisin in the Sun*.

One day during downtime in rehearsal, Tyrone said, "Yo, T, you should give up football."

"C'mon, T, don't start," Bo D moaned.

"Nah, man, hear me out," Tyrone insisted. "You already got a messed-up back. What's next? Your precious brain? CTE is real, bro. Football is a containment field, a hundred yards of gladiator glory the white man has turned into a harness for black male aggression and power."

"For real?" Bo D countered. "You seeing all that in a football game?"

"Man, that's just the tip of the iceberg."

This had not been enough to press Bo D's decision, but his sore back was. Amid disappointment from many, he dropped football, immersed in theater all of senior year, and began a love affair with prescription oxy.

And now, with help from Viagra, he shifted down to slow motion. LaChondra groaned, writhing. Then faster and faster, sweat mingling, until he finished with high-pitched hums.

"Ooo, Daddy!" she said, and tried to kiss him.

"What the fuck was that?" He pulled away. "Why you kissing me? You know we ain't about that."

She fell back as crimson light melted their brief, awkward moment. Still sitting up, Bo D looked around and thought of Indicca, his daughter's mother.

He met Indicca Bright in middle school. From day one, he had a weakness for her dark brown skin and dimples, but they ran in different circles, so he admired her from afar. By fall of junior year, 2005, their paths crossed often as he played his last year of football and she was cheering squad captain. He noticed how much her cheerleader's uniform showed off her breasts and thighs and tiny waist. These days she was nagging him to *stop acting a fool with Daddy Fletcher*.

This ain't right—this ain't right—he thought as LaChondra passed him a joint. He blinked once more to Othello:

She's gone. I am abused, and my relief
Must be to loathe her.

"For I. Am. Black," he said out loud.

LaChondra mumbled, "What you say?"

4
~

Over two years earlier, and a thousand miles north, dawn broke on New Year's morning, and dull, evenhanded light spread across the frozen river in Saginaw, Michigan. Giant snowflakes clung to his cashmere coat as Siman Miller exited a cab in front of the building he owned.

He worked as an independent CPA, and one of his clients took over a nightclub downtown to ring in 2010. This accounted for his raging hangover. Nonetheless, he paused in biting air blowing off frigid water to take in a radiant show of ice and sun. Such spectacles were a reminder of how much he loved this city whose native people, the Sauk, were driven out by the Chippewa, so—in Ojibwe—Saginaw means "where the Sauk were."

Icy air pricked Siman's face like needles, making his temples throb even more as his boots crunched through snow from cab to front door. His building was six stories of red brick standing on the Saginaw River's east bank like a medieval fortress. Gargoylesque eagle cornices adorned its top ledge, and lion-with-shield finials flanked huge windows on the first three floors. Siman took a top floor loft.

When he was a boy, this boxy structure, where Water Street met Genesee, had been an indoor parking garage. He tagged along as his mother did her banking across the street, and they often walked out onto Genesee Street Bridge to peer down at kayakers. Another west bank favorite was a giant neon bunny leaping through letters spelling *B-E-A-N-S* atop the Michigan Bean Elevator. Siman imagined those letters being taller than houses being built in the suburbs. The bunny lost its bounce years ago but continued as a red-neon night-sky event.

Saginaw sits just below the thumb's valley on Michigan's mitten. Growing up in the 1960s and 1970s—before auto industry jobs dried up—Siman dreamed of their family living in downtown Saginaw's hustle and bustle, his favorite being this section of Old Town. Across America, time and nature chiseled such rivers, shown on maps as thick blue lines that became red lines of lawful segregation. Invisible zones, political and absolute, bled into neighborhoods where races and cultures once mixed; they now divided east from west, rich from poor and Black from white.

Party music rang in Siman's ears. He lost his gloves, so his numb hands fumbled with keys. Snow-padded silence became a cavernous echo as huge lobby doors clanked behind him. A private elevator opened straight into his southwest corner loft with wholesale views of the river.

Siman took aspirin and went to bed. A few hours later, he woke, startled, dazed, and craving his favorite snack. He watched CNN with a bowl of crunchy Cheetos, then took a shower. Hot water rained over him and he scraped orange fuzz fingers across his teeth. He got dressed, feeling less pukish; refreshed enough to join his sister, Patricia, and family for New Year's dinner.

Waiting at his elevator, a gift bag in hand, Siman looked back at his two large computer monitors on his tall drafting table. Between them sat a tattered ring box, faded maroon with a fine gold line. Inside, nestled in tissue paper, was a monkey carved from a peach seed. Siman's birth mother had passed it on to his adoptive parents,

Jerome and Dorothy, the day he was born. She enclosed a note requesting that Siman be given the monkey when he turned thirteen. There was no more to her story then, and nothing had changed. This is why—as much as he longed to—the time was not yet right for sharing his monkey with his niece and nephew. They would rightfully cry out for details. He'd spent most of his life needing to know more but never getting satisfaction. He did not want to put Trinity and ThatcherJr in that boat.

When they were young, Siman's peach seed monkey always meant more to Patricia than it did to him. They were both adopted, and because she had no connection beyond blood to her birth family, she, and their parents, prodded Siman to cherish his talisman for its power to lead to his birth family. Then, seven years ago the family was thrown into an unimaginable abyss when Jerome and Dorothy died in a plane crash.

On January 2, 2003, the Millers were returning to Saginaw after spending Christmas with Dorothy's brother in Upstate New York. An attempt to land the small commuter plane in blowing snow failed, ending in a stall, barrel roll, and nosedive. Naturally, Siman searched in vain for numerical meaning—anything to explain thirty-nine people collectively dying. Having veered from his church roots, he now envied his parents' ability to place such woes in God's hands. He had no outside belief strong enough to go head-to-head with the anguish ripping through his body and soul.

Brother and sister spent two years in therapy, separately. Then, they met twice a month for dinner out, alone, in what Patricia called DIY therapy. Once their wrongful death case was settled, they upped therapy dinners to once a week, steering through a minefield of emotions as they accepted life rising from death's ashes. Siman bought the Water Street building, and Patricia and Thatcher bought in Bay City, thirty miles north of Saginaw.

For decades, without the internet, they had only his peach seed monkey to guide them: rich cognac color, back curled, holding his tail. The carver had given him teeny diamonds for eyes; eyes that harbored a story stuck in a lost past.

After spending 2008 working on Obama's campaign, one year later, he and Patricia dove into online research about peach seed carvings. They found very little.

Siman was headed to Bay City now to enjoy their traditional Hoppin' John meal: black-eyed peas and rice with collard greens for good luck in 2010. Since the plane crash, for Siman and Patricia, luck had taken on a different meaning.

&.

After dinner, Siman sat pretzel-legged on a floor pillow facing Trinity and ThatcherJr. Front and center was his Christmas gift to them: a LEGO Imperial Flagship. He watched as they tore into more gifts to find new mini figures: MLK as lieutenant, Bruce Lee, Pelé, and Mohammed Ali as soldiers. They put Langston Hughes at the map desk, and Prince—with pirate's sword—became the organist.

If his friends and relatives pitied him for being forty-seven, single, and childless, then Siman pitied them for shortsightedness.

After reveling in the new crew, the kids called on Siman, once again, to tell his story of being eleven months old when their grandparents adopted four-year-old Patricia. After bouncing from foster home to foster home, she couldn't believe it was possible to get a mother, father, *and* baby brother in one day.

When Siman turned six, he learned he and Patricia were adopted. By this time he required numerical evidence in order to trust existing conditions, and people. It had become evident that numbers were his best friends.

Where there was no proof through numbers, he relied on stories. His mysterious birth family was a missing story. Siman believed in kin folk he could count, stacked on chart lines connecting them to living, breathing uncles, aunts, and grandparents on both family trees, foldout charts in large Bibles where his name was next to Patricia's. Numbers gave him a place in the world, a how-to for making sense of Sunday school questions. But why were there no numbers to explain who he was? Why could he not count his blood relatives?

His first-grade brain could not reason why his parents told him he was adopted when there were no names stacked on lines for that other family, and no stories. No way for him to *know* them.

"And since the day Mama and Pop brought her home," Siman wrapped up, "Patricia and I have never spent New Year's apart." Even though it had no real ending, Trinity and ThatcherJr never tired of this story.

Thatcher and the kids moved on to Yahtzee, and Siman joined his sister in the kitchen.

"There you go, spoiling those kids again." Patricia spoke over the coffee grinder's whir. "Too many gifts!"

"What would I do if I couldn't?" he said, parking at the counter.

"You all right?" she asked. "You seem a little off—besides being hung over."

"I'm OK. Just not enough sleep."

"Yeah, partying is like a credit card, huh? Lots of fun until you get that bill." She sat a glass of water in front of him. "Dehydration. Drink."

When served by Patricia, a simple glass of water was an act of devotion.

"OK," she said, steaming milk for hot chocolate. "It's time for you to get on board this train! I'm setting up a Facebook group for you and me to help with finding your birth mother. All you need to do is get an account and accept my friend invitation. The kids can get you all set up."

"Doesn't being my sister make you my friend?"

"OhmygoodnessSiman. Left up to you, we'd still be chiseling on cave walls."

"Not so. You know I love smart data, but truly smart data helps decision-making by shining a light into a misunderstood lump of info. It's rare and disrespected. Angle the torch so the shadow it casts gives the clearest picture."

"I'm talking about friending me on Facebook, please don't drag me down your CPA road right now."

"Deal. If you stop trying to drag me into your social media hellhole."

"No deal. Just friend me. I'll make it worth your while."

"Fine, I'll play your game, but there's no data powerful enough to get a Black man closer to a mother who doesn't want to be found, not to mention relatives locked behind history's paperless wall."

She sat next to him. "You can't give up, not with three of the most awesome key words ever: 'peach' plus 'seed' plus 'monkey.'"

Once Siman entered genealogy and social media's online universe, he would long to slow his computer's lightning speed to the pace of microfiche and enumerator cards. His math brain needed to race ahead and codify what he called an *e-valanche* of data, while his literary brain yearned to slow down, devouring every story, every possible lead. Genealogy research became all-consuming; his two brains at war, burning through hours at his drafting table while Patricia worked after hours on her laptop at her kitchen table.

In 1996, all trails led to the great hope of DNA when online testing was placed within reach of those able to pay. When their children became adults, Jerome and Dorothy left decisions about their lives as adoptees up to them, but they stepped in to caution them not to venture into DNA testing and risk bringing to light birth family secrets that could cause more wrath than favor. Patricia and Siman heeded their advice, so his peach seed monkey became even more precious as their beacon of hope. Seven years later, the plane crash rocked their lives, and Siman's desire to find his birth mother was both driven and hindered by a myriad of possible outcomes.

"I know," Patricia said one day, early in their search. "You're afraid you won't find her."

"Of course I am," he replied, "or find out she's already dead. Too."

"Nobody should have to lose two mothers in one lifetime."

Regardless, his sister pushed them to follow the peach seed monkey's trail, turning up scores of images—from kitsch to exquisite—and bottomless chat room comments, but Siman found no match for his diamond-eyed monkey, a treasure that led nowhere, speaking in a tongue he could not decipher.

tucked
in the crease of
a waist cloth
in a ring box
a pouch
a cigar box
on a gold chain

we watch your worlds
unfold

you were born into the family
but apart from it
both you and family
never knowing

and so you ask
what is family

~

5

Distant tamarisk trees snaked and curled like ghosts, bent by heat waves rippling along the Sahel horizon. Rising from dusty, saffron-colored earth, a cluster of huts stood, shaded by acacia trees along the Senegal River.

All around, still, hot air cracked open a ballad of birds and sharp, chuckling barks from green monkeys. Malik Welé squatted in a tight circle with five sisters and brothers around a communal bowl, finishing their midday meal of millet, greens, and fish. Malik had learned from his older siblings to focus only on his section of bowl. Small hands mopped up hefty pinches of food, revealing more and more smooth iroko wood burnished with oil. Rich copper-red tones and swirls of wood grain excited Malik. He could not yet grasp the language wood speaks, he just knew he cherished listening. With his last bite, Malik peered out at brown grass clumps, undulating in torrid air. They were in the fifth month, and dry season would soon end.

Even though the terrain of memory had begun to shape Malik, he was unaware of the year, 1796, or the bizarre, relentless disappearances of countless Fulani men, women, and children. These were concerns for elders and had little effect on a boy, barely seven, growing up sheltered by his father, mother, and her sister wives.

Coming from a long line of leaders, Malik's father, Ibrahima, was revered as a master woodcrafter, sought after for his powerful incantations. Even though Fulani cattle and farmer castes looked down on them, the LawBe woodcarvers found strength in their spirit-giving power to turn wood into useful objects, and in prayers offered for fallen trees: kapok for pirogues; ebony and iroko for milk buckets, troughs, saddle packs, and many other wares and amulets. If customers refuse to pay, woodcarvers can render sterile cows whose milk will be collected in milking buckets crafted by their hands, or doom a pirogue to ill fate, even on calm waters.

Each morning and evening, donkeys bellowed as Malik and his younger brothers tended their small herd, which was used to haul wood and make deliveries. The boys carefully opened and closed a pen made of thorny tree branches. As seasons marked their days and years, from rainy to dry, they invented stories and created their own versions of elder myths honoring all those who came before: herders, farmers, builders, fishermen, and woodcarvers.

The clan was made up of Ibrahima, one older and one younger brother, their six wives and fifteen children. Their tiny village of thatched-roof huts with walls of mud, straw, and cow dung encircled a large communal house where adults gathered five times a day for prayers. To be close to the fisherman who bought their pirogues, they had settled outside Podor, an ancient town sitting at Senegal's northernmost point, between the Senegal and Doué Rivers.

Malik's mother, number two of three wives, was known to fellow adults as Dalanda, but the children called all the wives Yaaye. Although he had many other siblings, only he and his baby sister shared their Yaaye's hut. Right next door was his father's hut, where he lived with number one wife and three children.

The smell of warm, flaky grouper disappeared as Malik kneeled in river water, taking his turn using silt to scrub their large bowl. His siblings scattered, and his father and uncle returned to their work station behind his father's hut, hollowing out a giant kapok log. His father sliced a splinter from a stick to pick his teeth, resting it in the corner of his mouth.

Malik saw his father watching him, so he performed his bowl-drying duty with extra care—first shaking water from the surface, then holding the bowl out in front of him while he spun around and around.

"From time to time I see you sitting and staring, your mind wandering off," his father declared, bringing a hatchet down hard into pulpy kapok wood. They spoke Pulaar in an even, measured rhythm.

"Yes, Baaba," Malik said as his mother took the bowl.

"It is time you began learning your letters, studying the Qur'an, and drinking the knowledge of our trade," his father said. "If you are old enough for idleness, you are old enough for work."

Baaba was right. Malik had lost interest in catching worm lizards and dung beetles and was no longer in awe of bright yellow birds weaving basket nests that hung down from branches, beautifying trees. Since he was five years old and trusted to carry a bowl of cous-cous or yams to a sick cousin's hut, or collect aloe and herbs for his mother's potions, his daydreams competed with his duties.

While the men talked and worked, and their wives cleaned up, Malik looked out at baobab trees. As if they were growing upside down, their thick rootlike branches gripped a pale blue sky—a river-sky, his elder uncle would say.

"Bu!" his mother whispered. This was the family's nickname for him, meaning "child" in Pulaar—a word Malik felt he had outgrown. "Stretch out your arms."

Malik obeyed.

She tapped his fingertips. "Your work is right here, no farther than your reach, and *that* is where you must keep your eyes and ears. Baaba is preparing these hands to one day carve pirogues. And when that time comes, remember: you must let your thoughts be a feather so you can fly through your work."

Malik was already a master at focusing on his tasks while vividly holding a daydream. Older boys kept axes, adzes, and gouges sharpened, and as he and the younger boys cleaned and stored them in wooden crates, Malik imagined each family that would use their wares. As he chopped smaller branches from trees or collected firewood, he mused about the *open road* he often heard men discussing. This idea worked with his notion of a road: never ending, winding and winding, eventually bringing you back home. Always. Bringing you back home.

Blackened henna on Yaaye's lips framed her warm, bright smile. Malik giggled as she tickled him, burying his face in the folds of her cotton wrap. Yaaye air was always fragrant with potions and herbs. In no other place did he feel safer, even later, as he grew and thought of the dangers of visiting places where Podor's roads led.

Two seasons passed. Malik trained to carve mortars, pestles, and bowls, learning at last to speak wood's singular language. Malik's daydreams grew alongside him as he heeded his father's warning not to be stifled by the weight of wanting. He came to see his dreams as comfortable baggage and could not think of life without them.

Shortly before the end of a new hot season, *ceedhu,* the men prepared to deliver a pirogue commissioned by a Toorodbhe chief for his daughter's wedding. Malik led his younger cousins in collecting tall elephant grass blades to weave protection mats for their delivery. Afterward, he sat with Yaaye as she mixed her special black paint made from egg yolk and soot. Their Welé family's spirit animal, *taana,* was the green monkey. Yaaye designed a mother with baby encircled by mangrove branches. This she carved in relief, on each boat's west side, its forward point being north. She had trained three sister wives in her technique, which became their distinguishing mark for Welé pirogues.

Malik was nine now, old enough to join his father, older brother Bacary, and two cousins for a delivery trip upriver to Saint-Louis. Once there, Malik would collect riverbank stones for sharpening tools.

On the night before they left, his parents sat outside his mother's hut, talking. Malik crouched inside, watching through a thatch hole.

Yaaye was distressed. "What will it hurt to wait another year?"

"Would you have our son be stunted in his growth to manhood?" His father was stern. "We can be proud that *he* does not share your fears. The boy is ready."

In a gentler voice, his father repeated a Truth elders chant at Sharo festivals: *The kapok determines where to grow and we find it there, so it is with the virtue of men.*

ɞ

"Yaaye!" Malik yipped, bright and early, ready to go. "Baaba promised me we will see the ocean!"

"Yes." His mother drew circles on his back with her palm. "Baaba is good for his word, and you must be good for yours: stay with the men at all times. There are many dangers in Saint-Louis so close to big, big waters."

Evidence of these dangers was everywhere in and around Podor. With their men away and older wives occupied with other tasks, younger wives and elders kept careful watch over young children. Now Malik was old enough to be told why. For as long as their elders' elders could remember, no one was spared knowing friends or family who had been stolen, or killed resisting. Yaaye reminded her son to obey their Fulani laws of *Pulaaku*, to show proud reserve, a gentle demeanor, and to keep his distance from infidels.

"Remember, Malik," she said, fitting his elephant grass sack to his shoulders, "your time will be short for filling this sack with stones."

"Don't worry, Yaaye—I will be quicker than a cheetah can run!"

Baaba's convoy had two boats: one for men, and one for hauling the wedding pirogue, nested and padded with elephant grass mats and secured with rope. When they came ashore at Saint-Louis, Malik jumped into a whirl of activity around the port until Bacary scolded him for not staying close.

As Malik helped untie and launch the boat, he took in the sights and sounds around him: Baaba switching from Pulaar to Wolof, to French, in his greetings and dealings; men in boats of all kinds bartering and trading crops and wares.

Baaba blessed the wedding pirogue with libations. The royal delegates received the boat with much pageantry and formed a colorful processional downriver. Malik was mesmerized, his eyes flitting here and there.

Malik's business was stones, but his love was wood. He collected as many sticks and river-hardened wood as he did sandstone and quartz.

"Eh! Bu! Stones!" Bacary shook him playfully, sending Malik scurrying to an area near their boat. All around, people spoke in foreign tongues. He strained to hear familiar words. Two men speaking Pulaar discussed a university many, many miles to the east, where young men could learn letters and elevate their station.

Malik filled his sack, thinking about sinking in ocean water up to his knees, soupy sand oozing between his toes. He conjured up vast views of liquid blue stretching farther than eyes can see.

Baaba's crew navigated their pirogue through marshes that formed during big rains, headed for the Langue de Barbarie. This long stretch of sand was an island barrier separating lower Senegal River waters from Atlantic Ocean waters. They kept safe in mangrove cover, their pirogue gliding so smoothly not even pelicans and flamingos were disturbed. They stopped and peered through dense snares and tangles of mangrove branches.

Baaba placed his hand on Malik's shoulder, speaking softly. "So now you see this big water you crave."

"Yes! I want to cover myself with it!"

"Best you stay away," Bacary said. "That is too much water for a young boy to drink!" They all laughed as they turned around to head home.

Malik's elephant grass bag was filled with stones, and his heart with joy at being in the company of men. More and more their actions were no longer beyond his reach. Sights and sounds of his adventurous day kept him company as they traveled home. He would not know that at the beach, thick mangroves had sheltered from their view a large ship, anchored several yards out. Only a few hours before, down where sand met surf, a different story had unfolded: a handful of white men—known in Malik's family as *daneejos*—armed with rifles, packed several Black villagers into pirogues, like the one that ferried them home, to be hauled out to the ship. He would not be forced to ask Baaba who they were and why they were chained together. And Baaba would not have to answer with a heavy heart, *That is none of our concern, do not stray from Allah's teachings and you will not fall into the hands of infidels.*

Malik felt safe with Baaba and the others, eating kola nuts and drinking *bissap* juice. Today would not be a day to wonder why so many men, women, and even children could need such harsh disciplining so often. He had given enough thought to ending up captured by heathens; surely waters as vast as those he now held in memory would prove to be a road that winds and winds to bring him back home.

He collected one last view of endless ocean and tucked away fresh dreams of crossing the desert to learn to read and write. Could he not dream beyond his lineage, beyond his trade, or even beyond the Senegal River, a master they all served? No one he knew had ever spoken of life outside those boundaries. In time he, too, would learn to harbor secrets and never speak out loud of his longing for knowledge, or his growing love for water and boats that carried cargo and people to places he vowed to someday make his own.

❧

At sixteen, Malik prepared with his brothers and cousins for their Sharo festival, a rite of passage where boys endured flogging as a test of strength and manhood. He knew his family's pirogue business from end to end: starting with choosing a proper kapok tree to preparing sideboards for Yaaye's green monkey designs. His time had come. The elders matched him with his cousin Nbey (who had always secretly been his choice), and wedding plans were underway. He was ready to make pirogues under his own name. He needed only his father's blessing and at that time could choose his own spirit animal. He knew that he would keep the monkey, a symbol of honor, family, and unbound spirit.

Like a brazen coin, a dry season sun dropped into the horizon, nestled among clouds blushing from mango to guava. Malik and Nbey strolled hand in hand; their long shadows led them past a millet field, golden tassels waving in a hot breeze. Malik was enough at ease to break a vow he made as a boy, his first time visiting Saint-Louis; he told Nbey about his hope to go to the university in Timbuktu.

"You are too full of mind wanderings," Nbey said.

"And how do you *keep* your mind from wandering? This I cannot do."

"I tell my mind what my Yaaye told me," Nbey said. "*Wander too far and you will end up chained to a pirogue and headed out to sea.*"

"Heh!" Malik said, holding out his wrists, "there are no chains here, and yet that fear plagues my life, and yours. So to nurse it is to be a prisoner even without chains."

Nbey turned to face him, her smile filled with adoration.

"Let your mind wander," she said, playfully shoving him, "as long as the rest of you stays here—with me!" She chased him into the millet field and out again, both wanting to stretch their time together; after dropping her home, they would not see each other for twenty-four hours.

From that day, Malik knew Nbey would never fully understand this side of him. And so he returned to his vow, whispering his yearnings to soft wood as he hollowed out kapok logs.

At his uncle's compound, men slaughtered goats, and Nbey prepared to spend her wedding day amid festive chaos: cooking, gossip, dancing to trumpets and *gangan* drums.

Malik's three attendants joined him for his ceremonial river bath. With each step on the footpath, puffs of dust rose from bare feet, now powdery with red clay, headed to a gathering with elders for stories and prayers.

"My nephew!" One of his uncles greeted Malik with a firm pat to his chest. "You and Nbey are to be joined! And even the sky is vibrant with pride."

Leaving laughter and jesting behind, Malik and his attendants entered the clearing, each rubbing hands on a large ebony urn, carved by Malik's great-great-grandfather, showing green monkeys dancing and drumming; deep wooden grooves had been rubbed smooth from many, many hands. The circle of men fell silent.

"Once," the eldest uncle began, *"there were three Fulani brothers, all shepherds: Pullo, Bambado, and Labbo. There came a time of severe drought, destroying their herds. Pullo recovered and remained a shepherd, promising to give his brethren milk and meat—and they would never have to ask. Labbo and Bambado prayed to Allah to grant them other means to support their families. Their prayers were answered—Bambado became the storyteller and musician and Labbo received the craft of wood. As descendants of Labbo, we are unique from other Fulani only in our trades—we speak the same language, our physical traits and adornments are the same—and we are eternally linked by our beginnings."*

The storyteller called out: *"I wasn't there but somebody was"*—to which the circle responded: *"and passed this on to me."*

The day was unbearably hot, and Malik could not recognize Nbey, covered from head to toe in white robes and headdress. He wanted to rescue his bride from her shroud.

Guests arrived to food, music, and merriment. At sunset, before entering her wedding hut, Nbey splashed guests with water as she washed Malik's clothes in the river; she then tended to a child as he drew two buckets of water, strapping them to a donkey. Malik was relieved for her as she finally took off her bulky headdress and placed it on the donkey. In her honor, Nbey and her attendants stayed up all night talking and eating.

For three days they celebrated, and Nbey's joy was enough to cancel Malik's regrets at having to let his mind wander while the rest of him stayed put with his new wife.

≈

At seventeen, Malik was proud of his growing family and would soon choose a second wife from many eligible cousins. Nearby, Nbey turned her protruding belly sideways to lift their girl, Yacine, to a donkey's back. The child would soon be one year old and giggled as her mother led the donkey in a wide circle. In a few weeks they would welcome their new baby. Like their parents, Malik and Nbey modeled Fulani codes of behavior: patience, forethought, and hard work.

Malik's pirogues were in high demand, from Saint-Louis to Kaédi. One day, early in *dabbunde*, the cold season, he worked in the warm morning sun filtering through acacia trees, preparing a new pirogue for delivery.

A few days later, Malik, his brother Bacary, and two cousins headed out to a village near Sioure, three days east of Podor. A second wife would also ease Malik's mind for such trips, not having to depend on his father's wives to care for Nbey and their children.

On their return trip, the men set up camp on a straight section of river with good cover and views from all sides. These precautions, combined with taking shifts, kept them safe from kidnappers.

Morning light met river water in a bright gleam as Malik ended his shift, missing his usual breakfast of goat's milk and Nbey's warm millet porridge. He joined Bacary and the cousins, eating peanuts and dried okra. They made jokes that would prove impossible to recall in coming years as Malik went over every step of this morning countless times.

As if from thin air, two Black villagers and two *daneejos* rushed up on Malik and the others, thrusting knees into their chests and forcing icy rifle barrels across their necks.

Facedown, Malik struggled to flip over and was kicked back to his stomach. He raised his head to keep mud out of his mouth.

Over shouts all around him, with fear and fury ringing in his ears, Malik heard a blaring cry of rage. Gagging and choking, he strained to see Bacary, a few feet away, seize the rifle's ends and push up with all his might, throwing the Black villager to the ground. Through his own pain, blood in his mouth, *daneejo*'s rifle point digging into his back, Malik watched Bacary fight for life against a force he could not defeat. As Bacary ran, hot metal exploded and he dropped, shot in his back. From his view, eyes hovering inches above dirt, Malik saw no blood yet knew the river flowed red. Dreaming backward, he screamed his brother's name. Time was everted, and Malik's pain became agony. He and the others fought and were shackled by wrists and feet. Malik strained through mud and tears to see Bacary's body, left to lie where he fell, between earth and water turning to blood. He took what solace he could: his brother's stillness meant that he was no longer suffering. Though there would be many more, that would be the first time he asked Allah: *Why have You forsaken us?* It was as if, like Bacary, blood and breath had rushed from Malik's body, too.

After each raid, the convoy grew, hauling Malik and his cousins upriver in the pirogue built by their hands. Mostly young men, and a few women and children, were shackled and hurtled into the terror and mystery of *Why us? What have we done? Where are you taking us?*

&

On day two of their capture, Malik was separated from his cousins, his ankle chains joined to two men who did not speak Pulaar. From different villages, alien tribes, they had nothing in common except an arm's length of chain. What blacksmith would put his gift of taming iron toward this evil end?

Bearing upriver, his mind stuck on Bacary's body straddling

muddy bank and lapping waves, Malik silently kept to his daily prayers, according to the sun: dawn, midday, afternoon, sunset, and nightfall. He performed *ruku* and *sujud* in his mind, picturing Baaba and Yaaye bowing and prostrating for him. Bearing upriver, Malik clung to a truth he knew in his heart: the boat was protected by his choice of kapok tree. His hands on axe and hatchet had been guided by ancestors and blessed by Allah. He waited for benevolence to turn the boat around, or simply wake him from this nightmare. Instead, venomous hands shoved him into sand and wind on Saint-Louis Island. Hands that beat and shackle do the work of the fallen angel, Iblis, making good on his promise to Allah: *Now because You have sent me astray, verily I shall lurk in ambush for them on Your Right Path. I shall come upon them from before and from behind them and from their right hands and from their left hands, and You will not find most of them beholden.* Rough cold steel drew blood from Malik's wrists and ankles, and he knew this was not sleep. He must remain beholden. His faith in Allah must not be thin.

6

To Fletcher, nothing says *home* like a front gable roof, but because Olga's home, which had a side gable, was a Dukes family heirloom, he granted her a pardon. Olga was an infant when their modern Colonial house arrived in a boxcar kit from Sears, quite an investment for a sharecropper. Their father, Purvis Dukes, had the whole family scraping and saving for years. He oversaw the project, relying on his four eldest boys. Like many on Albany's tree-lined Whitney Avenue, Olga's wooden house was simple and elegant: sprawling single story, white with black trim, and a long screened-in side porch that kept passersby out of her business.

Even as a boy, joining his father and older brothers on construction jobs, Fletcher was always cognizant, collecting ideas. In junior high school, he found a job away from family working on a large peanut plantation, going from field hand to tractor driver in a matter of months. Olga prodded him to go to college. He was not interested. She loaded him up with homebuilding and architecture books, telling him he didn't have to go to college to educate himself. After high school he went back to working with his family in construction.

When he went out on his own, he had read many of the books and understood philosophies explaining why archetypal elements, such as front gables, stir in us a cultural feeling of home—*us* being those folk who lived in houses grand enough to have such gables and dormers and massive chimneys. Nonetheless, those designs inspired Fletcher in 1967, when he designed and built their house on the seven acres.

In 1961, Olga had been back from her expat years in Montréal and Amsterdam for six years, and for just as long, she had been Fletcher's guardian. Albany's Civil Rights Movement was in full swing. Olga taught science at Albany State College which placed her at the epicenter of student activism. She quickly took up a role as an adult advisor and her house became southwest Georgia's first Freedom House, home away from home for folks of all races who came from around the country to fight for civil rights with the Student Nonviolent Coordinating Committee.

Even now Fletcher never knew what to expect at Olga's and didn't know how she found the energy at eighty-eight with failing sight. Often, her house was jumping with volunteers, colleagues, and students working on academic or political projects, along with revolving shifts of nieces and nephews doing chores and errands for pocket change. One day Olga might Skype with folks in Europe about genetics and the next day host a phone bank for President Obama's second term.

In her front yard Olga bounced slowly in a metal garden chair, embraced by a small patch of sun. As Fletcher pulled his old pickup in, Sidney howled.

"No noise." Olga was firm but gentle, and the dog whined. "Thank you, Sidney—and you better not be wallowing in my lantana like it's grass."

"He ain't nowhere near your lantana," Fletcher said, slamming his truck door. "And if he was," Fletcher said, patting Sidney's chest, "how could you blame a beagle for being a beagle?"

"That's a good boy," Olga said as Sidney rolled onto his back on top of her feet. "I'll give you some Fritos when we go in."

Olga continued bouncing and Sidney went back to sniffing in and out of hydrangeas, camellias, and azaleas growing under the sprawling oak.

Weeks had passed since the towing and spotting Altovise in Piggly Wiggly. In every phone call he'd had with Olga since, neither of them mentioned Altovise. Even now, Olga only asked if Fletcher had heard from Bo D.

"Like I told you, he huffed and puffed and slammed doors like somebody crazy and I ain't heard from him since."

"Well, maybe he'll come tomorrow for dinner—it is Easter after all, one of his favorite meals." She reached for Fletcher's hand, and he helped her to her feet.

Fletcher led his sister up three porch steps. Straight ahead was her study, turn right for her large living room. They walked into a house humming with machines and spring-cleaning activity. To escape vacuum cleaner roars, mops, and brooms, Sidney made a beeline to sanctity under Olga's massive desk.

As she lost her sight to glaucoma, she outfitted her house with talking, beeping gadgets. Fletcher still had an '80s clap-on clap-off bedside lamp, so he was impressed by coffee mugs that announce a full cup, gizmos for reading money and broadcasting the time. Olga's iMac served as voice-command central, monitoring porches, opening and closing curtains, watering plants, and turning lights on and off. These electronics stood out in a house that in every other way was fossilized. Her two old favorites were a Chambers gas stove and—front and center on the living room mantel—a Zenith Cube radio.

When she turned thirteen, with money earned piercing tobacco leaves, Olga bought the Zenith Cube, a single trace of modern in their sharecroppers' home. The little radio could fit in a bread box and had a slick walnut veneer that begged to be touched. A big round black dial and three wooden knobs engraved with lightning *z*'s mesmerized young Fletcher. After fixing the stove, as was his practice, he would wipe the radio with an oiled cloth.

Fletcher was two years old when Olga began her expat years in Montréal. He watched their front door for days, waiting for her to walk back through, pointing to her pretty wood box as it sprouted music, singing, and men talking. His mother, Alpha, died when he was seven, and Fletcher wanted radio airwaves to magically bring back his mother's voice—singing as she worked, telling the children bedtime stories. To help Fletcher cut through his grief, Purvis taught his youngest child to whittle. And Olga's fancy wooden box sent Joe Friday to save the day. Once a week Fletcher and his siblings immersed in real-life crime in Los Angeles, a faraway place where *the names were changed to protect the innocent.*

The Cube held her place in the house until Olga came home in early August 1955 for their father Purvis' funeral. Fletcher's peach seed monkey rite of passage was one of Purvis' last acts. He died ten days later.

While Olga was home that summer, a fourteen-year-old from Chicago was brutally tortured and killed in Money, Mississippi. His mother, Mamie Till, insisted on an open casket so that the news and pictures of her mutilated son could be seen by the world.

Olga had said to Fletcher, "You're only one year younger than Emmett Till. That could have just as easily been you."

"When you going back over there?" Fletcher had asked.

"I won't be going back to Amsterdam," she'd said. "Turning this mess around is going to take a whole lot of us doing things we've never done before. You included."

Fletcher and Olga stepped into her study to a screen door screeching.

"I see I need to hit your hinges with some 3-in-One," he said.

"Don't you dare! That's my backup security system. You never know when technology might fail and the dog might be asleep. You can hear that door squealing clear down the block!"

"Not if your burglar hits it with some oil."

"They're not smart and handy like you!"

Ursula Kroon sat at her computer post amid neat piles of papers and files. She was Olga's assistant from the Netherlands, with one year left as a genetic research fellow at Albany State University.

"Hello, Mr. Fletcher!" Ursula chimed. Her short red hair exploded like fireworks and she spoke in a Dutch accent laced with southern Black vernacular.

"Have a seat, Fletcher," Olga said. "Can't wait to show you what Ursula and I have unearthed. Stove fixing can wait."

Olga sank into her high-back chair in front of the window. Sitting by the door, Fletcher studied his sister for any deviations in her routine; could she still hook her rhinestone sunglasses into her gray linen shirt collar, and then finger the silver watch she wore as a necklace? He didn't need to worry. Olga was as sharp as a pin.

"So, Ursula," Olga said, "you'll recall me saying my brother here refused to read or watch *Roots* back in '77 when the whole planet was talking about Kunta Kinte."

"Watching slavery on TV won't change nothing, so what's the point," Fletcher said.

"And yet it behooves us to study the past so we are not doomed to repeat it," Olga said, "so I'm not giving up on you, baby brother; any day now you will take up residency in this twenty-first century."

In spite of his poker face, Fletcher was intrigued as Ursula explained using DNA for searching ancestry. She handed him a sheet showing descendants of his paternal grandfather, Ezekiel Dukes, to be 89 percent West African.

"Your spit kit is all well and good," Fletcher said, handing the sheet back to Ursula and picking up his toolbox, "but I got a stove to fix."

Olga and Ursula followed Fletcher down the hallway, dodging spring cleaners. Olga continued, her voice aglow with excitement.

"Fletcher. You can't tell me you're not fascinated that we've traced our family back to the Fulani in Senegal. Granted, there are many, many diverse subgroups throughout the country, not to mention the whole continent, but this is a beginning."

"And y'all think you know all that from spit in a test tube?" Fletcher asked.

"These facts are as true as the blood running through your veins. Hell—they *are* the blood running through your veins!"

"And what about that eleven percent European I saw on your little map?"

"I know," Olga said, "you'd like your ancestry the same as you take your coffee—no cream—but there's no arguing with DNA."

"And consider this," Olga went on. "All our lives we've only had bits and pieces of our Isakiah Dukes story before hitting the wall of history. DNA can help us connect what science tells us about our Fulani ancestors to that piece of lore from the Sea Islands that we've held on to like a keepsake."

"What *will* science come up with next?" Fletcher said.

"More than you can imagine," Olga said.

Their parade had reached the kitchen, which, along with three bedrooms, occupied the back of Olga's house. Two great-nieces (The Twins) washed and dried dishes, plugged into music on their cell phones. Every generation in the Dukes family had at least one set of twins. These two, Mindy and Cindy, were juniors in high school. Olga hired them to help her with various chores and errands. Along with other young family members, The Twins took turns spending the night as Olga adjusted to blindness.

"I don't know why they need them earplugs," Fletcher said. "I can hear the music clear over here."

Olga said, "And these days we're better off not hearing foul and degrading lyrics. Used to be enough if you could keep young folks off the streets, but now the streets—and everything else—come straight to the palms of their hands. We should be doing so much more than living our lives through other people's lenses. It's a true tragedy how so much digital content is not worthy of its speed and storage."

Fletcher agreed silently. He was amazed at how Olga could find so many words to say *young folk done lost their minds and these cell phones are a waste of time.*

Standing on ladders outside, nieces and nephews cleaned windows as sunlight poured in, and brisk spring air made curtains ripple like gauzy kites. Fletcher approached the massive old Chambers stove with reverence. Cold white enamel was polished to a wax shine, but the chrome parts were dull. He began the laying on of hands.

A few steps away, Olga and Ursula sat in white wicker chairs on the screened-in back porch and Fletcher joined them, setting out polish, a cloth, and a toothbrush.

Ursula held up an oversize photocopy.

"What is that?" Fletcher asked.

"Copy of a slave-holding document," Olga said, "found at the East Point National Archives. Won't hurt you to have a look."

He put on his reading glasses, struck by the Declaration of Independence penmanship on the sheet. "'23rd day of June 1860, Dougherty County,'" Fletcher read. "Who is Edwin T. Dukes?"

"Oppressor," Olga said.

"I can think of a few other things to call him," Fletcher said.

"And I agree, but let's focus on the task at hand."

He noticed the row of ages, starting with sixty-four and ending with six months. He read other columns, with all blank fields: *Deaf & Dumb. Blind, Insane, or Idiotic.*

"What is this?"

"Classifying human inventory," Olga said.

"You saying I'm looking at the slaves this man laid claim to—no names, just numbers and these—classifications?"

"Yes," Olga said, "and we prefer to use *enslaved.*"

"Don't make no difference what word you use, a slave is a slave." Fletcher frowned, handing the folded sheet back. "I don't want this."

"Keep it anyway," Olga said, raising her palm. "It's possible that these were our kinfolks and—since this document was drawn up five years before emancipation—they could have surfaced as freedpeople.

This is an impossible puzzle, Fletcher, that we can never fully solve, which makes each piece priceless." Olga leaned back and asked Ursula to finish.

"In 1870, Mr. Fletcher, for the first time, your U.S. census provided details for Blacks. Cross-checking census records and documents such as this—together with DNA—is our best chance to trace your ancestors."

"Fletcher," Olga added, "we're outfielders, working for a long time toward a successful play." Her face lit up. "And then, bat cracks, little white ball flies, and a piece of our history comes home."

To Fletcher, this was more like the losing end of a perpetual no-hitter; but he liked the sport too much to compare baseball to slavery. After replacing knobs and cleaning pilot holes with a paper clip, he listened to Ursula give instructions on using the DNA vial and tucked the slaveholding document in his toolbox.

"She's good to go." Fletcher patted the stove.

Then he slipped the vial into his shirt pocket. "My mama didn't allow us to spit in public, so I'll have to get back to y'all with an answer."

"At least that's not a 'no,'" Olga said.

7

"Black Knight rides again!" Tyrone Bailey exclaimed, polishing the Mustang's hood with his sleeve. "Still looking good!" He turned to Bo D. "And why you got to make it so hard, T? Not returning my calls?"

"That Atlanta number threw me off," Bo D said, "until I finally listened to your voice mail."

"Yeah, well—being a Black man in the nonprofit world, I get more respect from donors, investors, et cetera, with that big city area code."

"I heard that," Bo D said, "and I-ain't-mad-at-you!"

Bo D had tweaked the necessary highball and was feeling the effects.

Blushing twilight clouds reflected off of Tyrone's Airstream trailer, which served as his office. Several yards across the parking lot, on the corner of Slappey Boulevard and Gillionville Road, stood a huge boxy building that was once Albany's main movie theater but had been empty for twenty years. Tyrone and his board members recently bought the property to transform it into his dream: Eusi Arts—a nonprofit youth center and theater for live performances.

"Oooo," Tyrone said. "I smell me some Jimmies!"

Bo D held up his backpack. "Half a dozen all the way, BBQ Lay's, and Miller Lite to wash 'em down. Can't remember when I last had one of these little pink weenies. Pretty sure they ain't even food."

"Taste so good, though," Tyrone said, "but before we eat, come with me."

Bo D followed Tyrone to a small storage shed behind the trailer. "Only you would have an Airstream trailer as an office—but what happened here?" Bo D motioned toward a section of missing panels.

"That's one of the things I need to talk to you about," Tyrone said, "but yeah, it's pretty cool, right?" Tyrone beamed. "A 1972 Sovereign. Nice couple up in Smyrna donated it. Then they had it gutted *and* delivered three months ago. My cousins and I are almost finished with inside renovations." He unlocked the shed.

"Whoa," Bo D said, running his hands over three new aluminum panels, polished to a mirror shine.

"Got to have everything around here looking good," Tyrone said, "to be taken seriously by donors. We have to change the thinking that nonprofits have to have a 'pauper attitude.' We're doing our part!" Tyrone slapped Bo D on the shoulder. "In fact, looking to hire somebody—like you and Anthony—to put in these three panels."

"You barking up the wrong tree, man," Bo D said. "I got a job. Besides, I don't know nothing about Airstream trailers."

"You and Anthony didn't know squat about restoring cars either, until you did. How's he been anyway? Haven't seen him since we graduated."

"He's fine. Working with his dad. Married. Having a baby."

"Cool!"

"—but we don't hang no more."

"No big. You can handle this by yourself."

Bringing up the tow truck mess was pointless. After what went down in high school, Bo D was surprised to hear Anthony's name on Tyrone's lips.

Freshman and sophomore year the three of them had been a uni-
fied front. The summer before junior year, when Tyrone officially came
out, Anthony told Bo D, "I can't be hanging round him no more, folks
be thinking I go that way." Bo D stuck by Tyrone but also saw this as
pressure to show he was not a mama's boy just because his father had
left eight years ago. His chance to prove this came when he accepted a
party invitation from a group of guys who weren't his friends.

One night they drove to a run-down mobile home in a walnut
grove and built a campfire in a bald dirt yard. As planned, Bo D was
introduced to a twenty-five-year-old woman who believed him when
he said he was eighteen—his mustache helped.

On the bedroom floor, a box spring and mattress stretched wall to
wall and thin wood paneling let in voices from outside.

"I ain't lying," the woman said as they shared another joint, "it's
hard to believe that was your first time."

Bo D had another first that night: rum and marijuana, a combination that made him feel loose-lipped and more invincible.

"I ain't lying either." He exhaled a plume of smoke. "I was a stone
virgin when I walked through that door—with no plans on leaving
that way."

The woman grinned. "Ain't no-body out here trying to brag
about being a eighteen-year-old virgin but, *you* so bold you ain't even
shame!"

"That's where you wrong," Bo D whispered and squeaked, his
lungs filled with smoke.

"What? You ain't bold?"

"I ain't but fifteen." He blew smoke rings.

"No you didn't!" She sprang up, naked. "You mean I'm up in here
with jail bait?" She laughed. "I'm gone have to call you my little Bold
Daddy from now on."

"Back up, back up!" Bo D said. "You and me both know you need
to drop that 'little' part."

"Damn straight!"

"But all this can be just between you and me, cool?"

"I'm down with that, Bold Daddy!"

But when they rejoined the party, she quickly spread Bo D's story, and later, around campus, his new cronies shortened *Bold Daddy* to *Bo D* and manufactured a legend.

"You don't have to answer today," Tyrone said, locking the shed. "Just promise to think about it?"

Bo D agreed, even though he wasn't the least bit interested.

Twilight faded as they entered the Airstream and Tyrone flipped a central switch, lighting his cozy office like a pricey restaurant. Bo D sat his backpack on one of two leather side chairs at a bistro table. Tyrone heated their fragrant chili dogs in his microwave and served them on square, black plates.

A brushed-steel stereo shuffled through hip-hop songs in languages that sounded to Bo D like Spanish or Arabic or he couldn't guess what.

For years, their friendship had hit bumps and rung bells like a pinball, always finding its way home. People thought of them as opposite ends of a spectrum, but since they were boys playing in her garden, Olga has said, *Terrence and Tyrone—two Ts—cut from the same cloth.* When they were into X-Men and Power Rangers, Tyrone's room was the coolest place to hang out. He worked wonders with cardboard, duct tape, and paint. And now, not a single item in Bo D's room at his mom's house could compare to what he saw around him. He was sure his G-pop would like how Tyrone matched light and dark hardwoods to play off the aluminum. He had throw pillows dressed in fabrics that TV lawyers wear, and an African rug covered his weathered wood floor.

"Makes a cool office," Bo D said.

"Secret is to look like Ralph Lauren on an IKEA budget," Tyrone said, "to surround ourselves with beauty and use the arts to lift youth above systems that fail them; back them in becoming agents of their own destiny—but enough about that, what's been up with you?"

With eyes cast down, Bo D talked about becoming a dad and

working at Hooper. Tyrone seemed genuinely interested in tire specs and presses. He compared something called a *corpus* to making steel radials. Bo D knew his friend was trying to make him feel better for not understanding a brochure he handed him: *endowments, best practices, and board governance.*

Tyrone graduated from Clark Atlanta University with a B.A. in economics, his master's in Performance Study was from NYU. He spent six months in Ghana and Kenya researching and writing his thesis: *Influences of West African Griots on the Diasporas of Hip-Hop Culture.*

"So, T," Tyrone said, before biting his chili dog, "our board of directors has a proposition for you."

"For real?"

"I'll roll it out after dinner."

They sat across from bookshelves filled with several copies of each book, some Bo D knew from high school: *The Autobiography of Malcolm X, No Name in the Streets, Their Eyes Were Watching God, Song of Solomon.*

"Dang, Man! You look like the library," Bo D said, dabbing grease from his mouth with a cloth napkin.

"I mostly give them away."

"Always liked this one," Bo D said, pulling down a copy of Italo Calvino's *The Baron in the Trees.*

"Yeah," Tyrone said, "we thought Songtree was crazy assigning that one—until we read it."

Junior year in high school, they took a literature class from a dapper Virginian named Lysander Songtree, a Tuskegee man. As they read Calvino, Bo D and Tyrone recalled how, as boys, they loved climbing the huge oak tree growing where Fletcher's road dead-ends. They'd lie on massive branches and talk about living up there, never touching ground.

"Remember?" Tyrone said, gathering up their dishes, "We always said *we* could've been Cosimo, living in the trees!"

Bo D replaced the Calvino book. "Yeah, I still park out under that oak tree and just chill, end up falling asleep."

"Sounds like your meditation spot."

"You could say that."

They moved to the snug conference room. A built-in sectional sofa surrounded an oak slab table. Tyrone sat beers on coasters, connected his laptop to a compact flat screen mounted on the wall, and queued up a presentation titled: *Altovise Benson: A Southern Icon.*

"You need to know about our national treasure from Albany, *G-A.* This soundtrack is her trio."

Tyrone turned up the volume.

"You kidding me!" Bo D said. "She's from Albany?"

"Born and raised."

"I been listening to her music my whole life at Auntie Olga's house and never knew that."

"Check this out," Tyrone said, pausing on a 1960s photomontage.

In a Polaroid of a group shot, Altovise and a young man held hands and protest signs in front of Shiloh Baptist church.

"Dr. B and your G-pop were tight in high school!"

"For real, dog?"

"Straight up," Tyrone said. "My aunt was in their class at Monroe and worked in the Movement with them. Back then nobody doubted that they would end up hitched."

"Daaang." Bo D leaned in. "I've seen another picture from that night on Auntie Olga's wall, with just the two of them and G-pop looking like the Putney Playboy, but I never knew who the girl was!"

All eyes in the photo are looking at the camera, except Fletcher. He is looking at Altovise. Bo D wondered how much his mom and aunts knew. And if his granmama Maletha had a clue?

"Dr. Al is awesome in the true sense of that word," Tyrone said, "internationally known academician in American theater—also a Grammy-winning jazz/blues singer. I've known about her since Clark and NYU, then met her two years ago at a theater conference in Las Vegas. She delivered the keynote. Man! To see that kind of dynamism coming from my own hometown blew my mind. Zero ego, totally accessible. Something went down and she moved north right after high school and stayed away—until now. Once I found out she was retiring back home I knew I had to make a move."

Altovise's deep, soulful voice rose in the room:

> It's halftime in heaven
> Coach wants to see you
> In the locker room
>   'Cause you need a talkin' to

"Love that song," Bo D said as Tyrone shut down the presentation and flipped through a binder on the table.

"I'm working on a play about Albany's long history of social activism. Listen to this—Dr. Al wrote it to help us get funding to buy this property.

"Through protesting, canvassing, and going to jail we shared experiences of the freedom struggle. To single out any one of us for praise—or blame—is to take the <u>act</u> out of the <u>activism</u>. The Albany Movement was the most famous branch of a struggle spanning centuries in southwest Georgia—one far-reaching story encompassing many parts, standing together to shine light on the whole. This history has been held in obscurity far too long. I implore you to help Tyrone Bailey bring this story to his community stage and to the world."

Bo D shook his head. "That's deep."

Tyrone said, "When I told Dr. Al and our Eusi board about *you*, they all said 'let's bring him in by all means!' So—this is for you." Tyrone slid the binder across toward Bo D. The cover read: STANDARD OPERATING PROCEDURES: AKA—HOW WE DO THINGS AROUND HERE.

"Just to be clear," Tyrone added, "this is me offering you a position at Eusi Arts as Makerspace Guru. Dr. Al has arranged for a couple of her colleagues who are top-notch tech directors to come in as Artists-in-Residence to mentor you until you're ready to fly solo as our head tech guy."

"You serious?"

"As a heart attack—and I know this is a lot to take in, but will you please give it some thought so we can discuss salary? Of course we can't compete with what you make at Hooper—but you have to factor in the compensation of having a job that feeds your soul."

"Ya'll got a 401(k) plan?"

"No, but we have 403(b) like a lot of nonprofits. And we have financial literacy support to help with investing outside of that."

"Now you sound like my mom. She tried to use that to get me to come back to church, only at Greater Goshen they call it Investment Ministry."

"Well, good for Greater Goshen," Tyrone said, "but not enough to get you back in the pews, huh?"

"Nope."

"Need to know in four weeks if I have to look elsewhere, and I sure hope I don't."

"OK, yeah. A month. Thanks, man." Bo D stuffed the binder into his backpack. "This is a lot—and amazing. But I'll think about it."

"We hope you'll do more than think about it," Tyrone leaned in, "c'mon T—the doors of the church are open!"

Bo D's mind raced, he scratched his forearms. Beer in hand, he ducked into the tiny bathroom, blew his nose, and washed down another oxy, counting brushed metal rivets around a fancy mirror. To his left, in a frame, was a line from James Baldwin's story "Sonny's Blues":

These boys . . . were growing up with a rush and their heads bumped abruptly against the low ceiling of their actual possibilities.

8

&

"Mama call it her Mother Rule," Patricia said, moving her queen.

"Patricia!" Siman squealed. "You can't do that!"

"You told me the queen can move any which way," Patricia argued.

"Yeah, that's right, but she can't be jumping over pieces." Siman laughed. "Only knights can do that."

They sat barefoot on throw pillows ten feet above ground in the backyard of their Saginaw home, surrounded by fresh wood aromas. That was Mother's Day, 1971. Each year, Dorothy had bread and butter waffles in bed, and Jerome occupied the kids all day to give her the gift of solitude. That year, their newly built tree house took center stage where Siman, being fourth grade chess team captain, gave his big sister a private lesson.

Siman studied his next move. "So—what's the Mother Rule?"

"It means if you decide to have a baby you better be ready to raise that child by yourself because you never know. That's what Mama said. That's the Mother Rule."

"Why?"

Patricia moved a pawn. "Because Mama said you can't know what plan God has for you, even when you married. Your husband might leave."

"I never heard about no Mother Rule," Siman said, leaning on a giant pillow to look down at the ground.

"Silly. That's because boys can't have no babies."

Siman looked seriously at his sister. "But when you get married the preacher say, *What God put together no man can take apart—*"

"I know that." Patricia sounded offended. "But Mama still say, remember the Mother Rule."

Siman cracked his knuckles.

"And what about our *real* mothers," he said, "they got a special rule for them?"

Patricia was silent, staring at the chessboard, and Siman knew that pointing this out had upset her, but he needed to discuss this, to learn from his sister exactly how he should feel. What was their mother, Dorothy, saying about *real* mothers—who choose not to raise their kids alone? Patricia remained quiet, as if at any moment she might cry. Siman had not meant to pick a fight, although he was angry, but not at his sister. He was angry at the part of life that makes some mothers not want their children. This wasn't Patricia's fault, so he changed his line of questions.

"But don't that mean there's suppose to be a Father Rule, too?"

"I don't know about that. You have to ask Pop."

They studied the board in silence, snacking on lemonade and potato chips, until Patricia smiled, moved a castle, and said, "Mate check!"

"Shoot," Siman said, slapping his palm to his forehead, "you threw me off with all that talk. And—you supposed to say 'checkmate.'"

For years after that day, the memory was like a mental greeting card Siman sent himself every Mother's Day.

As teenagers he told Patricia she was lucky to have the Mother Rule, a set of shoulders to build her life on. Their father, Jerome—the verbose lawyer—was ready with suitable quotes for any situation yet came up short on words when Siman asked about a Father Rule.

"Well, son, Proverbs tells us: *A wise son makes a glad father, but a foolish son is a sorrow to his mother.* I suppose that's as good a rule as any to live by."

Anybody could quote the Bible. Siman wanted words chiseled just for him; words from his father's heart, heavy words, like those often heard at dinner when discussions turned to important things, such as the Black Panthers' breakfast program or trying to make sense of busing to integrate schools. Siman never committed the verse from Proverbs to memory; it just stuck on its own. He had planned to check back with his father in a few years, maybe things would change.

℁

Now, forty years later, opulent spring light spread over Siman's warm, muted decor. Exposed brick, hardwood floors, and high ceilings helped him decompress. Shelves held books, photographs, and art pieces, including three handcrafted chess sets.

Siman stood at his drafting table, looking from river view to computer screen as he scrolled in a new woodcarving forum. For a few months he had visited many websites, connecting with veteran carvers, mostly commenting on tools and techniques. He was hoping to learn more about peach seed monkeys used in family traditions. Against all odds, he might find a path leading to his birth mother. Trying to find your birth mother may be an odd thing to do at the apex of life, but Siman agreed with Patricia: there's never a bad time for finding flesh-and-blood relatives.

He was adopted on the day he was born. Even though his birth mother kept her identity and the monkey's origin a secret, she left his parents a note with instructions, and they followed through, giving him the monkey on his thirteenth birthday in a rite of passage Patricia helped design.

Siman typed a fresh post in the new forum: *Seeking info about carving peach seed monkeys . . .*

The phone rang. He hit speaker and kept typing... *as a family tradition. Can anybody help?*

"Hey! I was just about to call you—Happy Mother's Day!"

"Thank you baby brother and you are full of caca: I know calling me is the farthest thing from your mind. Just like me: you got your head down at that computer."

"Right again. You still in bed?"

"Just finished my waffles and bacon, kids are washing dishes, then Thatcher's taking them bowling and to see *The Perfect Game*."

"—and you're calling to tell me about that blog."

"Yes, Si! I think 2011 will be your year!"

"That's what you said last year."

"Well, that was then and this is now. Have you even looked at it yet?"

"No." He stretched, walking his phone to the corner window to look north toward Johnson Street Bridge. "Go ahead. Tell me what you got."

"A blog out of southwest Georgia for the descendants of Ezekiel Dukes. The blogger, Olga Dukes, is old-school—her profile shot is a test tube containing a section of DNA chain. She posts about all kinds of stuff from genealogy and civil rights to recipes. Listen to these titles: *Brass Footprints, Bus Station Blues, Slap Yo' Mama Caramel Cake*—and my favorite is: *Thanksgiving: Never Been About Turkey.*

"It's been almost two years since we started searching in earnest," Patricia said, "and this is the most exciting bite we've had—"

"Patricia! There have got to be plenty things you would rather be doing." He was fearful of getting too excited.

"Si. Stop. Who are you to tell me how to spend my Mother's Day? Just check your email and our Facebook group. Please."

He promised he would but refused his sister's offer to stay on the phone to discuss this discovery from all sides.

Between his two monitors sat the maroon ring box. He turned it over in his hand like a worry stone as he perused Olga Dukes' site, which was flooded with political posts for Obama/Biden. As he typed in the SEARCH THIS SITE field, he heard these words in his sister's voice: "peach" plus "seed" plus "monkey" as this post instantly filled his screen:

Peach Seed Monkey—a Rarity

Like many, you have likely never heard of a monkey carved from a peach seed—or pit, if you prefer. Our family uses "seed," for this conjures images of life: growing, changing in a good way, while "pit" plunges you into an abyss. Peach seed monkeys have always been familiar to me, but I have never found them common. Growing up in the 1930s, our share-cropper's home was overrun with peach seeds—and men and boys teaching and learning an ancestral carving tradition, while we girls invented games to play with the rejects. From the age of four or five, I recognized the resplendence of the little gem and—like my sisters and girl cousins—was furious at a tradition reserved for boys. (Still not happy about that, B.T.W.)

My research journey mirrors technology's trajectory—starting with stories pulled from carvers I knew. Encyclopedias with wide, weak spines provided no data. As decades passed, I languished in libraries amid books and periodicals as the computer was born and grew up in the domain of busi-nesspeople, bank employees, university students, researchers, and the military—code for "mostly white folks." Meanwhile I read everything that crossed my path, hoping in vain to peer into the peach seed monkey's world.

In 1948, when Polaroid's Land Camera hit the market, and the world was recovering from World War II's devastation, I was a twenty-four-year-old expatriate in Amsterdam, a mesmer-izing city, in spite of the Dutch still claiming "we don't do race." I moved back home seven years later, the only family member with a camera, and became official photographer and curator for our monkey carving tradition, which hitherto had gone unrecorded. Through my transformation into womanhood— and from colored to Negro to Black—I embraced punched card classes, when computer programming finally entered even the smallest HBCU's syllabi. Right up until this Black woman became African-American, I have remained in awe of the simplicity and wonder of our family talisman. Not until zeroes and ones exploded into a handsome prince called Personal Computer and married the seductive Internet, did I finally learn things I'd longed to know and will share with you in future posts. Now, President and First Lady Obama are in the White House and I am back to being Black.

But questions still swirl around our peach seed monkey. Would that cyberspace were true space and fiction were fact. If only we had temporal distortions and rifts to connect us with the monkey's founding carver. Instead, we can only ask: On which shore? With what impetus? And which tools?

Olga Dukes wrote a lot but said little about the meaning her family took from carving and passing on monkeys. And why—after talking about the Polaroid—does she post no pictures of the monkey? There must be a reason for this, but he couldn't imagine what.

Other posts revealed Dr. Dukes' work in 1961 with the Student Nonviolent Coordinating Committee. Her alma mater, Albany State College, was now a university. Olga Dukes had been an adult advisor during the Movement. Her posts fervidly showed an inside view of sit-ins, marches, violence, and mass meetings, not only in southwest Georgia, but also from D.C. to Montgomery to Selma. Students as young as twelve organized and faced police with water hoses, dogs, billy clubs, and cattle prods. She posted a gallery of period Polaroids, including the first night Dr. King spoke in Albany. Different from timeworn public photos of the era, Olga's portraits showed King interacting with workaday folk who history would not remember.

From his parents' and grandparents' stories about dealings with racism before moving north, Siman understood why they pledged no allegiance to the South. Likewise, many of his cousins and friends who moved away now pledged no allegiance to Saginaw. They could not understand his loyalty to a city as segregated as any in the South. How can you explain that home is more than place, more than familiarity and routine? How here and now fills the void of an absent past? Having no comparison, they took blood for granted. With so many things in his past unsure, Siman's place in Saginaw was his main certainty. And yet, with this new lead, he scrolled, hindered and driven, and imagined where the road might lead. If it came to that, could he actually make a trip to Georgia, of all places, and meet strangers who might be as close as the blood in his veins?

In his distant view, beyond computer screen and window, the *BEANS* bunny flashed red neon. He was not in control of his fingers on his keyboard, going back to Contact Us and clicking on Olga Dukes' email: oalchemy@dukesmail.com. Even through the uncertainty that his little monkey's diamond eyes would solve this mystery, Siman wrote a query. He wouldn't spend time crafting a letter; this would not be much more than a question posted in a woodworking forum.

To his amazement, three days later, Olga Dukes replied, asking for more. Patricia stopped by after work and watched over his shoulder as he read:

Dear Mr. Miller,

Thank you for contacting us. We are intrigued by your adoption story and eager to hear more. Peach seed monkeys have been in the Dukes Family for three known generations, and certainly more that we haven't accounted for—yet—not even in legend and lore . . .

"I like the way she put that," Patricia said, "*not even in legend and lore . . .*"

"Pat! Quit interrupting—"

> . . . You say your birth mother gave the monkey to your parents. Do you know the town in which your adoption took place? It's unfortunate that the handwritten note was lost, since so much can be determined from a person's penmanship.

"You see! She agrees with me on that," Siman said.

"Now who's interrupting. Read on!"

> Nevertheless, your diamond-eyed monkey is most intriguing and may tell more than handwriting ever could. Please attach crisp close-up photos of your monkey: top, sides, bottom.
>
> I hope you understand the need for verification, so as not to waste your or my time. We eagerly await your reply and pictures and hope we can provide the answers you seek.
>
> My Best regards from Albany, (southwest) Georgia

"This calls for a celebration!" Patricia said, clapping her hands.

"A little early for that, don't you think?"

"Not at all—I'm excited for you, little brother! I have a strong hunch this Olga Delzina Dukes is related to you, and not very far down the tree. I can't give you any more than that. You just have to trust me."

"I do trust *you*. It's the rest of these people in cyberspace I worry about."

"How could this possibly be a scam? Dr. Dukes is not just in cyberspace; she's in southwest Georgia. Did you look up the town yet?"

"Didn't have to, she sent me a bunch of links to check out,

including one that says Albany is *not far from Plains, Georgia—Jimmy Carter country.*"

"I know you've looked at the numbers."

"Yeah." Siman found a note on his desk. "One year ago, the 2010 census, population was 77,434 and almost seventy-two percent Black, twenty-five percent white—and this is a telling stat: the national poverty rate was fifteen point three percent, and Albany was way more than double at thirty-nine point nine percent."

"Devastating numbers."

"I'll say."

Patricia lifted her voice. "But my guess is there aren't too many *Olgas* in that seventy-two percent, so she won't be hard to find when you get there."

"Hold on—nobody's talking about going to Georgia."

"Right. Not out loud, anyway. But I know you want to go."

"Slow your roll, Pat. Slow your roll."

9

Columbus, Georgia, is one hundred miles due north of Putney. During a rainstorm at Fletcher's, there could be a heat wave at Eunice Williams' house. He had been making this drive for two years— sometimes two or three times a week—since they met through a mutual friend when Eunice needed custom kitchen cabinets for her renovated house. He was pleased with her choice of cherrywood, which motivated him to replace his old cabinets with a custom set. Even though he could never justify such an improvement to his simple contractor's house, once he became enamored with her companionship, this seize-the-day attitude was the sort of thing Eunice brought out in him. And on top of that, she was tall.

By summer's end, frequent trips from Putney to Columbus had begun, a setup that worked well, since Eunice didn't like driving and he'd just as soon keep folks out of his business. In spite of all this, whatever you call what developed between them was no secret in either place.

Fletcher wiped his shoes on her front door mat, taking in the brazen spring day scented with dogwood and magnolia.

"Look at you," Eunice said, stepping aside and accepting a peck on the cheek. "Didn't think you'd make it by eight, but you right on time."

He stepped into the smell of her Lowcountry breakfast: shrimp smothered in an onion-green-pepper gravy served over creamy grits. And Eunice's rolled biscuits were almost as good as Maletha's drop biscuits. Almost.

"What choice did I have, woman? I know you don't serve breakfast past eight fifteen."

"Hot biscuits wait for no man," she said, "still—I'm always surprised to see retired people up-and-at-'em before the light-skinned part of the day."

Fletcher had a barbershop appointment in the afternoon, so he had time for only breakfast and a short visit, but he often spent the day with Eunice. They'd work in her yard, or shop for appliances at the mall, or take in a movie.

Eunice started working for Muscogee County's Division of Family and Children Services back when it was called the Welfare Office. During the week, she wore various wigs. They lived in her guest room on Styrofoam heads. When he visited, she kept that room closed off, but Fletcher could smell wig hair. He much preferred her close-cropped Afro, no guck or grease. She said, at sixty-four, she was too old to be bothered with looking cute; it was more important to be anonymous at the grocery store. Without a wig, she was less likely to be recognized as that woman standing between clients and their benefits.

"Black folk know who you are no matter how many times a week you swap wigs." She scoffed through lip air. "But you know our hair thing gets white folk all confused. And with my nappy hair, they're more apt to think I'm the one needing food stamps."

"Yeah," Fletcher said, "and that's just how messed up the world is."

"When I retire next year, I'm depositing all wigs in the trash."

"I look forward to the day," Fletcher said.

After breakfast he changed the batteries in her smoke detector and Eunice packed him biscuits and Lowcountry leftovers.

They took their leave as usual—with a peck on the lips. He said next time he'd like to stay through the dark-skinned part of the day. She answered with a tender shove out the door.

On the ride back to Albany, Eunice sat lightly on his mind and Maletha nestled in close, her shoulder touching his, as she had done when they first started dating. And the usual cross-firing began.

Even after two years, Fletcher had learned to live with Maletha making her presence known whenever he got together with Eunice. After nearly forty years of marriage, why wouldn't she hang around?

Fletcher was not impressed with Maletha when they first met, because back then he judged people by whether or not they worked in the Movement. Maletha did not, but he liked her reason—she was not nonviolent. Neither was he.

They danced a few times at the mixer, then found a quiet bench outside the gym to talk. Although she only drank root beer, that night she did not yet know enough to be opposed to Fletcher having a real beer.

She said, "Don't get me wrong; I have a lot of respect for Dr. King and his philosophies, but the first time a cracker lays a hand on me, one of us will end up dead, so I have to find other ways to fight for civil rights that don't involve being beaten, jailed, groped, raped, or starving myself. Getting an education is the most potent nonviolent act I can imagine."

"Dr. King would not argue with that," Fletcher said.

He had thought of Altovise, the one he was supposed to marry. She and Maletha had a lot in common: for both, a college education was as necessary as the air they breathed. They had similar grit. It was the reason Altovise left Georgia for the North and the reason

Maletha stayed. There were fancy words for southern versus northern segregation—de facto and de jure—but Fletcher and Maletha agreed the difference was whether bigots stabbed you in the chest or in the back.

Maletha added, "That's not to say I'm ungrateful to you and all the others who protest and risk so much."

"You're welcome," Fletcher said with a sly grin, already warming up to her charm and vivid, dark eyes. "Why you didn't go to college up north somewhere?"

"I love my home. Lord knows Florida has got problems, but my people fought hard for the little bit of Tallahassee real estate we own. Why should I leave?"

"Didn't say you should," he said.

"You think Black folk who leave the South are defectors of the southern Negro cause?"

"We helped build this country brick by brick, so we got a right to live wherever the hell we want. So naw, I don't think that no more than I think you and I are backwoods for staying."

"Amen!" She held up her root beer to toast. "White folks up north are bigots, too. Just not always easy to see. Down here people wear bigotry like a badge of honor, so you know exactly where the enemy lurks—for the most part."

"You can never destroy a target you can't see," Fletcher added.

"Amen again!"

By the end of the night, they had agreed on more issues than not, and moved to his Ford Fairlane, where they found much less to talk about. When he drove her home, he made up his mind to act quickly and not miss out on another good thing. Maletha was more cautious, insisting that he court her for the three years she spent getting her teaching degree before saying "yes." His family fell for her instantly, many claiming that Maletha's last name, Givens, was only skin deep—she was Dukes to the bone—to which she replied, *Y'all are way too impressed with yourselves.*

The bell above Harlem Barbershop's door rang as Fletcher rushed in from a downpour. Chatter and laughter never paused as the men waiting instinctively glanced toward him. Fletcher wiped his feet, shook off thoughts of Maletha and Eunice, and hung his umbrella on a hook by the door.

"What you say there, young man?" Fletcher said to his barber.

"Doin awl-right, Fletcher. How you?" Blue Jean said, shaving a young's man head. "You still dodging them church women?"

"Don't seem to matter that I don't go to church," Fletcher said.

"They don't care." Blue Jean was never in a hurry when he spoke. "If they missed you in the pews on Sunday, they'll try to catch you on a barstool next Saturday."

"That's why I avoid both," Fletcher said.

In chairs stretched along large picture windows, two men laughed and shook his hand as Fletcher joined them to wait his turn.

Fifty years ago the small brick building housed Dick Gay's Poolroom, where Dr. King connected with locals, rallying support for nonviolent protests. Anyone entering the barbershop steps on brass footprints embedded in the South Jackson sidewalk, marking the protestors' route from Shiloh Baptist Church to City Hall the night Dr. King spoke. Fletcher and Altovise joined thousands of people at that mass meeting, King's first of many in Albany. He spoke again that night, across the street at Mount Zion, and sidewalks bulged with people listening on loudspeakers. This was King after Montgomery and before Birmingham; King the man becoming King the legend.

In its heyday, four barbers worked in the shop, but now only two active stations were outfitted with vintage leather, brass, and chrome barber chairs. The same ancient shoeshine stand claimed the back end of the building.

The barbershop had its own incense, a mixture of decades: shaving cream, alcohol, and clipper oil mixed with a hint of aged cigar and cigarette smoke. Fletcher welcomed the mens' banter, a place to sink into as he was ambushed by memories that would have creaked like old knees had they made a sound. He brushed rain from his khakis, and revisited Monroe High School, freshman year.

1957. Summer had stretched into September that day in their airless homeroom class. Fletcher sat directly behind Altovise, who was famous for her collection of hair bows. That morning she had none to match her green-plaid box-pleat skirt, so she shaped a dollar bill into a bow. With her hair swept up off her collar, the second thing Fletcher noticed, right below the bow, was her strawberry birthmark.

At their segregated school, they shared a distinct brand of invincibility and strutted around inside a tailor-made experience: the 10 percent of their character above the surface, in full view—skin color, gender, clothes, music, religion—relating to everybody else's 10 percent. They knew from their all-Black teachers that, in spite of being cast out of history in cast-off books, if they believed it, they could achieve it.

Because Altovise lived in East Albany and Fletcher was on the southside, she only knew him as a star basketball center, like her older brother, Thaddeus. But like most folk, he knew her and her sister, Vada, from their singing—school and church choirs, talent shows, and eventually their own band. From the first time he heard Altovise sing and play piano, her music etched its way into his soul. They were dating by Christmas; he gave her perfume, she gave him a houndstooth shirt with mother-of-pearl snaps. That shirt was long gone, but she still buys Estée Lauder Youth Dew.

Their high school years were framed by bookend events involving Martin Luther King: Izola Curry stabbing him in New York City, and three years later, his trip down from Atlanta to help desegregate Albany. They would remember those years as a tornado of events: term papers, exams, courtships, breakups, mass meetings, and protests. On the eve of their first protest, like many of their friends, they wrote their last will and testaments; Fletcher ran drills in basketball practice, then shot hoops with Charles Sherrod and Cordell Reagon, who were new to town, college age, and working with the newly formed SNCC; he ran track and lifted weights in P.E. class, then trained in workshops to protect the women from mob and police violence; in choir and band practice, Altovise honed her piano and singing skills, then learned how to recast church songs as protest anthems from Cordell Reagon, Rutha Mae Harris, Bernice Johnson, and Chuck Neblett—the original Freedom Singers. In those cast-off textbooks from white schools—books that were never up-to-date, even when brand-new—they both scoffed at skewed versions of everything, and after school, they left behind biased mandates for a safety zone inside the 90 percent of their lives below the surface, outside of public awareness, by attending Olga's Institute for Etiquette & Equity. They practiced social skills, studied KKK church bombings and lunch counter sit-ins, along with Gandhi's Salt March. Their families skipped trees and gifts that year as part of the Black Christmas boycott of merchants in downtown Albany.

Amid fire and creative chaos, in meeting after meeting—even though Altovise was the chalk to Fletcher's cheese—they fell in love. Merely being near Altovise opened a portal between them. Fletcher peered through and saw them, gray-haired and still together, surrounded by many children and grandchildren.

Blue Jean called and Fletcher slid into the barber's chair. Memories followed, tucking in below each armrest. He readied himself for Blue Jean's barrage of questions about Altovise. Their conversation took a different turn.

"You here, but your mind off somewhere else," Blue Jean said, wrapping the barber's cape around Fletcher's shoulders.

"I was thinkin' about the SNCC days," Fletcher answered, facing Blue Jean's station wall, crowded with civil rights pictures and memorabilia.

"Yeah-yeah! I know bout *snick*," a young man in the next chair said. "That was the nickname for the Student Nonviolent Coordinating Committee."

Blue Jean said, "Wouldn't expect y'all's generation to know about that—not 'less you know somebody worked in the Movement, 'cause I know darn well they ain't taught y'all that in school these days."

"Not in school, but at church." The young man gestured toward the memorabilia, which included a recent photo of a Black teen in a light-colored hoodie, his vigilant eyes sloping toward the corners. "It ain't even been two months yet since Trayvon Martin was killed, but the deacons at my church already set up a ministry just for us men eighteen to twenty-five. We been learning about many Black boys and men killed by white terrorists, like Emmett Till, Eldridge Cleaver. Too many to name." He lifted his black hoodie from his lap, showing a bold logo: YBMM=Young Black Men's Ministry and a quote from 1960s Albany lawyer C. B. King: "*Find form for the expression of your discontent.*"

"Well that show-is a surprise," Blue Jean said, briefly resting his clippers. "They even teaching y'all about C. B. King."

"I always wondered," the young man asked, "was he related to MLK?"

"Nah—no relation," Fletcher said, "but C. B. was a king in his own right. A breath of air, just when we needed it. A Black man who knew the law and could stand up against them whites in *any* courtroom."

"Them white boy lawyers didn't know what had hit when C.B. let loose," Blue Jean said. "And now the courthouse named after him. 'Bout time."

"You in college?" Fletcher asked the young man.

"No, sir. I graduated from Albany State two years ago, but I read about whites speeding through campus back then, throwing eggs, ice, and urine on students. Even burned a cross in front of Gibson Hall. Girls' dorms didn't have enough security to keep white men from roaming the halls, propositioning our beautiful sisters."

"Sounds like you would've been involved back in the day," Fletcher said.

"Yeah," Blue Jean added, "and—you would've been shut down and expelled for it, too, 'cause that's exactly what President Dennis did to a bunch of students."

"William Dennis was a puppet, controlled by that all-white board of regents and scared of losing his job," Fletcher said. "Was a shame what he did."

"But," the young man interrupted, "President Freeman made it right! Last year he invited the expelled students from the class of '61 back and gave them honorary degrees."

"Fifty years after the fact," Blue Jean chided, "but I'm glad he did that—and he should've never had to."

His haircut finished, the young man took a chair along the window to continue talking.

"So y'all actually met Dr. King?"

"Me and Fletcher both, in this building right here when it was a poolroom."

"They called that a *day of penance*," Fletcher said, "the night before, police arrested protesters and somebody threw rocks and bottles. Next day, King and Abernathy came here to the poolroom, told us it was our right and duty to go up against segregation, but that nonviolence was the way of the strong."

Nonviolence had been Fletcher's biggest challenge. In every protest, he kept a roving eye, always marching directly behind Altovise, but knew he wouldn't be able to hold back if a cop laid a hand on her. It was one thing to role-play nonviolence in SNCC workshops with your friends shoving you, calling you names, and pretending to pour hot coffee over your head, or spit in your face; it was altogether different to face policemen or a mob that would just as soon see you dead.

Motivated by his audience of two, Blue Jean went on. "You see it was about leverage. King studied what Gandhi did overseas in India, and we did that here: protest, get arrested, and fill up the racist-ass jails to a breaking point. That give you leverage to start attacking problems."

"Makes sense," the young man said.

"But then," Blue Jean shut off his clippers, using them to punch the air with each point. "This how it really worked: Albany Po-lice Chief Laurie Pritchett studied Gandhi, too, and he bragged about outfoxing King. Albany po-lice was *supposed* to practice nonviolence. Where King went, the cameras went, and he stayed here—in Dougherty County—but that didn't keep them po-lice in *Terrible Terrell, Bad Baker,* or *Lamentable Lee* from beating up on folks once they knowed they wouldn't be on the TV." He restarted the clippers, focused now on the nape of Fletcher's neck. "Then, Pritchett didn't put nobody in jail inside Albany city limits. That sucker rented jail space all round, within fifty miles. Them empty Albany jails messed up that leverage idea and wore folks down."

"But Laurie Pritchett couldn't control everybody with a badge," Fletcher added. "He had no authority over Sheriff Cull Campbell when that joker used a cane on C. B. King's head. Campbell said: *I told the son-of-a-bitch to get out of my office, and he didn't get out.* Blood was all down C. B.'s shirt. No matter what he said, I bet you Pritchett's billy club got plenty wear and tear, too, when nobody was looking."

"Matter fact, we can go check!" Blue Jean said, "That billy club on display down the street at the Civil Rights Institute right now. One of them white girls smuggled it out in her jeans fifty years ago!"

The three men laughed.

"By the way, Mr. Fletcher," the young man said, "me and Bo D graduated the same year, only I was at Dougherty."

"I figured y'all might be same-year children." Fletcher had done the math earlier, thinking how much further along Bo D could be had he gone to college.

Fletcher was their age in 1965, married Maletha that year, and Altovise was nearly out of his system. He was filled to the brim with purpose and promise, despite having far too many doors close in his face. He never wasted time thinking about what might've been had *he* gone to college. What would college have been like back then if it could've just been *college*? Free and clear of boarding buses to test ICC rulings; not in need of biracial committees to negotiate bonds for students filling the jails? In 1965, he had a deferment keeping him out of Vietnam, and Cassius Clay was right: Black men didn't need to go to Southeast Asia; they were fighting a war every day on the streets of America. Fletcher had a PhD in everything he needed to know.

With no other men waiting, the barbershop fell quiet. The young man thanked them, gathered his hood around his face, and darted out through the rain.

Blue Jean gently whisked hair clippings from Fletcher's shoulders and removed the cape. Fletcher rose from the barber's chair and counted cash from his wallet.

Blue Jean's broom swished quietly as he swept the floor, never looking up.

"Well, have you heard?"

"Heard what?" Finally. Here it was.

"Tonk say somebody told him Altovise Benson back in All-beny."

"Is that right?" Fletcher said, laying the money in a small tray as he had done for the past thirty years.

"You know about that?"

"Nope." Fletcher added, "Take it easy," and walked toward his umbrella in a way that said the discussion was over.

Just like that. Altovise strutted back into his short term from their long-ago; back from stealing kisses in front of her locker, and holding hands in mass meetings. Teenage innocence and invincibility were luxuries they could not afford as they strove to be models of civil unrest.

Sooner or later he'd have to talk to her and stir all of this up like green-brown silt from the river floor. But not yet. He pulled his dripping umbrella into the Fairlane, keenly aware of each moment's passing in what would be his last days of freedom from their past.

Long after nightfall, he set his alarm and crawled into bed. Rockhudson circled three times and curled up, nose to tail on his bed nearby. The dog sighed. The man sighed and clapped his hands to turn out the light, ready to rest after several hours of memories riding his back like a spry little monkey.

10

~

April 1, 2012, nearly a year since Patricia found Olga Dukes' blog. Siman dreaded telephones and was waiting for a call from her. They had come a long way over many months of fits and starts, taking turns being on deck to move on with next steps.

When he was nervous, he often did *a quick buff*, as his mother called tidying up. He ran a feather duster over walls of books, which lead to his favorite chess set, displayed under a warm shelf light. The hand-cast resin set, which Siman commissioned from a Saginaw artist, pays homage to America's first Black union, Brotherhood of Sleeping Car Porters, men who worked 1930s and 1940s passenger trains.

Siman looked back on his year of waiting, grateful to focus on each chess piece, rendered in splendid detail.

♟ First, he buffed the pawns; which are period suitcases covered in travel stickers.

After Mother's Day 2011, true to form, in spite of his sister's prodding, Siman operated with an abundance of caution and did not send photos of his diamond-eyed monkey until three weeks later. By then Olga was immersed in planning the fiftieth anniversary of the SNCC Albany Civil Rights Movement set for June. Her assistant sent regrets at having to *postpone their missive* until after the celebration. Who calls an email a missive? He loved it and had come to expect no less of this force called Olga Dukes.

♖ Replicas of Chicago's Grand Central Station clock tower serve as castles.

The day his sister watched Oprah's last show, all teary-eyed, Siman had a rowing injury and tore his rotator cuff. Those early weeks of pain and inactivity led to doubt and setback, and he filed his binder labeled GEORGIA in a bottom drawer and rejected his sister's offer to take over correspondences with Olga. But he didn't unsubscribe from her blog.

♞ Knights are porters, outfitted in militaristic blue jackets or white dining car jackets with squared-off hats, each holding a passenger's walking stick with gilded horse-head finial.

Summer slumped by. Olga posted pictures and stories of her fellow SNCC Foot Soldiers who gathered in Albany, Georgia, from around the country. He figured she had enough to do without hearing from him about talismans and birth mothers. Patricia said, "Not true, baby brother. You're scared. I get it. But we can't give up."

♗ Bishops are engineers in dark denim or gray starched overalls, with plaid shirts topped by striped engineer's caps and finished with heavy gloves and boots, each holding an oil can.

Months later, his shoulder like new, Patricia pulled her brother from his gloom for Trinity's annual Halloween party. Siman donned his custom Vulcan ears and, in between jabs to get back to his search, Patricia told him he didn't need those extra ears, because his already came to a pretty good point. They laughed like old times and he finally conceded: he sent Olga the requested photos of his peach seed monkey.

♛ The kings wear charcoal or cream double-breasted suits, fedoras, and wing-tipped shoes.

Through the holidays, he and Olga had a lively, if sporadic, email exchange, but he was losing patience. How much did she know? Was *she* actually his birth mother? Who carved his monkey?

Then. Around mid-March, with no warning, Olga stopped emailing.

Patricia said, "Slow your roll, Si—what's a few more weeks compared to waiting your whole life?"

♛ He finished by polishing the queens, who wear charcoal or off-white Victory suits, with oxfords, tams, gloves, and fur stoles.

Siman stepped back, admiring the chess pieces standing at attention in golden luster. His desk space was prepared: ring box at its post between monitors, sharp pencils and fresh legal pad, and he printed out an article about Olga Dukes that he recently found online in *Science Woman* magazine. The interviewer painted a good picture of Olga's life, beginning with her birth in 1924 in Albany, Georgia.

In 1941, Olga turned seventeen and graduated from Madison High School in Albany. Influenced by her science teacher, who had graduated from Atlanta University, she was dreaming of genetics and DNA research, two fields far out of reach for her station. With the start of WWII, she considered joining the army at a time when white American soldiers would rather die than let a Black doctor or nurse touch them. Instead, she worked as a domestic to pay for college, and—for lack of any science courses—attended Georgia Normal and Agricultural College for a two-year degree in teacher training. She was elated when, in 1943, the school was renamed Albany State College and granted four-year status, allowing Olga to graduate in 1945 with a double degree in teacher training and home economics. Her science teacher arranged a job with a colleague in Montréal, where Olga joined a private lab backed by government funding to work on a penicillin project. The team included other young expatriates and refugees from Europe and Africa, including a young man named Levie Kroon who had escaped Germans occupying Amsterdam. The war ended and she moved with him to Amsterdam.

Science Woman made no mention of a husband or children, but when Siman and Patricia dissected the article, they had both thought it possible that Olga Dukes could be his birth mother. She would have had him at thirty-eight, after her time in Amsterdam. Not probable, but possible.

In the article, Olga Dukes said:

> *Travel to Canada for a twenty-one-year-old "colored" woman from the Deep South was the stuff of science fiction. The world was at war against fascism and from Maine to California nonwhites—as well as women of all races, from nurses to welders—stepped up to help with the war effort, in spite of having to still fight for human rights here in America. Of course, because Turner Air Force Base was in Albany, Southwest Georgia (SOWEGA) played crucial roles during World War II. While attending Albany State College, I cleaned houses and took in ironing while also helping on campus, which housed servicemen and was the residential headquarters for south Georgia and north Florida WACS. I had never heard the word expatriate; I only knew that I must seize the chance to leave Jim Crow Georgia. After graduation I boarded a Trailways bus to Canada. In Montréal I landed in an academic and professional oasis, working with a multicultural team of other young scientists. Having suffered the bigotry and misogyny of south Georgia, to be immersed in this diverse group of men and*

women in the middle of the war was unfathomable. We were experimenting on deep tank fermentation *to unlock the process for the mass manufacture of penicillin. You can see how crucial this was to the war effort.*

With only minutes before his phone would ring, Siman went back to work on his list. His word choices needed work:

~~Early Life~~   *Family*
~~School~~   *Childhood*
~~Work Life~~   *Education*
~~Work~~   *Career*

His list was complete. On his printout, he drew doodles around *Date: 4.1.12 = 8*. A good number. Infinity.

❧

"I always find concerns to be much worse in anticipation," Olga said at the top of their call when Siman told about his quick-buff introspection.

"My apologies," she said. "I'm afraid I added exponentially to your angst with my mysterious hiatus as I got ducks in a row for you. While that is an explanation of my rudeness, it in no way excuses it."

"Please, no apology necessary," Siman said. "I really appreciate this chance to talk with you. I was just reading about your amazing years in Montréal during World War II and Amsterdam after. You are as much a war hero as any soldier who held a gun."

"My-my," Olga said, "you have been excavating! That feels like a few lifetimes ago. There were so, so many around the world, working behind the scenes in the war effort. If one cares to dig, history will unchain what is left of those stories. More importantly, thank you for sending such detailed photos of your monkey. Quite exquisite!"

Siman felt pride! As if he had carved the monkey himself. A new sensation for him.

"Of course, they are all one of a kind, but yours is in a special class, with those diamond eyes. Would that I could give you more definitive news on how your birth mother came by the monkey—we're doing everything we can to solve the mystery."

"Sure. I wasn't expecting miracles overnight," Siman said, but in every way, he had been. So she wasn't his birth mother.

"But I'm eager to hear *your* side of the story," Olga said.

"I'm not much of a storyteller."

"We're all storytellers, Mr. Miller," she said.

Siman sensed that Olga Dukes knew more than she could—or would—share. She was evasive.

Siman added more doodles. Usually, he would decide his next move by answering his standard question: *What are the chances*? As he spoke, he slowly drew lines through each item on his list, and choosing not to be cautious, he pushed the note aside.

"To understand me you have to know why my life has two distinct eras: before and after the plane crash."

In the same way that first-grade Siman found no numbers connecting him to his mysterious birth family, numbers failed him again on January 2, 2003, as he and Patricia strived to make sense of tragedy.

"Since the crash happened on 01–02–03, I naturally looked for numerical meaning. Of course, I found many wonders in the power of three, and magic of six—sum of the date's digits—but—" He paused, looking away, relieved that Olga couldn't see how his face was betraying his stoic voice.

And then she added, "But in all that numerical splendor you found nowhere to hang your bottomless grief."

"No. I didn't."

"Deepest condolences, Mr. Miller. Your lives changed infinitely on that day."

"Thank you. Indeed they did."

And there it was. Infinity.

Silence hovered. Welcomed.

"But sometimes," Siman added, "even numbers fail us."

Siman wasn't sure what it was about this woman that compelled him to share more than he usually tells a stranger about his plane crash story. Maybe because he could sense, even over the phone, how intently she listened.

"There's not much more to tell," he summed up, "but I do have a request. I'm hoping you know my birth mother, or maybe you *will* know her soon and, even if she wants no contact with me, that you will relay my stories to her. I want her to see who I have become."

"Consider it done," Olga said.

Three nights later, Siman drove to dinner in Bay City, having made a crucial decision.

"Just so you know," he said to Patricia, waiting for Thatcher and the kids to serve dessert, "I'm telling them about my peach seed monkey later."

"Hold on," Patricia said. "We talked about waiting, until we had more answers from Olga Dukes."

"We know enough, it's time to pull them in."

Patricia was quiet.

"Trinity and ThatcherJr are as close as I'll ever come to having kids, so I thought you'd support me in this."

"I *do* support you," she paused and shook her head. "Just forget what I said."

Siman looked at his sister, who looked away.

After cake and ice cream, Siman sat his ring box next to his mug of coffee. Although he had renewed hope with this Olga Dukes connection, he felt a joy with his family that did not rely on DNA. He would share the peach seed monkey because Trinity knows carrot cake is his favorite; he can do no wrong in ThatcherJr's eyes, and Patricia and Thatcher support him even when they think he's wrong.

"Listen up, everybody." Siman tapped his mug with a spoon. "So! You know my adoption story, but here's a part you don't know."

He held his monkey between pinched fingers, carefully twirling it with his other fingers.

"Whoa! What is it?" Trinity asked as he placed the monkey in her open palm.

"Somebody carved this from a peach seed!" Siman said. "Can you imagine?"

"I wish I had a magnifying glass," Trinity said.

"We can fix that!" Patricia said, and left the room.

"I wanna hold it," ThatcherJr whined.

"I like the eyes," Trinity said.

"Trinity! Let *me* hold it!" ThatcherJr lunged, knocking the monkey from Trinity's hand onto the tile floor.

The monkey fell on the point connecting his tail to his body, bounced, and broke.

For a long moment everyone around the table sat frozen, speechless, staring at the two pieces.

"What's going on?" Patricia walked back in, magnifying glass in hand.

"ThatcherJr broke Uncle Siman's little monkey!" Trinity blurted out, shoving her brother.

"I didn't mean to! You wouldn't let me hold it. I was just trying to—"

"Calm down, you two," Thatcher intercepted.

"It was an accident!" Siman snapped.

Unaccustomed to petulance from their uncle, both children retreated into silence.

"Just a little mishap." Siman recouped and gently shook his nephew's slumped shoulders. "Don't worry, buddy, all is forgiven."

"OK, kids, let's bus the table," Thatcher said, gently ushering their sad parade.

Siman sat across from his sister, cradling his monkey in two pieces. He placed them in his ring box, unsure of how to feel.

"You OK?" Patricia asked.

"I was too huffy with the kids."

"Si—they broke your monkey."

"Did you see ThatcherJr's face? I wish *I* had broken the monkey."

"He's nine. He'll move on a lot more easily than you could."

She pulled the two pieces out of the ring box and examined the monkey under magnification. "Looks like a clean break. I bet superglue will do the job."

Siman cracked his knuckles, watching his sister place the pieces back in his ring box.

"I know what you're doing," she said, "you're looking for a sign in your precious numbers."

More silence. Where else was he to look for the way forward? His whole life his peach seed monkey had endured with minimal life support. And in the blink of an eye that changed.

"Let's see—what do we have?" Patricia went on. "Today is 4/4/12 and that equals 11, which leaves us with 2!"

"Good number." He gave up a half smile.

"Yeah, it is. And here's what I know." She closed the box and slowly slid it toward him. "Our little monkey is broken and your brand-new family in south Georgia is waiting to become whole."

"That's in no way an absolute yet."

"Feels that way to me." She smiled. "Just trust!"

Siman was smiling, too, thinking about his well-dressed chess brigade back at his loft, standing with all their bags packed, ready to march into some kind of action. Was it time for him to fall in line?

"Normal to be scared. I'd be scared, too." Patricia's voice trembled. "Shoot—I *am* scared, for what this means for you and me." She caught a tear.

"Noooo, Pat—"

Siman knew that all her life Patricia had a warm envy that was heightened as she witnessed his peach seed monkey tradition blooming.

Patricia said, "Let me finish—sometimes you just need to hear stuff out loud." She sniffed and wiped away tears. "Book your flights, baby brother! Something tells me they got superglue in Albany, Georgia."

Two *was* a good number, and for the way forward, he had only to look into his sister's eyes.

11

~

"You got my cobbler fixed so it won't spill?" Olga asked as Fletcher helped her into the Fairlane's passenger seat.

"Yep. Which library this month?"

"Tallulah Massey branch," she said, rolling down her window to let in a twilight April breeze. "I've got my phone. Siri will get us there."

"I don't need no computer telling me where to go." Fletcher started the engine. "I know Albany like the back-a my hand."

"And Albany is busy changing while you're studying the back of your hand."

"You might just have a point there." They shared a laugh.

Olga turned her face, as if talking to the wind. "Got a question for you."

"Awl-right," Fletcher said after she paused for too long. "What is it?"

"What became of that beautiful diamond-eyed monkey you carved in '62?"

He was surprised that she asked, since she knew this story better than anybody. Was that a sign of her memory failing?

"Well," he'd tread lightly, "remember I was boarding with you when I carved it?"

"And you were very secretive. I remember that." Olga held her hand out of the window, catching fistsful of wind.

The question would be out of the blue, if Altovise was not back.

Olga laughed. "And I also recall that you wore enough Old Spice back then to start your own trade route!"

"I think I had moved on to English Leather by then."

"I see. Guess I'm dis-remembering. But what about the monkey?"

"I gave it to Altovise," he would stick to what he knew she knew, "just before she left."

"I do recall you were lucky my little stray earring had two diamonds just the right size for the eyes."

She paused. Fletcher glanced over, knowing exactly who was on her mind.

"That was a trying time for you," Olga said.

"Must've been a pretty hard time for you, too."

Another topic that was off-limits. Levie Kroon—Ursula's grandfather—gave Olga those earrings for her thirtieth birthday in Amsterdam; an understated pair of two-stone diamond studs. The next year, her trip home for their father's funeral was marked by Emmett Till's murder. She was home only a couple of weeks when she lost one of the earrings. Back then Fletcher had not considered how much those earrings meant to her, since she was never a fan of diamonds, always said they have Africa's sweat and blood on them.

"That was a long time ago," Olga said, "can't remember that far back."

Content that his sister's steel-trap mind was intact, he tried to read her angle. She kept her face to the wind, steeped in fifty-year-old memories of her Dutch lover.

"I wonder what became of the little monkey?" Olga said.

"Maybe you should ask Altovise."

"Oh no you don't! You gave me strict instructions to stay out of it, remember?"

"Indeed I do."

"—so maybe *you* should ask her."

Fletcher didn't reply.

"Wish I had at least gotten a picture of it." She turned toward Fletcher. "Details may be fuzzy, but I'll never forget that one. An exquisite work of art."

"If that's true, it was your diamonds that set it apart."

For Fletcher, the entire event was as close as April's tepid breeze coming through his car windows. Everything had revolved around Altovise.

Fletcher and Altovise dated all four years in high school—deemed the couple most likely to marry. By senior year, fall of '61, youth in many cities had been mobilized by Black college students sitting at a Woolworth's counter in Greensboro the year before. On Shaw University's campus in Raleigh, activist Ella Baker harnessed this energy to create the Student Nonviolent Coordinating Committee. While Fletcher returned to construction work and Altovise prepared to enter Bennett College, they were both still immersed in activism.

During nine days in July after graduation, Movement activity surged. Local students were expelled from Albany State College for participating in the Movement and "literacy tests" denied Blacks the right to vote, prompting the start of Citizenship Schools.

Fletcher's tolerance for nonviolent direct action was tested again as he and Altovise joined a group protesting the Albany Theatre on Jackson Street. He prepared as usual, making sure Olga knew where he stored his will, savings passbook, spare key, and title to his Fairlane. He could not know this would be the last protest for him and Altovise.

Sparked by King's words from a mass meeting—*If they will not listen to our words, they will have to face our bodies*—on this day, the status quo would not stand. No line would form beneath a back alley COLORED ENTRANCE sign. Their small number had grown during their ten-minute march from Shiloh Baptist Church.

A group of whites standing in line parted like the Red Sea against an invisible force field surrounding the protesters as they moved toward the front doors, unruffled by sideline jeers, spitting, and obscenities.

Within minutes, police cars and paddy wagons arrived. With hands resting on billy clubs and guns, officers approached calmly, ordering all to disperse. Fletcher kept his eyes roving and saw a knot of preteen white boys throw rocks at the police, setting off an attack.

Pandemonium spread quickly as protesters fought back with silence and nonviolence.

An officer pushed Fletcher with the butt of a billy club and Altovise ran toward him. Fletcher yelled to the officer, "None of us threw them rocks. I saw those white boys over there throw them."

"Fletcher," Altovise implored, "don't speak, remember?"

"You talking back, boy?" The officer pushed Fletcher again.

Another officer wrapped his arm around Altovise's rib cage. Fletcher cupped her hand between his, afraid to pull.

"Let go, boy," the policeman drawled, "or I'll make you wish you ne-vah wuz born."

A second policeman stunned Fletcher with a cattle prod across his wrist. He lost his grip, sank to his knees in pain, and was grateful that Altovise's hand was spared.

The officer pushed Fletcher again. "Git movin, boy!"

"Fletcher! Don't resist!" Altovise's voice faded into the din as she willfully went limp and was dragged toward a paddy wagon. Fletcher's nonviolent training could not keep him from struggling against the policeman. Only the gashing billy club blow above his eye stopped him, his shirt instantly streaked red. He collapsed to his knees, writhing in pain.

He would lay down his life for her, but could only look helplessly through his bloodied eye at Altovise; same as a daughter or wife sold away, this wagon shinier, with much more horsepower, but nothing new. Seconds later, a policeman hit Fletcher again across his neck, and two others forced him into a different paddy wagon.

Shaking and rocking inside the paddy wagon, Fletcher raised his hand to his face to catch blood from his eye and nose. An older man handed him a clean, white handkerchief.

"Lean yo head back an' put some pressure on it, son. Lucky you ain't loss your eye. You'll be all right."

Blood trickled down Fletcher's throat. Voices around him singing freedom songs did not bolster him. How could he live if anything were to happen to Altovise?

After that protest, thirty-one girls were missing, including Altovise. Law authorities gave no information about where they were being held, or if they were alive. Along with many other girls, Altovise would spend over a month in the Larson Brig, a deplorable old prison, while their families worked frantically to rescue them.

The brig changed Altovise. And that changed Fletcher. Heartsick, he became an eyewitness to his life, replaying their brief four years together like a movie. He wanted Altovise to live her college dream, even without him.

Peach cobbler aroma filled the Fairlane as Fletcher pulled into Tallulah Massey's parking lot. He killed the engine, but before he could open his door, Olga said, "Wait. Before we go in, we need to talk. Altovise came to see me yesterday."

"Yeah?"

"She called in the morning, and by the afternoon she joined us for voter registration training, just like old times. She helped pass out Obama yard signs. And seeing her made a whole host of things come into focus. You saw her that day at Piggly Wiggly: the Volvo with the U-Haul and Michigan plates."

"You took longer than I thought to put that together," he said.

"It's only been about a week."

"With all your informants texting and carrying on, I thought you'd know by the time you got home."

"I've known for a few days, got tired of waiting to see when you were planning to tell me."

"I don't know."

Olga placed her hand on his shoulder. "I understand, baby brother. I'm sure you don't know."

"So?" Fletcher asked. "How is she?"

"First you tell me how she looks."

"Unfairly fantastic."

They laughed together.

"I had a feeling! But, of course, I couldn't grope her face like a cliché blind person in a movie, or feel up on her wrists like Ray Charles, to figure out her dress size."

"Nope. You couldn't've gotten away with that like Ray. So why the U-Haul?"

"She retired! And has moved back home—but you'll get the face-to-face 411 just as soon as you reach out."

Fletcher was quiet.

Cobbler balanced in one hand, he guided Olga toward the library doors.

"Speaking of Altovise," she said, "do *you* remember what I told you shortly after she left when you were grappling so hard with all of that?"

"Of course I remember," Fletcher said, surprised. She was referring to the one and only time Olga spoke to him about being raped when she was sixteen.

"Thankfully, Altovise never went through what I did, but after her time in the brig, she and I had both personally experienced stifling hatred growing like a fungus. That's why we left—and only forces much greater than our trauma would bring us back home."

"Did she mention the monkey when y'all talked?" Fletcher asked.

"No, but I'm sure you'll find out why once you get in touch," Olga said, "and I can arrange that."

"Nope. You stay out of this."

"Yes sir."

"If it wasn't seeing Altovise, then what made you think of that monkey out of the blue?"

"You won't believe me if I told you!"

"Try me."

"I couldn't believe it myself—but during spring cleaning, The Twins were helping me get things in order and one of them found that other earring!"

"You right," Fletcher said, "that is hard to believe. Where was it?"

"In one of many boxes in my study closet that I hadn't touched in years. Can't remember what I had her looking for, but there was the earring after fifty-plus years, must've slipped off and landed in that box—I was always losing things. But naturally, touching those little diamonds made me think of you carving the monkey that I hadn't heard of since."

"What are the odds?" Fletcher said, holding the door open.

"Indeed. What are the odds?"

12

$\sim$

Lately, Siman's ring box sat idle in its spot between his two monitors. Seeing the monkey in two pieces felt like a dreadful omen. Had he been too busy pushing away the only family he knew for a Georgia mystery family? Somehow quite the opposite was true. Searching for his birth family had brought nostalgia for his Saginaw childhood and the life his parents built.

Both Jerome and Dorothy migrated as teenagers when their families left Mississippi cotton and tobacco for Detroit sheet and tool. Born into the Silent Generation and making way for Baby Boomers, their decision to sever ties to southern relatives was a conscious choice filled with knots and tangles. Even though this meant no summer trips to the Black Belt, Jerome and Dorothy raised their children with a solid understanding of their roots and customs (such as what foods bring New Year's luck).

In those days, most of their family and friends worked for General Motors and had money to spend on new housing, cars, clothes, and recreation. Motown concerts brought many stars to town, which was much higher on his sister's list. Jerome passed his love of baseball on to Siman.

They lived in Saginaw's Buena Vista neighborhood, a few blocks from Vet's stadium. They could walk to the Negro League baseball games. Fans of all races came for comedy and stayed for top-tier baseball.

Siman liked swimming in Mershon pool, he and Patricia were excellent roller skaters, and their family often went bowling and had picnics in parks around the city; but nothing could top an Indianapolis Clowns game. They were the Harlem Globetrotters of baseball. Siman still had shortstop Birmingham Sam's autographed trading card.

In third grade, his parents forced Siman into Little League for social interaction. Even though he loved being a spectator, he had zero interest in playing and was well below average as a player. He joined to make friends with brawny boys and thereby win his father's adoration. Siman's failure to merit even a nod from those boys led to him devaluing friendships in general.

Noticing his son slouched on the bench, game after game, Jerome bought Siman a scorebook and introduced him to baseball stats, a universe unto itself. Siman found a new home for his growing love of numbers. From then on, he was fully engaged, smiling as he collected basic facts: *How many left-handed batters? Who runs faster: tall or short? How many first-pitch strikes?*

Baseball stats further verified his place in the world and brought order to randomness. But he still struggled socially. The art of conversation seemed to be about one person asking a question and the other answering, until people learned he was adopted, then they rarely engaged him. Was this because he had no answers to the questions flesh-and-blood families know? *Whose eyes do you have? Which side of the family has twins?* If asking questions is what people did, Siman was all for it—until he learned there were no stats for who he was; a vacuum remained where his birth family story should be. And his peach seed monkey was merely an empty token.

In spite of his introverted, awkward manner, his parents had hoped he'd become a lawyer like his father. But when he learned he could become a CPA and be paid for what he would gladly do for free, he dove wholeheartedly into numbers; he would prove that as a top-level numbers man he could deliver everything his parents wished for him. Since words put you at the mercy of rhetoric, he preferred the clarity of numbers, so he assigned math for his work life and literature for pleasure. In doing this, he dodged one of his greatest fears: being a disappointment to his parents by not becoming a lawyer.

His parents learned to embrace his hunger for stats, which made him more social, until they realized data was all he wanted from people. Patricia called him *the data dude*. He asked questions to keep others from interrogating him. His ploy worked well for a few years in elementary. He worked under the guise of "school projects," dazzling adults with his command of math and language. He was well on his way to renouncing the need for family, asking Patricia to join him as an allied force of two against the world, certain of their ability to take care of each other. Around this time everyone refused to play board games with him because he never lost—Go Fish: he knew the exact odds of you holding three 7s; Candy Land: he knew how many purple cards were still in the deck; Monopoly: only he could calculate the implied return on investment for Boardwalk versus Reading Railroad.

In high school, his journey into advanced stats began. He convinced the varsity coach that standard basketball stats, such as the number of turnovers, free throws, and field goal percentages—knowing that an opponent's star player was shooting 58 percent from the field—lacked specificity. Siman added nuances—such as where on the floor, against whom, and at what point in the game—then he analyzed results, and gave his team more knowledge than even the opponents had of themselves. He calculated that their increase in points scored plus increase in points defended contributed from nine to eleven points per game, more than enough to turn a tough loss into a solid victory. Once the coach bought into his analytics, he was recruited as stats guru. He sat next to the assistant coach at every game and was no longer teased for being "tall for nothing."

Statistics taught him that any balance consists of two parts: income and expenditure. As a boy, he was well versed in expenditure; he was not frugal with anticipation, wonder, adventure, peace, hope, and joy. This changed after his rite of passage left him counting on a much higher yield from his special amulet.

As college and freedom moved closer, he saw that, in searching for his birth mother, spending far outweighed earning. Looking across his life's scales and balances, he was compelled to avow his fear, regret, anger, and feelings of abandonment. He entered Howard University in 1980. College widened his world, but in order to make it through each day he pushed those burdensome feelings deeper and deeper down.

After college, his peach seed monkey went into a safe-deposit box, and Siman began living the new narrative he had spent four years polishing, one that did not involve searching for his birth mother. For a time, this released him from his other great fear: hurting his parents by searching.

Going from Saginaw to D.C. during Reaganomics pushed Siman into a deeper consciousness on politics and race. He and Patricia saw why their parents left the Black Belt to its own devices but also wondered how things would've been different had that mass exodus not taken place? Such discussions became a standard debate between brother and sister but never tainted their common goal of following his peach seed monkey in search of his birth family.

Notepad aside, he browsed bookmarks on his screen. During those early years, when Siman's peach seed monkey lay idle again, in the middle of his life, Patricia—being female and speaking a much more complex language—woke him up to a truth he had missed: family is not a birthright, it's a gift.

13

Second Sunday rushed up on Fletcher like a fish while you're baiting the hook. He and Olga made a rare appearance at church for Cricket's first Easter speech. She spoke bravely into a lowered microphone: "Easter, Easter in the air, Easter, Easter everywhere!" ending with arms opened wide to boisterous applause.

The ante was upped on dinner menu and outfits. After church, gospel music piped softly through Florida's house as Fletcher gently bounced and swayed, carrying Cricket, a bundle of poufed soft green satin, lace, and crinoline matching her mother Indicca's dress.

"Hey Gwan-gwandaddy." Cricket's voice was muffled, her thumb in her mouth, face buried in the curve of Fletcher's neck.

"Heee-y Cricket."

"Heee-y Gwan-gwandaddy."

Since Cricket started talking and dubbed him *Gwan-gwandaddy*, everything else played second fiddle in Fletcher's heart. As toddlers, Georgia and Florida were a united front, and in their first act of twin solidarity, they called their father *Ourdaddy*, and soon their sisters began using it, too. Those were simpler days, before Mozell settled in North Carolina and Georgia moved to Arizona. This left Florida as Fletcher's self-appointed keeper. He knew that someday Cricket would outgrow her nickname for him, which made it even more special.

Fletcher and Cricket bounced into the kitchen, where aromas made his mouth water: roasted chicken, ham, corn bread, collard greens, and peach cobbler. "Shieka, open wide," Florida said, "this is chicken."

"You like chicken," Fletcher added. Cricket turned her head away.

"She won't eat," Florida said, "'cause Bo D ain't here yet."

"Where is he?" Fletcher asked.

Florida returned to her pots. "Your guess is as good as mine, but don't worry, he'll be here. Free food."

Fletcher smelled lemon and Listerine on Florida's breath, which he let slide, struggling to keep calm. He had gotten worked up on the ride over, discussing Bo D with Olga. She told Fletcher once upon a time he, too, was young and didn't know a rook from a raven. He told her he still didn't know, and their laughter had been enough to momentarily cool him down.

In his pocket, Fletcher had Bo D's peach seed monkey, which he'd found in his punch bowl only a few days ago. He was confused but pleased to see it after so many years. He bought a new chain and had come prepared to return the necklace and make amends.

⁂

From his Mach 1, parked in her large circular driveway, Bo D counted twelve windowpanes in his mother's double front doors, watching as if walls, doors, and roof would tremble as his two worlds collided: family and things he was powerless to handle, versus all within his control—pills, beer, and pipe. In another five minutes his highball would fully kick in and make his family almost bearable. It's all about ratios; he could tweak proportions right up to the edge of withdrawal, depending on who he needed to be that day.

One of Bo's cousins, Nathaniel, with wife, baby, and young son, pulled in behind him. Bo D sat still and went unnoticed as they gathered themselves and their lively parade floated past his window and up the front steps as Indicca marched down, her face contorted. With her soft green silk dress she wore bedroom slippers.

On this end of his high, Bo D was a charmer, a lucid dreamer. He and Indicca once had that power over each other, high on love, magnetism, and weed. She got high mostly to please him. When they found out they were expecting Cricket, she gave him an ultimatum: give up weed and parties. They haven't been together since, and yet they haven't been apart.

One day, early in their senior year, he left play rehearsal because his back injury was flaring. He waited by his car for Indicca until cheerleader practice ended.

"So, you hungry?" he asked. "Come go with me to Krystal's and throw down some little square hamburgers."

"Can't. Got to go home and help my granmama."

She turned him down several times over three months, until finally agreeing to go with him to Winter Formal. They dated the rest of senior year. After the chase ended, Bo D did his usual—put distance between them. Three years after high school they ran into each other at a barbecue and shared a joint in the Mach 1. Nine months later he added child support to the things over which he had no control, and now he can't imagine life without Cricket and Indicca. She was still not happy with him, but the meth he added to his highball told him he could change all of that.

"Hey, you. Where you goin?" Bo D stepped out of his car and blocked her way.

"Shoot, Bo D!" She looked serious. "You scared me."

"Sorry, didn't mean to."

"Came out here to get that old stinking blanket." She moved around him to her car. "Where you been anyway? Everybody waiting for you."

"Had some business—I thought we were weaning her off that thing."

"One of us been trying to," she declared, "but Shieka always want her blanky when she missing her daddy. I think Auntie Olga is right—why not give it to her if it make her feel better?"

"Daddy is here now, so she won't need it." Bo D reached playfully; Indicca avoided him, cocking her head to one side.

"It's all good," he said, touching her hand.

"No, Bo D. It's not." She pulled away. "You think I can't see you high right now? I feel like a broken record that you ain't listening to. And I'm fed up with your mess! Daddy Fletcher tryin', Mama Florida, Auntie Olga—Lord knows I am. Everybody tryin' but you. That's got to change."

She walked away. He knew she was right and also knew his highball was designed to remove guilt from such moments as this. He felt for his necklace. This was where he would drop the monkey down his collar so his grandfather couldn't pass judgment on his pitiful life. He sniffed, rubbed his nose, and moved into the foyer like that lucid dreamer possessing power to fly above each moment.

He welcomed his mother's pristine house and Easter food aromas. Straight ahead, Olga sat alone on the living room couch. Indicca, Nathaniel, and his wife kept Florida company in the kitchen. Cricket was still in his grandfather's arms, clutching her blanket and sucking her thumb. They looked out at the pool.

"Hey, Auntie Olga," Bo D said, moving past her.

"Hello, but as you can see, I'm not the only one here."

"Day-oh's Daddy!" Cricket squeaked as Fletcher turned and Bo D caught her falling away from his grandfather into her father's arms.

"Hey, G-pop," he said as an afterthought while spinning a giggling Cricket around and around.

Fletcher sat next to Olga. "You can smell reefer and beer on him, walking around here with Cricket like nothing's wrong."

"Use your experiences to lead, not lecture," she said.

"Don't work like that," Fletcher said. "His sobriety can never mean more to me than it does to him. Nobody can do it for you."

"And yet it can't be done alone," Olga said.

Maletha knew about Fletcher's drinking from the beginning of their marriage because his private battle was taken public by trips to the Cabin in the Pines, a local nightspot he frequented in the early years. He only lost control once a few weeks after Altovise left and months before he met Maletha. One night is all it took for gossip to spread and last a lifetime.

Fletcher was out with two older nephews after a long, hot day on a construction site. He had too much to drink and took offense when another young man, also far gone on whiskey, said, *Y'all Dukeses thank y'all all that! Looking down your noses at folk. Y'all ain't shit. And you, Fletcher Dukes—you up in crying in your glass 'cause yo woman done left. That's what it's like to be pussy-whipped and lovesick.*

Fletcher went for the man's throat with his bare hands. His nephews stopped the fight and took their uncle home, but no one could stop rumors from leaking.

When Georgia and Florida were born, Maletha gave him a choice: get help or leave. After he tried and failed 12 Steps over and over, she softened and supported him in becoming a highly functioning drunk. When Florida gave birth to Bo D, Fletcher shocked people in his circles, both public and private; he quit cold turkey.

To his surprise, this infuriated Maletha. Terrence was their third grandchild, falling between Mozell's first two daughters and one that followed. Georgia's two girls came after that. Fletcher couldn't believe Maletha found a way to make even this a quarrel about peach seed monkeys.

"Fletcher Dukes. You mean to tell me this love affair with peach seed monkeys is strong enough to sober you up after all these years? Just because you got a boy at last?"

When faced with questions-that-aren't-really-questions, by nature, Fletcher always fell back on being at a loss for words. Once, during such a heated discussion—and only once, when they were newlyweds—he said to Maletha he didn't know what to say. That was a mistake he never repeated, since it only served to push her further up onto the hot sands of an island she felt she was occupying all alone.

"Don't get me wrong," Maletha went on. "I thank God that you are sober, and I never thought it would matter how or why you got there, but here we are with me trying to get a whole different monkey off *my* back."

"This ain't got nothing to do with Terrence being a boy," he said, "and I know there's no way for me to prove that to you."

"Maybe not," she said, "but try anyway. I'm listening."

"Like you always say, people will talk no matter what and onething-aboutit, gossip around this mess is still doing damage. But that don't mean I can't protect this family. And since I can't go back, best I can do from here on out is focus on every Dukes baby born. They don't need to be seeing any of us as a drunk or drug addict. Believe me, I ain't proud that it took me this long to quit."

Maletha was quiet, her head nodding slowly, her lips folded in. She walked closer and pulled him in for a hug.

Of the few rough spots in their marriage, his sobriety was the hardest. Fletcher took full responsibility for pushing Maletha out onto that island, and he also took credit for rescuing them both.

"Let's eat!" Florida rang her dinner bell.

Everyone joined hands around the table as Fletcher cleared his throat to say grace. "As my daddy would say, 'Dear Lord, come up through that crack. Bless the food and go right back.'"

"My favorite grace," Olga called out amid the din of laughter.

"You heathens will burn in hell," Florida said, "but don't drop hands yet, we ain't through." She closed her eyes and filled the silence this demanded with a proper grace: "Father God, make us grateful for this food we are about to receive for the nourishment of our bodies for Christ's sake and in His name. We praise you with—"

"—Amen," they uttered in unison.

Fletcher tried to balance his family on the scales of his mind.

Cricket refused her booster seat and sat too low in the chair between her parents, soaking up their mood. Tense air and forced small talk could not dull his anticipation for his favorite parts of Florida's massive Easter feast: glazed ham, scalloped potatoes, green beans, and creamed corn.

"Mr. Terrence!" Olga said. "Tyrone tells me they are in escrow on the building for his theater. Said he's hoping to get you involved."

Roasted mixed vegetables, candied sweet potatoes, and angel biscuits made the rounds as Fletcher listened.

"Yes, ma'am," Bo D said, drumming fingers. "I ain't trying to do no acting but—we did talk about me eventually running the tech shop."

"That's good news!" Olga said. "And don't cut yourself short on acting. I enjoyed your plays in high school."

"Yes, ma'am," Bo D said. "We'll see."

Fletcher had never liked deviled eggs, so he passed them on, as he did with the lighthearted conversation Olga managed to keep afloat throughout dinner.

The young folk helped Florida clear plates and serve peach cobbler with ice cream. Afterward, Nathaniel and his wife took the antsy children to the backyard swing set, leaving five at the table lingering over coffee.

"Fletcher," Olga said, "what you think of Bo D back on the stage?"

"Onethingaboutit, if acting like a man onstage will make you act like a man at home, I'm all for it."

In a white heat, Bo D sprang up, nearly knocking over his chair. Doc Martens boots cushioned his trudge to the kitchen.

"I don't know which one-a y'all is worse," Florida said to Fletcher, then followed her son.

&.

Bo D pulled a beer from the refrigerator.

"Where'd you have that hiding?" Florida asked.

He ignored her, popping the top.

"Well, you won't be drinking it here." She took the can.

"So now *you* judging *me*?" he snapped.

"We not going into all that right now," she said, pouring beer into the sink, "you need to get with Ourdaddy and clear up this mess between y'all. Don't make no kinda sense."

"Here we go! That's what this all about?" Bo D said harshly. "This whole dinner thing—just another dance for me and him?"

"Not so loud, Terrence." Florida's voice shuddered. "The kids will hear you all the way outside."

"But you didn't answer my question, Ma."

"That ain't no way to talk to your mama," Fletcher stepped in. "You got a bone to pick with me, here I am."

"I'm sorry, Ma," Bo D offered softly.

"Sorry on your lips ain't enough, Terrence," Florida said.

Bo D quickly turned to Fletcher.

"Five minutes. You couldn't give me five more minutes before you had my stuff towed? I was on my way."

"Five minutes?" Fletcher spoke firmly. "You showed up over an hour late. And didn't come with no tow truck to haul your stuff off my property, so exactly what were you coming to do?"

Bo D's eyes were cast down, his chest heaving.

"I gave you plenty warning," Fletcher added.

"You call that note plenty warning?" Bo D sneered. "Shiiit. I call that a cowar—"

The sheer speed and force of his grandfather's hands stunned Bo D.

Fletcher remained even, the veins in his arms swelling as he pinned Bo D against the refrigerator. "What you say?"

"Ourdaddy, no!" Florida reached for them. "Let him go, Ourdaddy! Let him go!" She yelled toward the dining room, "Auntie Olga, come in here!"

Time fused into immeasurable pulses. Fletcher did not recognize his hands on Bo D's neck, and Bo D did not struggle against those hands.

He was shocked at how instantly Olga appeared by his side.

"Fletcher." She spoke in a quick clip. "Remember what daddy always said—*being a man is more than a notion*—*this* is what he was talking about. Let him go, Fletcher. Please."

The touch of his sister's hand on his shoulder separated Fletcher from his anger. He loosened his grip. Bo D gulped, and—as if bouncing off thick air between them—braced himself with the counter. He rushed past his mother, headed for the front door.

"Terrence!" Florida yelled. "You come back here right now!"

"Florida—let him go," Olga said.

Fletcher crossed to the sink, breathing heavily. Florida handed him a wet paper towel. He refused.

"I'd rather cut my hand off than hurt a hair on his head," he whispered.

"I know," Florida said.

"But I'd do it again if I had to," Fletcher added.

"I know."

Olga sat at the counter, rubbing her eyes as Indicca rubbed her back. She looked very tired. And Fletcher thought how this added one more thing to wear her down.

"You OK?" Fletcher asked.

"I'm fine," Olga said, and then to Indicca, "go see if he left."

Fletcher dropped Bo D's peach seed monkey necklace onto the counter.

"How did *you* get this?" Florida asked, picking up the monkey.

"Was in my punch bowl. He must've snatched it off last time he was at the house. I guess he through with it now. You give it to him."

Indicca rushed back in. "Nathaniel's car blocking Bo D. He just sitting in his car, got the doors locked, and I'm feeling like he can get up himself and ask Nathaniel to move his car if he want to."

"You right," Florida said, "and Ourdaddy, you know he didn't mean none of that stuff he said." She looked at the monkey in her hand. "Yeah, Terrence was always good at hiding this little monkey from you. For years he kept it in that cigar box you gave him. His freshman year at Monroe, I bought a chain and he started wearing it all the time. I've seen him drop this monkey down his shirt many times to hide it from you. Bet you didn't know that."

"Had no idea," Fletcher said. "Why would he do that?"

Florida held the monkey in her outstretched palm. "Ask him yourself."

"Well," Olga said, "to the untrained eye this family must look pretty damn dysfunctional right about now."

Moments later, Fletcher stood by Bo D's car, holding up the peach seed monkey on its chain. Bo D unlocked the door.

They sat in silence, Bo D staring straight ahead, Fletcher cradling the monkey necklace in his palm.

"Your mama told me just now that you been wearing this for years and hiding it from me."

Bo D stared ahead.

"Why would you do that?"

Bo D sighed, snatched his keys from the ignition, and unlocked his door.

"Wait," Fletcher said, "hear me out and I'll leave."

Fletcher breathed deeply and draped the gold chain over the rearview mirror.

"This is a story I heard all my life. Happened the year before I was born, to my older brother, Rufus—he was with Olga, in our daddy's first set of kids. He went to fight in World War II and was stationed in Wyoming before they shipped him out. A white woman in the town claimed she was raped by a Black serviceman. They stopped everything for a week or more, set that woman up in a room, and had every Black serviceman in town paraded before her so she could say *yay* or *nay*."

Bo D cut his eyes toward Fletcher, then back out the window.

"Now you know Rufus was scared when his turn came to stand before that woman." Fletcher stared straight ahead, too.

"Did she pick your brother?"

"Yeah. She picked him, but guess what—" He cleared his throat, aware that there truly was no happy ending to such a story. "She picked the wrong man. Rufus' superior officer stepped forward and said, *I can vouch for the whereabouts of Private First Class Rufus Dukes, so I know this woman is lying.* They threw that investigation out."

Bo D leaned his head into his hand, saying nothing. Fletcher went on.

"Some people think this country has moved way beyond that sort of thing, but you and I know that ain't true. Looks different nowadays, sometimes. Then again it can look exactly the same. Point being: I worry enough about somebody else putting a hand on you to ever do that myself."

More silence. Fletcher hoped for deeper, more insightful words. None came.

Until Bo D erupted.

"I been wondering 'bout this for a long time."

"Yeah?"

"Ma's always saying you my role model, I'm like a *son* to you, and yet—you never call me son. You even call your *daughters* 'son'! Just don't make no sense."

Fletcher paused. His index finger set the little monkey swinging back and forth like a pendulum.

"Only one man has the natural right to call you son—"

"—and he don't deserve that right," Bo D said.

"That's only for you, as his son, to decide. For all his faults, nobody can replace him, and I won't try. Whatever is between you and him is for *you* to deal with, in your own time."

Bo D's honest reply was immediate: that man was as good as dead to him. *Bona fide bad wind.* He has no natural rights and there's nothing between them to even deal with. How could his grandfather not see that? All of this swirled and knocked against brain matter, never making it to Bo D's lips.

"So you think Ma and them like being called son?"

"Believe me—I know for a fact that they *did not* like it. Full-blown revolt when they were fifteen and thirteen. Right around the time the twins made Mozell stop calling them 'Lil Sis.'"

"Never heard about this." Bo D turned toward Fletcher, his shoulders dropped a few inches.

"It was legendary," Fletcher said. "Mozell told us the Supreme Court had elected Sandra Day O'Connor, the first woman ever, plus they had just read in school Angela Davis' new book about Black women power. And the twins," he stopped to laugh. "Bless their hearts; they said, *Ourdaddy! There's even a Black Barbie doll now!*"

Bo D tilted his head back and laughed. "Now that's classic—Ma and Aunt Georgia were trying to be grown, but not so much that they didn't still like their Barbies."

"Yep."

"Look like it didn't work, though."

"It did. They had two strong allies. Your Granmama and Olga made sure it worked. I was outnumbered and cut back for years. Now I just call them 'son' every now and then just to mess with them."

Fletcher moved on, car door open, one foot on ground, satisfied that they both felt lighter than when they started.

"You just promise me this—don't let nobody—not even me— decide for you how much of a man you are."

Bo D took a turn setting his monkey swinging back and forth. Then stared straight ahead as his grandfather walked away.

Later, Fletcher went home and dished up Rockhudson's dinner, scratching the dog's chest in thanks for uncomplicated devotion. He served up leftover peach cobbler, reclining and turning on the television—his main defense against demons and ghosts.

14

⁓

Pesticides and cow manure mixed with freshly cut grass and pinesap, saturating Putney's wide-open air. Fletcher took his midmorning cup of coffee down to check his mail. A hint of barbecue smoke floated over from a neighbor, anxious for summer on a late-spring Friday.

As he pulled out bills and junk flyers, a business card fell to his feet, buttered-side-down, showing colorful Muscogee geometric patterns floating on a turquoise background. He knew before flipping it over that Altovise had been there. He saw similar designs many times during their dating years: hair bandannas, dishes, napkins, and blankets in her family's houses and cars. On a light gray driftwood pattern, an oval-shaped turquoise stone floated above her name, *Ms. Altovise Benson*, and her phone number—a true retiree's calling card.

Back in the house, he stopped short of dropping her beautiful card in his punch bowl, and before he knew it, he was sniffing the small square of cardboard for its Youth Dew scent. It was only a matter of time before he'd have to face her and should really be thinking of this differently. Did he want the upper hand? Then he should make the first move. With business card resting on his placemat, he headed for the woodshop, grateful for many hours ahead working on Olga's bookcases.

Three days later, from his pickup's bed, he wielded a pitchfork, slinging straw around the chicken yard. He would leave a pile for Cricket to spread when she and Indicca came later.

Rockhudson's bark announced a car pulling in. Bo D, Fletcher thought, but knew he would've heard the Mustang's rumble even this far away. He looked up as Altovise rounded the corner of the house. She surveyed the property, then headed toward him, walking with purpose. He turned away.

Since spotting her in Piggly Wiggly, Fletcher's emotions had ebbed and flowed between ecstasy and despair. How could she know that she was walking into a moment of contempt because she was catching him dirty and sweating like a hog?

"I hope you don't mind me stopping by." She shaded her eyes from the glaring sun, catching Fletcher's glance.

Their eyes lingered too long for strangers and too short for old friends. So much for the upper hand.

"I guess you don't mind watching an old man sweat." He instantly regretted this rudeness.

"Old is a matter of perspective," she said, with cooing quail and cackling hens filling the silence, "but one thing's for sure: this south Georgia weather is *all* whacked out. Mid-April and feeling like late August. If this doesn't make you believe in climate change, I don't know what will."

"I suppose," Fletcher said, and in one swift move, flung his work gloves off and stepped down into the shade.

"Ice cold water here," he added and filled an enamel dipper from his hand pump.

"Humm. Thank you! I miss good ol' well water," she said after a long gulp. "Delicious."

As she held her head back to finish, holding contempt was not easy, looking at the line of her neck, her lips as she licked them, and almost feeling heat rising between them. All of this and the perfume made his emotions swing hard toward enthusiasm.

"What's going on over there?" She pointed toward the meadow.

"Digging a pond," he said.

"I see. That'll be good fishing right out your back door."

Would she notice that they were standing next to the pecan tree where he proposed on June 17, 1962? Back then his forest of Table Mountain and pitch pines wrapped around the young pecan grove; a shimmering mosaic of bright green leaves, stippled against dark trunks and branches. Months before, he had chosen this sturdy, straight tree as the site for his proposal, knowing that someday he would build a house twenty to thirty feet to the right, facing out toward Sumac Road.

He had expected the moment to be as blissful as a week before in his Fairlane's backseat. He etched a diamond shape into the tree, representing the engagement ring he wanted to buy her. This had grown far out of reach.

"You've always loved fishing," Altovise said, handing him the dipper, "sounds like a pond will be your dream come true."

Luckily, she kept talking as he tried to regain control of what came out of his mouth.

"If it's all right with you, I'll just walk around while you finish," she said.

"Be my guest."

This was a chance to watch her from afar, which she seemed to be granting him, strolling slowly. Maybe she was wondering, as he did for years after she left, what their lives would've been like together on this piece of land.

That day in '62, just before sunset, billowy clouds piled high in pinks, oranges, and soft yellows, a heavenly contrast to Albany police shutting down parks and libraries to keep Blacks out. Vigilante committees were formed to pinpoint Blacks shopping at boycotted stores. While Movement leaders were being arrested for setting up picket lines to promote the boycott, Fletcher and Altovise had run through the forest and grove like children, playing tag. They stopped at the pecan tree. She raised herself to tiptoes, pinning his hands above his head against the bark, and kissed him.

He turned her around to face the view, and wrapped his arms around her.

"All this is for you and me," he said.

"It is?" She sounded surprised and nervous.

"When my daddy died, this plot of land came to me."

"Why *you* over all your sisters and brothers?"

"So many families with no deed, no will passed on land and houses through something called heir property, but with nothing to prove ownership nine times out of ten they end up losing what's rightfully theirs. Daddy and Mama made sure they had deeds for the Sears house on Whitney and for this land. And they chose me because they knew I'd never sell. The pecans bring in pretty decent money, and I split that with everybody, but otherwise it's just been sitting here six years—waiting for me—and you."

As sharp blades of sunset cut through the trees, Fletcher pulled a ring box from his pocket: burgundy felt, edged in a fine gold line.

"Open it," he said.

He could see her struggling behind her eyes. This frightened him a little, but how could he know the instant surprise and regret that overtook her face would haunt him for five decades?

"Oh." She seemed relieved. "It's a key! She held up a tiny wooden skeleton key, polished to a shine. "Did you carve this?"

"Yeah," Fletcher said, feeling more embarrassed than expected at the mushy gesture, "since I ain't fool enough to pick out a ring—so when this boycott is over, we can go downtown and get the one *you* want—"

Her silence stopped him. "What's wrong, Veesy?"

"Wasn't expecting all this." Her smile was hesitant.

"But you can't say it's boring, can you?" he said. "That's just how I am!"

Altovise looked at her hands.

"That's the key to my heart," he said, "and if you will have me, I promise to always be there for you—with the motor running." His words instantly lost all warmth opposite her cold reception. Seconds ticked by, and he learned what she had known all along: unlike him, she had not been living each day since their beautiful night together anticipating this moment they now suffered through.

"So—when you want to go to Zales for a ring?" he asked.

Every word, every move slowly avalanched, but he was well rehearsed and had no plan B.

"I need to think about it," she said.

"What you got to think about?" Now he had to go off script. "Pretty clear-cut, ain't it?" And he spoke with a swagger, "Or do you need me to get down on one knee? Not my style but—I ain't too proud to beg!"

"No, no, no," her face relaxed, the smile was genuine, "you ain't got to go that far."

His script had called for them to be kissing again; instead, cicadas and mockingbirds barely held the moment together.

She simply said, "Fletcher, I'm so sorry—but—I can't marry you. I'm going to college, remember?"

Driving her home from Putney to Coachman Park, all that they could not say resounded through silence, but for her fingers tap-tap-tapping, playing his ring box like piano keys. That small, anxious action was an echo to her words: *I-can't-marry-you—just-take-me-home-Fletcher—*

From that day, he still marched behind her in protests, enduring the agony of seeing her, but not touching. They continued working in the Movement, and Fletcher watched as she rode the wave of her single-minded drive to go to college until the day of the march that changed everything. And from *that* day, he began his decline toward a seabed of self-loathing. Why had he believed she wanted him when she had sights on things far beyond Albany, while he couldn't see past a pecan grove?

Part of him was grateful she didn't notice the pecan tree, and another part wished that the whole afternoon had meant so much that she could never have forgotten. When she walked back to the truck, he had returned to baling, feeling menial and defenseless—and less contemptuous. He was surprised by her next move.

She stepped onto an overturned crate next to the tailgate and reached toward him.

He smiled, removing his glove. Their palms met and he pulled her up. He wanted to lift her wrist and kiss her medicine knot tattoo. Her face changed to distress.

"Fletcher. You still have it." She stroked the two-inch scar across his right wrist.

"Yeah, that's a cattle prod's job," he said softly, "to make sure you remember."

She quickly covered her mouth.

"C'mon now," he said, "we didn't get this far by letting any and every memory rip us in two. If that was the case, we would've given up a long time ago." She gently patted his wrist.

"So—I thought you'd call," she said. "My cell number is on the card I left in your mailbox."

Her card was still on the placemat.

He shook his head. "That's the problem with them dang cell phones; they give folks a false sense of popularity."

She dropped her head and chuckled. "True enough, I must say."

He pitched another forkful of straw. She looked around.

"You certainly did right by this piece of land, Fletcher."

"Been good to us."

"I—I know I must look like hurricane Altovise to you, but—" She took a deep breath.

"Not quite a hurricane," he said. "Maybe a tropical storm."

She laughed harder than his little tease warranted before succumbing to a threat of tears.

"Thissss—this is all wrong." She waved both hands in front of her. "I apologize for showing up uninvited."

She turned to leave.

The hot breeze shifted and brought a whiff of the perfume. Her head was lowered, ready to step back down. He wanted to kiss her kitchen.

"You any good with this thing?" he asked.

"What?" She stopped and turned, playfully mocking him. "You think you the only one know how to use a pitchfork?"

She began deliberately baling, and he wished he had a pair of gloves that fit her.

"Plenty of straw and no rush," he said. "Better pace yourself."

"I know that's right," she said, resting both hands on the handle.

Fletcher used his pocketknife to cut cords on another bale and broke up flakes with swift kicks.

"What do you intend to find back here in Albany now that you couldn't find fifty years ago?"

"Do you think I'm selfish to come back?"

"Guess we have to let the one who's never been selfish cast the first stone," he answered.

She went back to baling. "I don't believe that coming home can ever be a bad thing"—she stopped—"and I've had just about enough of this!"

They laughed as she handed him the pitchfork and sat on the edge of the truck.

"Look at you, woman. Done got yourself all hot and bothered."

"Excuse me?" She was plucky and waggish now, dapping sweat with her shirt. "This is my natural glow."

"Well in that case, you're more than welcome to come in and finish wiping that glow off."

She seemed to be weighing his offer. But against what?

"Don't worry. I keep a clean house," he added.

The girl was gone, but every trait that had made him want to settle down with her walked beside him in the woman, a force magnified many times. This made him rageful, and also, somehow, elated.

"You still like dogs?" he asked, gesturing toward Rock's pen.

"Yep, in fact I had a toy poodle named Si a few years ago."

"I don't know what to call a toy poodle, but it's too far from the wolf to be a dog."

"How you get off ragging on my poor little long-deceased Si that you never even met?"

"No harm intended—just warning you that Rockhudson might bark at you to say hello."

"Wait. Rock Hudson? Really?"

"Yeah. Down through the ages we've had Hazel, Mitch Miller, Dean and Jerry, Tom Cruise—"

This made her laugh again. "Time for some Black dog names, don't you think?"

"Olga took care of that already," he said.

"Oh yes! I met Sidney—"

She stopped herself.

"I know you been over there, Olga told me. I knew something was up since her mood's been swinging like a rookie at bat."

"Funny," she declared, "she made a similar comment about your mood! And, Fletcher, please don't hold it against her for not telling you. That was at my request."

"Is that right?"

"You needed to process the shock," she said, "which is why I convinced her to give you a pass."

As they walked toward the house, Altovise said, "Let me guess—Poitier, right?"

"That's right." Fletcher chuckled. "I tried to talk her into getting two from that same litter, so we'd have *Harry* and Sidney."

"Ya'll got it bad!"

Before entering the house, Fletcher noticed her car parked at an angle near slot #1.

"What happened to that red Volvo?"

"Ordered the Beemer months ago," she said, "finally delivered. I guess this is my old-age-crisis car!"

"Not a soul looking at you would think that," he said.

"Well. My body knows how old we are!"

He wasn't about to talk about anybody's body, so he opened the screen door and said, "After you."

They entered his kitchen, and Altovise smiled as he explained his table set with *Princess and the Frog* bowls and napkins for the weekly ice cream party for Cricket. While Altovise freshened up, he quickly set out ginger beer and peanuts in his south-facing living room, and immediately questioned the choice. At this hour there was way too much of the heavenly light of Maletha in there; she would hold them hostage. He relocated snacks to the den, then dashed to his bathroom to rinse straw dust off and change shirts.

She didn't have a wedding ring. Who had she made her life with? Was it a woman? He couldn't imagine that, but you never know. Either way, how could they know each other after half a century? In order to move forward, they would have to start right where they were, with no allegiance to the past and no promise of a future. He was rushing things. The woman had just dropped by. That's all. Probably out of curiosity more than anything. Still, he added a touch of Old Spice.

He walked back down his short hallway. Was she thinking the wood paneling in his den and avocado and orange in the kitchen had him stuck—classic southwest Georgia between 1970 and 1986? When he joined her, she was running fingers along his record collection.

"So you found you," he said, with just as much tenderness as he intended and felt.

"Yes, I'm so touched by this, Fletcher, that you have all six."

"Why wouldn't I?"

"May I?"—she held her hands in prayer formation, as if at an altar.

"Be my guest!"

She pinched and slid the stack out and sat down to flip through this personal and cultural chronology from 1972 to 2010. Their thin spines and spacious covers showed signs of the wear and tear of total recall. Each album was a time stamp of era and place. Fletcher had kept up with her life through cover art, fashion, hairstyles, and gaze.

She looked comfortable in his recliner, legs crossed at ankles, almost as if they had spent the night together and were getting ready to go out for a bite.

"What you in the mood for?" Fletcher moved closer.

"Let's see." She stopped on album number five, *Cabin in the Pines*. "This was our hard bop experiment, fused with Muscogee Creek hymns."

He moved ceremoniously; palms spread wide, not touching surface, album on turntable, cleaner on brush, needle in groove. They moved on to his kitchen.

She sat on a high stool at his counter. "Looks well-loved, like somebody actually cooks in here."

She was swinging one foot as she slipped peanuts in her mouth one at a time. He was not sure if *well-loved* was code for *old and run-down*. He let that slide.

"You mean to tell me you done forgot my salmon croquettes and biscuits?"

"I remember them well from back in the day, but you know— things tend to change over time."

"Then I'll just have to prove to you that some things never change." They shared another weighted glance, which seemed to make her more uneasy. He changed the subject, attempting to free them. They spoke about renovations on her new house at Cromartie Beach.

Small talk ended when she pulled out her cell phone, announcing that she had forgotten an appointment with carpenters and quickly excused herself, her ginger beer half gone. Fletcher stood in disbelief before following her out the kitchen door.

"Altovise!"

She was walking fast.

"Wait." He ran after her. "Why you leaving like this?"

She stopped and slowly turned.

"You're right. I can't leave without saying what I came to say."

"OK." He braced himself.

"Everybody's trying to make heads or tails of why I'm back—and you know I don't usually give a damn what people think."

"Always liked that about you."

"I came out here to say I'm sorry. Because I do care what *you* think. Leaving you in the dark that way was wrong and—" She rubbed palms together, then crossed her arms over her chest.

The Altovise he knew was always in control, of her emotions and her body, yet here she stood, searching for words and fingering the cell phone the way she had done the ring box the day he proposed.

"And—what?" he asked.

He let the silence hang open like a wound, hoping she wouldn't reveal an awful secret from their past, and also hoping this fleshy silence gave her permission to just say whatever she had to say.

"I had to leave. This town was on a mission to swallow up my dreams and leave me with nothing." She shook her head. "Nobody knows better than we do how crazy those white folks were."

"We went through a lot, especially you. But the way I see it, you can't hold that against every brick and tree in town. Always has been and still is a lot of good in south Georgia."

"I know, and I always envied you for your connection to this land and having such a clear purpose for staying."

"You did what you had to do," he said. "Tell you what—let me make you dinner so we can get off on a better foot."

"It's a busy time right now with the renovation," she said, getting into the car. "Can I get a rain check on that?"

He said nothing. Simply backed away with his palms in surrender mode and watched her drive off, taking his feel-good moment with her.

He let Rock out of his pen and had the distinct feeling that Altovise talked circles around what she really came to say. Rain check. Maybe she deserved hurricane status after all.

15

~

Last week's cool relief was a distant memory. The hot spell returned as April's heat pressed down like an iron, relentless and inescapable.

It was hump day; right in the middle of a three-day, 7:00 A.M.-to-7:00 P.M. rotation. It had been ten days since Easter dinner, and the whole family was back to treating Bo D as if he might break into a million pieces; a repeat of his first time in rehab but with some definite changes. He could feel the family building a new united front; because now he was a father.

He had not expected to still feel his grandfather's hand on his neck, but there it was, tied to a churning knot below his rib cage, spreading to other regions.

He felt a similar rising gorge after his grandfather left him sitting in the Mach 1, until Indicca came out and sat in the passenger seat. With help from his highball, feeling her next to him, both hugged by red vinyl, Bo D's lucid dreamer had returned. He reached over, caressed her inside knee, and she softened. She had been so cold earlier and he couldn't see yet that this was a little pity party she was throwing for him after watching his grandfather jack him up. She stopped short of inviting him to spend the night, which was fine: after all he'd been through, he knew that needed to be a party house night.

He was up a few minutes early to tweak a highball. After a few tokes on a joint, he shook a little meth into his beer. He had never done that before work. Should kick in shortly after he hit the plant floor. He'd be energized until halfway through his shift. At that point, music and his rhythm of work would be enough to carry him.

Corporate suits were springing an inspection, so the whole plant was on edge—from management to forklift. Bo D entered into the desired state of numbness to his cares about his grandfather, but he felt off and concerned about what to expect with this new highball.

Running too late for an exercise session, he picked up paperwork to start a new order: 50K / Radials / Pep Boys / for GM. This called for a brand-new mold, one of the few things to get excited about in his dead-end job.

Track after track blasted through his headphones—Flo Rida, Alicia Keyes, and Rihanna did their part to ease his worry. With his highball peaking, engulfed by factory noises, he sang along, loud and free:

> *Shine bright like a diamond . . .*
> *We're beautiful like diamonds in the sky . . .*

He was feeling overconfident. He greeted the start-up guy and decided to skip checking and rechecking his paperwork. On break halfway through his shift, he took an Adderall.

This left him still energized when he knocked off six hours later. He headed out to Nottingham Way, ate pizza at Mellow Mushroom, and went to the multiplex to catch Denzel's new movie, *Safe House*. He was looking forward to getting through Thursday, then starting three days off.

The next morning, he kicked off with a regular highball. The night shift guy would have put a nice dent in the Pep Boys order. Bo D parked the Mach 1 in his usual spot, ready to tag in and fall into rhythm. Lift. Walk. Bend.

Before he reached his presses, LaChondra tapped his shoulder. He slid one headphone to the side.

"Bo D!" she yelled, looking around. "Where you think you going? Didn't you get all my messages?"

"Nah. What you talking about?"

She pointed to his presses; a guy he helped train two weeks ago was already running them.

LaChondra pulled Bo D aside. "Don't know how, but that batch for Pep Boys got all fucked-up! Man! You must've been flying high to not know the damn mold was upside down!"

"What you mean?"

"I ain't got time to give you no details, Bo D, suffice it to say Rutherford is coming for you."

"I don't give a fuck. I checked my specs—"

"Bo D! You think I'm making this up? I checked, too," she said harshly. "All nine hundred and fifty came out upside down. And *you* in deep shit."

"Fuck that! I ain't the only one that missed it—"

"Oh trust me, many heads will roll, but yours is the one you need to be thinking about. How could you not look at your phone *all night*?"

"That was easy—I went to a movie, then I crashed." He pulled out his phone to check.

"Well, I can tell you that HR don't try but once, but I left you three messages." She sighed, a softness returning to her face. "Sorry, Bo D. But I got to escort you to Rutherford."

Inside the office, Bo D saw the man's mouth moving, heard each word, dragged out and nasalized, as if in slow motion. Charlie Rutherford was Bo D's first football coach in Parks and Rec and had helped him land the job at Hooper. This was the only thing keeping Bo D from telling him to kiss his black ass and walking out.

"Did you hear me, Fowler?" Rutherford squeezed his crystal blue eyes into a squint, causing wrinkles to convene all across his *Fistful of Dollars* face.

"Yeah, Coach."

"Then what you got to say for yourself, son? This ain't like you." He held up the envelope with specs: twenty to thirty questions Bo D had skipped. "How in God's name did you miss an upside-down mold?"

"What about Clarkson? He's the lead man, he missed it, too."

"Clarkson ain't none of your business. Now you know the drill, Fowler. Your shift, your responsibility. I thought you had the situation under control after your other rehab."

Bo D stood motionless, chewing on his bottom lip.

Rutherford tore a slip of paper from a pad. "Breaks my heart, son, but I got to send you in for a urine analysis." He handed Bo D the paper. "I can have you escorted now to the clinic. Results take twenty-four hours. You'll have to come back in."

After a few minutes, he left Rutherford's office with one more appointment: to talk to HR about cashing out his 401(k), a decision that went against Rutherford's advice.

Bo D rose early the next day after not sleeping well. He skipped his highball, convinced that he could stop anytime he wanted, even though, deep in a corner of his mind, he knew what a worn-out cliché of an addict that made him. He walked into HR skating dangerously close to the edge of withdrawal.

A beautiful queen-size Black woman with flawless hair and makeup greeted Bo D from behind her desk.

"Mr. Terrence, Mr. Terrence. Come right on in." She continued typing frantically, staring at her screen. "How is your mama?"

"She's fine."

"Please have a seat." More typing. "I'll be right with you."

He cautiously sat in a juvie chair facing her desk, hoping she was finished with niceties, since he couldn't be sure when he'd need to blow his nose or scratch. Itching always started on one side of his neck; but nothing yet. He didn't want to visit the red-and-white sorority tissue box on her desk. Too personal.

She stopped typing and laughed, focused on him now. "I don't know why I asked you about Florida, 'cause I just saw her in choir practice two nights ago."

Bo D knew this was her making an effort to cover up the trippy corporate version of juvenile detention that permeated the room. It wasn't working.

"As you know, your urine test came back positive."

Bo D took the sheet holding his test results. He wanted to hand it back. It mattered that this woman knew his mother well. There was no shaking his family. The only thing he wanted from this place was his 401(k) check.

"So, Mr. Fowler," she combined familiarity with business in a way that also felt trippy, "while we can make no assumptions about the extent of your drug use, a positive test does require that we inform you about our EAP." She pulled out a brochure and spoke as if she had a rat in her pocket. "We contract with excellent EAP advocates, and if you'd like, we can assign you right now."

"I appreciate that," he gently rubbed a spot on the side of his neck, "but I'd rather move on to cashing out my 401(k)."

"And we will get to that," she said. "But you should know that EAP services are free to employees, they take place off-site and—"

"I understand." Bo D sniffed, the itch spreading to his upper chest. "I just need to know how long it takes for me to get my check." He did the math overnight. With the $5,000 in savings and almost $45,000 coming after penalties for the 401(k), he'd have a nice nest egg to get him through whatever was next.

"Terrence, I would be remiss if I did not advise you—"

The woman talked, but he heard Rutherford's voice from yesterday, telling him the same story: *Fowler, after six years you got a nice portfolio to roll over to your next job, don't throw that away—*

"I understand." Bo D massaged his itchy chest. "Is there a way to expedite"—he knew she would like that word—"the process?"

"I'm afraid not."

The woman sat back in her chair, her arms folded in her lap. Who was she now? His mama's friend or the creepy HR lady?

"It will take three to ten days for your check to arrive." She leaned forward again and would not come up for air until the question mark. "You do realize, Mr. Fowler, that if you allow me to assign you an EAP advocate today, and you begin making use of the various resources we have available, you will not be required to lose your job?"

Rutherford had covered that, too. Corporate lingo for rehab.

"Thank you." He rose from the chair. "I do realize that, but EAP won't be necessary."

On his way to the door he used his sleeve to catch a dribble from his nose.

LaChondra had arranged to escort him to his car. After six years and over half a million tires, he walked across the plant floor for the last time. His eyes were on autopilot, ogling her station even as they walked side by side, as planned, so that she could give him the key to her house. It was just before 9:00 A.M. and he needed to be somewhere until 7:00 P.M. He would see her later at her place. Whenever they got together, they managed to find just enough to be happy about.

❧

"Daddy?"

"Yeah, Boo?"

"Way-oh we go-wing?"

"To see Auntie Olga."

"Why?"

"'Cause we love her, she loves us—and she got a surprise for you!"

The next day, the Mach I was parked in shade fanning out from Indicca's ancient elm tree towering over her mobile home. Bo D moved quickly through insufferable heat and gnats, carrying Cricket from air-conditioned rooms a few feet to his car.

As he buckled her in, Cricket's chattering ended, leaving quiet space he filled with flashbacks from earlier that morning: drug test and 401(k). A nice total blinked in his mind: $50,000. She settled in with her blankie, a lavender bow holding a puff of hair blossoming on top of her head. It was all he could do not to tell Indicca, but no one could know that he'd lost his job. Not until he could afford to keep her and Cricket in as many pretty things as they liked.

He cherished being with Cricket. Their time together, with its definite start and finish, was easy to manage. Now that he was not working, he could spend even more time with her. But Indicca had still not completely warmed to him since Easter, part of that united family front. Passing her inspection required careful tweaking of his Cricket highball ratio, which was pretty much the same for Auntie Olga: no smoking; swallow only one oxy for time-release effects.

When he started the car, a rap song blasted earsplittingly loud. Cricket screamed and covered her ears as Bo D rushed back to free her from her car seat.

"I'm so, so sorry, Shieka. You're OK."

She sat quietly, her face distorted.

He kissed her forehead and held her close, repulsed that she had heard the snippet of foul-mouthed, degrading lyrics. To him the words weren't even words anymore—just part of the mode and swagger of pretty much everybody he listened to.

"Daddy got you," he whispered, gently swaying, then returned her to the seat. "I know. It's hot out here! So let me get that air conditioner going."

Usually, Indicca watched them go from her window. He was glad she was in the shower and not seeing this.

Half an hour later, the Mach 1 rumbled through a tunnel of live oaks lining Whitney Avenue, a grandeur of leafy fingers weeping Spanish moss.

Bo D checked his rearview again. Cricket was dozing. He had

checked many times during the drive from Dawson. Finally, his heart was no longer racing. Forgiving himself would take much longer.

Father and daughter stood on the sidewalk in front of Olga's house. Cricket had moved on, and Bo D felt ashamed that he had no music clean enough for his three-year-old.

"Look, look, the wind, Daddy!" Cricket said, squatting and pointing to a small whirlwind of leaves.

"I see it," Bo D said, crouching down beside her.

"Less race that way!" Cricket chirped, her elbows pointing out like wings.

"Ready! Set! Gooo!" Bo D held her hand as they ran to the corner and back.

They were winded when one of The Twins opened Olga's door, saying, "Did y'all run all the way here?"

"We race the wind!" Cricket said, arms drooped forward, head tilted back, looking up at her cousin.

Bo D ushered Cricket onto Olga's large Persian rug. How many times had he walked on it barefoot? And driven his Matchbox cars along the vibrant highways of its curly design? His guilt from the car behind him, he focused on Cricket having her own loving memories of Auntie Olga, her house and gardens—his true childhood home— where he had found stability during his parents' stormy divorce.

"Little miss Bright Tarshieka Fowler! Come on over here," Olga said from her Mission chair, holding a small box out in front of her. "This is for you."

Cricket ripped paper and bow to find a pair of purple sunglasses with rhinestones, small replicas of Olga's current black pair.

"They sparkly!" Cricket said as her father slipped them on her.

"Yes—sparkly like you!" Olga said, lifting her great-niece onto her lap. "Ms. Tarshieka, you're not a trip, you're the whole journey!"

"What you say, Boo?"

"Thank you, Aun-tie!" Cricket sang.

"You're welcome, sweetness—now give me some sugar," Olga

said, and Cricket kissed her cheek. "You go follow Mindy and Cindy. I heard there's a tea party for you in the back garden."

Cricket trailed her cousins down the hall toward the back of the house, and Bo D followed Olga into the study, watching her vein-streaked hand feeling along wainscoted walls crammed with photos, art, and souvenirs. Her library and collections overflowed into stacks on tables, spilling over into other rooms: The *Southwest Georgian* newspapers, *Jet*, *Life*, and *Ebony* magazines, plus campaign swag from Truman to Obama. Bo D had trouble accepting that she couldn't see any of it anymore. But she also couldn't see how rough he looked, and he knew that feeling grateful for that made him a special kind of asshole.

"I been meaning to call you all week," Bo D said, "but work is crazy right now—and I've had other stuff going on."

"Don't blame you one bit—every now and then we have to shake family loose so we can breathe."

This was laughable coming from a woman who could only be shaken loose if she wanted to be, relying on her network of snitches to find any family member, anywhere.

During the Movement, when being Black and alone in southwest Georgia could be deadly, Olga instituted a buddy system for all Movement workers, which she later extended to family and grew into a network of informants the young nieces and nephews nicknamed Snitches Aplentymous.

"We've got a lot of ground to cover," Olga said, finding her way to her closet as if she could see.

It was stuffed with neatly organized boxes. She touched the fuse box, asking Bo D to be her eyes and start helping keep up the house. His first thought was, Why? This house never suffered from a lack of hands to help. What was her real goal?

"Your great-grandfather Purvis would be proud to see you learning about this house."

"The Sears Roebuck house! Solid built!" Bo D said, rapping a fist on the doorjamb.

"That's right. Back in those days Sears sold just about everything—from a paper catalog no less."

"Sears catalog was the first internet, huh?"

"I bet you could argue that. Would love to read that paper."

Bo D was quiet.

"As you know," Olga added, "I was a baby, so I only know stories, but I've always felt as if I toddled around watching every nail and screw go in."

"How much did it cost?"

"Anywhere from six hundred and fifty dollars to three thousand in 1924."

"That's crazy cheap!!"

"By modern standards, you're right, and I'm sure ours was on the lowest end, but still a colossal investment for your great-grandparents, Purvis and Alpha. They had been sharecroppers."

"So cool that this was their house."

"Delighted you see it that way." She patted his hands gently; hers were as soft as ever.

"Let's start here and work our way outside," Olga said. "I've got some rootstock roses I want you to meet—and annihilate."

They visited crucial systems first: main water shutoff, various fire extinguishers, smoke detectors, spare batteries, and phone lists for plumbers and such taped inside the kitchen cupboard. Out back, the tea party was a cheery backdrop. They stopped by the shed where he outfitted himself in garden gloves and chose a lopper.

Olga pointed her cane. "Smell those pink roses straight ahead."

"Humm, smell real good," Bo D said, even though his highballs were taking a toll on his sense of smell.

"That beauty is Madame Isaac," Olga said. "She's growing on her own roots. To the left is Garden Party, grafted onto a rose called Dr. Huey—he has sturdy roots but can't brag about his leaves and flowers; we call him a *rootstock* rose. You with me?"

"Sounds like Dr. Huey is the stud rose!" Bo D said, gripping the loppers.

"Never saw it quite that way." Olga laughed. "But that's certainly one way of looking at it."

While he was always happy to make his aunt laugh, he knew he needed to monitor how much his highball controlled what came out of his mouth.

"You see any shabby, dark red flowers mixed in with pinkish yellow ones?"

"Oh yeah, it's a lot of red ones," Bo D said.

"That's Dr. Huey. And left to his own devices, he'll take over. You show him who's boss of this garden." She touched his shoulder. "And watch for thorns—that rose is an armed angel. You just follow each stem and cut those suckers off where they shoot straight out of the ground."

"Suckers!" Bo D cried. "Now I know why G-pop like that word so much!"

Rootstock clipping finished, Olga had him pull dandelions and crabgrass before returning tools to the shed. She asked if he knew the definition of a weed. Not exactly, he admitted, but he knows one when he sees one.

"To be clear," Olga replied, "a weed is any plant growing where it's not respected." Even a precious rose can be ripped out as a weed if somebody doesn't want it there.

Back in the study, Bo D helped her sit at her boxy mahogany desk. He sat in the chair facing her, feeling like he was back in that creepy HR lady's office. His highball was holding, otherwise his paranoia would be roof raising at this point.

Before he could start counting books with blue spines, Olga said, "We have yet to discuss the incident with Fletcher on Easter Sunday."

"Yes, ma'am, I know."

"In spite of this temporary riff between y'all, you know you're like a son to him."

"Not this again." Bo D slouched back in the chair. "When G-Pop came out to the car Easter Sunday, I finally just point-blank asked him why—if I'm so much like a son to him, why he *never* calls me son."

"So you had that conversation again. It's been a while."

"What you mean? When did I ever ask him that?"

"I lost track. Was more frequent when you were younger, and Fletcher's answer has always been the same."

Bo D cocked his head like a puppy coming upon a curiosity. Was he a stranger to his own past?

"Why didn't G-pop mention that in the car? He just answered the question like it was the first he'd heard of it."

"Just as he'll do if you ever ask him again."

"But, Auntie! I would remember asking that!"

"Not if you'd rather forget. More importantly, you can learn from your Granmama Maletha. She blazed this trail a long time ago."

"I know both you and Granmama never liked only boys getting peach seed monkeys."

"We also led a revolt around Fletcher calling the girls 'son.' There was much more to Maletha's methods than met the eye.

"When Georgia and Florida were in fourth or fifth grade, Maletha drew the line. She wasn't studying about anybody's talismans or traditions—even though she kept up that lively quarrel with Fletcher. She enlisted me in focusing on girls all across the Dukes family, and of course your mama and your aunts got a bulky dose, bolstering them against patriarchy in their own home."

"Whoa! Y'all were poisoning girls against their own uncles and cousins and brothers? And fathers?!"

"Not at all. Since home is our first laboratory, we practiced the primary rule of teaching and parenting: *prepare the child for the road, not the road for the child*. So when they faced chauvinism—and all these other 'isms'—out in the world, they knew how to stand up and fight. Maletha turned what started out as a disservice, into something of value.

"But don't get me wrong," Olga added. "Boy-girl rites of passage would've been much more fair."

"I see you still haven't backed down!" Bo D said.

"Now what fun would that be?" Olga laughed.

She leaned in and extended both palms up across the desk. "Terrence. Every day, you live with the trauma of your father leaving. To a degree, the whole family does, especially Fletcher. You and he are not the first to face addiction and recovery in our family, and won't be the last. I'm asking you to look. Truly look. At all you have to lose and know that you're not alone.

"Yes, ma'am."

"We are your net, when you're truly ready to make the trip. Until then, remember. You have a space deep, deep in here," she patted her chest, "passed down like your little monkey. You can go there regardless of what's going on around you and feel safe, strong, and free. You believe that?"

"Yes, ma'am, I guess so."

Olga drew circles with her fist on her chest. "Grit, self-reliance, self-control; you have all that and plenty more, ready to be tapped. That space can never be taken from you—but if you're not careful you can give it away."

What she didn't know was that he frequently felt everything on her list, and then some, even faster than usual since he started chewing his oxy.

"How can you be so sure I haven't already given it away?"

"I don't doubt that you come close on a regular basis," she said, "but if you had completely given it away, you wouldn't be sitting here with me."

She sat back. "I came down hard on Dr. Huey just now, but actually, weeds are to be respected. Not to say I want a yard full of them, but—why hate them for being decisive, resilient, and hardheaded about survival?" She leaned forward again. "You feel me?"

"Yeah, Auntie, I feel you. Seems like a weed might be any plant growing on its own terms."

"Yes! I like that definition even better."

He couldn't believe it when she told him that he needed a win; that he had much to contribute to the family that nobody else could.

"You remember me telling you how after Daddy's funeral in '55, I didn't go back to Amsterdam?"

"Yes, ma'am, you said Emmett Till's murder changed everything and it changed nothing."

"Civil rights reached a fever pitch in many *public* places, but the most important place to be an activist is in your own family, as Maletha well knew. And that's what I'm asking you to do now."

She removed her sunglasses and lightly tapped a folder in front of her holding Siman Miller's emails and photos of his monkey.

"Not long ago, I received information that put me between a rock and a hard place. I need your help."

She slid the folder toward Bo D.

"Take your time," Olga said and sat back in her chair.

After reading the first email, he studied Olga's face and felt like a child, relying on adults to gauge how to feel about a situation. Lines of contentment across his great-aunt's forehead and around her mouth showed her faith in him. How could he ever be worthy of such trust? And then he saw a photo.

"Whoa. Auntie. Look at those eyes!" He had never seen a monkey with diamond eyes. In many other ways, this one was in the style of his monkey, with his grandfather's signature head and shoulders, so he was not surprised to see a tiny *F.D.* chiseled into the bottom.

"I know. You have lots of questions," Olga said, "these are early days and I need you to be patient. Not a word about this to anybody yet."

"Don't worry—but—somebody did tell you this monkey has G'pop's initials, right?"

"Yes."

"I guess somebody in his adopted family or his blood family, could've married a Dukes who had this monkey. Or do you think this guy is a Dukes?"

"Don't know of Siman Miller's full story," Olga said, "but whatever that is, once it's revealed, emotions will run high. I'm pulling you in now so you can help lead others—your mother especially—down the road to acceptance. You willing to do that?"

"Yes, ma'am, I'm all in."

"I was hoping you'd say that." Olga smiled, replacing her glasses. "I'll keep you posted on—"

"Day-ohs Daddy!" Cricket squealed, dashing around the corner and jumping into Bo D's lap. "Less go play, Daddy!"

"In a minute, Boo—"

"We've done enough for now," Olga said, "go play!"

As he carried her to the back garden, Cricket danced her fingers along Bo D's neck, feeling for his necklace. "Way-ohs yo monkey, Daddy?"

"I forgot it today, but, I want to know if you saved me any yummy tea and cookies?"

Bo D thought back to Easter Sunday when Auntie Olga had to talk his grandfather down. He'd never seen him that mad. He was surprised when he came out to the car to return the monkey, which Bo D put back in its cigar box. He wasn't sure if he'd ever wear it again. And now he had information even his grandfather didn't know.

The whole family believed that he didn't *want* to be a father. Not one of them seemed to get that he didn't know how.

Sitting in a child's lawn chair across from Cricket, Bo D smiled, listening to her nonstop snickers and chirps. New words marched through his mind—Siman Miller, Saginaw, Michigan, and a monkey with diamond eyes. Far too much to process, so he relaxed and sipped pretend tea, unaccustomed to being trusted with family secrets.

Act II

~

A young man can have fine cloth like an elder
but he can never have rags like an elder.

~ BERBER SAYING

16

Patricia was on her way. They had an hour before Olga's Skype call, and Siman was glad his sister agreed to join him this time. He spent too much time choosing slacks, and an eggshell blue shirt, then angling the computer's camera to show a wall of books. Morning sun sparkled on his stainless-steel bar cart, and cocktail glasses clinked as he set out a new bottle of Monkey 47, a gift from Patricia, saying *no* to slicing a fresh lime to make a gin and tonic. Olga would be introducing her great-nephew, so he was even more nervous than he had been on their first phone call four months ago. Not that Olga Dukes demands control, you simply hand it to her—gratefully—like a child, relieved that there's a grown-up in charge.

In their many emails, she confirmed that the mystery of who carved Siman's monkey was close to being solved. All the carvers are men, and there's a good chance that whoever he is, he knows Siman's birth mother.

Patricia put on tea water while he arranged and rearranged his legal pad, pencil, pens, and ring box.

"So, Pat. You're really up for this?" Siman asked. "I know Skype isn't your thing."

"I promised moral support." Patricia cuddled her mug. "I'm here to deliver."

"Here we go." Siman rolled his shoulders and started the call.

"Hello, Mr. Miller," said a white woman with short, shocking red hair. "Nice to finally meet."

"Good morning!" Siman knew all about Olga's Dutch assistant.

"I'm Ursula Kroon, we did not want to keep you waiting." She looked to her right. "She is almost ready—Oh!—here is Dr. Dukes."

Siman checked himself in the small square as Olga faced the screen directly, and adjusted her sunglasses. She explained that open-angle glaucoma runs in their family and had taken its toll on her vision. She said at eighty-eight maybe she had seen enough. Around her shoulders she wore a fashionably tied emerald-green scarf. In all their months of correspondence, she had never mentioned being blind. Her smooth skin didn't look a day over sixty-five, and she had thick, silver braids wrapped around her head like Frida Kahlo.

Siman greeted Olga, commenting on her sunglasses.

"Malcolm X had good taste," she said, leaning in. "When people look at me, I want them to say, *look at those cool glasses* instead of *look at that jive old lady*."

Siman laughed while Olga moved on, chatting about southwest Georgia's mid-April heat wave. He poured over the screen, hoping to catch her nephew in the background.

"We're lucky. It's a perfect seventy-two with a breeze here in Saginaw. I started my day before dawn with a cool, peaceful row on the river."

"That sounds heavenly," Olga said. "I trust you went easy on your rotator cuff."

"Yes, I did." Siman smiled, and his eyes met Patricia's, who raised an eyebrow and gave a thumbs-up. Siman introduced her.

"Pleased to meet you, Patricia. We owe a lot to your persistence."

Patricia stepped into the frame. "Dr. Dukes, it's a pleasure to meet you. I think you would've gotten equal results without me. And by the way, that pashmina is beautiful on you; it's Siman's favorite color."

Siman looked out over the river, rethinking a gin and tonic, returning to the bar. He peered inside the time being, focused on his sister's voice and Olga's laugh. He couldn't explain why, but he knew that—in one way or another—his life was about to change. In his forty-nine years he could count these moments on one hand—times that he recognized as pivotal as they unfolded.

Patricia ran over and poked his shoulder as Olga said, "There's no point in keeping you in suspense any longer. Siman? Where'd you go?"

"I'm right here." Siman rushed to his seat, gin and tonic in hand.

Without another word a young man sat next to Olga. His well-defined muscles showed under the Atlanta Hawks T-shirt he wore with slightly baggy jeans. His closely cropped hair lay in shiny black waves against his scalp. His eyes seemed tired and his shoulders slumped forward—all playing opposite his glinting smile.

"Siman and Patricia, this is my great-nephew, Terrence Fowler."

"—but y'all can call me Bo D."

"OK then," Siman said, gesturing to include Patricia, "we are truly honored to meet you, Bo D."

"Yes, we are," Patricia said. "I see you're a Hawks fan."

"All the way!" Bo D said. "Pistons for y'all, huh?"

"Only if I have to," Siman said, noticing Bo D's pointed ears. "Baseball is more my thing." He scribbled on his legal pad: *VUL-CAN EARS!*

"Truth be known," Patricia injected, "Siman likes baseball stats more than the game itself." She scribbled back: *DON'T GO THERE!*

"So you'll be interested in the Tigers versus Rangers game coming up in a couple of hours," Olga said.

"Definitely," Siman said. Baseball and gin combined to relax him, but he could feel Patricia's uneasiness as Olga quizzed her briefly about her family, so he put a check mark by Patricia's scribble.

He took a deep breath and focused on the beautiful wooden

radio on a shelf behind Olga. Everything around her transmitted an ease that carried into telling his birth story—directly from Jerome and Dorothy's memories and so well known to Siman he had come to see himself as an adult in that story instead of the seven-pound, seven-ounce newborn.

On March 9, 1963, rain had spread three hundred miles from Saginaw, Michigan, to Youngstown, Ohio. Jerome Miller dropped his wife, Dorothy, at St. Elizabeth's entrance and parked the car.

Thunder and lightning added drama as they stood in the foyer, shaking umbrellas and brushing rain from their Sunday best. Dorothy undid the chin ties on her clear plastic rain bonnet, trying in vain to keep her freshly pressed curls dry. None of that mattered as she stepped onto the hospital elevator, arm in arm with Jerome, stomping water from his wingtips like a child playing in puddles.

With paperwork complete, they were handed off to Nurse Snyder, whose hair was teased into blond cotton candy.

"Mr. and Mrs. Miller," she said, "right this way, please."

"I don't know why that little white hat didn't go flying when she whipped her head around," Dorothy whispered to Jerome, and they both stifled a giggle.

The nursery was crowded with clear plastic basinets filled with red fleshy-faced bundles wearing pink or blue caps. Black, white, or brown—each seemed to be a clone of the same baby, some sleeping, others crying.

"This one's your little Siman," Nurse Snyder said, lifting the only one completely silent with his mouth opened wide.

"Bless his heart," Dorothy said. "Is he hungry?"

"Not at all," the nurse said. "They cry when they're hungry. He's just mouthy, hardly fusses, very alert. It's as if he wants to swallow up the world with himself in it!"

Dorothy sat in a big, white rocking chair to receive Siman. Jerome scooted a chair close, and they unwrapped Siman's swaddling to count fingers and toes.

"Hello, son." Jerome offered his index finger to a tiny clinched fist.

The baby's sloth-like moves did not match his dark quick eyes.

"Hello, Siman," Dorothy cooed. "We're so glad to finally meet you."

Jerome whispered a prayer of thanks, both following with, "Amen."

The nurse, who had been waiting in the doorway, handed a bulging manila envelope to Jerome. "The birth mother left this for you."

The first time he heard the story, variations of that one sentence played over and over in Siman's head:

*"The **birth** mother left this for you."*
*"The birth mother **left** this for you."*
*"The birth mother left this for **you**."*

His whole life seemed wrapped up in that one sentence.

From the envelope, Jerome pulled out a burgundy felt ring box trimmed with a fine gold line.

"My goodness! Look at that," Dorothy said as Jerome lifted the peach seed monkey. "I've never seen the likes of it."

The birth mother had written inside a thank-you note in beautiful cursive:

> *To Siman's Parents,*
> *This is a big day for all of us and there are at least four very different reasons. Though we will never meet, I want to thank you for making Siman's transition as short as possible. This is one of my many hopes for him. I chose the name Siman for its meaning—he who listens and hears—because that is also my lifelong hope for him. And I wanted "man" in his name. Of course, you may want to choose another name; I do, however, ask that you honor this request:*
> *Please give him the enclosed peach seed monkey on*

his thirteenth birthday along with these words: <u>This</u>
<u>will keep the monkey off your back, because being a</u>
<u>man is more than a notion.</u>

 I'm not at liberty to say any more than this, and I
trust that today's beautiful blessing will be enough.

 I send this with my eternal gratitude.

Siman had fallen asleep. Jerome and Dorothy silently watched his peaceful face. Jerome twirled the monkey gently between his thumb and forefinger, marveling at the diamonds catching fluorescent light.

"Whoever carved this did a perfect job," he said, "little fella even has an expression on his face."

"Looks like he's waiting for somebody to answer a question he just asked," Dorothy said.

"These diamond eyes must have a huge significance," Jerome said.

"I wish we could meet the mother," Dorothy said, "because she's right. God has blessed this child: the way Moses was blessed—with a mother who loves him enough to send him to us but not without a tar basket."

"I like that," Jerome said. "This little monkey is Siman's tar basket and we are pulling him from the Nile."

All four sat silently before their screens as Siman pinched tears from the corners of his eyes.

"Fascinating story, Siman," Olga said. "And you tell it beautifully."

"Thank you, but I'm hoping that you have a story for me."

"Indeed we do." Olga bumped shoulders with Bo D. "We are certain that your monkey came from our Ezekiel Dukes family."

"Wow. Not sure what to say!" Siman looked at Patricia, smiling.

"Understandable," Olga said, "even though we don't know exactly who the carver was yet, the initials *F.D.* on the bottom are a sure sign that he's from our encyclopedic family with its many arms and legs and incarnations."

"I see," Siman said.

"As soon as we know more, we will let you know."

"That's a promise," Bo D added.

Siman scribbled: *SHE'S WITHOLDING!*

"Thank you so much, Olga and Bo D," Patricia said, cupping Siman's hand. "This is more than we could ever have hoped for."

Siman insisted on exchanging cell phone numbers with Bo D. They hung up, and Siman jumped up from his chair.

"Everything she just said she's known for months! Since the day I sent the photos!"

"You're right," Patricia said. "She definitely knows more than she's telling—and—I'm sure she has a very good reason. This is major stuff, Si. All of this is the very reason Mama and Pop didn't want us doing DNA testing. You have to let it unfold at its own pace."

"—and you know Bo D had to notice that he and I both have Vulcan ears! I wonder if he'll tell her?"

"The assistant was in and out of the frame, making notes. I bet she noticed."

"I doubt that," Siman said. "When did white folks ever look that closely at Black folks?"

"I'd say a Dutch woman hanging with Black folks in southwest Georgia ain't exactly your garden-variety white folk."

"True. At least Bo D's my new ally. I'll send him a text right now."

> SM: Hey Boe D!
> (Did I spell that right?)
> It was an honor to meet you! 👊 👍

❧

"Dag!" Bo D stood quickly as Ursula ended the Skype call.

"Tell me," Olga said.

"Can't believe what I just saw!" Bo D paced. "Siman Miller has pointed ears!" He turned to Ursula. "You saw, right?"

"Yes, I noticed this. A genetic trait."

"They look like mine," Bo D chimed, "—and G-pop's!"

"Right," Olga said. "Your great-grandmother Alpha had the same ears."

"Wait. What?" Bo D said.

"That's strong evidence that Mr. Miller *could* be related to you through your great-grandmother Alpha." Ursula said.

"For real?!"

"For real," Olga said. "You'll recall Fletcher and I had different mothers, so I didn't get those ears. We need DNA testing as proof of kinship, so let's not put the cart before the horse. At this point, the only thing we're sure of is that Fletcher carved Siman's monkey. It has his mark—and my little diamonds. And now, after all these years, it has led Siman to us."

"So why didn't we tell Siman?" Bo D asked.

"These are delicate matters. Need special handling."

Ursula put files in her briefcase, confirmed their next meeting with Olga, and said her goodbyes, which pleased Bo D. He didn't want to share his aunt for this next part. And he was reaching the edge of his carefully orchestrated buzz, which made the meeting with Siman go smoothly, but now needed tweaking. He went to the kitchen and popped an oxy, feeling like Judas when he came back and saw his auntie sitting in her high-back chair by the window, Sidney at her feet. She looked helpless to him, fingering her silver watch necklace. He cleared his throat, and she turned to face him.

"So! Auntie," Bo D rolled the office chair over, "now can I ask my questions!"

"Ask away."

"How did Siman's birth mother get the monkey?"

"Not sure. We can only speculate."

"OK. So you have to be thinking what I'm thinking and what anybody looking at this would think, since G-pop carved the monkey."

"Go ahead. Say it."

"Got to be his outside child."

"That would be a logical deduction, but even logic can be overrated."

"Then what about the ears? Don't you think if we saw his, then he for sure saw mine? And his sister did, too? I bet you they having this same conversation right now! They ain't stupid."

"Here's our situation," Olga said. "Until we have blood proof, we're dealing with false hope."

"Hold up." Bo D checked his phone. "Siman sent me a text."

"Tell me." Olga smiled and leaned toward him. She looked less helpless to him now.

"Dude said he was *honored* to meet me." Bo D rocked back in the chair.

"Of course he is—*Dude* knows good character when he sees it."

"And he used thumbs-up and fist-bump emojis."

"Not surprised."

Except for Lysander Songtree, who actually stood at his classroom door every Monday and shook every student's hand as they entered, Bo D had never had anyone even act like they were honored to meet him, let alone say it. Especially when that person had good reason to believe he was lying by way of withholding the truth.

His fingers sailed across his phone. It wasn't his style but he threw in an emoji.

> BD: yo siman ditto
>
> and its Bo D . . . drop the e
>
> 👊

17

Fletcher slung a dish towel over his shoulder, standing at the small island in his kitchen, and set out his assembly line for salmon croquettes: three shallow bowls holding flour, egg, bread crumbs. This was two weeks after Altovise rushed away, leaving him standing in his driveway. He had convinced her to join him for what now felt like a blind date with a woman who knows your oldest secrets but has no clue who you are now.

He had to get a burning question off his chest tonight: Was she sick? There was no ideal time to ask. He moved deftly from stove to refrigerator, eyeing the back door and feeling elated and guilt ridden for feeling elated. A few minutes later, Altovise caught him with his fingers covered in egg and flour as she approached his back screen door.

"Hel-looo," she sang, clutching her purse and a bottle in a brown paper bag.

Rockhudson blocked her entry, sprawled in front of the door.

"Rock, go to bed!" Fletcher commanded. The dog rose slowly and moped off down the hall.

"Got my hands full so c'mon in," Fletcher said. "Sorry about that—sometimes Rock takes up more than his fair share."

"Looks like your movie star isn't much of a watchdog!"

"Right—he'll watch a thief walk away with the house." Fletcher chuckled.

Her light blue sundress looked cool and refreshing.

"Hmmm, smells good up in here!"

"Cheese grits—just wait 'til I put my scratch biscuits in the oven."

"I see you're still bragging about your cooking," she said, "and I don't blame you one bit, if I could cook—I'd brag, too."

"What's in the bag?" he asked.

"Just a bottle of wine. White goes with fish, right?"

"Wait-a-minute now, them honkies in Michigan got you drinking white wine with croquettes and grits? We got to reconnect you with your roots."

"I'll just put this in the refrigerator," she said, shaking her head. "Maybe I should've gotten beer—"

"I'm just joking with you. Don't matter either way. Me and alcohol parted ways years ago."

"Oh. I'm so sorry, Fletcher. I should've asked."

"Feel free to pour whatever you want. Won't bother me. Got plenty to drink. My tea is so sweet it pours slow."

Their laughter came as easily now as when they were young. Her sassy energy filled his outdated rooms, and he felt old and slow in her presence. Didn't much matter what they talked about—or if they talked at all. He was having trouble focusing on timing his biscuits to come out when the croquettes were finished. They nearly collided when she scooted past him headed for the refrigerator.

"Woman, you got to find somewhere else to be," he joked. "There just ain't enough room in here for both of us."

"Yessir—you don't have to ask me twice to leave a kitchen," she said and wandered off toward the living room.

This, of course, was another chance to look at her.

To Fletcher's surprise, seconds later she was singing and playing his little spinet:

> *Life is a funny game*
> *Not fixed in my favor*
> *I make moves that*
>> *Aren't part of a plan*

Fletcher had not heard her sing live since their last mass meeting at Shiloh decades ago. Then, as now, with each zest of air, she sang toes to her brows. He wiped his hands and parked in the archway to listen:

> *Like bubbles in a bar of soap,*
> *Or a book that ain't been wrote;*
> *These things cannot be counted.*

> *Taking my time now,*
> *I'm in no hurry.*
> *Looking over my shoulder*
> *At where I've been*
> *Trying to figure what to do ~*
>> *With so much I never knew I never knew.*

In high school, he'd spent many evenings at her house where her musical family delved into spiritual celebration, and was envious of how much history she'd learned from grandmothers on both sides, from Yoruba drums, chants, flutes, and banjo to Black and Muscogee hymnal line singing. Blended vocables lived at the ready in Altovise's throat, fusing with southern vernacular, giving rise to her own brand of scat. Fletcher had watched her learn from generations of herself during her short journey from girl to woman.

"I like it." Fletcher applauded as she finished off with an easy, rhythmic slide.

"Very early stages—but always good to see if I've gotten notes and words down in the right order."

"You got a title yet?"

"'Things I Never Knew I Never Knew.'"

"Got a nice ring to it. Can't remember the last time somebody played that piano. Needs tuning."

"My sister and I grew up playing a little Winter spinet just like this." She closed its cover and stroked the shining mahogany. "She's fine—but we *do* have to get her tuned."

Fletcher liked the sound of "we" in that sentence.

He led the way back to the kitchen. He had spread a lace tablecloth and brought out Maletha's silver flatware, crystal stemware, and good china. A mason jar of fresh garden roses replaced his punch bowl, and his one emergency candle was in a fancy holder from fireplace mantel knickknacks.

Fletcher served dinner buffet-from-the-stove and relaxed, seeing that his meal had turned out as planned. He watched with joy as she settled into her seat, quietly taking a moment, eyes closed, her lips uttering a quick grace.

During dinner, if he brought up the Movement, she talked about phone banking with Olga for Obama's reelection; if he mentioned their high school days, she praised Tyrone Bailey and his new nonprofit. He followed her lead, knowing that the past is patient. Every second of avoidance drew them closer to memories their younger legs could outrun, camera-eye images that were as robust as they had been during their youth.

And he, of course, held on to the question of her health. How could you ask somebody that looks that good if she's sick?

"It's been a long time since somebody made me breakfast for dinner," she said, "and I take back every joke I made about your cooking."

"I'm glad you enjoyed," he said, and then added, abruptly, "you not sick, are you? That's not why you came home?"

"Boy-o-boy you still know how to cut to the chase! No, no. I'm not sick." She cupped his hand in hers. "You're sweet to be concerned, but I assure you, I'm fine."

Now he felt like a sucker for agonizing so long, especially since any fool could see he was a lot more decrepit than she was.

"Be right back," Fletcher said with a sly glance. He returned with a small, flat box.

"What's this? It's not my birthday!"

"Yeah, but these might come in handy."

"Sunday comics! I like your wrapping paper," she said, ripping. "Yes!" and slipped on a pair of leather work gloves. "I can do some serious hay-baling with these."

"I hope so," he said.

They scraped and washed dishes and Altovise was prepared to forgo opening the wine—no corkscrew—until he led her to his woodshop.

His Christmas tree lights amused her, but not nearly as much as his woodshop curiosities. While Fletcher looked for his Swiss Army knife, she ran her hand across the smooth ebony wood boards ready to be assembled, then paused before the shelf of half-carved peach seed monkeys. She looked at them and said nothing.

Most folk come back home for forgiveness. If that was so for Altovise, there wasn't much point in sitting down to a candlelit dinner in hopes of being washed clean of the past. Even though the story hovered heavily between them, neither talked about the night he gave her the peach seed monkey.

That sweltering night in late July 1962, Movement activity rolled out at a maddening pace. Fletcher attended a mass meeting that was not the same without Altovise. He stopped by home to change, then drove to her house in Coachman Park. Not a breeze stirred, and he was roasting in gray sharkskin pants and his favorite olive-green Banlon shirt. Only three weeks before, she had rejected his proposal, so he wanted to at least look good on his way down.

Altovise sat alone in her porch swing, sucking on a softened lemon.

Moths fluttered around a bare, swaying light bulb. Her surprise showed in her feet—quickly stopping the swing when she saw his car. He walked somber-faced up the stairs.

"Missed you at Third Kiokee," he said. "Dr. King really preached. Talked about Gandhi's Salt March, the power of the human soul, and how we have to mobilize that soul force right here in Albany. I wish you had—"

"I'm not going to any more mass meetings. Olga tries that same tactic—pretending everything is the way it's always been. Doesn't work with me anymore."

How could he blame her for being mad after spending over a month incarcerated? He was mad, too, that she had endured the filthy prison instead of him. One of the first things he'd learned from Charles Sherrod was to protect her, so Fletcher was prepared to give her plenty of room. Still, there was one question he had to risk asking.

"I thought about you all the time while you were in that prison. Tore me up."

"Yeah. Me, too." She seemed to shift. Looked softly into his eyes.

"I worried that them A-holes laid hands on you."

The swing was parked at high arc, her feet apart, planted. She crossed at the ankle using both hands to squeeze lemon juice into her mouth.

"They didn't, did they?"

"Why you ask, Fletcher? Is it because you care if I was hurt, or you want to know if you should bother laying down with me again?"

He could not fathom the depth of her hurt after all she had been through, but was she mad at him? They had both wanted everything that happened in the Fairlane's backseat that night. Altovise was as strong and fragile as the monkey he had in his pocket to give her.

He was silent. He could not think of his needs; that would call for him to go down on his knees and beg, and he surely didn't beg. Not even for the thing he wanted most in the world.

The swing still paused in high arc, she shifted her legs, now standing straight and firm—a warrior's stance. His hand deep in his pocket, Fletcher hung on to the ring box that had held the key to his heart. Not wanting to hammer home any of this, he got straight to the point.

He took out the ring box. "You going off to college and won't be wearing my ring—so—I made this for you."

She walked down from her warrior's stance, porch swing slowly dropped to make a seat, and the lemon fell into her lap. Her hand trembled as she accepted the same ring box she'd left on his dashboard after he proposed.

Pride, anger, and shame collided in him as a mountain of hurt swelled between them.

She smiled, confused, and lifted out the little charm with its delicate gold chain. "Fletcher. This is so beautiful. I just don't know how you could carve a peach seed so intricately. Look how the grooves fit down his little back, and you really got his tiny monkey head and arms perfectly."

She caught a tear before it fell. "Thank you. Where on earth did you get these tiny diamonds?"

"Olga had a stray earring."

"But are you sure you want me to have this? I know it goes against your Dukes father-to-son tradition."

He had shared the details with her not long after their first date—when he showed her the peach seed monkey his father had given him.

"This one is yours," he said.

"How is it I deserve this? I don't know what to say." Her voice was heavy with tears.

Her face glowed. He wanted to kiss her and say, *I'll go wherever you go and wait however long you want me to wait.*

She held the monkey by its chain like a silent metronome to Fletcher's final words before he turned and left.

"I think everything's pretty much been said and done—except for this—" He pulled up a little straighter, changing the words to fit. *"This will keep the monkey off your back, because being grown is more than a notion."*

Altovise followed him down into the yard as he got into his car, not looking back. Engine on. Radio on.

"Fletcher. I'm so, so sorry."

"Yeah. Me, too."

He fought his volition to look at her. Love is patient; wielding power over feet to move or stay put and exerting dominion over hearts to break and change. Actions of our mind have speed, but actions of our heart have endurance.

With eyes focused in his headlight beam, he drove away.

He never saw her again until that day in Piggly Wiggly.

Altovise meandered around Fletcher's woodshop, a conservatory of his life.

"There you go," he said, wine bottle uncorked.

"This doesn't seem right," she said. "I'm really fine with iced tea."

"Look—I've been sober since Bo D was born." Through his crooked smile he added, "Never was a wino anyway."

"Excuse me? Who you calling a wino?"

She faked singeing him with a glance, then touched his hand. "Since you insist—I *will* have a glass, and we can serve your ginger beer in a wineglass."

They moved to a bench a few yards from his pond site, drinks in hand. A large backhoe was silhouetted against a night sky spotted with stars and filled with crickets in metallic ensemble.

"So peaceful here," she said, their faces lit by bright moonlight.

Once again, Fletcher launched straight in. "On the first Friday every month I take Olga to her library meetings, and this last one she asked me about that monkey I gave you. She gave me some story about finding her other earring."

"And—let me guess: you're thinking my showing up is somehow connected and it would be hard to convince you otherwise."

"Not hard. Impossible. But," he entwined their fingers, "I'm willing to spend a lot of time letting you prove me wrong."

She took a deep breath, looking out into the silver-lit darkness.

"When I dropped by the other day, we stood in front of that tree," she pointed into darkness, "drinking well water. The tree where you carved that diamond."

"So—you *do* remember."

"Of course. I never forgot a single detail of that horrid day."

He turned, shifting his weight toward her. "Do you remember what I promised?"

"Yes, I do." She placed a palm on his chest. "Is your motor running now?"

Their kiss came easily, the climax to flirting that had started among straw bales on his pickup and reached its peak tonight at dinner.

Back inside, they talked and laughed, listening to her albums, mixed in with other greats: The Meadowlarks, The Penguins, Martha and the Vandellas. When he suggested that she stay, she said, "There's no rush," and they walked to her car.

"I hope your monkey held up?" he said. "Been a lotta years."

"Sad to say, I don't have my little monkey anymore," she said, hesitating, then getting quickly into her car.

She seemed tense, stroking his hand, resting on her closed door.

He needed to talk about that night on her porch and knew they wouldn't. Why hadn't he walked past himself to keep her from leaving? Why hadn't he begged?

He moved aside, hoping her driving away from him was not becoming a habit. But this time he also stepped out of his own way, so that he could fall again—deeper into the love he had carried for this woman for half a century.

Seconds later he stood in his bedroom in front of Maletha's jewelry box. He didn't know where things were going with Altovise, but it wasn't fair to take Maletha with him.

With soap, water, and some work, his wedding band finally slipped off over swollen knuckles. He turned the tiny jewelry box key, placed his ring safely inside, to keep company with three unclaimed peach seed monkeys. He waited for a different feeling. Gold band or no gold band, he felt Maletha's presence, knew her voice was still in his head. And the ether of Altovise's words was also present: *Sad to say, I don't have my little monkey anymore.*

18

~

"They here, Terrence!" Florida yelled after banging on Bo D's door. "Terrence? You hear me?"

"Yeah, Ma. I hear you." Bo D sniffed and wiped meth powder from the back of his hand.

"Well, come on out then!"

Timing was off. His hit needed five minutes to kick in. He shook his head briskly and popped up from the bed, knowing he could fake it for five.

It was the last Sunday in April, a roller-coaster month for Bo D. And now he was headed for a sit-down with Indicca, which Florida had skipped church to arrange and he reluctantly agreed to after she threatened to put him out and change the locks. He believed she meant every word. To maintain the pretense of work, he would up his weekly CME visits. Auntie Olga had a Berber saying: *My dog is hopelessly phony; he's always glad to see me.* That described the party people—always looking for a bone—so why did he prefer their company to almost every soul in his family? Where else could he go?

He threw a T-shirt over his sweats and put drops in his eyes.

"Where's my baby girl?" Florida said at the front door. "Indicca, I thought you said you were bringing Cricket with you? Where is she?"

"I don't know," Indicca said, with Cricket's pink crinoline dress spilling over on both sides of her mother.

"I know where she is." Bo D peeked from behind his mother.

"He-oh I am, Daddy!" Cricket ran into the foyer and wrapped herself around her father's legs. She was wearing her sparkly purple sunglasses. This had become a regular thing.

"OK, Cricket," Florida said, kneeling to smooth crinoline and lace, "let's go to the mall!"

Cricket clung tighter to Bo D. "You go, too, Daddy," she whined.

Bo D handed her a five-dollar bill from his pocket. As Florida picked her up, the bill floated from Cricket's hand.

"She's fine and we'll be back in a couple of hours." Florida carried the whining bundle quickly from great room to garage. The muffled cry pierced Bo D's heart as he walked toward the kitchen.

"The other day it was candy and now this," Indicca said, following him, holding the money, "even though I told you over and over and over not to try to buy her love."

"Damn! Indicca! She three years old. Give me a break," he shouted, because Ritalin was surging.

"I looked up to my daddy same way she looks up to you, and he gave me love and guidance—not gifts and money. That's why I can take care of me and my child."

"Hold on. She's my child, too!"

"And—like it or not *you* set the tone for what she'll be looking for in a man someday. You be teaching her even when you not trying.

"She just want to be with you, Bo D. So stop throwing money at her." She threw the crumpled bill at him.

Bo D caught it, then dropped his head, shyly, and gave the signal for time-out.

She walked slowly toward him. "We only got two hours and already off on the wrong foot. I'm so tired of fighting."

For that fleeting moment, seeing her see him, her readiness to fight for them, Bo D believed in the impossible—a feeling he wasn't used to. He still loved Indicca, as messy as that could be at times.

"OK then." He smiled. "Let's start over. You hungry?"

"I could eat." She opened the refrigerator. "Really, Bo D?" She held up a milk carton with TERRENCE written on a piece of duct tape. "Some things never change."

They sat side by side at the counter with ham and cheese sandwiches. Bo D pushed his plate away and pulled a beer from his backpack.

"How come you not wearing your monkey?" She took a bite. "Daddy Fletcher got that new chain."

"Don't know." He shrugged.

His mother's huge kitchen seemed to swallow them up. The ceiling was too far away. He wished they were sitting in Indicca's tiny kitchen, at her little table for two. As she ate her sandwich, he tapped his teeth with a fingernail then broke bread crust into pieces. He wanted to swim to the top of the silence and stick his nose out for air. He wished he could tell Indicca about his new uncle, but he had promised, and couldn't risk a leak.

From the looks of things the family pity party was over, so he knew what was coming from Indicca—like everybody else, she wanted to know his long-term plans. He wanted to know his plans, too. He pivoted in the swiveling stool, jingling keys in his pocket.

"Bo D. Don't you even think about leaving. We need to figure this out—for Shieka's sake."

She swerved around to face him, her palms rubbing her knees, calmness replaced with strictness. The change in her surprised him. He placed clasped fingers in full view on the marble, listening as she confided in him. He had not known of her fear that he would walk away once he found out she was pregnant. Seems all women might worry about this, even in a supposedly happy marriage. Look what happened to his mom.

"I was ready to be a mother," she said, "but that first time I was by myself, holding little tiny Shieka—"

"She wasn't so little," Bo D said, "weighed eight pounds nine ounces!"

"But she looked so helpless that first feeding after we got home. And even though my mama and them were there helping too much, I felt like I was all alone. I don't know why. That's when I got scared."

"Of what?"

"Going over the edge and not being able to take care of me and my baby."

"How come you never said nothing?"

"'Cause, boy!" She punched his arm. "I could see you was more scared than I was!"

"Yeah." He laughed with her, even though it wasn't funny. "You right. One of us needed to step up and be grown."

Was it out of love that she reminded him how he'd texted her several times from work that first day, and he dropped by right after work to see the baby? He could feel the chill from her family and knew he hadn't earned the freedom to come and go. He was the reason she felt so alone in trying to work out being a mom on her own.

"Not running away ain't the same as stepping up, Indicca. I'm just Shieka's *sometime*. You're her *nonstop*."

"Don't be dissing yourself," she said, her serious tone returning, "you did step in—now we just need you to step all the way *up*." She caressed his hands. "I know you don't like pressing tires." He wanted to tell her he was fired, wanted that kind of closeness again. Instead, he listened.

"And I know it's hard, everybody putting pressure on you, but Bo D. Taking them pills, smoking, and drinking is not your answer."

He pulled his hands away, rose, and walked to the sink. "You know I still have to take them pills for my back."

"Don't do that. This me you talking to. You high right now. I can smell it and see it in your eyes. So that beer is the last thing you should be drinking. You need help."

"Here we go again." He paced. "So that's really what this little meeting is all about. I thought you wanted to talk about us being a family together."

"Can't talk about one without the other. 'Cause we can't be together until you get yourself together—keep up child support and see Cricket on a regular basis like you used to. The whole family know about that alley house. And it's time somebody came clean with you so you can get help again. Look like that's gone have to be me."

Indicca wrapped his sandwich in foil and moved on to washing plates.

"You giving away your soul, little by little, every time you go to that drug house."

Bo D did not look at her. He dried and put away dishes. She put the sandwich on the shelf next to his milk carton and leaned against the refrigerator.

"I'm not scared anymore," she said, "but just because I know I can raise our daughter on my own don't mean I want to. And as much as I feel blessed for help from your family and mine—me and Shieka want *you* to be a family with us."

Bo D had never heard Indicca say those words out loud, even though they had rushed silently from her since Cricket was born; they had been evident in the way she had done without so Cricket could have, and in her bottomless patience for him. She was always speaking on behalf of the one person who was most justified in hating him. One day Cricket would be able to speak for herself. Would he then be on the receiving end of the kind of contempt he holds for his own father?

All these things sickened Bo D because he saw his failures in Indicca's strengths. He didn't hate her for this; he hated *it*. The big *it*. The subject of the sentence: *It's hard out here . . .*

"I'm here to find out if you really want what we want," she said.

Bo D did want to be a family—in that space Auntie Olga talked about where he can protect Indicca and Cricket. Still. He just didn't know how to get there.

Indicca went on, "'Cause if you want to be with us you have to get some help and get off all them drugs. Otherwise, I can't let you be around Cricket. You a father, Bo D, and you need a plan. Period.

"You say you don't have no passion, but you do. Making stuff and restoring cars—even acting."

"Yeah," he said, knowing she'd have no comeback, "but a passion without a plan is a pitiful thing."

19

In the month since salmon croquettes, Fletcher and Altovise had spoken by phone several times, gone to House of Jazz, out to dinner, and two movies.

In every situation she dodged conversation about their past. This changed on the day she joined him to deliver Olga's bookcases to Albany State's library. Turning off Oglethorpe onto what was now College Drive, they entered times long gone, when the street was called Hazard Drive and was a microcosm of Black culture in Albany.

Fletcher drove slowly down the street, where, in less than a quarter of a mile, a universe once unfolded. Now a shrunken replica of itself: maintenance buildings, institutional lawns, checkpoint huts, and parking lots replaced the simple wooden houses—some owned but most rented—where folks raised families, leased rooms to ASC students, and got on with life. Now, a row of well-behaved city trees stood at attention where Mrs. Clara's plums once stained the sidewalk and fingers and lips of neighborhood children, until she chased them away.

Without the big mimosa tree, who can be sure where Hazard Laboratory School once stood, lost to Albany's Great Flood of 1994?

Hazard was a K–7 school where children of white-collar academics and blue-collar workers in the houses blended, and where a hidden yet absolute line was drawn between those who brought a check for $1.25 each Monday morning to cover a week's lunch, and those who brought cash.

For Olga, as an ASC faculty member, the campus was her second home, and many Movement leaders were students. Altovise spent a lot of time with her aunt and uncle, who lived on Hazard Drive. Fletcher called on Altovise many nights at their house—a parking lot now—directly facing one of the girls' dorms.

The dike still stood, a long grassy swell, slopping up gently along the parking lot's west end. This was meant to hold back headstrong waters of the Flint River, only two blocks beyond the dike, but it failed grandly in '94. Tropical Storm Alberto unloaded over two feet of rain, flooding many buildings up to the eaves, uprooting tens of thousands across Georgia. In Albany, instead of July Fourth fireworks, freed from rain-soaked earth by the pressure of merciless rain, hundreds of caskets blasted off like rockets, sky bound for six feet before splashdown. Horrors of disinterred bodies ensnared on fences would forever haunt loved ones and volunteers. Southwest Georgia bounced back stronger for having, once again, survived the worst of times.

Fletcher and Altovise walked around, stopping first at a pink-and-green Alpha Kappa Alpha plot in front of Gibson Hall. A wave of imposter syndrome hit Fletcher, the way he felt walking around this campus during the Movement, when he was the age of students now flouncing past him and Altovise as if they were invisible—two senior citizens who had apparently lost their way.

"It's like it was yesterday," Altovise said. "Vada and I thought our Albany State friends were rock stars back then."

"I remember that," Fletcher said, "y'all wanted to be Rams even though Thaddeus graduated from the arch rival Fort Valley."

"Yeah, he couldn't wait to leave home and play basketball for the Wildcats—but Vada and I were Rams at heart—helped decorate homecoming floats, cheered at games and concerts. Hip young pledges dressed in those tailored suits, pumps, and pill box hats—pink and green, red and white, blue and white. Oh and the step shows! Ohmygoodness. We had no idea what it meant to *cross the burning sands* but we knew it was a thing."

"But what you didn't know," Fletcher said, "is that I came close to enrolling just so I could pledge and be in them step shows!"

"You're right." Altovise shook her head. "I did not know that."

She stood, pointing across the campus lawn. "Our cousin's house stood right over there and I remember early one morning, after Vada and I spent the night, we woke up to deep voices chanting way off in the distance and ran out onto the porch just in time to see a single file of men, like living bronze statues, appearing out of a ground-hugging fog; marching; shaved heads, each carrying a brick sprayed gold. No shirts, bulging muscles—"

"Watch out now," Fletcher said, "don't let me have to pour some water on you!"

"I'll be all right," Altovise snickered, fanning her face with a hand as she went on. "Heavy work boots stomped to that bass chant: *O-may-gah—psi-phi! O-may-gah—psi-phi!*" She bent at the waist, arching her back to mimic their moves.

"Little did I know," Fletcher quipped, "all I had to do to keep you was become an Omega man."

"It's true that even the Temptations couldn't hold a candle to the Omegas back then," she took his hand, "but you are everything I need in this moment."

They walked on to find the library.

⁂

Buying a bottle of California chardonnay was a first for Fletcher, and yet, three days later, there he stood, at Altovise's hotel room door, holding a brown paper bag shaped like a wine bottle and understanding that he was in her grips again. Tomorrow's move into her lake house would give them plenty to talk about. Her sister Vada's husband, Roscoe, was a general contractor and had been working on the renovation for months, so it was too late for second opinions, but, out of curiosity, Fletcher had accepted her invitation to visit the house.

He had put his boat in at Cleve Cox Landing many times, but never knew anybody with a Cromartie Beach address—especially in a house like this: sitting on close to an acre surrounded by oaks and evergreens with a lawn sloping down to the water. He thought her bungalow style would fit well in California, or somewhere else he'd never been. Three bedrooms seemed way more house than she needed—but how could he not be impressed by a full-width front porch, bevel wood clapboard, most likely cedar, which makes up for high maintenance with good looks. Both stories had big sash windows, and her vaulted great room was a festival of wood: walls, stairs, banisters, and exposed beams and rafters.

Her back deck jutted out over a boat port, even though she had no boat and no clue what they fished for out there. A low river rock wall bordered her private beach and matched the massive chimney. Their last stop on her tour was her screened-in dock patio with kitchen, dining area, and four Adirondack chairs facing Cromartie Lake. He had not been very talkative that day, in awe of her house, silently critiquing Roscoe's methods, and still in shock that she was actually standing in front of him.

He twisted the paper tighter around the wine bottle and made a deal with himself: once inside her hotel room he would steer clear of those stories—both dull and fiery—that her return had stirred in him. He would not recall how, even though she was known for being wise for her years, her impersonation of Donald Duck would make him laugh until his side ached. And at all costs, he would avoid calling her *Veesy*, since that would take them back to stealing kisses between classes in front of her locker. The past was off-limits, but everything else was fair game. He was blowing into his cupped palm to check his breath when she opened the door.

"Hey you," she said, stepping aside.

"Hey yourself." That perfume was always a problem. If she didn't want to visit the past, why did she keep wearing it? He handed her the wine.

"Thanks, Fletcher, you didn't have to do this."

"I wanted to." He looked around at the candles and fresh flowers. "Looks like you expecting company up in here."

Boxes and suitcases were stacked on one side, covered with Muscogee patchwork quilts. On top of this sat a bowl with several pairs of reading glasses. A turntable, tiny speakers, and crates of albums lined the other wall.

"I know. Candles are too cliché," she said, "but I drew the line at satin sheets. I figure at our age we might slide outta bed and not be able to get up!"

"I bet we'd figure out what to do while we're down there." They laughed as she opened the wine.

He fished out a pair of reading glasses and knelt before her vinyl collection, scores of albums in alphabetical order: Etta Baker, Barbara Dane, and Sister Rosetta Tharpe, but also Earth, Wind & Fire and Cyndi Lauper. She poured wine and ginger beer.

"What we drinkin to?" he asked.

"To surviving tomorrow!"

She put a Mildred Bailey album on the turntable and stepped back, swaying to the sultry piano intro.

Fletcher rested both their drinks and stepped up behind her, swaying in unison. He kissed and gently stroked her kitchen, finding a knot of worry there. His thumbs worked tenderly on that gnarl. She purred.

"Seems to be where I store everything," she said, rolling her shoulders.

Then he slowly turned her to face him, quick-stepping into a twirl that made her laugh out loud.

"Can't say you're short on talent." Altovise smirked, quoting the lyrics. "Look at you—still got them moves."

They fell into a two-step, her face resting on his chest. Her back, too, was tense as he ran his hand gently along her spine.

"My grandmother Arnela used to say, *never get in the way of a blessing*," Altovise said, "and you definitely look like a blessing to me—just not sure how I turned into the girl nobody asks to the prom 'cause they think she's already going."

"You been single all these years?" They had never discussed this.

"Yes, I have."

Fletcher was silent, waiting for her to elaborate, but since he had opened the gate, she seemed to be waiting for him to keep walking through. All this was stiffened by their rhythmic two-step.

"Granmama also said it's good to have somebody in your life to leave a light on for you."

"Like Motel Six, huh?" He tried to clean up this lame reference. "After Maletha died, I took to leaving a light on for myself."

"Not quite the same though, is it?" She stopped and stepped back, sipped wine.

"Not quite."

"I came very close to the altar once," she said, sorting through her albums.

"What? You left another poor joker standing there with his ring box in his hand?"

"Just the opposite—*he* got cold feet before we even booked the venue."

"What happened to that plan you had for six sons?"

"You mean my basketball team and water boy." She hung her head and sank into a quiet laugh, which he matched.

"Truth is," she said, "I've seen it too many times: children grow up and out, then parents seem to be left with nothing but pet peeves and a mutual ire, if not full-blown contempt. It's as though they poured all their love into bringing those children into the world, and when the children leave home, the love goes with them."

He searched for what to say again. His mind was still working when she put on a Bertha Hope Trio album, sat on the couch, and went back to her drink.

"I guess I reaped what I sowed for walking away from you," she said.

"Wasn't all on you." This was not enough, but all he had. "I'm the one who walked off your porch that night."

"Let's not do this, Fletcher. If we pick up shovels and put on boots there's plenty of blame to spread. We were young and had been through a lot."

Abandoning caution, he sat next to her and took her hands in his, not giving up on words and the power of a whisper. "We both want this, so what could be wrong in making that happen?"

"I'm used to being in control," she said, lacing her fingers, "and suddenly we're together after so long and I don't know who you are anymore." She quavered, "And I sure as hell don't know who I am with you."

"You know me, Veesy." The word had slipped out. He kissed the medicine knot tattoo on each of her wrists. "I'm Fletcher Dukes."

Like a decrescendo, they were reduced to murmurs as hot bodies met cool sheets and Fletcher was lost in that space called skin-to-skin.

They were almost eighteen again, except he knew not to expect certain things. Speedy was nowhere to be found. This was not a problem because he was in no hurry. And neither was she. Their grunts and moans incited each next move, and they rode a slow glide to ecstasy.

After, they lay tangled in sheets, like tethered rafts, floating on waves of pleasant exhaustion.

"Damn woman," Fletcher rolled onto his back, "you're like the U.S. Army."

"How so?" The pillow muffled her voice as she said, "And this better be good."

"You make a man wanna be all that he can be!"

The bed shook with laughter.

"More, more, more," Altovise said, drifting off.

Each had met the other halfway, and what had happened in the middle was now beyond words. And so they slept.

Fletcher would miss this minivacation at her hotel: waking up to a Flint River view and free copies of *USA Today*, not to mention home-cooked café food. From their window seat, as families and businesspeople buzzed around them, he and Altovise looked out at bronze Ray Charles sitting at his piano and morning traffic whizzing by on Oglethorpe. Fletcher finished an omelet, she drank coffee and picked at a piece of toast. The newspaper rested on the booth seat beside him. To keep away from their past, he'd avoid discussing the sickening child sex case at Penn State and went instead for President Obama rightfully attacking Romney's wealth. But Altovise had changed overnight. She was full of thought and spoke as if she were talking to herself.

"My last day on campus I stood at my office window looking down on students in the quad—so young and invincible, like we were during the Movement. Seemed like I could smell Georgia in the Michigan air, and just like that I jumped back to the Larson Brig. I hadn't thought about that place in years. Invincibility vanishes once you face the real fear of harm or death. And that's the thing—we don't have innocent thoughts of our teen years that aren't attached to some terror from those racist assholes," she turned to Fletcher, "and this is why I never like talking about the past."

"I can understand that," Fletcher said, thinking of a few private memories he would take to his grave. Even so, he favored the past where nothing was left to chance. Unless it's a piece of the past heavily soaked in secrets, like a ceiling plaster so flooded by slow leaking rain it comes crashing down.

Back then he had wanted a world with Altovise, a chance to simply be *in love*, uninterrupted by protests and bigotry.

Before he could fill the backward silence, she followed a memory back to riding with Olga to the first Albany Movement meeting at Slater King's home. She slipped into lecture mode.

"Remember? It was about a difference in tactics and strategies: the NAACP Youth Council preferred dismantling segregation through the courts. Because I was young and stupid—I thought Olga was right to switch to the brand-new SNCC and *direct* action, but she later pointed out that we needed both."

"I remember." Fletcher smiled wistfully. And as easily as that—in morning's forgiving light—their past was no longer off-limits.

She even brought up their first date. 1957, county fair. That night was heaven: her hair tied back in a turquoise bandana, which he often swept aside to softly kiss in her kitchen. If they weren't holding hands, he had his arm around her, and she slid her hand into his back pocket, until both their arms filled with stuffed animals he won shooting hoops. One by one she handed them off to random kids.

"We got grown very fast," Altovise said, "holding on to each other through all that chaos."

Memories don't unfold in a linear fashion. They roll out in lumps, like soft, heavy rocks, or appear in flashes that you must grab before they burn out. They talked about their past like siblings, growing up under one roof, often coming at details from different sides. But they had an unspoken accord about their love, a shared keepsake from the four veriest years of their lives, now with two separate lifetimes built upon them.

〜

Altovise's car and Fletcher's pickup pulled up behind a huge moving van parked in front of her lake house. A swarm of helpers came and went, unloading. She stepped out of her car and Tyrone introduced Bo D.

Tyrone greeted Fletcher and helped him fold the tarp from his pickup.

"I see he's lucid and calm," Fletcher gestured toward Bo D walking with Altovise into the house, "which means he's high. That's so he could hold it together in front of Altovise."

"Yeah," Tyrone said, "too much at stake. He was psyched to meet Dr. Al 'cause he now knows how much she means to you. Still not talking to you, huh?"

"Nope."

"Like I told Ms. Florida, I got his back. Always."

"Means a lot to us, Tyrone, I just wish that was enough."

"Yes, sir," Tyrone said, "so do I."

"Take it from somebody who knows: when it comes to helping an addict get clean, you might have better luck getting a mockingbird not to sing all night in June."

"Yes sir, I hear you."

The conversation was shifting the young man's mood and that was not Fletcher's intent, so he patted Tyrone's back. "I heard Altovise made you chief bottle washer, so what's my assignment, boss? Put me in the background somewhere."

Tyrone sent Fletcher to join a young couple on the back patio breaking down boxes. Both were actors who had just joined Eusi. They ignored Fletcher, which suited him fine. He took a bottle of water from a cooler. Several feet away in the great room, Altovise and Bo D unpacked books and found more to talk about than Fletcher expected. He wanted to be a fly on the wall. Mostly, Altovise talked and Bo D listened, and they both laughed a lot. If Bo D smelled of beer and reefer at this hour, then she'd know, having dealt with college students and their mess. She would think Fletcher was a failure as a grandfather. Their wave of joy from last night might come crashing down around him. He wished Bo D had not come.

Altovise handed Bo D a book. He smiled, flipping through it as she went upstairs. He put drops in his eyes, slipped the book into his backpack, and headed toward Fletcher.

"Hey, G-pop!"

"Hey." Fletcher tried not to look as puzzled as he felt.

"Can't believe Tyrone got you on box duty."

"I wasn't drafted—I volunteered. What you been up to out there?"

"Unpacking books. I like Dr. Al. She cool—and man! She *got* some books!"

"Yeah, all those years teaching."

"Like Granmama Maletha."

Bo D popped the top on a can of root beer.

"Why don't you come help me?" Bo D said, glancing at the actors, still keeping to themselves.

"All right," Fletcher said, following him back to the great room. It wouldn't hurt for Altovise to see them together, but more important, the feud seemed to be over, in which case, Fletcher was convinced that Altovise was a miracle worker.

20

~

Bo D had a headache. His mother no longer did his laundry, so he also had slick sheets and pillows that smelled like sweat and drool. He wasn't sure why she'd stopped. Somehow, she must know he lost his job. And it's not her style to just come out with it right away.

The bench press held a pile of dirty clothes. He gave his pillow an upper cut, his eyes were half-mast. A blur, directly in front of him, one of his pill crushers sat on top of a copy of *Invisible Man* on his nightstand. This was the book Altovise gave him on moving day just over a week ago, which seemed like an eternity. When she shook his hand, he instantly saw why his grandfather was in love. She pulled you in, like a magnet. She had facial features and expressions set from birth; if you saw her baby pictures, you'd see a grown face on a baby's body, looking like she knew way too much. He had seen this face all his life in a Polaroid in Auntie Olga's study.

His mom hadn't left for work, but the house was too quiet. From his nightstand drawer he pulled out his last joint. He would light up out by the pool after she left. Leading up to moving day, Bo D made sure his Altoid tin was well stocked so that he could feel smart and in control for meeting Altovise. He tanked up with a perfect balance of weed, meth, and beer. To the unknowing eye he was just another upbeat helper, ready to work.

His grandfather—on the other hand—was a fish out of water, breaking down boxes with those wannabe movie stars, who were putting on airs, having no idea they were in the presence of a national treasure who has his own side to stories Auntie Olga and Altovise Benson tell about the Movement. It wasn't even about ending that feud; he had to step in. He couldn't stand seeing those two disrespecting his grandfather.

He and his mom avoided each other as much as possible. Since their schedules fluctuated, managing the illusion of working had been easier than he thought.

He sank into a pit of big, fluffy throw pillows on his bed. TV's hawkish light flickered across his face. His headache was worse and his skin itched because now his Altoid tin was empty.

"Terrence!" His mother's voice punctured his closed door seconds before she marched in, turning on the ceiling light.

He sprang to his feet. Through all their scrimmages she had never barged in on him like that.

"We need to talk," she said, throwing a plastic bag with empty prescription bottles at him. "Pull yourself together and meet me in the kitchen."

She stopped and added, "And put some Vaseline on them chapped lips. You look like I-don't-know-what."

Ashy skin was the least of his problems, but he stopped by the guest bathroom for Vaseline. Ten minutes later he sat watching his mother rewipe her spotless marble counter. With gospel music turned off, silence permeated every corner.

Between brewery and tire factory hours, over the years they'd both done their share of graveyard shifts, but there was a time when he and his mom always ate dinner together at a table fit for company. She kept up a tradition she started when he was a toddler: ringing her dinner bell, even when it was just the two of them. After Cricket's birth, she held it against him for not marrying Indicca, and their cozy mealtimes dried up. She reserved bell-ringing for large family meals only. He'd take a plate to his room or eat alone, standing at the sink.

Now almost everybody was moving away from the pity party that started Easter Sunday. Auntie Olga was the only one on his side. He was trying hard not to mess that up. She probably knew through her snitches that he'd lost his job. Her tactic was to sit on things to see if he would come clean, ask for help. This time he would keep his cards closer to his chest. As promised, he texted regularly with his shiny new Uncle Siman. That was a high point in his days because no one else had a clue.

In kindergarten, Bo D had collected new pennies in a mason jar on his nightstand. He liked that they were not mucked up by buckets of crud sticking to everything else within his reach. With carefully chosen emojis he could keep Uncle Siman exactly where he needed him: hundreds of miles away thinking his newfound nephew was special.

He had seen this talk with his mom coming. Every movie has a climax, where the good and bad clash. He and his mother saw each other as the villain. Whoever is closest to you gets most fucked up by your crud.

"I want things to be different between you and me," she said, still wiping. She was calmer than before.

He sighed, arms folded tightly over his chest.

"OK. I'm trying, Terrence," she stopped wiping, "trying to be careful what I say and how I say it so you won't do what you're doing right now."

"What? What did I do?"

His mother was only forty-four but she was starting to look old, worry lines getting deeper and deeper. He had never considered how much he had contributed to each and every one of those lines. He softened his stare, both palms spread on the cool marble, realizing that his mother could be privy to whatever Auntie Olga's snitches uncovered about him; in which case she might know a lot.

"You still taking them painkillers they prescribed when you hurt your back. That was over six years ago."

"You been messing around in my room," he snapped.

"Let me remind you: *your* room? Is in *my* house."

He opened the refrigerator and drank from his milk carton. This was mainly an excuse to walk past her to see if he could smell gin. He couldn't, but sometimes she drank vodka.

"I suspected you hadn't been working and come to find out it's been two whole weeks! What kind of fool do you think I am, Terrence?"

Bo D had learned from an early age that when a mother asks a question, she already knows the answer. This is called entrapment. His mother was an expert.

"How'd you find out?"

"Boy, please. You do realize Hooper's HR director goes to Greater Goshen? And we sing in the choir together. So it was just a matter of time."

Bo D cracked his knuckles, wishing he'd managed this as well as he did his highballs.

"Looks like that meeting you and Indicca had didn't help, but I'm not here to fight, just concerned about you. Do you understand that?"

Bo D paced. "I know where you going with this, Ma. Yes, I *was* an addict but I recovered. Remember?"

"You know full well that ain't the way it works."

"Regardless of what them psychiatrists say—I'm in control, so forget all that once-an-addict-always-an-addict bullshit."

"So now you know more than *all* them experts?" The dishrag was a wad in her closed fist.

"Have *you* been to rehab?" he needled. "If you serious about things being different then let's talk about some stuff *you* need to change. Are *you* in control of your drinking?"

"Don't do that, Terrence. Don't make this about me. You need help—"

"And *you* don't?" he yelled. "We were planning on telling you together, but I might as well do it now: Indicca and I cutting you off from driving and watching Cricket."

"Why you always got to raise my blood pressure?" Her voice rose, too. "I'm trying my best—truly—to keep this from happening. You can start by coming back to church."

"Yeah-yeah! Let's talk about church." His hands punctuated each word. Florida stared into the sink.

"Ma," he walked closer, "you know what I learned two years ago in rehab? God is a Group of Drunks, and the Gift of Desperation and Grace over Drama. That's what God is. Not a trinket trapped inside a fancy church."

Bo D jingled keys in his pocket.

"And don't you even *think* about walking out," Florida said. "You open all this up and think you can turn around and just walk out?"

"You think you're invisible stashing gin bottles all over this house?"

Florida created order: dishrag-over-faucet, walk-into-greatroom.

"So now *you* the one walking away?" Bo D followed her. "It's a simple question, Ma, and if you don't have a simple answer then I guess you a hypocrite—"

"That's it." Florida threw her hands up as if testifying in church. "I have had E-NOUGH. You hear me? More than E-NOUGH!" she yelled, facing Bo D. "You know what, boy? I got mine. This house is paid for. In a few years I can retire and be very comfortable. I'm here trying to help *you* get yours, and this is how you show thanks? Throwing a few cocktails in my face and keeping me from my grandbaby?"

Bo D stared down, rubbing both palms back and forth across the do-rag on his head.

"So you listen to me," his mother went on. "Number one: you do not stand in my house and attack me and my God, and number two: if you think I'm such a hypocrite then you can just pack your shit and git out of my house! You ain't got to eat my hypocrite grits no more, or my hypocrite fried chicken and collard greens either. And you definitely ain't got to listen to this hypocrite trying to help you get your triflin'-ass life in order." A simmering vapor trailed after her up the staircase. Seconds later, she slammed the door to her room.

"Fuck it then!" he yelled. "I'm outta here!"

21

To throw off snitches, after his blowout, Bo D parked his car in a friend's garage. He bummed a ride to the party house, where he slept on the couch. Three nights later, LaChondra gave him a ride to pick up his car and he left his friend's house in pounding rain.

Under a moonless night, buildings, gas stations, and trees appeared ghostly, familiar yet foreign. Wyclef Jean's song *Hendrix* blared, drowning out the wipers' frantic rhythm. Stopping at a traffic light, he turned on the dome light to check his reflection and brushed away paper towel lint clinging to his whiskers.

He was driving to Dove Cove now because he knew his mom was doing a graveyard shift. Breathing into a lingering buzz, he looked forward to a shower and a few hours in his old bed before her shift was over. Beyond that, he had no plan.

Headlights beamed through blurred rain and Bo D stared at what he saw piled in the driveway. Everything he owned had been reduced to a duffel bag, a suitcase, and three giant black leaf bags.

Pulling his sweatshirt hood over his head, he stepped out into the torrential May night, and within seconds he was drenched.

"Really, Ma!" He screamed up at the windows, rain filling his eyes, "this is how you gone do me?!" Mostly, this was meth and beer conspiring to make him puff up like a lizard and lash out.

"Ma! For real?"

Had she changed the locks? Didn't matter. She wasn't home, and even if she was, she would not be listening for his car to pull in or watching from an upstairs window. He also knew she would have been hitting her gin stashes pretty hard.

Gooseflesh rose on his arms as he moved through pouring rain, hurling slick, wet bags into his car. No need to hurry; he couldn't be any wetter. His car was filled with his earthly belongings, so he could not risk sleeping at the CME house. He thought of only one person to call.

A little while later, he parked behind Indicca's mobile home. He glanced back as he ran around to the front. Sitting in a pool of lamppost light, his Mach 1 was almost erased by slashes of rain.

Before he could knock, Indicca opened the door. He stepped in, emerging from the shelter of his hoodie. He exhaled slowly, seeing her in her cozy living room, carefully made sofa bed and beach towels as a rug for his sneakers and soaking wet socks. He dug in his backpack for phone and charger.

"So, I see push done come to shove with Mama Florida." Indicca's voice was low and unshakable. "We all been worried sick about you."

"I know. Sorry. Really appreciate this. Had nowhere else to go."

"Mama Florida been calling and calling, Daddy Fletcher in Atlanta don't even know even know yet. At least I didn't lie when I said I didn't know where you were. Where you been for three whole days?"

"I stayed with—"

She lifted her palm. "On second thought, less I know the better—and like I said, this is just for tonight." She shook her head. "You can't be staying here with no job and no rehab. You understand me?"

"I know, I know. You think I want Boo to see me like this? I'll be gone before she wakes up." He plugged in his phone. "How she doing?"

"She misses her daddy. *That's* how she doing."

"I'll make this right, I promise."

Unlike his mom, Indicca didn't have to utter a word about money spent on his Sean John hoodie, True Religion jeans, and red leather Big Sean sneakers. She folded her arms again tightly across her chest. That said it all.

"You know she can sleep through a train wreck if you wanna take a shower. I left towels in there for you. I wake her up at six, we leave the house by six forty-five, but I want you gone by five thirty just in case."

"OK. I'll set my alarm. Don't worry. But there is one more thing you could do for me."

"What."

"When they ask you, don't tell them I was here."

"No way, Bo D. Your family is good to me and Cricket, so I'm not about to lie to them. They love you and deserve to know where you are and you tryin to drive all of us crazy with worry."

"You don't have to lie, just delay the truth for twenty-four hours. I just need time to figure things out."

"Now you *know* that will take more than any twenty-four hours."

He put his face in his palm and let out a puff of air. Things worked better with her if he didn't try to explain too much.

"I'm telling them you're OK, you just need some time to yourself. They'll back off 'cause they don't want you to do nothing crazy." She let the pause hang there. "You not planning on doing nothing crazy, are you?"

"No!" He looked at her with genuine surprise. "What the fuck, Indicca! I ain't mental!"

"OK, OK. I'm just sayin—the only way I'll agree to this is if you promise on our daughter's head that you will keep me updated. Text me so I at least know you're alive somewhere. I don't need to know all your business—just that you're OK."

"I can do that."

Indicca spread his jacket over the back of the rocker.

"Thanks, Indicca."

"You welcome. Good night."

"'Night." He wanted to scuff down the hallway with her.

He took a shower and put on clean sweats, draping his wet clothes over towel rod, curtain rod, and sink. He tiptoed into Cricket's room. She was fast asleep and her night-light was too dim to show her face. Her breathing, fast and shallow, was a sweet sound, like a bird.

Sprawled on the living room couch, in soft light, he could barely make out the smiling panda face in the fiberboard ceiling. One day, when they were lying on the floor side by side, he had tried to show Cricket, tracing the outline with his fingers, *Where it go Daddy, where it go?*

He tried to imagine the three of them living here as a family until he got back on his feet, but this was not a picture he could hold in his mind. Indicca had not uttered one word about pills or pot. He knew how she thought. She was scared of pushing him to some edge and she was also tired of putting up with him. She figured his mom's move was speaking loud enough. She was right.

"Wake up, Bo D! Bo D! Wake up!" Indicca shook him and whispered loudly.

Bo D's dream instantly vanished as the room came into view. That he had slept in his clothes came as a surprise at first.

"It's five fifteen," Indicca said, "and you forgot to turn the light off last night. Running up my bill!"

"Shit. Sorry." He moaned.

"You got to leave. Thought you said you was setting your alarm?"

"Yeah, sorry. I meant to. No problem—I'm outta here." There was no time to look in on Cricket before he left. Why had he come? He wasn't thinking about the worry this places on Indicca.

He slipped into his damp sneakers. As he put his jacket on, she stuffed his soppy clothes into a plastic bag and held the door as he squeezed past.

"Thanks again, Indicca, and sorry about your light bill. Let me know how much."

"You welcome," she said. "And Bo D?" She gently touched his arm to stop him. "You know you got too many people who love you to be out here acting like you homeless."

"Homeless!" he spurned, "ain't nobody out here trying to be homeless. I got a nest egg—I can keep up my child support, so don't worry. This right here what you see? This is not a thing, OK?"

"I know you, Bo D—you getting ready to let your pride get the best of you again. I hate putting you out but like you said, Cricket—"

He stopped her. "I'm just glad that she's got you."

She smiled and softened. "God is good. You'll get it figured out."

"Yeah. I will. I promise."

"Keep your phone charged—and text me."

No more rain, but the air was still and heavy and as quiet as night. With sleep still clutching him, Bo D walked like a zombie to his car. Indicca had put a small umbrella in with his wet sweats. He had no idea where to find his toothbrush.

He watched sunrise from a table at IHOP. After splashing cold water on his face in the bathroom, he ordered breakfast, his eyes heavy. He took a third cup of coffee to go and thought about driving to the big oak, but couldn't risk going past his grandfather's place in daylight.

On his front seat, *Invisible Man* and Tyrone's Eusi binder showed from beneath his backpack. He took a small notebook from the glove compartment and drew four tally lines—one for each day since his mom put him out. He was too humiliated to call Tyrone or any of his relatives—who would take him in without a problem. LaChondra's little Waycross house was two hours east. She'd help, but could he ask? He had his savings and could check into a hotel if he needed to, but why waste money on that? All of this was temporary, to give him time to think. His Altoid tin was low, and he had no more weed. A party house trip would remedy that. Indicca was wrong. He was nowhere near homeless.

He would drive to a quiet, air-conditioned library to regroup. He wanted to look for more books by Ralph Ellison anyway.

On his phone he typed: *Going to Waycross*, but didn't want Indicca to know where he was. So he backed up: *Told you! I'm OK* with a smiley emoji. He added a heart.

were I of flesh, blood, breath and thought
I could not hold this story
because
thinking is trouble

your story is my story
mine yours

22

A biting harmattan wind blew dust from the Sahara across West Africa, muting December's sun at the Langue de Barbarie. Pushing up from shifting sand, Malik looked back, in pain from manacles on his wrists and ankles, yet taking pride at how well his empty pirogue handled turns where the Senegal met the Atlantic. The Welé family's unique raked hulls kept their bows riding high enough to prevent getting stuck in shallow waters. A tall young man—a villager like himself—smoothly guided the beautiful pirogue, a boat made by Malik's hands, and also of his body, having been measured by his own paces, cubits, and feet. A tear slid down Malik's cheek, eyes fixed on his Yaaye's sideboard design: green monkey mother and baby, encircled by mangrove branches. He thought of his mother, with other wives, singing and laughing as they carved and painted. Malik could not know this would be his last time seeing Yaaye's work, for in the end, his boat held no power against Black villagers and the daneejos they served. Malik watched his boat disappear and knew he was living the horror and mystery he had witnessed since his first visit to Saint-Louis, and now, his family was sick with worry.

Nine years ago, on their delivery trip for a wedding pirogue, Baaba gave Malik his first glimpse of these ocean waters. His same two cousins, who were now missing, had joined Baaba, Malik, and Bacary—dear Bacary—already a husband and father by then, same age Malik was now. On their ride home, they had laughed and joked and eaten good food.

Now, he squinted from glaring white sand whipping around them like tiny tornadoes and stinging like a thousand insects. He winced from pain and, as he had done that day with Baaba and the others when he was nine, longed to wade in the water.

Mostly strong young men, but also women and children, huddled near a line of pirogues bobbing in shallow waves. Their various tribal robes had been replaced by waistcloths for the men and sack dresses for women and children. Daneejos, pallid faces wrapped in scarves, took cover from the wind among mangrove trees, while Black villagers coughed and spat sand, walking among the captives, wielding whips and sticks. Malik wondered again: Who were these villagers speaking Pulaar and many other patois capturing their own countrymen?

With his back to the wind, Malik shielded his face, parting fingers to make bars in a tiny window. His breathing was amplified and rebreathing warm air soothed parched nostrils. Were his cousins among that human tapestry silhouetted against the blinding sand? The huddled mass would suffer a merciless night sharing what heat their bodies produced and praying to their various gods for a miracle: rain during dry season.

§♣

By morning, a lifeless haze sat over the Langue. Powdery sand mixed with dew making a pasty layer that clung to bare, curled backs in shades of iroko wood: from copper to ebony. Given scarcely enough water to wet their parched throats, they passed among them buckets and ladles to eat. Unable to wash his hands as Allah requires, Malik refused food and water. He gave in only to avoid the humiliation of having watery boiled mush forced down his throat with a funnel.

Delirious from hunger, thirst, and lack of sleep, Malik shifted constantly. He looked back at the river, beyond rows of mangrove trees. He could not run, but he could stand. Better to be shot like Bacary than face whatever lay ahead. *Stand up!* his heart commanded. He struggled to dig his feet in. Men on each side shuffled and mumbled. Determined, Malik dug in. His foot sharply hit against a small stone. He fell back, his foot throbbing. His neighbors pulled on the chain, throwing him off-balance, foiling his plan. He could hardly blame them, knowing from experience that his dead body would become *their* inconvenience until daneejos cut him loose. He dug into firm, wet sand and found a hard, tawny seed laced with deep grooves like their ancestral urn, now—like Podor—a distant mirage. Strange seed, of a fruit he could only imagine, fitting like a worry stone in his palm. In spite of weeping cuts on his wrists, he was intrigued and tucked the seed into his waistcloth. He would find a use for it later, maybe a knob for a special box for Nbey to welcome the new baby, or a charm to wear around her neck.

Down where sand met water, a commotion rose as each human link was paraded into crashing waves to wash away dust and sand.

One by one, a hot iron burned a mark onto arms or chests as men, women, and children cried out in agony. Malik had stood strong when flogged at his Sharo, and he did not cry out now. He blew cooling breath on his chest and tried to conjure the joys from that week-long festival—dancers, tricksters, delicious food—but this failed against blistering, oozing skin: the shape "C" enclosed in a square. His group was hauled out to a ship like those he had seen in the distance his whole life. Malik counted twenty-four other men crammed into a large dugout bobbing and skipping over waves. The ship flew two flags over its main mast: one with a red cross and diagonal white stripes on a blue field; the other solid golden, faded to pale yellow with black symbols: C A M I L L E.

For many, many days, sailing up and down Senegal's coast, *Camille*'s hold filled beyond capacity. Destination: Charleston, South Carolina. These facts and so many more would become parts of a history the captives would never know, or understand, even if they knew.

A vile darkness reigned below deck, and yet sun rays bled through ship plank cracks laying glowing lines across tortured faces. No breeze moved to displace rank, stifling air.

Stretching down the center of this hold were several blocks of shallow shelves packed with captives lying on their backs in filth; itchy, ashen skin pulled tight. Each block was three men wide, three men long and seven high. Men were shackled to shelves and each other at their necks, wrists, and ankles, and shelves above were only inches away from their faces. More blocks lined side walls all around. Malik would learn to count himself lucky to be bound to the top tier of his block, for there he caught precious sun rays, but could not bear to glance to his right and see rows and columns showing tops of heads and soles of feet. He gagged and feared losing his sanity as splash after splash, briny water often rained down, stinging noses and eyes. Were they to be eaten? Used to fatten animals?

Although Malik's days and nights no longer belonged to him, he controlled that which he could, ordering his mind to count cyclical passages of light across his face. Now his memories were his only possessions, and the peach seed still pressed against his waist. His LawBe powers and prayers would ground him during the demonic voyage. For many, the ship's relentless rocking brought on dry heaves or retching, already wallowing in their own waste.

Malik rarely slept. Beneath constant mewls and groans from others, his body screamed with pain from cramps, blisters, the brand, and other raw, oozing wounds. During morning hours, he imagined that his sun-marked face matched those around him, as trade winds pushed this vessel of death west across the Atlantic. He called upon his Sharo training again and again and prayed to Allah not to forsake him.

After fifty-five days, memories of Yaaye and her playful green monkeys became his muse. He never had a problem that she could not make better. After his Sharo, her special salve healed his flogging welts, and would quickly heal his chest sore. He could only hope that she would never learn of his plight, or even conjure such horrors as he now lived every day, for his family's own horrors were enough: losing four vibrant young men on the same day.

§▲

On the sixty-first day, the *Camille* met a smaller ship and took on extra water and increased rations: beans, potatoes, and dried beef. From this point on, captives were brought up on deck more frequently for exercise. Malik was more certain than ever that they were being moistened and fattened like goats and he questioned how long before he was meaty enough for slaughter?

Two weeks later, far more rain than they had prayed for on the Langue de Barbarie, mixed with seawater and bodily waste, poured through floorboards and trickled down to lower tiers.

So many days at sea had taken them farther from Podor than Malik could imagine. Many died. Bodies meeting water now a sound etched into memory. He had wished more than once to be among them, death would be his peaceful freedom, but had somehow survived a journey too brutal for words, too evil for memory.

As rain fell, crewmen rumbled deck boards, shouting, whistling, lowering *Camille's* sails and dropping anchor. Being better nourished and less delirious gave Malik an inexplicable veneer of hope. He thought of how much he had nursed dreams of travel and his longing for education. But was all of this punishment for giving in to daydreaming against his father's counsel? If so, what was the price of atonement? He would gladly pay. *So, let not this present life deceive you, and let not the chief deceiver deceive you about Allah.*

Above deck, a large vat filled with palm oil waited. Malik fell in line, rushing, pushing, dipping arms and hands to cover themselves from head to foot. Their desert-cracked skin at first refused to drink, but as pummeling rain washed away salt, their bodies were fed by oil and ablution.

And what of Bacary's bloated body? When he was found, did anyone know who he was? Did anyone know who he was?

A whip cracked above his head and Malik moved back to the dungeon below. In his bleakest hours, he closed his eyes and summoned images of Nbey; the soft terrain behind her knees, beneath her breasts, and along the nape of her neck. Against darkness, he sanctioned light, willing hobbled hands to lift his baby girl, Yacine, feet fluttering, delicate chest quivering with giggles. He spun her around and around and around—

23
~

At dusk dark, Fletcher pulled into his driveway and saw Florida's white Mercedes. She was inside for her weekly cleaning, which was odd for a Sunday. After three days in Atlanta with Altovise and her band for a jazz festival, he had looked forward to a quiet night in his own bed. He came in carrying a bag of groceries and found Florida in his recliner by the window in the den, fast asleep, a photo of Maletha in one hand, a dust rag in the other.

"Boo!" Fletcher said.

Florida's eyes sprang open. "Ourdaddy." She slowly shifted, sitting up, her voice cracked and dry. "You scared me."

"Never has been hard to scare you," he said with a simper.

"What time is it?"

"Time for you to go home and go to bed."

Florida gently wiped the photo.

"Mama knew what she wanted." Her voice seemed too fragile for the seven years her mother had been gone. "That one thing made her liked by everybody."

"I know," Fletcher said, collapsing onto the love seat next to his recliner. "She pulled me along for the ride of my life for thirty-five years."

"If you were grown, and standing in her way," Florida said, "she wouldn't run you over."

"Huh-uh, she'd just navigate around you. Plenty times she left me standing there until I either turned around and saw her and ran to catch up, or stood there 'til I was lucky enough to have somebody come by and say 'what you waiting for man!'"

Florida returned her mother's photo to the mantel. He had smelled mouthwash and chewing gum. "You ain't got to keep coming over here cleaning this clean house."

"Already finished," she said, "waiting to talk to you about Terrence." She wiped the television screen. "But I guess you still distracted by that dark blue BMW."

She followed him into the kitchen.

"Onethingaboutit, that BMW is the least of your problems." Fletcher hung bananas on their hook. "You drinking and driving—again?"

"I had one cocktail after work, Ourdaddy, and I ain't trying to get in your business. I just worry when you don't pick up the phone, that's all. I—"

She sat down, elbows on table, head in hands. Her whole body shook as tears fell.

Fletcher stopped putting away milk and eggs. He knew he should go to her, rub her shoulders or pat her back. He'd seen Maletha do this countless times.

She recovered for a moment, wiping her face. "Terrence needs help, Ourdaddy, and I just made things worse."

"What you mean? What happened?"

"You always hear about how people have to hit rock bottom before they change. I knew he'd never get there sitting up in my house, well-fed, no rent, spending his money on parties and drugs." She blew her nose. "So I put him out."

Her breathing was choppy—the way she had cried as a teenager after a breakup, or when friends wronged her. Of all three daughters she had always been first to stand up to a crisis and first to break down under its pressure. He had not seen her this way since her husband left, but Maletha was around to deal with that.

"He disrespected me and I put all his stuff in the driveway. I didn't know it was gone rain, or that he'd be gone three whole days."

She was shaky and sweating, red flags Fletcher knew all too well.

"That was Thursday night and here it is Sunday, we don't know where he is and it's my fault."

"This ain't your fault. Bo D is a grown man," Fletcher said and stood to get two glasses of water. "It's time for him to start acting like it."

"I messed up." She sipped water and blew her nose again. "And my son is out there doing God knows what."

Fletcher had more on his mind. This moment was clearly not right for mentioning that she needed help, too.

"How come y'all didn't call and tell me about this? You had the hotel number."

"We thought we'd have it handled before you got back, but even Auntie Olga can't get a lead on where he is. Not usually this hard to find Terrence. Only good thing is, he's been texting Indicca to at least let her know he's OK; bless her heart, she made him promise."

"We'll find him," Fletcher said. "His car ain't hard to find once he slips up on hiding it. Bound to sooner or later."

After walking to the trash with wadded-up paper towels, she sighed and stiffened.

"I tried my best to get you to talk to him, man-to-man instead of jacking him up by the collar."

She took her purse from its backdoor hook.

"And when you home? Just answer the damn phone. You ain't even got to talk to me. Just pick up and hang up so at least I know you ain't laying up in here dead."

❧

The next morning, Fletcher woke more tired than when he went to bed, and found his quarrel with Florida waiting next to his slippers. He knew alcohol paranoia firsthand. One thing he had kept from his failed 12-Step meetings was the wisdom to know the difference between things he could and couldn't change. He'd give Florida a little more time, but at some point, they had to deal with her drinking.

❦

On Friday, during his morning rumination, Fletcher settled on calling Indicca. Saturday was her salon's busiest day, but she agreed to talk to him before going in. He drove thirty minutes north to Dawson to set in motion a plan he had been thinking about for months.

Since the day she announced her pregnancy, Indicca had lived rent-free in a mobile home next to her uncle and aunt's large old farmhouse, the same double-wide that Fletcher and Maletha had lived in on the seven acres for six months while he built their house.

Before he could knock, Indicca invited Fletcher in. On wood panel walls, framed pictures of both families were arranged in a circle around Cricket's newborn picture.

"Where's that Cricket?" Fletcher announced, stepping in.

"You *just* missed her," Indicca said. "Mama picked her up ten minutes ago. Since Bo D still being a fool, I'm not surprised Mama Florida put him out. If you push her too far, we all know that woman will knock the taste out your mouth without laying a hand on you!" She smiled nervously. "I didn't want to have to, but I revoked his visitation rights. And we had just cut Mama Florida off from driving and watching Shieka alone."

"I don't blame you. You did what you had to do," Fletcher said, not taking lightly her respect for him. In spite of being young and afraid, she sat there with her back straight, wisdom in her spine. She showed him every day what one can do against all odds.

Indicca rubbed her hands and said, "I been gettin' texts all week from him—but he just says he's OK, so I still don't know where he is—and he turned off 'find my phone.'"

She rose and went a few feet to the tiny kitchen. "The other day he dropped by my uncle and aunt's house while I was at work to leave a big fat child support check. Three thousand six hundred dollars. That covers three months." She slipped a note from its refrigerator magnet and handed it to Fletcher.

Bo D had drawn two hearts and written: *One for you, one for Cricket.*

"Sound like he making plans," Fletcher said.

"Surprised me," Indicca said, "but I don't know if I'm happy or sad. Bo D always been good about saving, but I know he burning through money fast out there. So where did he get that much money to send us? I prayed and prayed that we had made progress after we met at Mama Florida's, but—Bo D do what Bo D wanna do."

They sat for an awkward moment, staring at the floor a few inches in front of them, as if the problem lay there, in triangulation, waiting to be solved.

"Onethingaboutit, there's plenty family to go around," Fletcher assured her, "on both sides."

He laid out his plan to have Cricket spend the two days each week she would've spent with Bo D in Putney at his house. As suspected, Indicca tried to refuse his offer.

With titled head and crosswise smile, Fletcher said, "Now wait a minute; you not gone stand in the way of my blessing, are you?"

"No, sir, I'm certainly not. Thank you."

❦

Altovise helped childproof his house and shop for crib linens and stuffed animals. Although Cricket called herself a big girl, refusing high chairs and booster seats, he was sure the new golden oak crib would make her feel safe while surrounded by unsteadiness.

They shifted furniture in Georgia and Florida's old room, making space for Cricket's crib. Altovise took a break, sitting on one of the beds. Maletha never liked people sitting on her beds, considered it bad manners. She had many rules.

Details were vague from the early years, before Fletcher's heart closed to any thoughts of Altovise. Right after she left Albany, he started working in construction and insisted on paying Olga rent. He regularly took on double shifts to bring on fatigue. He measured time in chunks based on whether he was dripping sweat or rubbing numb fingers over an open barrel fire. He refused to think about getting over Altovise or making even the smallest step away from their past.

"Fletcher," Olga had told him over supper one night. "This is what grief looks like."

"What you mean—ain't nobody died."

"Doesn't matter. It's the same when love dies," Olga said. "You have to allow for process—the same way Daddy had you carving when Mama Alpha died. For a long while all you can do is put one foot in front of the other until you can do better."

"That's why we have work," Fletcher said, focused on the fried pork chops smothered in gravy.

"But work is not enough," Olga said. "You've got to balance that particular past and whatever kind of future you hope to build."

Nevertheless, work became a callus he built up against the hurt of Altovise. He worked until he was reduced to muscle aches and falling into sleep.

While ignoring Olga's advice he met Maletha, and she slowly opened him up to accepting love. But to his surprise, once his heart cracked open, his locked-out feelings for Altovise flooded in. For a while he quietly dealt with dueling emotions—with help from vodka, straight or disguised in any number of mixers. After marrying, he and Maletha quarreled mostly about the peach seed monkey tradition, but sundown always brought an end to their disagreement. In their early days he was afraid the quarrels would eat away at their solid foundation, which—as is true of any marriage—had its secret cracks and dings. If Maletha had ever learned that he gave Altovise the diamond-eyed monkey, he still couldn't imagine what she would've done.

"Fletcher, what's wrong," Altovise asked. "This looks good. Cricket will love it."

"Yeah—I believe she will." He prepared to swerve. "I'm trying to figure out where I went wrong when Bo D's daddy left. Maybe if I had stepped in far enough back then, I wouldn't be repeating myself now."

"Trust me," Altovise said, rubbing his back, "any regret you're holding will shrink in the face of all you're doing for Cricket."

Altovise left well before Indicca and Cricket showed up.

As Indicca unloaded her car, Cricket ran toward Fletcher, her dingy blanket bunched in one hand, a new backpack bouncing with each step.

"What you got there, Cricket?" Fletcher asked.

"That's my backpack. It's *my* backpack. It's pink."

"I like it," Fletcher replied.

"Way-oh WokHudson go?" She looked around.

"He's in the house, looking for you."

They dropped off packages in the kitchen and headed to Cricket's new room, with the dog in tow.

"Daddy Fletcher!" Indicca said, catching her breath. "You didn't have to do all this!"

"Now that's where you're wrong," Fletcher answered, lifting the child into the crib, shoes and all.

Cricket burst into tears, reaching for her mother.

"This is because we just got her a big girl bed at home," Indicca whispered to Fletcher. "I should've told you. I'm so sorry."

"That ain't no problem," Fletcher said, lifting Cricket from the crib and letting her bounce on one of the twin beds. "'Cause we got nothing but big girl beds in this house!"

Gathering eggs distracted Cricket from crying while Indicca snuck away. Then they threw stones into the pond. From that moment Fletcher was on duty nonstop: weeding, making mud pies, and giving Rockhudson a bath. While he made spaghetti, she played with pots and pans.

After a bubble bath using a surplus of towels, she stood in footie pajamas on the toilet seat, toothbrush in hand.

"I bwush my teeth," she said, pointing, "and Gwan-gwandaddy bwush his teeth."

"That's right, you and me brushing in harmony."

"Is that way-o we live?"

Fletcher laughed. "I hope so, Cricket. I sure hope so."

Fletcher read *Goodnight Moon*, watching for her eyelids to droop, but instead she asked for "Anothe-o mow!" and they moved on to *Flossie and the Fox*.

He moved her into Mozell's room. As he pulled back covers to tuck her in, Fletcher said, "Tomorrow when you wake up, I'll be right here. But if I'm still sleep, you call my name, OK?"

"OK, Gwan-gwandaddy."

He stretched out on the bed next to her, too weary even for television news. In one afternoon they had gone through every activity he'd planned for three or four visits.

In an early morning dream,

Fletcher stands on the edge of a beach cliff where a sheer wall of sand drops for hundreds of feet into an abyss. Inside a cave carved into a cliffside, he lies in a fetal position with wet sand molded to the shape of his curled body. Waves crash in, washing away more and more sand, pushing him farther and farther in.

He hears Altovise singing, her voice mixing with the babel of waves. He calls to her. She answers, and they seem to be in caves right next to each other. They make a plan to dig toward each other, but with the echoes they cannot discern which

direction. Altovise starts singing again, this time her voice
morphs into a wee phantom voice that seems much closer.
"Gwan-gwandaddy! I'm cal-lin yoooou!"

Fletcher bolted upright to the distant sound of Rockhudson howling. Fully clothed, he had slept on top of the covers and was at first unsure of where he was.

"Cricket?" She was not next to him. "Cricket!"

Rockhudson howled again. Breathless, his heart was beating in his throat. Legs rubbery, he ran room to room, calling her before finding the back door standing open. He sped into the yard and found Rock sitting like a sentinel by the woodshop door.

Dizzy with fear, Fletcher rushed past the dog and saw light shining under his workbench. Cricket sat pretzel-legged at the small table, pretend-sipping from a wooden teacup. All around her she had arranged wooden chess pieces, animals, and other shapes Fletcher had carved.

"This tea good," she said.

She didn't turn when Fletcher called her name. "This tea can make you be warm."

"Lord have mercy, Cricket!" He knelt beside her, rubbing his face with both hands and catching his breath. "I was looking everywhere for you!" She looked at him with concern.

"Did you call me when you woke up?"

She nodded slowly, staring at him.

"You're OK." Fletcher smoothed her rumpled hair. "But next time when you wake up you better shake me or tickle me, OK?" He chuckled nervously, looking around at saws and knives. How could he forget to padlock the woodshop?

Cricket handed Fletcher a peach seed monkey she had climbed on a chair to take from the shelf.

"OK, c'mon," Fletcher said, placing the monkey back. "Time for breakfast."

Cricket screamed when he lifted her, reaching for her wooden tea party.

"What's the matter?"

"I need Monkey, he's mine. I need him," she cried.

Fletcher's hands still shook as he emptied a flannel drawstring bag still holding Maletha's sewing tools. Cricket filled the bag with her tiny table, king, queen, and monkey, holding on tight as Fletcher carried her to the kitchen, his heart still pounding.

Before they reached the door, Fletcher noticed her tiny hand clinched tight and asked, "What you holding?"

She said, "It's mine, Gwan-gwandaddy, I fount it."

In her palm she held the tiny wooden key Fletcher carved for Altovise. He hadn't seen it in years.

"It's mine," Cricket repeated.

"OK, baby girl, it's yours."

By early evening, beyond sore muscles, even Fletcher's attention span hurt. He tucked Cricket in and called Altovise.

"I'm not cut out for this," he said.

"As Olga would say, taking care of a three-year-old is more than a notion. Your body may not be as able, but your heart's in the right place."

"Not right now, 'cause it's still stuck in my throat. I don't know what I was thinking. I sleep like a dead person, so the child could be out in the middle of Sumac Road and I'd never know!"

"I'm a light sleeper."

"That's precisely why I'm calling."

"Be right over."

24

~

Day 17. Being awake at sunrise was a rare event. Bo D missed his bedroom with heavy drapes keeping it dark. Light spread like golden, liquid glass from cloud to cloud. In the parking lot of Flash Foods near Lee Avenue Library in Waycross, early risers came and went while he drank Coke and ate potato chips, adding to a sea of carry-out garbage collecting on his passenger-side floor. He was shocked at how much his nice safety net had dwindled after only two weeks.

Albany, Bainbridge, and Waycross formed a triangle that had become his new territory. He stamped out days like tires, except the mold never changed. With no reason to punch in, he felt free, but not always in a good way. He was most grounded when driving, connecting through car and tires and road. How many people drove around on tires they pressed themselves? With meal and bathroom breaks in Valdosta, Thomasville, Cairo, or Moultrie, his full triangle course easily ate up eight or nine hours. Normal job hours. He spent too much on gas avoiding familiar ground as much as possible, then put down temporary roots in Waycross; eating in restaurants and acting like a tourist one day at Okefenokee Swamp. LaChondra owned a nice little house and was good about letting him shower and do laundry.

He spent the day at the Lee Avenue Library. Getting a library card had been easier than he thought, but no books by Ralph Ellison. Dr. Al had him looking for books he couldn't find. He read Tyrone's Eusi binder, watched Airstream videos on doing patch panels and skin repairs, and scrolled job listings. What skills did he have besides restoring cars and pressing tires? He was becoming expert at dodging snitches, and sometimes drove as far north as Macon to park and sleep. He had to admit: that job offer at Eusi sounded tempting. But what if he took it and failed? How could he ever live that down? Tyrone kept calling him *a maker*; if so, he needed to make himself over into a new man. He left the library with a stack of books.

If he ate two decent meals and did not give in to self-loathing and guilt: that was a good day. The days when he scored his magic trilogy were worth risking his grandfather seeing him drive past to park under the oak tree, which felt most like home. There he could privately jubilate. On either end of his high, he could be intrigued by his new life, because an ultimate test of will and fortitude had a quick lesson to teach: what creativity can't muster up, the streets hand over with no problem.

Bo D had learned in Sunday school that suffering leads to endurance, and endurance produces character, and only then can there be hope. With each gruesome day, hope dwindled, but he knew enough to see suffering as his atonement, his way to wash his hands clean. Auntie Olga had said many times: *families are messy, like life; sometimes you just have to get in there and get that stuff all over you before you find what's worth keeping. Only then do you wash your hands clean of muck and mire.*

In addition to child support (20 percent of his income, which was now zero), he had highball inventory, car, clothes, and food costs, and the continued expense of hangers-on and parties. These burned hot and fast, down to a stubby wick, but gave Bo D a home base and people to pose as family, seeing to his basic needs: food, drugs, and sex.

LaChondra took him in for five days until he couldn't stomach how much she had changed. She was not willing to just get high and hook up anymore, and was too into fussing over him. She agreed to store leaf bags so his backseat was clear, washed his clothes, and sent him off with leftovers.

On Day 23, his first sunny morning back on the streets, he drove to the big oak early, before his grandfather was up feeding chickens. He lay faceup on his backseat, glad to be clean with a fresh pillowcase on his nevertheless grungy pillow, which technically belonged to his mom. The fact that she had packed it meant that she really does love him. He came from a strictly monitored world: tidy houses, neat yards with grown folks paying attention. The night he received his nickname was the first time he had touched a bed with grungy sheets. That proved to be practice for scenes he repeated many times on Fellowship Alley, becoming immune to piles of dirty dishes, thick, hairy rings around bathtubs, sticky carpets, and dust bunnies trying to grow to the size of real bunnies.

He pulled himself across the console and counted three–six–nine decorative holes on his steering wheel posts. His highball waited, a quiet, comfy promise, while he ate cold chicken and rice. Oak branches were too many to count, so he focused two-by-two on lateral lines in his red tufted upholstery.

His life was a giant contorted tree, branches stretched every which way. He had misjudged, walked out at first, then crawled, and finally scooted—like a baby—to the edge, where he was now. On a limb too weak.

A surplus of plastic straws overflowed from his glove box as he carefully lifted out a ritual: small mortar and pestle, smooth, cool marble like his mother's kitchen counters. This heavy chalice ordained a formality reserved for this practice: Crush an oxy. Use half a straw. Snort.

In a matter of seconds he was speeding, and notions of his father paralyzed him like a bad dream.

Where was he? How did he look after twelve years? Would I recognize him if he stepped on my foot? G-pop was always saying it's a bad wind that never changes. No shit. Walter Henry Fowler was a bona fide bad wind. And nobody cares. Even if I wanted to tell his pathetic story, who would listen? A real dick. How can he call himself a man? Me and Ma did just fine without his ass. Ma made it work. I shoulda done more to help. What was I supposed to do? Wasn't my job. Like Auntie Olga said, that's a father's job. He went off somewhere with his other family. New woman, three kids—did he even marry her? Ma still don't know that I know. I heard her on the phone with Auntie Georgia right after Asshole Walter left. Got the whole story. So—I'm not an only child—another fact nobody talks about.

"Fuck!" Bo D punched the dashboard, licked his finger, and wiped clean his marble bowl. Ritual back in glove box, he finished breakfast. A joint beckoned from the driver's side ashtray. He lit up, sank into red vinyl ease, and allowed snippets from high school orations to rivet through his half-lucid thoughts.

Freshman year, Young Baptists Spoken Word contest, James Weldon Johnson's "Prodigal Son":

Young man
Young man
Your arms too short to box with God . . .
. . . you just slip and slide and slip and slide
   'Til you bang up against hell's iron gates.

Oak branches looked like powerful arms that could break through glass. His first time climbing the tree, he reached a branch only about six feet up, but his grandfather helped him feel like king of the trees.

His red vinyl seats ambushed him, their memories of sexual exploits fighting against Cricket in her car seat: *Way-oh we go-wing, Daddy?—We race the trees!* At least Indicca let him talk to Cricket on the phone; he missed her monkey hugs, that fluttering little heart. He should bring her out to this tree, teach her to climb. Someday. That's a father's job.

"FuckFUCK!" He hit his fist against the steering wheel, then filled his lungs with cannabis smoke, and cried.

25
∼

Olga called Siman on his cell. He excused himself from a meeting with his law firm client, bummed a cigarette from the receptionist, although he hadn't smoked in years, and went for a walk toward the Saginaw River.

"Siman." Olga's voice was energetic yet laced with fatigue. "I have good news."

He wanted this to be a reverent event, and after lighting up, in blazing midday heat, he realized that smoking did not fit. He snuffed out the cigarette before walking out onto Court Street Bridge.

"I'm all ears," he said.

"We have found her."

"Seriously?"

"Yes. Your birth mother is Altovise Benson, and life works in such a circular way sometimes—she is from Albany. I know her well."

Siman had heard nothing beyond her lyrical name, *Altovise Benson*. As children, Patricia kept a list of names she had picked for her birth mother and father. Siman never dared. Hearing the musical word now—*Altovise*—he could never have guessed it in a million years.

"Are you there?"

"Yes, yes! Sorry. I'm here. Please go on."

Olga paused. "Pardon my manners, I should've asked, is this a good time?"

"This is the perfect time."

"As I said, Altovise is from Albany, born and raised, and just so happens that she only recently moved back home for retirement."

"Really? What sort of work did she do?"

"She was a theater professor and she's also a Grammy-winning jazz musician and singer." Olga paused again. "And this part will shock you: she spent a good portion of *your* life living in Ann Arbor."

Her pauses, although awkward for Siman, with his disdain for phones, had been normal, conversational breaks, but the pause they were in now was cavernous. Traffic whizzed by behind him, as Siman stopped and looked down the river, his mind almost afraid to picture Altovise Benson, so he reached instead for familiarity: *presiding judge, opposing counsel, quality of evidence, legal precedents*—reliable data he had collected, analyzed, and would compare to his proprietary database of past Michigan cases, calculate the probability of success and likely financial payout, and present to his client, waiting for him to return. But who will he be in five minutes? When he walked back into their high-end conference room, those five men and women in suits will have no clue that he now has to find a place in his psyche for jolting new data: all his life he had been only an hour-and-a-half drive from his birth mother.

"Are you OK, Siman?"

"Excuse me again. I'm sorry."

"No need to apologize. This is a lot."

"So, what about the—my—father?"

"As you suspected, he is my younger brother—"

"Fletcher MacArthur Dukes," they said in unison.

"We all know the Vulcan ears sealed the deal for you early on," Olga said, and they shared an easy laugh, like kinfolk in the aftermath of a funeral.

"As you can imagine," Olga said, "the situation down here is delicate. As a young man, before marrying, it was no secret in our family that Fletcher intended to father many sons, and, of course, had three beautiful daughters."

"Does he know about me yet?"

"He has not been told yet. Altovise wants to handle that herself."

Siman wanted to ask how long Altovise had known, to confirm that he and Patricia were right about Olga withholding on the Skype call with Bo D, but he didn't see the point. Olga Dukes deserved as much grace now as she had granted him through this whole process.

Olga went on, "But she knows everything that I know and is excited to meet you and ready to connect on whatever terms you set. And I've been cleared to email you her contact info."

He had come to know and respect Olga over the past three years, since first contact, and now, she was officially his aunt.

"I can't thank you enough, Auntie Olga—and it feels good to call you that!"

"I like hearing it! We'll talk again, soon. Before I let you go, let me be the first to say, welcome to your families!"

"And I like hearing that!"

They said their parting words; Siman tucked his phone away and sank cautiously into new thoughts.

He had many relatives and friends in the area, so he was no stranger to Ann Arbor and had spent time both in town and on campus. He and Altovise could've passed each other on a street, or at a museum, in a restaurant, a play, a concert, or at a football game—if she's a Wolverine fan. He had reached the end of the bridge and turned to pace his way back. He couldn't wait to begin searching for her albums.

A name bears so much, and that day Siman had spoken his mother's name for the first time. He always cherished his name story, knowing that even the spelling had been part of her plan for him: she wanted him to grow to be a *man* who *listens* and *hears*.

After work, he joined Patricia and her family for dinner. She made him a birthday cake and said, "If this isn't what it means to be born again, I don't know what is."

❦

Roasting in summer heat, Siman wiped hot dog grease from his hands, sharpened his pencil, and prepared to record the bottom of the ninth. Olga followed through on having Ursula email Altovise Benson's contact info and Patricia joined him in tracking down her albums; three down and three to go. Beyond several unanswered texts and one failed video chat with Bo D, Siman had yet to make a move toward his new family. Olga had been strangely quiet about Bo D.

The smell of outfield grass and home plate dust took him back to his agonizing days on the bench. Now, except for the sweltering heat, sitting with Patricia, Thatcher, and Trinity at ThatcherJr's games was a relaxing diversion from the growing situation down in Georgia. Unlike people all around him, Siman did not keep records on a laptop or tablet. Numbers were meant to be drawn, transforming each numeric idea into a carbon mark on paper; the glorious Ø, the graceful 7, and 9 curling into itself and back out again. He ran his hand over neat columns with boxes and tiny diamonds waiting to be filled in.

But numbers were useless in dealing with Altovise Benson. He would have to rely on his gut to calculate the implied return on investing in new blood relations.

Their team was up 3–2. He didn't have to feel bad for his nephew; dusty and sweating between second and third base, no matter the weather, ThatcherJr loved this game. If asked, Siman will claim to show up purely for moral support, record keeping, hot dogs, and beer, when in fact—despite his lackluster history as a player—baseball was under his skin. His collection of baseball books was proof: from *The*

Natural to *Shoeless Joe* to *Only the Ball Was White*. From his early days he had always grasped the power of pitcher against batter, and fielder against ball, shortstop being his favorite. Although Siman was never good enough to play the position, at nine years old, ThatcherJr was already showing signs of having what it took to master the art: the ability to repeat each move with numeric, machinelike precision, understanding that the shortstop is where all things converge in an instant of agility and speed. Siman watched pure choreography, his nephew's baseball dance of pregame fielding: stepping up, looking left, looking right, then throwing the ball to meet a catcher's glove with a *WHAP!* Boys practicing to be men, and each coach reliving his own boyhood.

"Let's go Bucks!" Patricia and Trinity shouted as their batter walked up to home plate.

Siman recorded the base run, his thoughts not having to slide far to land again down in Georgia. How exactly do you tell a man who wanted a son and had three daughters that his wish has finally come true, half a century late? Players ran bases, fielded balls as if his life had not completely changed. A journey that began in 2009 when Patricia found Olga's blog had delivered both parents.

The news was only two weeks old, and there were still days, like this one, when conflicted feelings overwhelmed Siman. As game action unfolded, to navigate his upset, Siman scribbled madly in his baseball journal and focused on the certainty of here and now.

The game ended and he carefully packed supplies into his satchel, and Bucks and Cubs formed high-five lines, followed by coaches dousing nine-year-olds with ice-cold water from Super Soakers.

"So, Siman," Thatcher asked as they waited on the sidelines, "have you contacted your mother yet?"

"No news on that front," Siman said. "Altovise Benson, and everybody else down there, is still waiting for me to make a move."

"These things take time," Thatcher said. "How about your other nephew? You like him, right?"

"Yeah, cool kid. His name's Terrence, but he goes by Bo D.

Don't know that story yet. He's twenty-three. Bright kid. He calls me Unc."

"Can't get more southern than that!" Patricia said.

"Yeah," Siman said. "He's *way* into having an uncle after being smothered by two aunts."

"That's the wildest thing," Thatcher said. "According to Jerome and Dorothy, you wanted a brother more than anything when you were a toddler."

"Really? I don't remember that."

"I sure do," added Patricia. "You thought being adopted was like shopping for kids, told Mama and Pop to go buy a baby brother!"

Thatcher said, "And here's your chance at last and what do you get? Three sisters!"

Patricia shook her head. "I can only imagine the conversations *they* have about you."

"I don't have a clue," Siman said. "For the time we were texting, Bo D steered clear of talking about Fletcher Dukes and his daughters. His texts can be sporadic and cryptic. I think he's going through a rough patch."

"Maybe Uncle Siman is just the distraction he needs," Thatcher said. "Don't you finally want to make the trip to meet these folk?"

"Now you sound like Patricia."

"That's because Patricia is right," she chimed in. "All this talk about the nephew is because you can't even bring yourself to believe WE FOUND YOUR MOTHER!" She shoved him. "How can you not go meet her?"

"I know." He nuzzled his sister with an elbow embrace. "But I want to know how *you* are doing through all this?"

"It's not a bad question," Thatcher said, "and maybe she'll give you an honest answer—because I've tried."

"Don't be ganging up on me!" Patricia said.

"And don't you be trying to change the subject," Thatcher insisted. Siman increased his squeeze.

"I'm actually OK," she said, "not saying it's always been easy but, helping you has helped me. I made peace with closed adoption a long time ago. Mostly anyway. But yours has always been something else altogether. Ms. Altovise closed the door, but she didn't lock it. She put the little monkey there like a placeholder for her foot—just in case. So don't worry about me. I'm fine. And so happy for you, Si. This is a win for us all."

❦

Later, with an instrumental mix of world music floating through his loft, Siman stood at his drafting table. He had played and replayed the idea of going to Georgia. All his life he'd seen himself as a victim, his adoption happened *to* him, and him alone. Now he saw that there were no victims because there were no culprits. This explanation worked momentarily. Tomorrow he might be back to thinking of Fletcher Dukes as the biggest victim. Or was *he* actually the culprit? What had he done—or not done—that left Altovise Benson feeling she had only one choice?

He drafted a letter on a yellow legal pad.

> Dear Ms. Altovise Benson,
>
> I appreciate you (and Auntie Olga) leaving the ball in my court, and I am here with my opening serve.
>
> Where to begin?
>
> That's a question I've asked myself repeatedly over the past two weeks since Auntie Olga called me with the news. Finally, today I came to this conclusion: ~~this~~ no letter could ~~never~~ ever hold the volume of ~~feelings~~ emotions I imagine we both ~~are~~ carrying, so I might as well start with this one as ~~an inevitable icebreaker to us finally meeting~~ a prelude to the day we meet.
>
> ~~I'm curious to know if Mr. Fletcher Dukes has been told about me yet?~~ My next move, of course, depends on when and if I hear from Mr. Fletcher Dukes. From where I stand, the

time seems right to make a trip to Georgia to meet the Dukes and Benson families. (I almost ~~feel like~~ want to type that one more time, it's hard to believe—both families with this one effort. What are the chances?!) But I know there is much more to consider than my own POV.

That said, late September or early October could work for me. I hope that 3–4 months is enough leeway on ~~that~~ your end. Otherwise, I've waited 49 years, what's another few months.

Your most grateful son,

Siman

He had expected to send this letter c/o Olga, but his mother emailed her home address, which he assumed was her new beach house Bo D had often mentioned.

He loaded his favorite fountain pen with sepia ink and chose a crisp linen résumé paper in eggshell blue. Words rolled off the nib in his best cursive, which was far better than average, and he began to peel back layer after layer: his feelings of abandonment, betrayal, and self-doubt. But Olga had shared with him this truth at the end of their call: Altovise Benson had been young and afraid, ladened with her own set of problems, and had done the best she could for herself, and especially for him.

26

Afternoon sun beat down across Cromartie Lake. Fletcher saluted his buddies, Deke and Tonk, standing on the shore, and throttled up steadily to cruising speed, wind and thrust a fitting end to his long, trying day. All three daughters had converged on a Skype call at Olga's to discuss Bo D's situation.

With Tonk and Deke taking care of his animals for two nights, Fletcher yielded to a promising forecast: going fishing with Altovise.

Lately he had sensed a worry buzzing around her like a mosquito. Over dinner a few nights ago, he caught her staring into space, claiming that nothing was bothering her. They talked about wanting this second chance to last and walked back through their short history, from the moment he had spoken to her in homeroom (about wearing a dollar bill bow in her hair) to their first roll and sway on the Fairlane's backseat. Then they each got answers to half-a-century-old questions:

Did he ever consider living anywhere else?
Why would I? This is my home, no place better.

Did she get any of the notes and letters he left on her porch?

Got every one. Still have them.

Did he work in the Movement much longer after she left?

We never stopped working, one way or another. Even now.

&

"Hey-hey!" Altovise called out as Fletcher maneuvered his boat into her covered boat dock.

"Hey yourself!" She looked cool and collected in spite of fanning away heat and gnats with a Pistons' rally towel.

He killed the engine, "Catch this," and threw her the painter line. "I'll show you how to tie off," he said, then hurled his overnight duffel onto her dock.

When it came to music, restaurants, and theater, she was boss. This was his domain.

She watched over his shoulder as he knelt, his moves automatic, coupling rope around cleat into a hitch knot.

"Ah-ha! We use a similar knot in theater."

She laid her hand over his. "Thanks for coming, Fletcher. I know how hard it must be not knowing where Bo D is."

"Yeah—he's all right or we would've heard from a sheriff or somebody." He tightened the knot and stood. "His mama put him out about a month ago. Bo D told Indicca he needed time to think. I feel for him—Florida can use up all the air in a room better than anybody I know."

A cumbersome quiet dangled for a moment, then he moved on. "And thank you again for pitching in with Cricket. Onethingaboutit—I was a fish outta water for those two days."

"You did fine by Cricket. And I was glad you called me. She's such a cutie."

Sun rippled across the lake with pastel radiance and the sky seemed boundless. Altovise moved like a teenager in cropped jeans and a floppy gray T-shirt with inside-out seams. Why could she get away with that at their age? If he dressed like his nephews, he'd end up in a paddy wagon for impersonating a minor.

Fletcher fingered a feathery bait on her straw cowboy hat. "Look at you, don't know nothing about fishing!"

"Are we even using these lure-thingies?"

"Nope, using night crawlers—nice, fat worms." He circled her slowly, taking in the perfume. "Got any shot sinkers on this hat?"

"No clue." She laughed, hands on hips. "But I do know there's good channel and flathead catfish out there. And crappie, which I have to say, does not sound tasty."

"Is that right?" He almost beamed like a proud husband.

She stared at the sky, fanning her face and reciting, "Plus bluegill, three kinds of bass: largemouth, shoal, and striped."

"I see you been talking to your neighbors."

"Or better yet—the Georgia Department of Natural Resources website," she proclaimed and laughed.

"You can't fool me." He pulled her to him, ducking under her hat's brim to plant a peck on her lips. They strolled toward the house, shoulders bumping.

"Nice boat. What kind is that?"

"She's a sixteen-foot V-hull bowrider, fifty-to-ninety-horsepower outboard."

"I like that you named her *Cricket*, and I've always wondered why they give boats female names?"

"For protection, so that the water will keep the boat safe on its journey, same way a mother watches over her child."

Altovise's pensive silence left Fletcher wondering if this was not a thing to say to a childless woman.

❧

"You cooking up a storm in here," Fletcher said later, walking into her kitchen.

"Not really, we're eating light; I just create a storm no matter what I do in the kitchen."

"Well, I do recall that you and a stove have never been the best of friends. What you making?"

"Chicken off the bone with asparagus and a watermelon, walnut salad. Nothing fancy—but—life's a special occasion, right?"

"It is when certain folk come to town." He smiled, and they returned to the weighted glances of the past few weeks.

They had drinks out on her screened-in kitchen dock, and she chatted nervously about chicken taking white wine, so she opted for a pinot grigio, and she hoped he was fine with sparkling grapefruit. He was OK with anything she did.

Her food was delicious, and he was amused at dinner by more cooking show talk about asparagus and truffle oil—which sounded like a cure for a faulty engine.

They were both worn out, so their platonic evening planned itself: he read through a stack of the *New York Times* in her library and she nestled in with a book next door in the movie room.

Once in bed, only their legs entwined, a gentle embrace between two people learning again to speak without words.

As they drifted off, he said, "Now remember, no perfume tomorrow."

"Right," she mumbled, "it'll cost me bites." She sprang up. "But that won't matter 'cause *I* will *not* be actually touching anybody's worms or crickets, right?"

"We'll see about that—"

Well before dawn, still wrapped in toasty quiet, they filled a cooler with ginger beer, water, ham and cheese sandwiches, and slices of Vada's famous pound cake. They motored upstream to the islands on Lake Chehaw.

"Look at that," Fletcher said over the motor, pointing to a flagrant sunrise. She gave thumbs-up and walked through to recline.

After dropping anchor in cool, heavy air, Fletcher revisited the question he had asked weeks ago. "You told me you didn't have that diamond-eyed monkey I gave you, but you didn't say what happened to it?"

"Oh," she said, "are we back to that?"

"I never really left it," he said, "just left it alone."

"I don't like to say it's lost—sometimes things resurface after years of being tucked away. We were going nonstop during the Movement. And when I left for college, I was exhausted from it all. I misplaced more than a few things. So at Bennett, I started over. That's college's biggest gift—you get to reinvent yourself."

"Woolworth's in Greensboro was ground zero. Tired as you were, it's hard to believe you weren't active at Bennett."

"Oh, I never said I wasn't active. I was there during the last four years of Dr. Willa Beatrice Player's term. She was known as the 'activist president,' so for anyone trying to hide from Civil Rights, Bennett was not the place to go! Woolworth's was Phase 1. By my time we had moved on to theaters and cafeterias. And we Bennett Belles had also moved on from dresses, hats, and gloves; we were preppy, wearing knee socks, loafers, and sweaters; sometimes we wore flats and stockings, so we were still very well-dressed walking picket lines and stepping into paddy wagons. President Player visited us in jail, brought our assignments so we wouldn't fall behind.

"But I'm afraid our exquisite little monkey was one of the things that didn't make it to my dorm room, but not because I didn't want it there."

"Can't hold that against you. That little monkey ain't hard to lose." He was satisfied and would leave the matter alone.

"Time to get serious," Fletcher said, rubbing his hands in a bucket of fresh grass to remove traces of unnatural scents.

"But I don't need that, because I have these," she said, pulling on the leather work gloves he gave her.

"You planning on baling hay?"

"Well, I guess not!" She smiled, slipping off her gloves and gently massaging fistfuls of grass into her hands.

He explained barrel swivels, slip bobbers, and how to crimp on shot sinkers. He dialed the radio to jazz and focused on making worm balls on each hook.

She turned away. "I can't even watch you do that. Why aren't we using my beautiful lures?"

"Catfish don't care nothing 'bout your lures. That's for bass, and you not ready for that yet. Need a different boat, too."

"Do you have one?"

"Yep. I keep it out at one of my nephews' house. I first fished for bass back in the early '80s. The Albany Mall opened in '76, and a few years later I partnered with some white fellas to build a little shopping strip out there. They were into bass fishing. Back then it was catfish or bream for me. But man, I was hooked after I caught my first bass! I'd rather fish all day for a bass and never catch it than fish for bream."

Heat blanketed Cromartie Lake, awake now as white people screaked by on Jet Skis and inner tubes. Their cackles and yelps rebounded, and six-pack picnics unfolded by the water's edge.

"Seem to me you got a heavy burden on your mind lately." Fletcher readjusted his pole and advanced with caution.

"My mind's always churning," she threw out again, wiping sweat from her forehead with a bandanna, "but I wouldn't bore you with Eusi Arts fundraising problems—why spoil our lovely time out here with these fish that don't want to bite?"

As soon as she said that her bobber sank.

"Omygoodness! Omygoodness! Did you see that, Fletcher!"

"Oooooo yeah, yeah!" he whispered, leaving his pole to help her.

Heat mounted as they headed back before noon with seven breams and four channel cats. When Altovise caught a six-pound catfish, Fletcher swore she could be heard yelping back at Cromartie Beach.

After sunset they ate fried catfish sandwiches under an indigo sky dotted with stars. The lake was an inky reservoir reflecting lights from distant shores. Later, as they lay skin to skin, all her moves were clearly forced.

He drew circles on her shoulder, feeling like a John Shaft imposter in the silk pajama bottoms she had bought for him in Atlanta.

Just before lights-out, her face was a conflict of worry and contentment. When he asked what was wrong, she said, "Just can't believe this is happening; *you* are happening." And she lifted her face and kissed him.

As usual, Fletcher woke first as day broke. Her back was to him and his eyes followed her spine up to the strawberry birthmark. He held back, letting her sleep.

He threw on a T-shirt over the silk pants and went down to start breakfast.

"Nothing like waking up to the sound of Fletcher Dukes cooking," she said a short time later, hugging him from behind. "Wait a minute—do I smell biscuits?"

"Yes, you do. They'll be ready in about five, but I couldn't find no coffee in this fancy kitchen."

"I gave it up in the '90s for green tea," she said. "Good source of antioxidants."

"Antioxygen? Now what have you got against oxygen?"

"You haven't changed a bit. Still getting pleasure from working my last nerve!"

He turned, holding his hands aloft, caked in cornmeal, preparing fish to fry. "I'm much more interested in working a few other parts," he said, then kissed her softly.

All through breakfast she wrapped her robe more and more tightly, as if holding herself together with terry cloth.

"You'll have to teach me how to make those amazing biscuits," she said, handing him the last plate to dry.

"Drop biscuits are one thing," he said, "but what is eating away at you, Veesy?"

She dried her hands and touched his face lightly. "I'll be right back."

Fletcher neatly folded the damp dish towel and draped it over the oven door handle. He could feel his heart beating in his throat. He sat back down at the table.

She returned with a manila folder. Medical records? Had she lied about being sick?

"I didn't lose my peach seed monkey," she said, placing the folder in front of him, and sitting across from him.

"I gave it away."

"To who?" Fletcher looked puzzled.

"I don't know how to tell you except to tell you. When I left Albany, I was pregnant." She sat up straighter. "And we have a son."

Those four words were in no way unclear, but still he asked, "What did you say?"

Her years of silence turned into a river of words. She looked everywhere but at him as the story flowed from her like a dream you have no chance of forgetting when you wake.

"The day he was born I put him up for adoption."

How could this be? He was seventy years old, three daughters, six grandkids, one great-grand, and yet here he sat, feeling his heart in his stomach like a sixteen-year-old praying his girlfriend counted her days wrong.

"I'm so sorry, Fletcher. For keeping you in the dark. You had every right to know back then. I hope you believe that there's so much more to the story—."

This shocked him. *How much more could there be?* He shouted the words in his mind, *I loved you, was ready to marry and make a family with YOU—*

Altovise went on, "For years I imagined that if we ever came to this, it would be an interrogation; me answering all of your questions, knowing there is no match for the guilt I've carried—even though I still know I did right by Siman."

"Simon?"

"Close, but with an *a,* S-i-m-a-n. His last name is Miller."

Fletcher walked to the picture window.

"Where does he live?"

"Saginaw, Michigan."

"Michigan?" He hit this like a punching bag.

"Yes. Only an hour-and-a-half drive from Ann Arbor. All these years."

He did not turn to face her. Every answer led back to the question he could not ask: Did she know she was pregnant that night on her porch when he gave her the monkey? His inner voice shouted, *Just ask her!*

"You were sure," he asked instead, "I mean, that I'm the father?"

The sixteen-year-old asks this question under pressure from his parents. He wished he hadn't asked.

"Positive," she replied, as if it were the most natural question he could ask. She looked fragile, a word he had never associated with Altovise, but she collected herself and spoke as if delivering a lecture for her students.

"The day I left Albany, Mama and her sister, Aine Lou, drove me to the Atlanta airport and I flew to Youngstown, Ohio, to live with their brother and his wife, who were childless and happy to help me. I spent eight frightening months in their loving care. I begged them not to come for the birth, knowing it was going to be hard enough dealing with Mama and Aine Lou trying to convince me to keep the baby. *We always take care of our own,* they kept saying; *let us raise your child until you finish college.* But I told them if they ever wanted to see *me* again, they had to honor my wishes."

Fletcher rubbed his face with both hands, unable to snuff out another burning question: *What did I do to make you hate me so much you didn't want my son?* He tuned back in.

Altovise looked briefly at him, then back down at her hands.

"Siman was born and adopted on March 9, 1963. I had the nurse deliver your peach seed monkey with a note card to his parents.

All these years I had no idea where he was. He has an adopted sister, Patricia. They were searching online for info about peach seed monkeys—hoping it would lead to me—and she found Olga's blog. I learned all this when I visited Olga about two months ago."

"Two months ago?" That was around the time he took Olga to her library meeting and she asked him about the monkey. Things were coming together for him and Altovise. Olga claimed she found the other earring. She would call that a white lie.

"I've wrestled and wrestled with how to tell you. And like you, Olga is still not convinced that Siman Miller surfacing now had nothing to do with my coming home."

Fletcher said nothing.

She opened the folder and pushed two sheets toward his empty chair. "I can see how it would be hard to believe, but the real miracle is that the peach seed monkey has not only led Siman to me, but to us. Olga wondered how we were going to tell you. I told her there is no *we* in this, and made it clear that she was to let you and me handle it. I didn't want him to know any of this yet. Not until you and I have a chance to discuss how to move forward."

He sat back down, slipping his reading glasses from his shirt pocket, feeling like a drowning man looking for a raft.

"That's the second email Siman sent to Olga," Altovise said. "First he sent a quick sentence about getting a peach seed monkey as a rite of passage. I guess he didn't expect the lead to go anywhere. But Olga asked for more details and he sent this to her."

Fletcher's eyes sailed across the text.

Dear Dr. Dukes,

Thank you so much for your reply requesting more details. Even though we were very excited to find your family blog— actually my sister, Patricia, found it—I must admit, I was not expecting to make contact.

I live in Saginaw, Michigan. I was born on Saturday, March 9, 1963, and adopted the same day. My birth mother (unknown to us) gave my adoptive parents a handwritten note (which sadly has been lost) and a peach seed monkey, which I still have. The carving is quite exquisite, with tiny diamonds for eyes. The note gave instructions for me to receive the monkey on my thirteenth birthday in a rite of passage. My parents (both now deceased) and Patricia followed through.

You can imagine our excitement when I read your post about peach seed monkeys on your family blog. You write that you are no stranger to the monkey tradition in your family. I'm hoping the monkey I've owned my whole life can lead me to my birth mother. Perhaps you have answers? In all my research over the years your blog is the most promising thing I have come across. I look forward to your reply.

Fletcher pored over the photos, gratified by his handiwork, recalling this monkey's special traits. This story was also his story, and there was a forty-nine-year-old man in Saginaw who still had no idea about him.

"When Olga showed me this email, my first thought was that Siman's parents carried through with my requests; they even kept the name. I wrote in the note card that I chose Siman for its meaning: *he who listens and hears*—and pointed out that I wanted 'man' in his name."

If she had been speaking about somebody else, Fletcher would have smiled at the intentions behind her actions in naming the boy, but his face was frozen.

Neither of them spoke. She took slow deep breaths. All of this, Fletcher could see, was a dam she built against breaking down. His heart broke watching her.

"You were young," he finally said. "You did what was in your heart to do. Can't nobody hold that against you. Least of all me."

He was grateful that she somehow knew what to do next: answer questions he didn't know how to ask.

She breathed up into a straight back, her mouth quivered into a smile. She rearranged the saltshaker and pepper mill on the table. "He was a *beautiful* baby. Biggest, brightest eyes I'd ever seen."

"You—you saw him?" Fletcher drummed his fingers gently. "Not usually done that way, is it?"

"No. It was definitely not the way adoption was done back then. This was also not what I imagined back in Albany when I envisioned college. As I waited for labor to start, the ring box with your peach seed monkey was in my hand. And it comforted me. Had no plans to give it to our baby; brought it to feel closer to you, even though I could hardly bear to think about you, about us. I've never been able to say why I knew I had to see him, or when it became clear that the monkey should go with him. I ended up keeping the gold chain, not even sure why. And since I was so young, those nurses, and the other mothers, fought me tooth and nail on my decision to see him." She paused to honor a deep exhale.

"Anyway. I finally had to raise my voice and practically fake a seizure to get them to butt out! But I knew I had to see him alone."

"That was rough," Fletcher said.

"It was. But I held him. Big, beautiful eyes looking right at me." Now she rocked with tears.

Fletcher wanted to hold her, but did she want that? Then he saw that she didn't need him to hold her, the story lifted her.

"I told him he was from good stock, that we all loved him more than he could know, and now he would have another family loving him, and with that much love coming from all sides, he was going to be just fine." With her fluffy white sleeve, she wiped tears.

Fletcher brought Kleenex and rubbed her back as she sobbed.

His body was like lead. "We don't have to do this now."

"Yes. We do," she said, patting his hand. With a giant inhale, she went on. "They took Siman back to the nursery and I was left in the big room with three other new mothers—white women, their families coming and going—so much excitement, so much joy. Mama and Aine Lou acted like we were at a funeral, and all my certainty vanished. Well, almost all. Now I was certain of only one thing: I was making the biggest mistake of my life and it was too late to turn back."

"But I thought they give you a few days, in case you changed your mind."

"Yes, but I could never crush the hope of the couple after all they'd been through.

"The adopting parents were on their way. They were in their late twenties. I remember thinking that's where you and I would be in eight or nine years. I didn't meet them. Siman was born that morning at nine ten, and his parents picked him up early afternoon. I left Saint Elizabeth's Hospital the next morning. Spent my devastating summer in Youngstown. My aunt was a cook at the State University and got me a job washing dishes. I had deferred enrollment until that fall and told myself repeatedly: at least you're working on a college campus."

Fletcher felt her looking at him, but he was looking out at the lake.

"You have anything else to say?"

"Don't know what to say." He turned to face her. *Ask her! Now!* He kept his eyes on her but still couldn't find the words.

"On the back of the envelope I gave the parents, I wrote a proverb I grew up hearing from Grandma Onawa: *The ones that matter most are the children.* There's not much more to tell."

She leaned back, wrapping her robe tighter, her hands folded and quiet in her lap.

Fletcher paced, unable to look at her filled with apology and agony. How could she hold their son, give him a name, and let him go? Finally, he asked, "Did you know you were pregnant that night on your porch when I gave you the monkey?"

"Yes. I did know. I was just over about two weeks pregnant. I found out in the brig, and at first thought I was late because of the stress of being in that dreadful prison."

Her answer had come so quickly, sinking his regret even deeper for having walked away from everything he had ever wanted.

"But how could you be so sure you were pregnant at that point without a test?"

Altovise shook her head. Her face was an improvisation. "Because. I had *the spits*. Excess salivation. I knew about it because Mama had it with all three of us, and her mother had it, too. It's a rare side effect of pregnancy. Scientific name is *ptyalism*."

"Sounds bad."

"Believe me—it's even worse than it sounds!" Her smile faded quickly. "And of course, one of the worse moments of my life was when I looked through the broken windows of that brig and whispered to Mama that I had the spits. That's all I had to say for her to know. She never judged me, though. I guess she felt I was suffering enough in the brig. She just came back about an hour later to bring me a care package, including a cup of ice, a few fresh lemons, chewing gum, and a big plastic cup with paper napkins in the bottom. I used it as a spittoon."

"Wait," Fletcher said, "so that's why you had a lemon on the porch that night?"

"Yep. That's why. So. Disgusting. But somehow I made it through."

Learning all the details, it hurt too much to look at her. His eyes grazed the floor.

"Are you angry?" she asked, "because you have every right to be."

"No." He really wasn't. Anger would have been easier than the abysmal sorrow he felt. "Mostly, I'm confused. Why couldn't you tell me this then? How could you think I wouldn't want you and our son?"

"It wasn't so cut-and-dry," she said. "That June was both beautiful and terrible for me. Starting with graduation and then—not even a week later—the night in the backseat of your Fairlane. Then, when you gave me the monkey, I felt even more awful for turning down your proposal. Going to college was not optional, and I had to get away from southwest Georgia. Then, of course, to add insult to injury, the summer ended with me in the brig, and I just couldn't find a way to make you and me and all those things line up.

"It's been hard for me to accept that I settled in Ann Arbor, and all his life Siman's been in Saginaw, only eighty miles south as the crow flies."

Fletcher needed to leave. Out of habit, he patted his thighs for car keys. He forgot he was wearing John Shaft pants, feeling like even more of an imposter.

He listened to her talk around the edges again, wishing it were within his power to catch and release the misery now circling them both.

"Onethingaboutit," he said, finally looking her in the eyes before walking upstairs to change, "there's a lot about this that's harder to accept than those eighty miles."

~

is blood family
running like
a river
carrying all that you are
like sand stirred from
low land
growing richer
deeper
with each baby's breath

~

27

After sixty-four days at sea, Malik was one among hordes of captives packed in a fleet of canoes leaving the *Camille* headed for South Carolina's southeastern shore. Malik bowed his head and closed his eyes against a spring rain, coming down in sideways sheets, washing his body clean of the ship's filth. He looked back toward the ship, a spectral mass, hovering and threatening once again to swallow him whole. The sound of bodies hitting water resounded in his memory. How and why had he survived? Muscles in his core quivered at sitting upright, his branded chest still oozed and stung, refusing to heal. Fulani codes and his faith in Allah often shuttered but did not perish. Through all he endured over more than four months—Bacary's murder, his own capture, the ship—his peach seed had been an anchor, a bewildering glimmer of hope.

The man to his left tugged at their shared chain. Head still bowed, Malik glanced over. He was an elder, but not of many years, who spoke in his tongue above shouts from the crew and rain noise. Malik's face registered no understanding. The man gestured with eyes, and face, and head, lifting to the sky and bidding Malik to join him in drinking from pouring rain. They shared an ephemeral smile.

Hordes of captives spent twenty-one days quarantined on ships or on *jamesisland* in *pest houses*, crammed into windowless brick fortresses not good enough for animals. Malik slept on dry, scratchy grass he would come to know as *hay*. He listened with intent to the daneejos' language; verbal wordshapes with no meaning. Since the moment he was separated from his cousins, Malik had spent his days in silence, like a child, filled with wonder and curiosity, waiting to be understood, and like a man prepared to kill with his bare, shackled hands. He could not know this yet, but he and others would use silence as a weapon, a new common faith. For many days and nights, thunder rattled tin roofs and rain beat down, through sheets of humidity. Mosquitoes covered his body with welts. He wanted nothing more than to stand free outside, to let water wash over him and drink again. He was now chained to a single man closer to his age. This man bore wretchedness on every surface of his skin like a shield, and it traveled through the chain to threaten what solace Malik sought to conjure. Malik fought this and wondered where his previous neighbor, his rain-mate, had ended up.

The rain stopped.

Once again from a canoe, Malik looked out on a gauzy haze lifting to unveil freshly scrubbed blue skies. April's tranquil light sparkled on the water with purpose, prompting Malik to wonder if he would ever again find his. The mighty Atlantic, Malik's unwitting nemesis for many months, surrendered her powers to ever narrowing estuaries, ending at *cooperriver's charlestonharbor*. Malik could bear no hatred toward these innocent waters, like the Senegal and the Atlantic, forced by daneejos to do their bidding. They could just as easily be used to bear him back home.

But for the scourge of infidels, Baaba would embrace this wharf named *gadsden*, alive with men and boats of every stripe: oar-powered plantation boats, topsail schooners, side-wheel ocean-going steamers. Had this been a joyful journey, an arrival at such a port would be triumphant, as he had felt many times at home delivering pirogues. The wharf, an eight-hundred-foot-long, very wide wooden expanse, was capable of docking six large ships at once and led to cobblestone streets and massive brick structures. *Holdingpens.*

Captives passed through the outer gate of one such building, into a hall sixty feet by twenty feet with tables and benches lining each side and a bare floor covered by moldered hay. Iron-gated windows, crusted with dirt, let in paltry light. At one far end, a brick wall served as backdrop to an elevated platform eight feet square. *Auctionblock.* A door led into a yard surrounded by tall brick buildings. In an anteroom, captive women had been stripped naked to please infidels.

Each morning captives were doused with buckets of cold water, given rough rags to scrub from head to toe, then oil their bodies from vats—smaller versions of the one on the *Camille.* This oil's magnolia scent mingled with disease and death tinged with wine and ale, refreshments traders provided for their customers. From another vat they applied scoops of wet, pasty clay mixed with crushed chickweed. At last, a soothing balm for Malik's branded skin.

Malik was issued a pair of short breeches made of a rough fabric Yaaye and the wives used to store yams at home. He quickly freed his peach seed from the soiled, odorous loincloth and tied it into the hem of this new garment. All around him, men were plunged into pits of self-loathing. Malik fought this with prayer and plans to build a boat and escape. A pirogue was not big enough, this much he knew, but beyond that his mind stalled, swirling around images of different types of boats he knew from home or saw in *charlestonharbor.*

Being young, strong, and healthy, Malik spent only a week in this holding pen, where many more captives died, their bodies piled on wagons bound for mass graves, prompting Malik to rehear the splash of bodies hitting open waves. He stood on the auction block, with fear bubbling over in his stomach and working its way up to become bile in his throat. He pushed sore, calloused feet deeper into the platform's grain so that he did not collapse, and faced a bitter truth. There were no roads winding and winding to take him back home.

In a transaction not unlike many he had performed selling pirogues in Podor, he was sold to a bulbous man with massive, pillowy hands. The man was accompanied by three other daneejos, all dressed more shoddily than he, who addressed him often as *mrcalhounsir*. The well-dressed man placed his hands on Malik's face, one on his forehead, the other on his chin to force open his mouth. Malik clamped down hard on the blubbery thumb, hooked over his lower teeth.

"Son of a bitch!" the man cried, drawing back and cradling his hand.

The backhand blow to Malik's face came from one of the other men. It rattled his teeth and drew blood.

"That's the last time he gone do that," the large man smirked through a grimace, "just needs breaking in. We know how to do that. Put him in the wagon."

Malik watched from the buckboard as Calhoun completed his transaction. The hulky man put folded papers in his suit's pocket as he walked over to the wagon.

"Call this one Sawney," he said to the driver. "Git him on home."

Calhoun owned a large rice plantation on the Ashley River, a few miles northwest of Charleston. Alone, sitting awkwardly, with buckboard splinters cutting into his skin, Malik adjusted his hands to ease the cold wretchedness from shackles on raw wrists. Showing more mercy to a horse than to a man, the slight daneejo, whose backhand blow still stung, constantly turned his head to let go streams of brown spit, laughing as he sang repeatedly, *sawneycalhoun-lookatyounow*!

For this wagon ride, rice fields and majestic trees veiled in gray moss greeted Malik with beauty and torment. Hawks and turkey buzzards orbited above lush woods and an unburdened river, reflecting a rain-washed sky.

Although palmettos, beaches, and pompous clouds reminded him of Podor, he could see no parallels between these people and his home. Never had he witnessed brutalities equal to those he saw at every turn since Bacary was murdered before his eyes. Had daneejos no code to live by? Did they answer to no God?

It was midday when they arrived at Calhoun Plantation. Inside his silence, questions in Pulaar raced loudly through Malik's mind. Within a few months he would have a working handle on the daneejos' language, but on this day, only gestures and hand signs told him the knapsack thrown at him was his to keep. Inside was meat and bread wrapped in oilcloth, and a neatly folded shirt made of unbleached, coarse linen, long breeches of a darker shade, a straw hat and a new pair of shoes, unblackened leather with no steel toes or buckles and very different from those worn by nearly every daneejo. Malik had not worn shoes since that day on Langue de Barbarie, when he was stripped of his sturdy leather sandals, pants, and favorite blue tunic. He had been well-dressed to deliver his final pirogue, needing to represent his family well.

He was assigned a bed in a small three-man cabin. He gladly traded itchy breeches for his new clothes yet longed for a bath. At home, each day as he bathed in the river, his naked body was worshipped. Here, for the first time, he found shame in it. In spite of the magnolia-scented oil, his skin was cracked and ashen like earth in a drought. He needed Yaaye's shea butter. He tied his peach seed into a section of his new shirt. He could not yet know these clothes and shoes were meant to last all year.

He laid claim to the empty bed: a four-by-six-foot wooden box, too short for his frame. Straw mattress transferred to the floor, he sat. He ate salt pork and bread. Exhausted, he slept. He woke covered in strange new bites, greeted by his two cabinmates.

"Oonuh got to curl up on that trifling box to block them blood-sucking spiders," Horace, the elder man, explained, pantomiming as he spoke. "Them too dumb to crawl up the side. They hits it head-on and turn right around."

Horace was born on Saint Simons Island and had never been sold more than two or three plantations away. He seemed close to Baaba's age and carried himself in a similar manner, upright and focused. From their first meeting, Malik had utter respect for him.

Born in the Louisiana bayou, Crayfish was purchased a few months before Malik, and they were close in age. He welcomed Malik with a tune on his harmonica, and Horace gave him a can of salve for his wound: elderberry bark and beeswax.

"Me and Crayfish is *Beenyas*." Horace smiled warmly, slowing down his quick Gullah accent and adding hand gestures. "And oonuh is a *Comya*. Us aims to make you welcome!"

"Them buckruhs done told us to call oonuh *Sawney*," Crayfish said with a grimace, shaking his head and palms.

Malik heard that word, remembering the slight daneejo's song, and welcomed this denouncement.

"Horace," he said, patting his chest.

"Crayfish" raised a hand.

"Malik Welé" smiled, head bowed.

"Then that's how it is," Horace said, pointing to each man, "Malik, Crayfish, and Horace. Ain't no Sawney living in these walls."

Although he understood none of their words, Malik was well versed in reading what he saw in his cabinmates' eyes. This took him back to *Camille*'s hold and deck and he became wise to all he could not see while depleted and submerged in terror. In those rare and cherished moments gathered around palm oil vats, or eating special rations, when Malik gazed into the eyes of other men, he now fathomed that even though they spoke different dialects, were of foreign tribes and faiths, all those things became secondary. He could now name what he had felt: through horrific shared experiences, a person's soul can rise through tyranny. As the beneficiary of Horace and Crayfish's good graces, Malik carefully deciphered this rise—this link, this net—silently connecting him to others who were learning to speak their newly forged language. With each step, from hold to pesthouse to holding pen, he had not looked far to find in other faces what he would eventually call the Rise. This new primary focus would guide each move forward. With every new person he'd meet in this devious land, Malik would start with their eyes.

The next day, Malik was assigned his quarter-acre task.

"Oonuh done come new just in time for the sprout flow," Horace said, "us plantin' rice seed."

His cabinmates used hand signs and facial expressions to show each step in the process: point flow, long flow, lay-by-flow. He learned to manage being up to his knees in boggy, bug-filled water, swatting eyes and ears constantly against *gnats* and *mosquitoes*, words for two things delivered from hell.

In the coming weeks, he met other African captives, working in various jobs on the huge farm, fighting to forget or hold on to their memories of home. Many were born here, like Horace and Crayfish, knowing Africa only through stories, songs, remedies, and customs. Because neither man could read or write, they were envious and amused by Malik's fluency in Arabic. On rare nights by candlelight, with paper, pen, and ink secured by Crayfish from his main house sources, Malik regaled his cabinmates with written and spoken demonstrations, recalling the Qur'an's *surahs* and *ayats*. This reconnection with his faith and language lifted his spirits and gave him a much-needed sense of autonomy. Newly armed with tactics for preserving his knowledge, Malik would write in the sand when taking rice field or boat workshop breaks. This would grow into a plan to add secret schools to the Rise.

Before his first visit to Saint-Louis when he was nine, Malik had never traveled as far as two hundred kilometers from Podor. That harbor flourished with languages he had never heard and was a marvelous unknown from which he could retreat into conversation with his family. Inside this new, horrid unknown, he met inconsolable silence, confusion, and loneliness. He struggled to repeat meaningless phrases shouted at him. But anger and torment could not quell his curious mind. New words did not fit well in his mouth, yet he found them intriguing: their *canoes* were inferior to his pirogues. The many boats he saw had names that slipped and tore through water: *schooner, sloop, cutter, ketch, yawl.* He had yet to learn which would be his salvation. Horace owned a ripped and stained calendar showing that months had passed since the *Camille* docked, and now Malik saw that this place called *charlestonsouthcarolina* was the animal they had all been fattened to feed. The beast had many stomachs: *auctionblock, pesthouse, holdingpen,* and *ricefield.* But only one head with two faces. On one side, he knew the daneejo *calhoun*—who Horace called *buckruh*—deemed himself *master* and that he, Malik, was labeled *slave.* Opposite of this was pure majesty: *palm trees* and grand buildings; horse-drawn carts piled high with strange, colorful fruit, a dark crier singing their names: *Me got pee-chis fuh oonuh! Paw-paws! An plu-ums!* And between these was *atlanticocean*, open, fair, and underhanded. The same water that bore him away and fed local creeks and rivers also washed up on Senegal's shores or flowed upriver to Podor. He could see Nbey there, washing their new baby's blankets, months and miles across water. He could not think too long of his family's agony, left to suffer his mysterious disappearance. His life gone. Reduced to vapor.

One evening Malik and Horace walked through stifling air back to the compound, aching and hungry after working the lay-by-flow: flooding fields to cover the plants.

Malik untied the section of his shirt where he kept his peach seed.

"Oonuh know?" he asked, holding the gem in his palm.

"Let's see what that is." Horace squinted. "Ooh! That be a peach seed."

Malik stared ahead, remembering a crier's song—*Me got peee-chis!*

"—done seen peach?" Horace leaned forward, pretending to bite into the fruit, wipe his lips, and slurp juice "flavor so good it make yo mout leak!"

"Heh! Where us git peach?" Malik asked.

"Ain't likely, brother!" Horace shook his head. "Old man Calhoun won't be giving no peaches no time soon, but oonuh glimpse them ever-where round here."

Horace was right. Now Malik saw daneejos everywhere eating peaches. Satan on horseback, whips thrown across saddles. He often came across seeds underfoot—dropped by hands, carried by birds—but did not dare touch them, for they had been sucked clean in the mouth of evil.

Horace handed the seed back to Malik.

They had reached their cluster of weathered shacks where neighbors gathered cheerfully outside around firepits for their evening meal.

Malik saw his peach seed differently now. Was this one also sucked clean in the mouth of evil? Had it come from this very place and now was being returned? He would run the seed through an open flame for purification, knowing that carving would further release any bad spirits.

"Them buckruhs been plantin Oldmixons since my pa was a boy," Horace said, "and they in season right now. Look to me like it's gone be a juicy ripe peach in your near enough future."

28

Day broke with dull rays, settling on Fletcher's pink bathroom sink. He flipped on the light switch to radio music tucked on top of his medicine cabinet. Bo D was still flying under Olga's radar, and with each passing hour since he'd learned about Siman Miller, emotions piled up around Fletcher like scrap cars. If he stood still, he risked being crushed in his own wreckage. So he kept moving.

White, frothy lather grew in the cup under his shaving brush. Each razor stroke exposed a straight, smooth path of skin. If only he had such clarity. Maybe he should take Altovise's advice and call their son. Talk man-to-man. But there's nothing more useless than a telephone when you don't know what to say to somebody. He and Altovise have a son. He still had not said the words out loud. After splashing with witch hazel, he patted his face dry.

Having a familiar, weathered, and battered piece from your past pop up unexpectedly is one thing. But having this unknown blind-side him at his age—that was regret by a different name. That was straight-up grief. He had lived a lie only because she'd kept their truth from him.

Unlike a mother, a father's presence is insignificant to the birth of his children, and on some days, even seems immaterial to their lives. As long as Fletcher was there for his girls providing armor against the world, there were times when even he took his presence for granted. But now, learning that he was denied a chance with the son he'd always wanted, he fully grasped the waxing of a father's love.

He was ashamed that it took longer than he imagined to rejoice in the glory of three beautiful girls. From time to time he winds Maletha's jewelry box and a sad tune plays for those three pristine monkeys still locked inside.

He set a fresh pot of coffee to brew then mixed Spam with kibble in Rock's bowl.

"Don't look so sad, nobody's dead," he said. Rock's eyes were filled with mercy. Man and dog made cursory rounds from finished pond, to garden, to coop, ending up in the woodshop. No sanding to do and Fletcher didn't dare put hand to saw; there were no straight lines in him. His familiar, cluttered room felt too small. He put Rock in his kennel with a fresh beef bone and called Eunice. No one else had proper distance to deal with him in this state.

Ninety minutes later they sat at her table, playing gin rummy.

"You certainly have your hands full," she said, dealing cards.

Fletcher smiled, collecting a run of hearts.

"I know what that's like," Eunice went on, "to have everything closing in. That's when you know you need a change of scenery."

"Well I'll be." Fletcher spread his cards and sank back. "Gin!"

"What! That fast?" Eunice said.

"You dealt me a pat hand!" He felt relaxed, glad that he had come. Three days ago he had been sure he and Altovise were headed for this level of easiness. And now, who could say where they would end up.

"So—have you got a trip in you?" Eunice asked, pouring root beer into frosted mugs, "Somewhere you've always wanted to go?"

Fletcher shuffled cards. He couldn't imagine a trip with Eunice being their best move right now.

"Always does me good," she added, "to get away alone so I can hear myself think."

Fletcher stopped dealing, dropped his head, and laughed. "I thought you were talking about us going somewhere together."

"Oh no, honey child!" She laughed, too. "I got enough drama of my own without getting tangled up in yours—all your wives are lining up at once: the deceased wife; and me: the wife-that-was-never-to-be; and now Altovise, the wife-you-could-have-had. It's too much!"

"I don't know what I got to laugh about," Fletcher said.

"Leverage," Eunice answered, "that's what you call that."

After cards, she made tuna sandwiches and he set the table and poured sweet tea. Over dinner, they talked about locations for a road trip before he drove back home.

The next morning, he was up earlier than usual, in no mood for breakfast. From the girls' rooms, to kitchen, to den, all corners of his empty house pushed against him in new ways. After rounds and chores, he found himself driving his pickup on Highway 19 North. A few miles farther and he'd be at Florida's house. He picked a random exit, Nottingham Road, and explored streets he never had reason to visit: Whispering Pines, Westgate, Westover. In the 1960s, way before the expressway went in, he and his friends said all those *W* streets stood for "white." He turned off the radio. Worn-out songs worsened his mood, but he found so much noise inside the quiet that he opted again for music.

At a hotel on north Dawson Road, a large, noisy bar was shaped like a track. Fletcher sat in one of the curves. The straights spilled over with conventioneers—Black and white—men and women—about Bo D's age, dressed for business, and sitting in segregated groups. He ordered a cup of coffee, thinking how his life felt like a snapshot taken from high, high rafters. He looked down and wondered, who is that old man? The one with a grandson he no longer recognized and a son he never knew about?

Voices clattered, chairs scraped, laughs pitched up and over the din and crept up his back like a sleepless night. Perched like a watchman as commotion roiled, Fletcher sipped coffee. He was a stranger in his own city.

"More coffee?" the bartender asked.

"Why not?"

A new wave of Black professionals was at the opposite curve, as decibel levels reached a crescendo. Fletcher ran his fingers over condensation on his water glass. Everyone he saw was younger by many years. Fifty years ago, his generation had sat at counters in order to stand up against bigotry. Back then, he could not see past mass meetings, protests, or voter registration drives. It was enough to make it through a day. He could not envision this present where young folks still sat in segregated clumps, waited on by Black bartenders and waitresses, where public schools were back to being Black. Like his barber, Blue Jean, said, "Us Foot Soldiers and Freedom Riders, we the only ones what really know all that was gained by what we gave up." There was no need to bemoan shortcomings of the Movement, it was better to keep asking the questions SNCC leaders taught: *if not this, then what; if not now, then when—and if not me, then who?* In Fletcher's mind, the young folk around him did not have much to laugh about.

And now, here was Altovise, showing him how much more was lost. He couldn't call her, and didn't want to face his empty house.

A lively group of Blacks near him discussed the difference between Gullah and Geechee.

"It's Gullah in South Carolina," one man offered, "and Geechee in Georgia and Florida—and don't y'all be arguing with me 'cause I got plenty kinfolk on Saint Simon and Jekyll."

A month ago Fletcher and Olga had talked about Ursula uncovering facts supporting a story that had floated around the family for generations. Isakiah Dukes had been enslaved in Cusetta, Georgia— seventy miles north of Albany. He was about twenty-one in 1862 when Union warships took control of Georgia's coast. He and many of the state's enslaved made their way to Union lines. A Union general issued an order to free the enslaved in three southern states, then formed a black regiment on the Sea Islands. An escaped preacher from Savannah recruited Isakiah to serve in that unit. Isakiah was one of thirty-eight men sent to Saint Simons Island to help other Black escapees fight Confederate attack. Olga added a new designation to Isakiah Dukes' name in their family Bible: Union Army hero.

Fletcher had driven north, south, and west of Albany many times but never due east to the coast. He had grown up with family and friends using "Geechee" to describe coastal Blacks as "loving rice and talking fast and funny." What little Fletcher knew about the Georgia Sea Islands he'd learned through Olga's years teaching about how their history and customs stretched directly back to West Africa, evident in indigo, rice, and cotton, and in the Gullah language—a mix of English and African dialects. He never joined Olga on multiple field trips she led to show what public school curricula didn't teach about generations of enslaved Americans whose descendants became the landowners, leaders, artists, and hardworking folk who built the islands. Now, the fact that their family had roots there was reason enough to drive over.

It took as much time as it would've taken to drive back home for Fletcher to find a pay phone to leave a message for Olga.

Just past noon, he drove past the Marine Base on Highway 82 East, headed toward the coast. Uniform rows of pecan trees disappeared into a hazy distance. Familiar things were like water to a man with rabies. He was back to radio scanning and settled on country western, agreeing that you *can* make it out of hell before the devil knows you're there.

After nearly three hours, Fletcher felt he had not left Putney—Highway 82 was lined with the same pine trees, kudzu, and broken-down sharecroppers' cabins from his childhood: tin roofs, wooden clapboard sides, and chimneys. Most were abandoned, engulfed by vines and weeds, but some were still occupied, one car in the well-swept yard. And Fletcher imagined one or two immaculate rooms and something savory on the stove.

He sped on, waiting to be changed by a foreign landscape. Memories continued, too, like a hurdler, jumping over time. He had no plans, no real destination, just a will to shift through muck and mire and get to clear waters.

From town to town, chain stores repeated like wallpaper finally ending at the coastal city of Brunswick. Pulled by one word—"Island"—Fletcher turned right onto the causeway leading to Jekyll. Marshland and palm trees turned him into a foreigner at last and he looked for a beach to release his churning, tumbling thoughts into rolling waves to be worked smooth like sea glass.

29

~

Up the coast in Darien, fishermen sat on white plastic buckets and tourists milled about taking pictures with an Altamaha River backdrop. Fletcher walked along shrimp boat docks eating a catfish sandwich. Every sight and sound seemed drained of first impressions. Had he become a tired old man? Was he unable to see things new and fresh unless Cricket was there to point them out? There were only so many times a person could get excited about restaurant food and shops filled with junk nobody needs. Artifacts in an antique shop window—depression glass, plumb bogs, enamel bowls and ladles were carbon copies of many in his house and shed. Relics like him. Why had he survived lynch mobs and protests?

He rested on a bench, squinting at the horizon, his mouth a worried line against thoughts of calling Siman Miller and finding Bo D. A few feet away, an elderly man sat on a stack of crates rolling a cigarette. With skin the color of topsoil, his straw hat threw his face into deeper shade. His hand-rolled cigarette hung loosely in his mouth as he struggled to stand.

Fletcher walked over. "Need a hand there, partner?"

The old man accepted, his large hand, cracked and calloused, matching Fletcher's palm for palm. Fletcher braced himself and heaved him to his feet.

"Much obliged." He removed the cigarette. "In pretty good shape for the shape I'm in." His voice was raspy. "Done got stoved-up— didn't think much about ma gittin' up when I did ma sitting down." He coughed a phlegmy smile, showing a few missing teeth.

"Catch any-thang?"

"Beg pardon?" Fletcher said.

"I seen oonuh pondering that water. Catch any-thang?"

"Naw-sir, didn't bring my pole."

"I can see that. A man ain't need no pole for the kinda fushin oonuh doin."

Fletcher sank his hands into his pockets and the man pulled a box of matches from his.

"Naw suh." He pinched the jouncing cigarette with his lips as he lit it. "Just need the right bait."

The man lingered, making for an awkward moment.

"Smoke?"

"No-no," Fletcher said, "gave that up twenty years ago."

"That-there was a terrible idea." The man pushed his sun hat farther down over his eyes and hobbled past Fletcher toward the shore.

Then he turned and asked, "Oonuh drive?"

"Where you tryin' to go?"

"Not far—bout eight miles to Meridian ferry. Goin' over to Sapelo to see me daughter. If it ain't no bother, I can show how to get there." He pulled out a pocket watch. "Still time. Us can make that three thirty."

"No bother at all," Fletcher said, "that's my old blue truck over there."

"They call me Pops." He extended his hand.

"I'm Fletcher Dukes." Two callused hands met. "Pleasure's mine."

Pops told Fletcher he grew up in the 1930s on Sapelo, a small island in a string off the coast of South Carolina and Georgia. But for those who stay to carry on with legacy, salt air trembled with the presence of a people almost erased, their footsteps becoming a faint whisper among private beaches, hotels, and golf courses. Many young folk become city dwellers, finding traditional ways a loose fit on modern skin, often missing connections between hip-hop and the hambone from which it sprang. Those who stay understand that their island home is closer to the source of everything others were running toward.

Pops' grandparents had been enslaved on the island, same as their parents. Fletcher had never met a Black person who could go back five generations and envied Pops knowing them all by first and last name. This man's enslaved ancestors were a source of pride Fletcher could not share, for all of Olga's relentless trying. He had names—if not faces—on which to pin his history.

"Yes-suh—I's raised right there in Hog Hammock," Pops said, "and my daughter live there right on. Oonuh huntin' a place to stay tonight?"

"Might be," Fletcher answered, "hadn't got that far yet."

"Welcome to come on out with me. Ferry don't cost but a dollar, and my daughter—name Naomi—and her husband, Chester, they rent out rooms. A fine place called the Wayfarer. And her cooking gone flavor your mout, that's for sure."

"Don't I need a reservation?" Fletcher asked.

"Yeah, and now you got one." Pops rested his hat in his lap and his head against the window until needed for directions.

They joined a handful of people silently watching the ferry pull in until a squat man, his face mapped with blood vessels, walked up holding hands with a twitchy woman wearing a matching wedding band; tourists from London. They geared up for what would be the British Husband and Wife Show.

Standing too close for comfort, the man said to Fletcher, "Fine day for a trip, wouldn't you say?"

She intercepted cheerfully. "We missed that last boat, now didn't we? Because this one took a wrong turn. I mean who can get lost in teeny-tiny Meridian except us?" She laughed too hard at her joke. "So we have to take this three thirty."

He took over. "And, of course, you know Sapelo has limited access. So if you were taking the five thirty out—that's the last boat—you better have a reservation or you'd be outta luck, now wouldn't you, mate?"

Why were these people asking and answering questions in the same breath? Pops had conveniently drifted behind.

Fletcher let a small people-wave carry the couple ahead, and he drifted back to his hitchhiker. He wondered what prompted the man to strike up a conversation with him when he was minding his own business? Maybe his height—at least a head taller than most in a crowd—or a look of conviction? He needed to know, so he could change whatever drew strange white people to him.

A young Black man with a clipboard quizzed each rider on who would be meeting them.

"He with me," Pops said.

"OK, gotcha, Pops."

After a U-turn, the ferry snaked through viney creeks, rocking and droning, then picked up speed when they hit the sound. Pops resumed his nap in a window seat and Fletcher went up top. Rows of cotton ball clouds streaked a clear blue sky, and wind played with people's hair. Fletcher followed a tinny, jiggy tune to a man below, who looked a lot like Pops, standing alone, playing a harmonica.

When they docked on Sapelo, a woman with ebony skin and a cropped blond Afro waited next to an early-model Buick as Pops made introductions.

"Welcome to Sapelo, Mr. Fletcher," she said in a quick Gullah clip, shaking his hand.

"'Preciate y'all taking me in."

"Any friend of Pops is a friend of ours."

"What kinda Beenyas would us be," Pops added, "not to open us doors to a Comya like oonuh?"

"Y'all must be hongry," Naomi said, "but nothing fancy at the Wayfarer tonight, no time to make provisions."

"Fancy or no," Pops said, fastening his belt, "I done already told him he fixin' to eat good."

"Sit up front, Mr. Fletcher."

≀&

Fluorescent lights and fatigue ganged up on Fletcher in the Wayfarer bathroom. He looked as tired and jittery as he felt. Perched on a high, fluffy bed, he left a message for Florida with the Wayfarer's phone number.

Drawn by home-cooked aromas, he joined Chester and Pops at their kitchen table.

"Smells mighty good," Fletcher said, steam rising from his bowl of tangy tomatoes, shredded beef, and corn. "My mama used Brunswick stew to catch my daddy, along with fried chicken one Easter Sunday on the church grounds."

"That would work for me any day of the week," Pops said, and they all laughed.

Fletcher twisted his invisible wedding band, thinking of Maletha and Altovise, an odd feeling in the company of people who knew neither of them.

"Mr. Fletcher," Naomi said, "we don't need your room until Monday, so tomorrow I'll set you up with a bicycle and a map. Plenty to see: Chocolate, the Light House, the beaches, the mansion."

"An if you take pleasure in the fish, you kin head off to the salt. Just make yourself to home," Chester said, leaving with Naomi.

After finishing his bowl of collards, Pops sipped pot liquor as if it were whiskey. Struck by how short the distance between stranger and new friend can be, Fletcher was emboldened to ask about Isakiah.

"Say he from slavery time?" Pops asked.

"Right after slavery, during the Civil War. He was in a black regiment on Saint Simons."

"That just south from here. Heard tell of plenty blockade running around these parts during wartime, but that name ain't ring no bell. I used to know a fair amount, but I disremember. You done come too late."

The next morning, Fletcher sat at a picnic table out front, sipping coffee. Heavy fog made a cow's bellow and a strange bird's call seem an arm's reach away. In spite of worrying about Bo D, he had slept soundly and woke thinking about Altovise. Two things that were becoming a habit.

He pedaled a chunky old Schwinn painted periwinkle blue. Bulky tires bumped from sandy path onto smooth main road, lined with a tangle of Spanish moss and vines. He welcomed being engulfed by discovery, and after three miles, reached Nanny Goat Beach, with gentle waves and clean white sand dusted with crushed seashells that resembled sawdust.

With not a boat or person in sight, a white ember sun seared through. Fog rolled over grassy dunes and a massive driftwood tree that had beached like a whale. Fletcher sank ankle deep in raking waves—the right music at last—and seagulls emerged from a blurred horizon as if by sleight of hand.

He picked up a thick driftwood piece that would make a perfect handle, already sanded by time and waves. His trials and tribulations seemed paltry against this fresh slate of ocean and sky, which made way for a memory that he hadn't hosted in years. Since Altovise's return, he'd fought each time it tried to etch its way forward.

After Altovise rejected his proposal, she moved further and further away from Fletcher, and he blamed himself for their separation and suffered through being near her but not with her. When SNCC workers boarded the red, white, and blue bus traveling to various counties for voter registration, Fletcher opted to ride in one of the cars to avoid the pain of her presence.

Before long he saw a way around his pain in glances from Tammy Sue Harold, the daughter of a prominent white lawyer and socialite, with southwest Georgia roots steeped in plantation bigotry. They were close friends with local politicians, so Tammy Sue was privy to conversations around their dinner table that were pertinent to the Movement. Without her parents' knowledge, she had helped engineer plans for the Black Christmas boycott. Many felt her presence was too volatile and questioned her motives.

One evening, to the beat of rain on the tin roof of SNCC's tiny office, a group of workers ended a planning session with laughs and jokes. Altovise was now avoiding close meetings such as this. After Fletcher returned her glance, Tammy Sue walked closer and whispered, "You could come by sometime, you know."

"What about your parents and all this so-called undercover work you doing here? How you go from that to just letting me 'come by'?"

"It's called a shed, behind my house. My parents won't even be home. Plenty trees, won't nobody see you."

This would be an act of pure lust and intrigue on her part, and for Fletcher a kind of poison in just the right dosage to cleanse, not kill.

In broad daylight, Tammy Sue picked up Fletcher behind the post office on West Broad and drove north to her house near Lake Loretta. The Harolds' garden shed was several yards from their back door. Sweat, cologne, and perfume mixed with kerosene, soil, and mold. Neither of them spoke as she worked. Unbuckle. Unsnap. Unzip.

He massaged her breast through crisp cotton. She purred and he slipped sleeve and bra strap away, jolted at first by her pale, freckled shoulder. Seconds later, he ignored the warning of crackling tires on gravel, but Tammy Sue pulled at her blouse, frowning and pushing away to look through a dingy window.

"Son of a bitch, that's Mama!" She fumbled with buttons. "Git up, Fletcha! Git up!"

A muffled voice laughed and talked with Ann Harold.

"Hurry up, Fletcha, button your shirt." Tammy Sue paused to listen. Voices fell silent. Screen door slammed.

"For God's sake, Fletcha!" She ushered him out to hide in a rusted pickup a few feet behind the shed.

"You must be crazy," he said. "I ain't hiding like some jailbird."

"Please!" Tammy Sue whispered loudly. "Just lay down in there 'til dark—I'll come back after dinner and let you know when the coast is clear."

"Like hell," Fletcher said, tucking in his houndstooth shirttail.

Tammy Sue let out a hoarse bark. "She might see you!"

Fletcher did not think further than his feet moving him along the garden path with Altovise beating in his chest. He was fully wise to reality: if Charlie or Ann Harold found him that would be all the poison a young Black man looking for self-revenge could ask. He moved cautiously through steamy, crescent-moon darkness, fighting mosquitoes. His three-mile walk to Whitney Avenue took over an hour. He was ready to fight for Altovise but was too late. She had not left town but was already gone.

Fletcher tapped the driftwood in his palm. Since only he and Tammy Sue knew what took place—and never took place—inside her shed, as usual, this ghost was easily returned to the vault. This time that wasn't enough. He turned it over to the sea.

He threw the driftwood as far as he could, and held on to one thought that had come with it: Siman Miller's story had played out for forty-nine years without him and would carry on still without him. He found solace in the fact that no one, especially Altovise, ever found out about Tammy Sue.

After parking the bicycle, Fletcher joined Chester in his walk-around to check fishing-boat-to-Jeep rigging.

"Slept clean through that first ferry and tuck that as a sign to head-off fushin," Pops said, pulling slowly up into the Jeep. "You share that sentiment, young man?"

"Yep, believe I will," Fletcher said, "as long as I can still make that last ferry."

"Shouldn't be no problem." Chester patted Fletcher's shoulder. "You can handle this V-hull, can't you?"

"Give me a navigator and we good to go."

"I'm your man," Pops said. "We gon try for yellowtail and trout over at Ark Dale or Salt Pond—either one."

Fletcher started the engine. "What we using for bait?"

"Shrimps."

After an hour, Fletcher dropped anchor and Pops swiveled in the bow seat like a schoolboy. Water lapped the sides and marsh hens squawked, measuring time as Pops caught the first three yellowtails.

"You must be taking my luck," Fletcher said.

"Not about luck," Pops said, "you ain't fushin yet."

"What you call what I been doing the last hour and a half?" Fletcher asked.

"Mere fact you know puhzac'ly how long us been out here say it all," Pops said. "My pa and maamy always tell us: *worry 'bout what you kin worry 'bout.*"

Fletcher had heard the saying all his life, enough to know that many things fall in between. He wasn't accustomed to talking about his business—inside or outside of family—but in his state of mind, Pops brought the whole story out of him: Altovise returning home, delivering a grown son, and about the diamond-eyed monkey.

"Never hear tell of any such-a thang," Pops said, "but a curiosity like that is true as blood running through your veins"—he sipped Colt 45. "But one thing I know for true. Us done loss too, too many—lost to the salt, to the whip, to the noose, to hard, hard labor. And to the gun. But praise the Maker, your son won't never loss. Just been raised by your brethren. Time done come for him to make it home to you."

Fletcher reeled in and rested his pole.

"Aint for me to say whether your son's mama is your friend, but she ain't your enemy."

Fletcher was quiet, thinking of Olga saying their little monkey doesn't know how to lie.

Night fell on their drive back. Fletcher was eager to get back home and knew he had missed the last ferry. His place now was to keep Indicca and Cricket stable while they found Bo D and got him back on his feet. As he and Pops pulled in, Chester approached the Jeep as if he had been waiting.

"Mr. Fletcher, call come for you about forty minutes ago. From your daughter." He handed Fletcher a note.

Fletcher rushed, fearing the worst for Bo D.

"Auntie Olga had a mild stroke," Florida said on the phone.

"What?"

"God is good: The Twins were with her. They had just got back to the house from school shopping. She was sitting on the couch and the left side of her face went limp."

"Can she talk?

"Oh yeah. She can still talk. Mainly affected her left arm. Doctors say that could change for the better with therapy."

"Where is she?"

"Out at Phoebe North. They keeping her at least five to seven days."

"You all right?"

"I'm fine. When you coming?"

"Be home in about four hours."

"OK—You drive safe through all them little speed trap towns."

Beneath a country dark Sapelo sky, with hands still smelling of fish, Fletcher sat tense and worried in Chester's cousin's boat headed for the mainland. He was so concerned for Olga that he'd forgotten to ask for an update on Bo D.

During the commotion, Pops had hopped a ride to Saint Simons, and Fletcher regretted not saying a proper goodbye.

Light from a small oil lamp lit his driver's sable face. As he turned the boat around, Fletcher was mesmerized by an electric green and blue light show in the water.

"Them's sea sparkle," the driver explained, "that's a algae and they glow attract they predator's predator."

"Never seen it, but I heard about that," Fletcher said.

"On the island us say—*the enemy of my enemy be my friend.*"

Driving along 82-West back to Putney, black trees and a deep cobalt sky formed a tunnel pulling Fletcher back through towns he knew only through stories: Willacoochee, Alapaha, Enigma, and Ty Ty. He rolled down his window. Night wind blew on his face but could not blow through his tenseness.

He should have stayed home. At a time when Olga needed him most, he's off gallivanting like a twenty-year-old. And yet, there was no denying, Pops had shed light on a few things. Fletcher had been his own enemy long enough.

The old man made a lot of sense and had used three words foreign to Fletcher: *your son's mama.*

Beyond those in his family, Fletcher thought of all the men he knew lost to the mess Pops listed. If his son wanted to meet him, how could he stand in the way of that blessing?

30

〜

"Good to see you, Big Sis," Fletcher said softly, not sure if he should sit or stand.

"Good to be seen—not viewed," Olga mumbled. Her words had lost their pep and lyrical follow-through.

She attempted a smile that slid down the left side of her face, and a stream of drool escaped. Florida caught it with a tissue. Fletcher turned away. The woman who helped raise him was not there. He felt selfish and ashamed to be looking for the other sister instead of finding a tissue to wipe drool from this sister's mouth.

"Sit, Fletcher," Olga said. "Tell me 'bout Sap-lo. Isa-kiah?"

"Afraid not." Fletcher pulled up a chair. "My one and only source told me I came too late. But you know, nothing beats a failure—"

"—but a try," Olga said. "Glad you went."

"Seem like I needed to be here, so you'd behave yourself."

Olga smirked again, dismissing him with a shaky wave. He had given his Altovise and Siman worries over to the ocean to handle and it sent back an answer. Those matters paled in comparison to seeing his sister this way, in a hospital bed.

Florida held a cup. "Here, Auntie Olga, drink some water."

"Too loud. Not deaf," she grimaced, "already had water."

"Have some more." Florida was stern, gently touching the straw to Olga's lips.

"Yes, ma'am." Olga took a sip, drooling again. "Got a hole in my mouth."

Fletcher, with hands clasped and elbows on knees, cast his eyes down. He never liked hospitals, and after Maletha's death, didn't care if he ever set foot in one again. Maletha left far too soon, only sixty-two. Never even saw retirement. He and Olga were in good enough health not to have spent much time inside these bare, sterile walls. He would've at least framed the windows in a nice warm wood.

"Diiing-dooong." Altovise walked in, singing softly, holding a bouquet.

"Come-on, Avonlady." Olga perked up.

Fletcher stood as Olga slurred under Florida's heavy sigh. "Altovise, meet Florida—about time."

"A pleasure to meet you, Florida." They shook hands.

"I'll see if I can find a vase," Florida said, walking out quickly.

"Thank you," Altovise said.

"Smell like glads." Olga's right hand shook as she reached for the flowers.

Altovise laid them across her chest. "You know I had to bring your favorite, lavender and chartreuse, of all colors."

"Hard-to-find," Olga said, gently touching the flowers, then added after a pause, "Florida will come 'round in time." She pointed. "But—you two found middle ground?"

"Not for you to worry over," Fletcher said. He had returned to his answering machine filled with messages from Altovise, which he had yet to return. That all had little meaning now.

"That's right," Altovise said, "right now we need to focus on you."

"No," Olga said, "on Bo D—"

"They don't have a vase big enough," Florida interrupted.

"No problem," Altovise gathered up the glads. "I'll find one and bring these by the house maybe?"

"That'll be fine," Fletcher said, averting Florida's scoff.

"They want us to leave so you can get some rest, Auntie Olga," Florida said.

"Can't rest," Olga said, "need Bo D update."

"All right. I can see you not gone leave this alone." Florida pulled out a notepad and flipped through. "Terrence has been out there about a month."

She paused, used a tissue to wipe drool from Olga's mouth and continued.

"Praise God for Indicca. He was still texting her regularly for a while. But now she hasn't heard from him in over a week. He's been keeping up his child support checks; she just don't know where he is." She choked on her words. "So this morning I filed a missing person report."

"Missing person?" Fletcher asked.

"That's right." Florida tucked the pad in her purse. "Been over seventy-two hours and he's missing, ain't he? So they should be looking for his car all around southwest Georgia right now."

"We'll find him," Olga said.

"He ought to get in touch," Florida added, "'cause both me and Indicca texted him right away about the stroke. He didn't reply to me. Just texted back 'Damn' to Indicca."

"Our Bo D is scared," Olga said, and no one spoke for a long moment.

"I just hope he won't stop paying for his phone," Fletcher said, "to have more money for drugs."

"Terrence got plenty money," Florida said, her voice as thin as tissue. "He cashed out his 401(k)."

"What!" Fletcher said.

"That's right."

"How you find that out?" Fletcher asked.

"Auntie Olga not the only one with intel sources. Plus Terrence got savings, so he can afford his phone. He's just ignoring us."

"Told Fletcher bout Loblolly?" Olga asked.

"Getting ready to." Florida sniffed and rubbed her eyes with a knuckle. "It's that fancy rehab place, Ourdaddy—"

Olga turned toward her niece's voice, slowly extending her right hand, which Florida accepted.

"Not to worry," Olga said.

Florida patted Olga's hand. "Right now I'm gone talk to the nurse about your prescription list." She turned to Fletcher. "So I'll call you later, Ourdaddy," and she walked out past Altovise.

Olga closed her eyes, resting her head on the pillow.

Altovise moved to the bedside and whispered, "You sleep tight, Olga. See you tomorrow."

Olga's nod was barely perceptible. Fletcher gently stroked his sister's feet through the covers. Then he saw Altovise out to her car, gladiolas in hand.

☙

Earlier that same night, in Waycross, Bo D was on Day 32. LaChondra scored oxy for him at Hooper, so his Altoids tin was stocked. She was on night shift rotation, so he was alone. Balmy June night air felt good on his skin. He did some jubilating in the library parking lot, watching people drop off books: dads with kids, teenagers, elders. No one noticed him, even in a black car with red racing stripes running along the sides. He and the car, shrouded by night, were invisible.

As he walked toward the library with his stack of books, a text came in from Indicca.

> IB: Auntie Olga had a stroke. Left side
> paralyzed but otherwise she OK.
> At Phoebe North. We need you to come home.
> Please.
>> BD: damn
> IB: Shieka miss you. 🖤 Me too. 🦋

His highball was full force now, telling him they were all better off without his drama. But Auntie Olga. Even a stroke was no match for her. He inhaled deeply, spreading what he'd come to call his Holy Trilogy across all bodily systems. He dropped books in the return slot and walked one block down to Flash Foods for more beer to go with the pizza he had planned for dinner.

An older Black man approached him at the corner, begging. Bo D put five dollars in his pie pan. "Mare-sea, mon-frair," the man said.

Bo D exited the store carrying a Miller Lite six-pack. Somehow struck by the man's aura and his bad French, he offered to buy him dinner at Pizza Hut.

He had not considered having the man's strong smell in close quarters. As his passenger settled in, Bo D went around, rolling down windows.

"—looky at you." The man rubbed cracked, sooty hands across the dashboard. "Here come the king! Your solid upbringing is in these here red leather seats."

"Not leather. Authentic vinyl." Bo turned the key, already feeling nauseated at rancid urine and foul breath filling the air.

The man ranted for one mile to Pizza Hut. As Bo D figured, they were refused sit-down service, so he bought two pizzas to go and shared his Miller Light, using the Mustang's hood as a table. The man's stench mixed with onions and pepperoni and repulsed Bo D. He pushed his pizza box over toward the man, who grabbed it.

"KING is here!" He gulped pizza and slurped beer. "Once upon a time   I was like you   young king   testing these waters   Good folk.   my family   fuck them.   I made River Street my domicile—"

"You talking about River Street in Savannah?"

"—she was queen to my king played a little mouth organ for our subjects." Pizza oozed from the corners of his mouth, muffling his words. And there were so many words.

Bo D stepped farther back and looked away. Another text came in from his mother. Same info as Indicca's with a lot more words and emojis. His highball kept her at bay. She was definitely better off without him.

His dinner guest paused to swallow, then went on. "You cruise past your subjects like you somebody." He rapped knuckles on the hood. "Bat car gone bring a pretty penny when you ain't got one."

"You crazy, man!" Bo D yelped. "Never selling this car."

"Never say never." The man gently stroked the side mirror. "Vintage from the Bat Cave   '67? '68?"

"'69."

"Yeeeessss! Yeeesss!" The man did a quick step in place. "1969! Thirty years after bat car was born   I'm in the air for real   watching the millennium die   with my mouth organ on River Street   manufacturing hardship   just so I could overcome   plain life wasn't hard enough   for this Negro man   so selfish I still won't give me a chance   properly armed with facts about myself in order to survive   if I'm looking for sobriety first   that ain't happening   you got to know the difference   between triggers and excuses "

Triggers and excuses, jargon Bo D knew from his first time in rehab, when he was sixteen. How many hours had this half-sane street philosopher spent in rehab programs, wasting his good family's money?

"No excuses!" The man yelled, "playing Russian roulette with six bullets   misfire   wasn't my time   up against yourself   but you can't beat yourself by yourself   you have to have a higher power so they say   have the willingness to live instead of the voracity to die"

The man carefully sat the empty beer can near his foot, crushed it, and slipped it in his raincoat pocket.

"Pretty penny!"

He talked and talked, guzzled and slurped, until pizzas and beer were gone, each time crushing a can. Bo D was afraid he'd choke. He tucked one pizza box under his arm like an oversize book.

"I was like you king." He backed away, wagging a finger. "But you ain't like me   not yet   got no PhD in hard knocks."

Bo D spotted a police car cruising past like breakthrough pain, as the man raged on.

"White pillagers pay high bounty for the new black slave   months and years   and life $600K 900K   many millions to keep me locked up   for however long   can't deal with me out here."

He spread his arms, looking around. His pizza box fell. The police car circled back.

"But looky here Mr. Charlie!" he whispered, fist-beating his chest, "here's me   black son of a bitch   never been behind your bars not one day." He pinched air between his thumb and index finger, and looked directly at Bo D. "We know young blood   we know the only difference between you me and our in-car-cee-rated brothers is the thickness of the bars."

Pizza Hut diners walked to their cars—mocking heads turning. Bo D hoped the man would not vomit.

The police car hovered.

"You got a place to sleep tonight?" Bo D asked. "Can I drive you somewhere?"

"You out here faking   I did that too   king for a while   king for a day   king for a minute   king is dead ding dong."

He lumbered away, rank, ghostly gray against asphalt and street-light, yelling over his shoulder, "fuck you king   drive your bat car   back to your side   I hear mama calling you—" He nearly fell hurling the pizza box and disappeared into the nothingness of night.

Bo D turned and saw two officers approaching on foot, one shin-ing a flashlight in his face.

"Eeeve-nin," said the one with the light.

"Evening," Bo D said, squinting but keeping his hands out in front of him, palms out.

"We have to bother you for some I.D."

"Is there something wrong, officer?" He'd had only one beer. His guest had finished the other five and taken the evidence with him. But what if they searched his car?

"I.D. please-suh."

Bo D slowly pulled his license from his wallet. The other officer, who seemed younger, read it.

"Yeah," he said. "That-there's him. Terrence Fowler."

The senior officer lowered his beam. "Mr. Fowler, your family filed a missing person report on you. Seeing as how there ain't no crime in buying a bum a pizza, we won't take you in, but you get in touch with your family ASAP."

"I will," Bo D said, being careful not to glance toward his car. "Thank you, officer."

"You have a nii-iice nii-iight and be safe out here."

Bo D's knees felt weak, but not too weak, because even his waning highball was just that good. Still, nothing shakes a blissful oxy high like a cop's flashlight in your face.

Not having his car searched was just dumb luck. But now he was on the radar in Waycross. He could drive two hours north to States-boro, or an hour south to Valdosta. He started the engine. No matter where he went, for a Black man, there was no such thing as lying low enough to be completely safe from police. His Mach 1's roar swad-dled that worry like a mother's voice, fighting with the homeless man's stench and words clinging to everything inside the car: *a pretty penny when you ain't got one.*

"Fuck that!" Bo D said out loud. "Money may get low, but it'll never get that low."

He drove to an empty self-serve car wash. His knee bounced. He reached for his stash in the glove box; crushed and snorted, then licked powder residue from the back of his hand, a familiar, bitter embrace.

Using paper towels and window cleaner, he wiped down his pas-senger seat, seat belt, and dashboard. From a vending machine he bought a bottle of air freshener and sprayed the interior, top to bot-tom, and finished up with a thorough vacuum.

When he was in Albany, he could drive five or ten minutes to any one of many kinfolk who would take him in or take him home—to his mother. He didn't need that, or an end game. He felt good about the missing person report, proof that he was beating the snitches. The streets were a test, his true rite of passage. And he would never be like gray-haired pizza man, a lifetime out here, his arms like tree limbs gnarled and knotted from shooting up. *Got no PhD in hard knocks.* Bo D was a master at tweak and balance: his highballs, his car, his life. He would stay far ahead of rock bottom.

In order to do that he needed to put distance between him and everything familiar, especially the party house. It was only a matter of time before somebody came at him when he was least expecting it—on behalf of the family.

He filled up with gas and picked up Highway 16 North to I-75 North. In about three hours he'd be in the Atlanta area. A CME dealer had given him a solid referral in Decatur, where hours would grow into days; days into months.

Act III

~

what didn't you do to bury me
but you forgot I was a seed

~ Dinos Christianopoulos

31

Day 124 was a Tuesday. September 4. But for Bo D, days no longer had names. Names were not vital to a man in complete overhaul. He was a much earlier model now, pure reptilian, answering primal needs: feeding, fighting, fleeing, and fucking. No reason to include family in that list. He had a new family. He had moved around metro Atlanta inside a sad, hopeless freedom that had become his new skin. Whatever had tied him to blood he had deposited weeks ago, into book return slots at Lee Avenue library. He had a new party house (even more grungy than Fellowship Alley) and new friends, but he was the same. One hundred and eighty miles from family was far enough; and three months was time enough to get used to turning a deaf ear to his mother's messages sitting in his full voice mail box; and ignoring texts from Uncle Siman, who wouldn't give up; and to not care about all the messages he had not sent to Indicca saying *I'm still OK!* When he felt regret around Auntie Olga's stroke after they had such a good visit that last time: *a weed is any plant growing on its own terms*, he tweaked his highball and moved on. Turning his back on Cricket was hard. His necklace was ever present now, solely because the monkey whispered Cricket's sweet voice: *You got your monkey, Daddy! . . . Way-o we go-wing?* For all he knew she had found her *r*'s by now and sounded completely different. Cricket had been his motivation to send Indicca monthly checks until he came up to Decatur. He switched to money orders that couldn't be traced. People who think he is dependent on drugs don't understand the concept. His Holy Trilogy was his second dependent, after Cricket, and would not be put on a back burner. Spoke a language he couldn't ignore. *Get your ass up NOW and take care of business for us.*

How was he any different from Walter Fowler? Too often he wandered through the maze that question created, a dead-end street paved with overwhelming guilt for leaving Indicca and Cricket. Those were barbed wires not even his most well-tweaked highball could handle. And so he stopped asking questions, and stopped visiting answers. It was all becoming easier and easier.

His little tally notebook was looking raggedy, but he still marked every day.

His phone had gone without a charge for nearly four days, and when he finally plugged in at a Caribou Coffee, he was surprised to find several voice mails from LaChondra. She wanted his stuff out of her garage, and must've been serious because she didn't text.

He called her back.

"Hey! Yeah, sorry about that," he said, "had to charge my phone. You know it bees that way sometime."

"Ain't no problem, long as you come get your shit out my garage." It was actually good to hear her voice.

"You can just throw that stuff away. I don't even know what I left there."

"Fuck that, Bo D. I ain't your private garbage collector. You need to come take care of your business yourself."

"OK! Chill! Didn't know it meant that much to you."

"Besides," her voice softened and he imagined her black-lined eyes and belly button ring, "you been gone a long time."

"Sooo! This is about you missing me, huh?"

"Ain't nobody said nothing about missing *you*, but—"

"But what?"

"But yeah, I guess so—just git your ass back here. You working?"

"Working hard at not working."

"Then you ain't got nothing else to do."

He felt strong in their decision for him to come in three days. He knew he could slip in and out of Waycross overnight and the family would be clueless. While he was at it, he texted Neeshah, an alley house regular who's always down for a good time. He still owed her some oxy, and he liked to pay his debts. At the rate he was going, his nest egg would be gone in another two months, so he had started skimming off the top, selling from the oxy and weed he scored. This left him well stocked for paying back Neeshah.

Late on Day 127, he drove across familiar ground: the CME tracks on North Davis Street.

A few folks sat on porches in muggy September air, swatting bugs and kicking off their weekend. Too tired to care about hiding his car, he parked around the corner from Fellowship Alley and walked to the party house, carrying a KFC bucket and beer. Music, talking, and laughter spilled out onto the tiny porch where, as usual, a man sat smoking.

Bo D stopped, placed an order, and waited.

"Yo man!" the smoker said, his red-tipped cigarette glowing as a joint and payment exchanged hands. "I ain't seen you in a month of Sundays! Where you been, man?"

"You seen Neeshah?" Bo D asked.

"She here." His words rode an exhale of puffy smoke. "Y'all need anythang else let me know. Welcome back, man!"

Bo D made his way through the crowded kitchen, a few hands reached for chicken from his open bucket. There were many new faces, and he was glad not to have to talk to them. Most of the regulars he saw were too stoned to care who he was after so many months. He accepted a joint.

"Hey!" a beer-hugging man yelled over loud music, "ain't your name Terrence?"

Squinting from swirling smoke, with no interest in this talking face, Bo D took a beer and piled a paper plate high with hot wings.

"You don't remember me, do you?" The young man spoke in a rapid slur, moving closer. "I-was, I-was a year behind you at Monroe. My-brother, my-brother name J. D. Breedlove. He-graduated-with-you. Yeah. Your name Terrence Fowler. I know you."

"Shut up, fool!" said a slightly more sober voice. "He go by Bo D, errbody know that! Where you been, Bo D? Ain't seen you in a long time."

Bo D took a long toke and passed the joint.

J. D. Breedlove's brother wasn't finished. "What the fuck kinda name is Bo D anyway? Bo D. What the fuck—"

"Told you to shut up!" the sober voice said. "Where you been that you don't know that stand for Bold Daddy?" He bumped fists and laughed with his buddies. "Yeah, Bold Daddy is back! You gittin ready to do some triple time on that backroom mattress? That's his office, y'all." More laughs and fist bumps.

On a night like this, Bo D hated his nickname—sliding off the parched lips of drunks and addicts. But what could he expect from a nickname with origins like his?

He paused outside the bedroom door. Even though Neeshah seemed to be a permanent fixture at the duplex before he left, he hardly knew her—had only hooked up once before because she had scored oxy and was in a generous mood. He liked to pay his debts, even if it took a few months.

Through a window, streetlight flowed in, and an oscillating fan circulated sticky air smelling like Safeguard soap. He did like that about Neeshah. She had a foul mouth, but she was clean. Nothing had changed.

"Long time no see." Neeshah's pillow voice was hoarse and dry. "I'm ready for you."

Bo D rested his beer and hot wings on the bedside table, littered with remains of other parties. Neeshah didn't move, breathing heavily behind him. Ever-present music quaked through walls and door, lyrics and beat becoming one sound. Bo D swigged beer and licked chicken grease from his fingers.

Neeshah stirred. "That smell good. You brought me some?"

"Nope. Plenty more out there." He wiped his hands on new Sean John jeans, then peeled them off along with shirt and Calvin Klein briefs. Shopping made him feel better and meant he didn't have to find a laundromat. Beer slid through his veins, chilled and buoyant, releasing him of cares that would keep him from joining Neeshah between the sheets.

Payback pills rattling inside his Altoid tin triggered Neeshah to sit up on her elbows, grinning. She swallowed a pill as he lit up a half-smoked joint, blowing a plume of smoke toward her face.

"Ummmmm, that smell good, too," she cooed accepting the joint.

In early morning darkness, the room's sweltering air had not changed. Neeshah slept loudly, each foul puff made Bo D happy that this time she had not climbed all over him, even though the rest of her smelled antibacterial. They simply shared the bed. He went in and out of sinking and nodding, his body a heavy plank somewhere beneath him unable to move when there came a hard knock on the door.

Bo D thought he heard his name, but whenever he added Viagra to his mix, it took longer to gather himself into one mostly coherent space. But this was definitely his name being shouted. Neeshah was even slower to wake up.

"Bo D! You in there? It's T. I'm coming in—"

And before Bo D could respond, Tyrone flipped on the ceiling light. Too bright.

"What the fuck—?" Bo D said, moving slowly. "—You crazy, man?"

"Clearly I have lost my mind," Tyrone said, passing Bo D his jeans. "And you're coming with me. Get dressed."

Neeshah struggled to sit up.

"Ah HELLLL naw!" Bo D clambered out of bed, naked, and slammed into Tyrone. "You crazy motherf—"

Tyrone spun Bo D around, pinning him against the wall.

"Calm down, T. And trust that you're in no shape to come at me right now. So. I'll let you go. You get dressed. We leave together. Cool?"

Bo D swayed and Tyrone loosened his grip. "Let me go," he snapped.

When Tyrone let go, Bo D shoved him against the wall. Tyrone calmly recovered, showing his empty hands. The friends stared at each other, one with contempt, one with compassion.

Quickly turning, Bo D did not fumble as he wrapped his lower half in a bedsheet.

"Ain't this some shit—" Neeshah said, naked, leaning against the opposite wall.

"Excuse me," Tyrone interrupted, turning his back to her. "What's your name?"

"None of yo GOT-damn BEEN-ness," Neeshah hissed. "He may be scared-a yo ass but I ain't sca—"

"Her name is Neeshah," Bo D answered, looking around for clothes.

"Thank you," Tyrone said to Bo D, gesturing toward her. "With all due respect, Nee-sha, I kindly ask that you get dressed and leave."

"So *that's* what this is." Her laugh was scornful as she stumbled, pulling on jeans. "Bold Daddy my ass—let me get the fuck up outta here before I catch me some AIDS—"

"Save it," Tyrone said firmly, swinging the door open. She wobbled through, stopped, and turned. Tyrone stepped back.

"Y'all Dukeses think y'all all that! Y'all ain't shit. Yo granddaddy ain't nothing but a straight-up akaholic. My uncle know all about—"

"What you say, bitch?" Bo D sprang to life as Neeshah staggered off.

"Nothing, T." Tyrone closed the door. "She said nothing."

"Didn't sound like nothing to me!"

"Whoa, T, your nose is bleeding." Tyrone looked around.

Bo D lifted his hand to his nose as blood dripped onto the sheet.

"I'll be right back." Tyrone left quickly.

Bo D held his head back, gathered a ball of sheet, and pinched the soft part of his nose.

Tyrone walked back in. "Bathroom and kitchen out of everything."

"What you expect, Egyptian towels?" Bo D barked, wiping his nose with a wad of sheet.

"I see you got it under control."

Bo D's vibrating foot shook the bed as he glared at Tyrone's face. As usual, he itched, like every morning, but the commotion had distracted him from it.

"I won't leave here without you, T. One way or another," Tyrone said. "We'll take your car—I'll drive, come back tomorrow for my Camry. But we leave together."

Bo D cinched the sheet tighter around his waist. "You gone step out so I can get dressed or you hoping to get another look at my dick?"

"I'll be right outside the door. Don't tarry."

The hairs on Bo D's arms stood on end. He gazed from floor to door to window, which he knew was painted shut. He got dressed and saw that his Altoids tin was not in his backpack.

"Fuck," he hissed, "that heifer!"

He had paid her back, but that wasn't enough for Neeshah. Now he had nothing to see him through the night.

Tyrone fell in line behind him through the quiet house. Neeshah was nowhere to be found.

The Mach 1 smelled of sweat, beer, stale food, and cannabis ash. Bo D sank into his seat, shoes wading through fast-food trash that was spreading to the driver's side.

The morning was still. Tyrone exhaled, his hands on the steering wheel.

"Did you know that about G-pop?" Bo D asked.

"I still don't know. And neither do you," Tyrone said. "C'mon man. Why would we trust the word of a woman *that* pissed off *and* high?"

"Because she ain't got nothing to lose or gain by lying."

"Well T, if you believe her, you just have to ask him."

"I guess you think this is rock bottom?" Bo D said.

"I wouldn't know, but it looks to me like a good place to turn around."

Bo D opened the glove compartment.

"For real, T?" Tyrone said. "Are you seriously looking for pills in this moment?"

"Notebook," Bo D said flatly and flipped to his tally page under a rhythmic pattern of streetlights streaking by. He made a stroke for Day 128, aware that he stank; which only mattered because his former best friend was ignoring the fact that he was wearing brand-new clothes, and yet he stank.

"I just know it's damn good to see you in one piece. We've all been worried sick about you, man."

"Can you even drive a stick?" Bo D asked.

Tyrone laughed and started the engine. "Guess you gettin' ready to find out."

During the twenty-minute drive to Mock Road, Bo D nodded off, waking to Tyrone shaking him gently.

"Hey T, wake up, man. We home."

"And by the way," Bo D said, in a groggy voice, as if finishing a sentence he had started before he dozed off, "you won't have to bother picking up your Camry, 'cause it won't be there, or if it is, the tires and about everything else will be gone."

"That's why we drove the Mach 1," Tyrone said. "Have to take care of the Black Knight, right?"

"My car used to sit on that street all the time," Bo D said, "and didn't nobody mess with it 'cause they know me. But see—you? You ain't got it like that."

He may have been a failure at everything else, but the streets had become Bo D's expertise.

"Make yourself at home," Tyrone said as they entered the house. "Plenty to eat and drink in the fridge."

Bo D threw his backpack to the floor and collapsed onto Tyrone's black leather couch, taking off his shoes and socks. The curly-haired throw rug tickled. Like Tyrone's Airstream office, this room was an ensemble of sofa, chairs, rugs, and walls, black and gray tones held together by hammered and brushed gunmetal tables, cabinets, and shelves. Tyrone was the only guy Bo D knew with real framed art on his walls, each piece had a spotlight on a track attached to the ceiling. This was a page from a magazine and magnified Bo D's reality: almost everything he owned was crammed into his car.

"Be right back," Tyrone said, pulling out his phone.

Bo D listened outside Tyrone's bedroom door, missing a few words of a muffled conversation.

". . . yeah, yeah . . . fine . . . was there, just like she said . . . push back . . . not bad. He's here . . . come by tomorrow . . . don't worry Ms. Florida. I got him . . . later . . . and . . ."

Bo D quickly disappeared, running bathroom water, and met Tyrone seconds later in the hallway.

"So T." Tyrone smiled. "Fresh sheets on the guest bed, towels in this hall closet. You hungry? 'Cause I make a mean omelet."

"Not hungry, need some sleep," and more important, he wanted to know the name of the person who set him up.

"Sleep as long as you want. It's Saturday, so I don't have to go in until late afternoon—and—we do need to get what will be left of my car at some point."

Even in the air-conditioned coolness Bo D's skin was hot and itchy. There were only two people who knew he would be at the party house. He wanted to sleep standing up with cool shower water washing over him. Pickpocket Neeshah was bad-mouthing his family, so it had to be LaChondra. She was always safe because she didn't know anybody in the family. But before he left, she had been acting different. Getting too clingy. Somehow they got to her. Shouldn't have taken her call.

He woke from a fretful doze on what had been crisp sheets that reminded him of his mother's house, minus that sickening dryer sheet smell clinging to everything she touched. Now the sheets were clammy with sweat and a thin, salty saliva flooded his mouth. He needed to find as much of a highball as he could. Tyrone had no beer but probably expensive wine or tequila somewhere; plus the car keys were nowhere in sight. Bo D couldn't risk rummaging around for booze, but luckily still had his spare key hiding safely in his wallet behind his driver's license.

After digging through ashtrays, he singed fingers lighting a puny roach in his car. The nice long toke gave him an illusionary high.

His phone vibrated a text: Uncle Siman. The dude won't give up.

> SM: Hey Bo D—you there?
>
> BD: what up unc
>
> SM: So glad to hear from you!
> Sorry to text so early, but been
> trying all hours.
> Was worried.
> You OK?
>
> BD: yeah cool
> bout 2 make a change
> my buddy tyrone waiting 4 me

Bo D revved the Mach 1, hoping his loud muffler woke Tyrone.

As sunrise broke through pines, he drove back to Fellowship Alley. He had no choice. Withdrawal was knocking, and that was his best chance of scoring. When Tyrone came to pick up his car—if he was crazy enough to come looking for him—he would make him sorry. And LaChondra. A snitch. Fuck her.

Bo D knew that everybody was sure he was headed in the wrong direction. And that may be true, but at least *he* was at the wheel.

32

Trouble mostly chooses odd hours. Baby announcements and invitations to a graduation or wedding can afford to take their time, showing up in fancy envelopes. But severe chest pain, devious viruses, or strokes demand speed. Even email and texting fall short, so the telephone is still king.

All hands were three months into a new regime after Olga's stroke, and now Fletcher's heart pounded as he reached toward his nightstand, knowing that a ringing phone at 2:00 A.M. is never good news.

"Ourdaddy." Florida's voice was strangely calm.

"What happened?" Fletcher's feet hit the floor.

"Bo D left that party house about twenty minutes ago too stoned to be driving and nobody knows where he went."

"On my way."

Murky September air was still and quiet. Machinelike, powered by a dread emanating from his core, Fletcher somehow arrived at his car. He joined nephew Nathaniel, along with four others, Florida, and Tyrone in Olga's living room, car keys in hands.

Olga stood slowly, her left arm hanging loosely, her right hand on her cane. She sounded tired and yet her voice was a comfort. Fletcher knew this was too much for her and also knew he was powerless to stop her.

Florida did the talking. "The call came around one forty-five from LaChondra at the CME house."

"Wasn't she the one helped get him to come back?" Nathaniel asked.

"Yeah, she was his inspector at Hooper," Florida said. "She heard him say he was up in Decatur all this time; said Bo D was drunk—and had been smoking. They couldn't stop him from driving off."

"Why didn't she follow him?" Fletcher asked.

"She had been watching him but went to the bathroom, and when she came out, he was gone."

"Yeah," Florida said. "Both police and sheriff on the lookout for his car, and we called Loblolly. They got a bed for him and an aid car that can pick him up and take him straight there."

"Why not to the hospital?" Fletcher asked.

"Loblolly *is* a private hospital and rehab," Olga said, "got everything out there."

Using texts and calls, they quickly expanded into a Dukes family posse and divvyed up areas Bo D frequented, scouring within a fifty-mile radius.

Florida said, "Auntie Olga and I will be here with cell and land lines open, plus connected to Loblolly's Aid Car. Don't y'all worry. We'll find him."

"Move out," Olga said.

Tyrone rode in the Fairlane with Fletcher.

"Maybe the whole thing with LaChondra and the HR director was a bridge too far," Tyrone said.

"Come again?" Fletcher said.

Tyrone explained how Florida arranged for her HR director friend to enlist LaChondra's help in getting Bo D back to Albany.

"I'm so sorry," Tyrone said, "I assumed you knew."

"Not your fault. Florida knew better than to tell me 'cause I'd never go along with it. Last thing you want to do is blindside an addict, even with the best intentions."

"Yes, sir, I see that now. And to make it worse, I'm the one who betrayed him, busting in on him like that. I was way out of line."

"You were trying the best way you knew how." Fletcher saw no point in harping on the issue. "When you dealing with addiction, you can get to a point where you'll try just about anything. And it's natural to be second-guessing, but I wouldn't if I were you. We'll find him."

They rode on in silence, under the weight of an unthinkable outcome.

For Fletcher, a memory is a pulsing mirage hanging on him like humidity in August. He can touch it with his whole being. Neither of them spoke as they drove along Newton Road past the airport. Fletcher unpacked visions of Bo D like delicate goods from a suitcase; he and Maletha rushed from waiting room to nursery, grandparents again, their only grandson a ten-pound-one-ounce newborn in Walter Fowler's arms, a man who in their minds was unworthy of such a gift.

﹖

They were headed to Bainbridge and sped through the flashing yellow light where Newton Road meets Lily Pond when Tyrone said, "Ah!" and drummed both hands on the dashboard.

"I know where he is, Mr. Fletcher!"

Fletcher made a U-turn, and made his way back to Highway 19 to Putney.

"You say he spends a lot of time out there?"

"Yessir, back in April, before all this, we talked about how we used to climb that old tree. Can't believe I didn't think of this before."

They drove past his house to the end of Sumac Road.

The Fairlane's headlights reflected in the Mach 1's shiny black finish parked under the oak tree.

Tyrone's fingers moved like lightning on his phone texting Florida. Fletcher left his headlights on and took a crowbar from under his seat.

Bo D lay on the backseat with all doors locked.

"T! Wake up, man! Wake up, T!" Tyrone's voice shivered as he banged on back windows while Fletcher smashed the driver's-side window and unlocked doors.

"Terrence!" Fletcher yelled, slapping Bo D's face.

Fletcher's hand trembled as he put two fingers on Bo D's neck. "He's alive. Wake up, Terrence! Wake up, son!" He rubbed four knuckles above the clammy, cold lips.

"Ms. Florida replied. They're on the phone with the Aid Car."

"Firehouse three minutes from here on Antioch," Fletcher said, using his sleeve to wipe vomit from Bo D's face. "Tell them we'll meet the Aid Car there."

Tyrone sent the text then spoke sternly. "Mr. Fletcher, let's move him to your car. Mach 1 may be low on gas."

When they lifted Bo D's limp body, an empty Altoids tin fell to the ground. Fletcher's voice strained and shook with each step. "Let's turn him on his side."

Tyrone slid into the backseat, cradling Bo D's head in his lap. Fletcher sped off.

Tyrone used his cell phone torch. "Pinpoint pupils—and you felt how he's clammy and chilled. Mixed oxy with booze and pot most likely. LaChondra said he calls that a highball, and that's good info for the doctors. Don't worry, Mr. Fletcher. We got him in time."

Fletcher gripped the steering wheel, steadily pushing the pedal to the floor. They sped along on fast exhaust, suspension, and tires that were all due to Bo D's prodding a few years ago. *C'mon G-pop, let's soup-up the 500!*

And now, Fletcher endured the longest three minutes of his life, sickened further by the fact that Bo D had driven right past his house while he was home.

Within the hour, Fletcher sat next to Florida in Loblolly's antebellum waiting room in their main house, converted to serve as ER and hospital. He wanted to call Altovise but couldn't expect Florida to hand over her cell phone, and he didn't dare leave her alone when she was looking for an opening to sneak a drink and smoke.

Her Bible, in its tan leather cover, was open on her lap. She was doing as her mother did in times of crisis, murmuring scripture and wringing her hands.

"Y'all did the phone tree to update your sisters?" Fletcher asked.

"Yeah, told them he gon be all right." She rocked back and forth. "Ourdaddy. Terrence gon be al—"

Fletcher put his hand on her shoulder as she shuddered with tears.

"He's alive," he said, "and that's more than a notion."

The suitcase of memories he unpacked earlier was now a house of spongy, crystalline walls where he walked from room to room, recollecting Bo D's twenty-three years. He regretted every hour they had recently spent feuding.

"How could I ignore the signs?" Florida said. "I hope God will forgive me for putting my only child out on the streets. In the rain."

"From what I understand," Fletcher said, "God has already forgiven you. Now you just need to forgive yourself."

Doctors gave him naloxone, and Bo D responded well. He would spend two to three days in the medical unit before they checked him into his cabin.

The sun was just rising when Fletcher and Florida pulled into Olga's driveway. Her house was lit up with breakfast and kinfolk. Fletcher wandered around, under the care of women once again.

With soppy eyes, Florida walked directly over to Olga and hugged her tightly. "God bless you, Auntie. You got Terrence into the right place."

"Top-notch docs. He'll do well. Once he gets past most folk out there being white except the help."

Olga ordered Florida to rest in her guest room and sent everybody else home. Then she and Fletcher sat in her study. She asked him to read out loud through a stack of brochures and flyers from Loblolly on crisis intervention, peer counseling, and suicide.

33

Bo D woke up. He breathed evenly, as if asleep, and kept his eyes closed. He smelled his mother's perfume, but other scents were still unfamiliar: bleachy sheets, distant food—pork chops this time—with weird spices. Nice bed, supported every part of his body. Many details slipped through his fingers of memory like water; from yesterday, and last week, or the past few months, and yet he had an odd feeling of déjà vu just before opening his eyes. He remembered his little tally notebook in his glove box. But where was his car?

He hesitated, knowing that his mom had been waiting for who knows how long. On a deep inhale he opened his eyes and saw a tall, stout white woman in a nurse's uniform, her back to him, head bent over a medical cart. She smelled like everything on her cart plus some kind of mint gum. Probably why he thought he smelled his mom.

This hospital room tried to pass for a nice hotel: high ceilings, hardwood floors, soft white walls, and everything else blue: drapes, comforter, and throw pillows. Bright sunlight seeped in around long, heavy drapes, mixing with the cold fluorescence. Rehab again. Like in a movie, he checked in with his mind: *Who is the president*: Barack

Obama; *What time is it?* No clock, no clue; *What day is it?* That was a good question.

"Nurse Reynolds?" Bo D said, sitting up slowly on his elbows, not sure why he remembered her name.

"Well, hello, Mr. Fowlerrr." The woman moved toward him, giving each *r* and each vowel more than its fair share. "How are you feee-lin today?"

"Like I could sleep twelve more hours."

"That's typical, but better if you get up and at 'em! Walk around our grounds after lunch, get some fresh air and exercise."

"My mom was in here, right?" He looked around.

"She *is* here—in the dining cabin, but no, she hasn't been in this room. Strict rule."

Sunlight overtook fluorescence as Nurse Reynolds turned off bedside lamps and seemed to have eight arms: flinging open curtains, fluffing pillows, filling nightstand cup with water, adjusting bed to a sitting position, and setting out a white bundle sealed in plastic.

"Not unusual that you're having spontaneous olfactive memory." Then she whispered, "Fancy words for smelling smells that aren't really there." Her eight hands disappeared into two that rested on her hips. "Just the other day I smelled that white paste from kindergarten. If you got it on your fingers—which you always did because you're five—it would dry and flake off like dandruff. You wouldn't know about that, since you're of the glue stick era," she snickered.

"Is anybody with her?" Bo D asked.

"Your mama? No-no. We only allow one visitor your first seventy-two hours while you settle in."

"What is this place again?"

"You are at Loblolly Grove: hospital, residential rehab ranch, and farm. Started by Dr. Gwen Yonkers twenty-five years ago." She returned to her cart, her back to Bo D, reciting her rote speech: "Access to the best docs and psychiatrists between the Panhandle and Atlanta." But all her words after "residential" became background noise as Bo D's heart raced, his mouth went dry, and he gasped for air. He was trapped here. He tried to remember what had happened as the walls and ceiling began to spin and the nurse's warbled voice seemed to be underwater.

He gladly gave in to Nurse Reynolds' big hands pressing the middle of his back and just above his navel, lifting him to sit up straight. "OK, Terrence." She put pressure on his diaphragm. "You're OK, breathe so you make my hand rise." Her warbled voice was firm and soothing, becoming more and more clear as she coaxed him.

She eased his head onto the pillow. Her octopus hands were back as she coached his breathing and made more notes on the clipboard. He coughed and recovered, even more eager for answers.

"What day is it?" He strained. "And how—long have I been here?"

"Today is Thursday, September 13, 2012." She looked directly into his eyes and spoke slowly, as if he might not understand. "You're in the Main House now—checked in about 3:00 Monday morning. Any of that ring a bell yet?"

"No!"

"It will. Give it time," she said.

She handed him water and watched as he drank, then refilled.

"You're OK, few more sips, and breathe into your belly. It'll pass; walking around, having some food, that'll help." She stared straight at him again. "You may have trouble remembering certain things or recall things out of order. Frustrating but temporary. The past three days will slowly come back to you. You had a rough start, but that's all behind you now."

Bo D felt at his collar and blurted, "My necklace! Where's my necklace? It's a gold chain with a little peach seed monkey—"

"No worries. Your family was given all your jewelry when you checked in."

She hung the clipboard on a hook. "OK! Take your time getting dressed, and after lunch you'll jump right into your first session with Dervin, who is fa-aantastic by-the-way." She pushed the cart toward the door, whispering, "Red button by the commode if you need us."

And she was gone.

Bo D practiced bench-press breathing into his core. This stopped the spinning walls and ceiling. He kicked off bedcovers, glad a bathroom was right there. When did he ever own matching pajamas? At a few points in the room, giant red buttons labeled NURSE could only be for people who keep their teeth in a jar.

Behind a sliding closet door sat evidence of his mother's handiwork, a duffel bag filled with somebody else's new clothes: two pairs of Lee jeans, a pair of twill cargo pants, Champion hoodie and sweats, another PJ set, two pairs of Everlast basketball shorts, fresh six-pack Fruit of the Loom T-shirts, two six-packs of Jockey boxer briefs, crew socks, a pair of Reebok running shoes. And a new black backpack that would never work. He had to have his camouflage.

He walked out dressed in sweats and sneakers. At least he would not see a soul he knew, except his mother, who was sitting on a couch facing the archway he walked through. She rushed to meet him.

"Hey, Terrence," she said softly, the way she spoke whenever he stayed home sick. He expected that voice back in the room when he opened his eyes.

"So you here to visit the sick and shut in." He couldn't look at her.

She pulled him gently into a hug, whispering, "You listen to me. Like I told you that last time you went down this road, there ain't no shame in it. If you broke a arm or leg you'd do what it takes to heal it. This is no different."

She held his shoulders at arm's length. Her perfume comforted him, but still, he pulled away.

"How you feel?" she asked.

"I feel OK. You got my necklace?"

"Yep."

"And my camouflage backpack Cricket gave me with a little notebook inside?"

"All in your room at home. Safe and sound."

She said, *your room* like he would ever step foot in *her* house again. What did she think? They could go on from here as if she didn't put his stuff out in the rain? He did remember that. But in spite of everything, here she was smiling and trying. How could he hold that against her?

"Why you got me all new stuff?" he asked, feeling like memories were puzzle pieces thrown high in the air.

"So everything fits OK?" She stepped back, examining him. "You were in no shape to shop, so I did it for you. Your things we found in your car were beyond dirty so—" her eyes became watery.

"That's all right, Ma." He guided her to sit back down, handing her the tissue box from the coffee table. "It's all good. Thank you for the clothes."

"I know I bought the wrong stuff, but once you get better, we can go shopping for all them brands you like."

She had put a few puzzle pieces in a pile, but they were not making a picture yet.

"You'll get past this." She stifled tears. "I know you got a lot of questions, but let's eat first, OK? They said you wouldn't have much of an appetite yet, but you have to eat."

She was right, he had a lot of questions and even thinking about food repulsed him. He wanted to keep making her feel better so he said, "Yeah-yeah—let's eat."

Knotty pine walls sent voices bouncing cafeteria style. Everyone busing tables and serving food was Black. A mix of old and young— all white—sat at chunky wooden tables in high-back chairs eating and talking. What would become all too familiar in the coming weeks was right now a game to Bo D: Who was the addict and who was the family member?

They took their seats and a young man walked up, looking like Malcolm X with sandy-colored shoulder-length locs. He introduced himself as Dervin and told Bo D that his first group session would be at 14:00 hours. "Plenty of time to take a walk with Mom around the grounds before she leaves. Nice to meet you, Mrs. Fowler."

He shook her hand and left.

"That's a breath of fresh air," Florida said. "Somebody Black that's not the kitchen help." She turned to watch him walk away. "Educated young brother. Cute, too."

"OK, Ma—TMI—" They both laughed.

"These pork chops don't look half bad," Florida said. "You need to eat, Terrence."

"Not hungry."

"I know, but eating right is a part of any kind of healing—"

"Ma!" He shouted and pounded the table. He and his mother looked around but no one else had bothered.

He bit into a dinner roll.

"That's all right. I understand," she said.

"I don't think you do, Ma. I don't even think you *can*."

"Try me," she said, putting her fork and knife down.

"What happened to me in those seventy-two hours I just lost? And why did you put my stuff out in the rain?"

"OK. So—" She pursed quivering lips, hands stacked as if in confession, and went on. "The doctors said you might have trouble remembering things, but that'll pass. And," she added a bouncing knee, "that night you're talking about happened back on May third; a day I wish to God I could take back. Believe me, I thought I was helping, but just made matters worse. I'm so, so sorry, Terrence. So, so sorry."

In this strange place, surrounded by foreign food and white people, he was too tired to fight but couldn't stop himself from going further. "Then let's just start with the past seventy-two hours: Were you, or somebody, with me that whole time?"

"None of us were allowed in your room after you were admitted. They call that the mandatory induction period. But every chance I got I made them nurses give me a blow-by-blow. We were so lucky we didn't lose you."

Bo D sank down into the chair, as if he wanted to disappear as his mother kept talking.

"Me and Auntie Olga did the intake assessment while Ourdaddy and Indicca sat in the waiting room. Her mama kept Cricket that night. But let me back up. It all started when somebody called from that CME house and—"

"You mean LaChondra called," he said firmly, "and y'all turned a good friend into a snitch."

"We all did what we had to do, Terrence. And it's pretty clear that young lady thinks of herself as more than just your friend—but that's neither here nor there—we appreciated her help."

"Go on."

"About nine or ten of us split up and went out looking for you. Ourdaddy and Tyrone found you—"

"Damn!" Bo D pushed his chair away. "Tyrone was there."

"The family thanks God for Tyrone. He figured out where you were. Him and Ourdaddy found you and drove you to that firestation on Antioch, and the Loblolly Aid Car was waiting when y'all got there and brought you straight here. We sent Tyrone home 'cause he just wasn't handling seeing you like that. He told me to tell you he's sorry for the way things went down the other night in the CME."

"Yeah. He ought to be sorry."

"Terrence. It takes a true friend to do what Tyrone did. Why should he be apologizing for saving your life? Will you please call him? Let him come see you?"

"Just finish your story, Ma."

Bo D rubbed his face with both palms. He could almost piece together driving to the oak tree, but nothing before or after was clear until he woke to the backside of Nurse Reynolds.

"Nurses said you tried to leave to avoid that withdrawal."

"So what kept me from leaving?"

"You were too uncomfortable. Irritated, snappy, couldn't sleep. It was like you had the flu, you were real weak. But even if you had the strength, ain't no buses way out here, and you didn't have your car. I thank God for all of that, too. So they started you on Suboxone, and that knocked most of the symptoms back.

"It's been so hard not seeing you for the past three days."

Pork chops, mashed potatoes, and green beans, which weren't half bad, sat mostly untouched. His mother stopped talking, as if mentally walking back through the night had worn her out. Again.

They rose from the table in unison and Bo D said, "I'm sorry, Ma."

"I know."

Loblolly's wide stone staircase felt important and led down to a football field lawn. Summer air was shifting. Bo D could almost believe fall was coming—and yet tomorrow the same air could be hot and filled with humidity, as close to rain as possible without raining. But for now, cool air sat lightly on his skin.

Mother and son stood looking up at the two-story wooden mansion, painted haint blue, trimmed in white, a far cry from Pine Avenue Rehab where Bo D went in high school. At least he hadn't been the only Black face in those sessions.

The deep front porch had a row of white and black rocking chairs between five white columns with two more flanking double front doors. There were six floor-to-ceiling windows on the first floor and five shorter ones upstairs.

"Easy to see this was once a plantation," Florida said, "like them fancy quail hunting resorts you see in magazines in a doctor's office—so we would never have a reason to set foot in a place like this. But it sure is beautiful. And I heard they did all kinds of ceremonies—Indian and African—to bless the land, since slaves lived here."

"So what am I doing here?" he asked.

"Auntie Olga. She knows the head psychiatrist who started this place, worked with her in the Movement. Took one phone call."

"How come we can't use that place on Pine?"

"This is one of the best in the country, Auntie Olga said. Maybe if you had been here before, you wouldn't be here now."

"Yeah, so that means this cost a fortune."

"Look at me."

He looked away.

"Terrence."

He turned reluctantly.

"That is *not* for you to worry about, you hear? Auntie Olga is helping me take care of this because she wants to and she can afford to. When you're ready—and *if* you want to—you can come back home to figure out your next step. If you can forgive me for what I did, then we will move on from there, because 325 Dove Cove Drive will always be there for you, you understand?"

Bo D recalled Step Nine—Making Amends—and figured, Why not start there this time?

"OK, Ma. And I hope you can forgive me for all the crap I probably said to you that night."

"We both said things to be sorry for," she said.

"You mean like *hypocrite grits*?" he teased.

"Of all things," she shook her head, smiling, "leave it to you to remember that. Thank God it's in the rear view now."

She put her arm around him, and he automatically tensed up. She stepped away and strolled farther out, alone, looking around. Another puzzle piece fell into place. One that needed an answer.

"Ma?" He walked toward her, still a bit wobbly.

"Yeah, love?"

"There's something I need to know."

"OK."

"Is G-pop in recovery for alcohol?"

"Who told you that?"

"Doesn't matter. Just answer the question."

"It's not my place."

"You do realize that right there *is* the answer?"

"You have to take it up with Ourdaddy." She hugged her purse. "I need to get going and you got that session with Dervin."

She hugged him, and he ran a mental inventory of the many ways that was a cowardly move, asking her when he should face his grandfather. No more secrets.

❦

Day 150 was a Sunday. After breakfast Bo D sat on Spruce Cabin's screened-in back porch inhaling crisp September air as sunlight glittered on Small Pond. He rocked back in one of four white rocking chairs, reflecting in the glossy, teal-colored floor. Spanish moss dripped from pines and oaks, filtering morning sun. During these three weeks of rehab, he made a habit of hitting that patch of sunlight every morning. This made him think of Auntie Olga. And Sidney, always chasing the sun. He rocked, trying to prepare his head for Indicca, Cricket, and his grandfather visiting after lunch.

How can 1,500 mostly unspoiled acres and all that sky still leave a man feeling trapped? His first week had been hard, not being able to leave at all—because of suicide watch. The family danced around that word, but the one thing he had been sure about through all that happened is that he never wanted to die. He only wanted to not feel what he had been feeling for so long. At least now he could get permission to leave. But still. Trapped. He missed his car. They had become inseparable on the streets.

A mockingbird ran through his repertoire and Bo D thought how much like this bird he was, except his songs were a stockpile of emotions. For the first time in a long time he felt everything in its raw state, not fried by highballs. It was good and it was too much.

Inside his backpack were his main possessions: little tally notebook, pens, colored pencils, and a sketchbook filled with notes and drawings of trees. This was thanks to arborist Ranger Ben, whose tree class was the highlight of Bo D's week. He had learned more than he could imagine about trees he'd been looking at his whole life: growing habits; leaf and needle formations. Their names were like lyrics he drew with flourishes across sketchbook pages ∼ *maple* ∼ *longleaf* ∼ *loblolly* ∼ *sumac* ∼ *sweet gum* ∼ *pitch*. Leaves would not be changing for another two weeks, and even though tourists do not flock to south Georgia for fall color, once you know what to look for, there was plenty to see. Bo D had learned from his mother to watch for fall's fiery shock of color amid evergreens, so it's never wasted on his eyes. Soon autumn would tinsel summer's decline on water oak, laurel, and pecan leaves as trees took stock of their season, preparing to flush with pride or blanch from modesty.

The whole mess with junk cars, Anthony, and his tow truck hardly moved the needle compared to Tyrone and his grandfather pulling him out of the Mustang. And now he would face G-pop to ask him about his own demons with alcohol. No way to imagine that stubborn man in a rehab circle. Good thing Indicca and Cricket would be here. To keep things from getting crazy.

Bo D rocked back, closed his eyes, listening to the mockingbird until his two cabinmates interrupted on their way out.

"Hey, Bo D," Lester said, "soaking up some rays?"

"Yep."

"I know dang well *you* ain't tryin to git no tan," Brad scoffed as he walked out.

Lester shook his head. "The guy's a bipolar asshole, don't pay him no mind."

"He ain't bipolar," Bo D said, pulling his backpack into his lap. "He's just a straight-up asshole."

"Can't argue with that," Lester said.

Brad was reddish blond, about Bo D's age, and at least half a foot shorter. He wore his bigotry on his shoulders. Lester was tall, gray, and balding with years of drinking written in tiny red veins across his doughy face. He coached middle school football and tried too hard to hide signs of any bias. Bo D tolerated Lester and trusted neither of them. Loblolly was a cross between prison and high school, where even trees seem to stand guard, so Bo D was in no position to be choosy about allies.

"I'm about to take a walk," Lester said. "You wanna join me? Plenty more sun where that little patch came from."

"Nah, I got plans."

At any moment the Spruce house phone would ring to announce his visitors. Bo D was nervous to confront his grandfather, and was worried about how all of this was affecting Cricket. When she saw her cousin's tent at Girl Scout Camp, Cricket was very excited, so Indicca told her that Daddy was at another camp. She was eager to see the ponds and chickens—and Daddy's *tent*.

Bo D was eager to see Indicca. She still had power over him. He wished she were there now, sitting alone with him. He would rock her back and kiss her. Hard. Because of him, they hadn't been together as man and woman since Cricket was born. They had become a tag team. All that time on the street was supposed to be for figuring how to make that better, not worse. Some men used having a kid as a reason to walk away. Bo D was ashamed to admit understanding that feeling, and proud that he had never left for good. Auntie Olga said to him many times, *We can't have you fathering a child, but not raising that child.*

Even when he was on the streets, not once did he stop child support. Nevertheless, he saw clearly that even though he was coming back, there was only a thin line separating him from men who didn't, like his father. It was never optional: he had to be a better man than that.

About an hour after lunch, Bo D sat talking with his grandfather under the main lawn gazebo. A few feet away, Cricket was wearing her sparkly purple sunglasses and being pushed on the swing set by Indicca. Bo D had planned to jump right to discussing what Neeshah said, but his grandfather had a plan of his own.

"I won't say Tyrone went about it the right way at the drug house that night," Fletcher said, "but he had nothing but your best interest at heart."

Cricket squealed a giggle. Bo D was silent.

"You believe that?" Fletcher asked.

"Yeah. I guess."

Fletcher was silent.

"I'll call him," Bo D said.

Bo D then kept to his plan, refusing to name who said that about his grandfather because he'd rather no one knew that he had any reason to be in Neeshah's company.

"You're right," Fletcher said, "it don't matter who you heard that from. I was wrong not to tell you, and I hate you had to find out the way you did."

"It's like you think I'm made out of glass, and I'll break into a million pieces, and on the other hand you think I need toughening up."

His grandfather's exhale had an all-too-familiar timbre. Silent, piercing overtones Bo D had read, and misread, his whole life. This triggered, as always, a quick pulse surge, turning on the motor in his leg. Now, watching his own daughter giggling so hard she might fall from the swing, Bo D understood his grandfather's overtones to mean, *I have no words for this moment.*

"High-o, Mommy, push high-o!" Cricket squealed.

"That's high enough, Boo," Bo D called out.

Then he pulled out his little notebook.

"What's that?" Fletcher asked.

"I been keeping tally of the days."

"Since when?"

"Since that night Ma put my stuff out—in the rain."

"So what day is this?"

"Today is Day 150." Bo D made his mark. "Nice round number."

"And how you feeling now?" Fletcher asked.

"Like I need to be through with counting days and focused on making the days count."

"Sounds like a good plan to me."

"Also feel like a damn fool. I don't even know what to say to Auntie Olga. I ended up piling misery on top of misery and she almost died!"

"Ain't nobody dead and ain't nobody to blame," Fletcher said.

They both leaned forward, elbows on knees, hands clasped, and shared a look of affirmation, a mutual validation of all that was unspoken between them. Bo D was tired of punting, so he went back in.

"So—how did you beat your drinking?"

"First thing you need to know is that it damn near beat me, so that includes my family, too. Had it not been for your granmama, it would have. I tried Twelve Step. A couple of times. At least. Can't really recall. But in the end, it was you."

"Me?" Bo D sat back on the bench and almost laughed.

"That's right. When you were born, I quit cold turkey."

"Wow."

"Don't mean that can work for you."

"I know."

"Or even that it could work for me again if I needed it to."

"Right."

"You in a good place, Terrence. Proud to see you sticking with it."

"Yes, sir."

Fletcher sat back, his arms stretched across the bench back. "Your granmama and your mama can just put things in God's hands, and I used to wish I could do that. When I got back from Sapelo, I could testify even more to one thing: whatever gods may be, they have no hands—they work through ours."

"I believe that," Bo D said, feeling good that they had always seen eye to eye on this, when so many in the family didn't.

"And G-pop, I know you worried, but I got this."

"Who said I was worried?"

"You can't fool me," Bo D goaded. "I know what worry looks like on your face."

"Yeah?"

"Yeah!"

Cricket ran over and crawled up into her father's lap. Fletcher tickled her tummy and Bo D reveled in being clearheaded and present. Cricket delicately pointed at his peach seed monkey.

"Daddy!" Her whisper was urgent. "You way-wing yo monkey!"

"Yep. I sure am, Boo."

34

~

"Car is dark, dark blue," Bo D said to Olga, "almost black." They were standing shoulder to shoulder on her front porch.

Bo D was about one month into rehab. So much had changed since the stroke. In addition to her left arm hanging lifeless, she had an ever-present white handkerchief in her right hand. As usual, her linen layers and cashmere wrap were meticulous, and beneath slurred words she was his Auntie Olga. And this was Sunday dinner.

"Sweeeeet!" Bo D sang. "They call that color deep sea blue—with white interior, BMW 650i—Convertible—That is one niiiice car!"

"Fletcher left space?"

"He did." Bo D wasn't sure he should bring it up, but he was more interested in Siman Miller's latest email. "Did you reply to Uncle Siman yet?" he whispered.

"Not yet. Need to make—"

The screen door screeched open. Olga patted Bo D's shoulder.

"What y'all two cooking up out here?" Fletcher said. "Got your heads together like Wink-em and Blink-em."

"Are you Nod?" Olga nudged Bo D.

"Oooh no." Fletcher grinned. "Don't try to pull me into your conspiracy."

Altovise pulled into the driveway, and Bo D leaned toward Fletcher. "You don't see that blue-white combo every day in Albany, huh, G-pop?"

"You got that right." Fletcher beamed, walking down to meet Altovise.

"How y'all?" Altovise called out.

Olga smiled and dabbed her handkerchief around her mouth. "Sounds like you never left south Georgia!"

"You know how that is," Altovise said, "once it's in your DNA—it's there to stay."

Bo D took note as his grandfather kissed Altovise's cheek, then rubbed his hand along her lower back. His face changed to that of a man looking at the object of his desires. Like a road that had been dimly lit and was now washed in high beams. He took her hand and led her up onto the porch. In these moves, Bo D saw himself with Indicca. Was he more like his grandfather than he was willing to admit?

"It's good to see you," Altovise said, caressing Olga's right hand and softly kissing her forehead.

❧

Day 164: the middle of October. Like Bo D's sense of smell and taste—which were heightened now that he was sober—fall colors looked more vibrant, especially at twilight. For those few precious minutes before sunset, all of nature was phosphorescent, as if throwing back sunlight it spent a whole day collecting.

He strolled through the Whitney Avenue house, plucking memories from nooks and corners purely for the joy of remembering. Auntie Olga's house was filled with people who cared about him most, shown in so many ways: G-pop had Anthony replace the broken window, service and detail his Mach 1, which his mom had kept in her garage.

Tyrone drove out to Loblolly today to pick him up. An awkward ride at first, but how could he stay mad at T? He wondered what everyone really thought of him. And struggled to see this old house—and himself—with new eyes.

He had been high the last time he'd stood on Olga's Persian rug or leaned against her old pedestal bathroom sink. His lucid, sober self was ashamed of that other Bo D and didn't see how he could do what his therapist Dervin said they all must do to move forward: make peace with their addict.

Respect! He heard Dervin's voice in his head, *it literally means to see again!*

Bo D kept a close eye on his mother, prepared to do what he'd done all his life: make his next move based on hers. He found her in the kitchen, looking above the sink at a rack displaying Olga's legacy of cast-iron skillets.

Since Altovise pulled into town, Bo D could imagine his mother avoiding conversations at work, at choir rehearsals, the beauty parlor, and instigating texts and phone calls with her sisters. Not being sure how to reply to his uncle Siman's texts about his mom and aunts, he punted, and no more questions came. His mom was so alone—no man and both sisters in different states. That was sobriety's downside: things becoming crystal clear—except the solutions to your problems.

"You need help, Ma?" She seemed surprised that he asked.

"Thank you, Terrence. Could you get that big skillet down for me?"

There was no smell of lemon or Listerine, which accounted for her jittery mood, and buzzing around always helped anchor her. In a huge porcelain bowl, a wooden spoon stood straight up out of stiff biscuit dough. With her index finger, Florida pushed spoonsful of tiny white mountains into the skillet. On the street, Bo D had missed her drop biscuits almost as much as her corn bread. But what he had craved more than anything was collard greens and ham hocks pot liquor. This is what she always made him when he was sick: brought to his bed in a big mug with steam rising.

It was in this kitchen a few months after his father left that he first started counting things. What is hardwood now was linoleum then, a grid with large pink and gold roses. He was a big-time second grader; walking around and around the kitchen, stepping on the gray lines and counting each rose-filled square over and over.

As much as Florida was nervous, Olga was calm, asking if she needed help.

"I'm fine," Florida said. But Bo D knew she wanted to fake a grocery store trip for a smoke and a drink.

"Bo D," Olga said, "my study, please."

"The air around my mom is thick enough to cut," Bo D said, helping Olga into her Queen Anne chair, "but that's no surprise."

"Protecting Maletha's memory."

"But G-pop and Dr. Al don't even be disrespecting."

"A fact daughters can't so eas-ily see."

"Didn't look like Ma said hello to Dr. Al."

"She did. But—haters hate—"

He remembered the rest of the sentence: *haters hate you more when they find nothing to hate.*

"Remember Mama Alpha?" Olga said.

She had told Bo D his great-grandmother's story many times. Being the youngest of Purvis' first set, Olga was only seven years old when Alpha, Fletcher's mother, became their stepmother. Olga was missing her mother and took to *Ma Alpha* right away. The older siblings thought Alpha was too young and too spirited for their father. Alpha's answer was to embrace them all with open arms and stern love.

"Altovise," Olga said, "same big heart."

"I like her," Bo D said, "too bad she and G-pop couldn't cut it. But then again, that's a statement against my own existence!"

"That's true." Olga chuckled and clasped her hands. "Now. Uncle Siman?"

"We've been texting on and off. I keep it light," Bo D said. "And you know he's thinking about coming to Georgia for Christmas, right?"

"Little birdie told me," Olga said, and squeezed his hand.

"OK—and how we feel about that?" Bo D studied her face.

Olga smiled, gave a thumbs-up, and quickly asked, "So—no rehab talk?"

"Right," Bo D said. "Should I tell him?"

"Up to you."

After dinner, two cars drove to Gillionville Road for a tour of Tyrone's Eusi renovation. Indicca drove the Mach 1. Bo D sat up front; Olga and Cricket quietly sang and clapped backseat songs.

"I tried to get Ma to come," Bo D said to Indicca.

"Like Auntie Olga said, she's not ready to be around Ms. Altovise. Plus—you know she's scared she's gone cause you to relapse."

During his highball years, nothing had been easier for Bo D than ignoring his mother's addiction, and it was impossible for her not to focus on his. This new, sober Bo D could hardly believe his mother's sad, lonely life since his father left. There was an oblivion inside the Dove Cove house that created a fog of mother-son ill will until Bo D's rage set hers loose and changed everything.

Bo D felt Olga's hand on his shoulder, as if she could sense his dejection from the backseat. "Not giving up on either of you."

Tyrone led the tour; Fletcher carried Cricket, strolling next to Altovise, and Bo D sandwiched himself between Indicca and Olga.

"We're halfway through Phase One," Tyrone announced as they entered the main auditorium. "Finishing this house and stage means we can go into production, generate revenue, and attract funding for next phases."

Altovise made eye contact with Bo D, raising her eyebrows and pantomiming applause. He jotted down ideas in his sketchbook. In his backpack was the book on restoring Airstream panels, even though he had said nothing to Tyrone.

They entered a large room that was stripped down to studs.

"Yo T!" Tyrone called out to Bo D. "This will be our tech shop."

"Looking good!" Bo D answered.

"Fantastic!" Olga said.

"And meantime," Altovise added, arms outstretched, pointing toward a section of wall, "we're close to getting two shipping containers donated to expand this workspace through here out into the parking lot."

The others milled about the space, and Altovise pulled Bo D and Tyrone aside.

"We were lucky to have my colleague come in as interim," Altovise said, "and now the board hopes you will reconsider our offer to head up the tech team. You'll be able to design this space and the shipping containers anyway you want."

"No pressure right now for an answer," Tyrone said.

"Are you kidding me! The answer is yes and thank you!" Bo D bumped shoulders with Tyrone and shook Altovise's hand.

"I finish up rehab this week and move right into ninety days of sober living, so to come into that with a solid job offer is way more than I could ever ask."

"And exactly what you deserve," Altovise said.

~

i know
and you will learn

family is both
blood and duty

those who
deliver you to the world
and those who
hold you
feed you
mend you

~

35

Malik welcomed September and the promise of coolness. He pulled a sharp, crescent blade across a bundle of golden, brown rice plants, and prayed again to Allah for Baaba to find another cousin to marry Nbey, and that she would be blessed with more children and sister wives. He was thankful that his children were too young to know his name. They would not miss him.

He pulled the sickle through another bundle, laying each on top of uniformly even stubble about two feet high, what's left in fields after harvest. Dried rice was tied into sheaves and hauled by canoe to the threshing yard, where flailing separated seed from grain. Each new tool built fresh calluses on a different part of Malik's hands.

After harvest, daneejos turned to duck hunting. When their flat-bottomed canoes got stuck in shallow, muddy waters, Malik and other young men were left with sore shoulders and backs from lifting and pushing boats, men, and gear to deeper water.

In their compound on Sunday morning—their single day of rest—Malik, Horace, and Crayfish mingled with neighbors, young and old, singing, eating, telling stories. Crayfish played a high-pitched, prankish tune on his harmonica, recasting traditional lyrics with coded messages for the Rise to inform captives of next steps. These new songs were quickly carried on breezes far inland and up and down the Sea Island chain. A one-man show, Crayfish played while teaching a dance called *calenda*. Eager couples took turns in the dirt clearing, slapping thighs, writhing hips, quick-kissing faster and faster.

Malik picked his teeth with a splinter he found sticking out of a log. This brought thoughts of Baaba, a double-edged sword, because recalling home always lead back to Bacary dying in blood and water at the river's edge, sights and sounds that were frozen around Malik's heart, his joy forever stunted.

Off to one side, Malik smoothed a silty dirt patch with his hand. Crayfish took a break near Malik, watching him draw with a stick.

"Well I'll be!" Crayfish said. "What oonuh know about a pirogue?"

"My family, we make in Podor. The best from Saint-Louis to Kaédi."

"Good!" Crayfish pointed to the raked bottom, tilting his hand to mimic the bow's slope. "She riding up at a good angle. Higher than what I seen."

"How *oonuh* know this pirogue?" Malik asked.

"Er'body where I'm from know about pirogues. Onliest way to get through them shallow bayou waters without hauling a canoe under your arm."

Having no daneejo words to describe his boat's size, Malik sprang up, took a stick, and marked the sand. From there he walked off a line four paces and two feet long, made another mark. He connected these marks with a graceful arc, marked its center, measured a width of two cubits and drew another lengthwise arc; the two lines came together in sharp points on each end. He drew lines for two seats, climbed in, and finished his plan by resting forearms on invisible edges, showing the boat's sides to be three hands high. Crayfish climbed in with him, pretending to rock from side to side, and they laughed. Horace left the group's merriment to join his friends.

"Which tree in your Bay-you?" Malik asked, knowing nothing could replace the mighty kapok.

"We call it BY-you," said Crayfish, who had a great love for words and the sound of his voice, "and the Choctaw been digging out cypress trees since before God was a baby." He knelt to draw the tree with its bulbous roots.

"CY-PRESS," Crayfish said. "Swamp tree, already used to water—them grow round these parts, too." He pointed again at Malik's drawing. "So oonuh make these?"

"I make—with good cy-press tree."

"Well, son," Horace squatted near the boat, "Calhoun got all that and then some."

Calhoun, dim and heartless in all matters, could be a man of reason where profit was concerned. Horace encouraged Malik to show his design to Calhoun. A young house servant, who had an eye for Crayfish, supplied pencil and paper for Malik. He presented his designs after their next hunting trip and Calhoun was intrigued. He assigned an overseer, arranged for Malik to fell a cypress, and gave him hatchets, adzes, and drawknives to build a pirogue. This brought Malik a step closer to his dream of escaping, a plan he knew to be fraught with obstacles. Who could he trust to help him learn to build a big enough boat? Where could they get supplies? Where could they hide? All questions he only discussed outside the Rise with Horace and Crayfish.

By winter, Malik, Crayfish, and Horace were hired out to build custom boats and allowed to keep a portion of their wages. This work was added to their daily acre tasks and took them from Charleston to Sullivan's Island, and as far as Pawleys Island, over seventy miles up the coast.

It was during this time that a somber veil seeped like smoke up and down the coast as captives mourned the death of over eight hundred men, women, and children. They died while quarantined in a holding pen at Gadsden's Wharf. Their frozen bodies were buried in a mass grave. Malik thought back to his days only a few months ago in the same wretched building. Inside cabins and praise houses, sitting on stumps and standing in clearings, with song, prayer, and ritual, Low-country captives honored the nameless, now faceless dead. Buried with them were pained and conflicted hopes held by many: the off chance of looking upon even one of those new faces to confirm that their loved ones might still be safe at home in Africa.

36

~

Rockhudson watched Fletcher step on a large roll of chicken wire, clipping with tin snips. Raccoons were dexterous beyond belief with fresh eggs and chickens at stake; Fletcher had a mangled section of fencing as proof. Through his open kitchen window, he heard the phone ring. Olga no doubt. Calling about the World Series tomorrow. As usual, just the two of them would listen on her vintage Zenith, which still had a nice, cushioned sound. They were looking forward to having a detailed talk about Siman. Things had settled into a rhythm with Bo D in rehab and doing well, mostly.

"C'mon, Rock," Fletcher said, resting his tin snips on the picnic table, "let's see what Olga wants."

"Hello, Mr. Dukes," said the voice on his machine, "this is Mrs. Ida Culpepper on Whitney, next door to Dr. Dukes. I had so hoped to catch you. The dutiful Sidney has been howling for almost twenty minutes—very unusual. I knocked on the front door and no answer. And of course, the curtains are still drawn. You'd better come."

As Fletcher unlocked the door, he could hear Sidney howling above faint radio music. In her dimly lit living room he immediately saw Olga, sitting in her easy chair, her head resting on a throw pillow. The Cube was tuned to a classical channel, and Sidney sat at her feet.

Fletcher's heart jerked. He rushed to Olga and felt her neck for a pulse, even though he knew she was not sleeping. She was still warm and he was grateful she had not been there long. He let the radio play.

A little over a month ago he had made this same move for Bo D. This time he was robbed of the chance to make a deal with whichever god was listening.

Fletcher knelt to rub Sidney's chest. "Good boy, you did a good job. You coming home with me for now. Ol' Rock will be glad to see you."

When Fletcher stood, Sidney leaned into his leg, looking up at his face. The dog was silent now, his eyes missing Olga. Fletcher wiped his own eyes with the back of his hand.

He laid Olga on the sofa; her face was restful, at peace. What had gone wrong? Since her stroke she was never left alone. Florida would know who didn't show up to relieve The Twins for school. Olga would've insisted that they not be late, but the girls should have called somebody. Why hadn't he run in to pick up the phone? What if she had been calling for help? Sometimes his bullheadedness amazed even him. If he had a cell phone in his pocket like everybody else, Ida Culpepper could've reached him. But Olga had not called, and there was no sign of struggle. She was sleeping peacefully, already dressed for her day. He thought back to their many conversations about death from year to year and how he coveted his sister's comfort zone with the idea. *All I ask of whoever's in charge is that I have fair enough warning to put my house in order.*

The Twins had done their job; the coffee table was arranged for tomorrow's game: bright blue Fall Classic program, a fresh pack of number two pencils on top of a Giants lineup sheet and scoring chart. In happier times Olga would've drawn smiley faces next to Casilla, Mota, and Posey. She and Fletcher have had this tradition for over thirty-five years: he brought soul food carryout. During lulls in the game, they worked through family problems away from the Dukes family echo chamber. Now that Bo D's dilemma was under control, they had planned to make a decision about Fletcher contacting his newfound son. Fletcher shook his head, his lips trembled. Then he flinched at the sound of Olga's drapes opening. It was 9:00.

Vibrant blues and oranges on her Persian rug pulsed under his feet, and in those first few moments, holding an audience with death's face, Fletcher became acutely aware of life—his life, life around him, life gone—until grief's empty agony attached like a leech. Everything and nothing had changed, electricity still moved through lines, and birds had not stopped singing. Olga's house had instantly transformed itself into a monument.

Fletcher shifted into dazed automation, only knowing his next move as it happened. He called Altovise first, wanting her there but knowing how much this would upset Florida. Altovise told him she would come as soon as he gave the word. He called the funeral home, and then Florida.

"Hey. I'm at Olga's." He knew he didn't need to finish the sentence. All was said in his fractured voice, his pause. "You better come."

Florida left work immediately, and Tyrone drove out to sober living to pick up Bo D.

Later, with the hearse waiting in the driveway, they all stood silently in an arc around Olga.

Sidney followed as they rolled Olga's body out. This reminded Fletcher of himself crawling into his mother's deathbed. Before she died his days had passed as if nothing would ever change; no one close had died and everyone dear lived within walking distance. He was too young to appreciate how life and death ruled his small world.

Fletcher beckoned Sidney to follow him to the kitchen. He opened a bag of Fritos into his bowl, then sat in the breakfast nook with Florida to the sound of teeth crunching on corn chips.

"You saw how quiet Terrence was?" Florida said. "As usual, he won't cry. That's not good, holding all that in."

"Nothing wrong with a man showing strength," Fletcher said.

"Right. He's like you; always letting his tears fall on the inside, where they do damage. Auntie Olga always said: Let those tears fall outside where they belong. They help wash away pain and polish up memories."

Fletcher thought the opposite. He had taught Bo D what he'd learned from his father, Purvis: When you fall, pick yourself up and keep going. *Don't waste time on water*. He was pleased to know the boy had taken that lesson to heart.

At Fletcher's insistence, they all left, and he found a small carry-on bag and went to the study.

Among organized papers on Olga's desk, he flipped through a file folder labeled SIMAN. His sister. Always giving, giving, giving. And now she would not be here to reap what she had worked so hard to sow.

Through all of life's upheavals Olga had been his constant. What would the world be without her? With each death he conjured every unthinkable scenario for his family.

He packed Olga's Zenith radio with towels in the carry-on and called Altovise.

&

Olga's cremation shook Fletcher more than her death, with Florida reluctantly leading her sisters in the task and Fletcher not accepting any part of it.

Mozell flew from North Carolina, and Georgia from Arizona; both checked into their rooms at Florida's palatial house. Since Thanksgiving was Olga's favorite, they began planning her memorial for that week.

For the crematorium trip, all three ordered Fletcher to ride with them in Florida's Mercedes. As his daughters went in he paced outside, searching for a peach seed to worry, but these pockets were empty, leaving him adrift in thoughts.

Fletcher had not listened to the World Series this year. He was quiet during barbershop antics over the Giants sweeping. On her coffee table, Olga's still life with pencils waited. She would be happy with the score. She would also not be unhappy that *her* final inning had come to a close; field lights were out, and he prepared for a world without her.

For so much of his life he'd refused to fathom this non-Olga place. Her long Amsterdam years felt like a dry run for this real event. As a toddler, he could only wait and watch; thinking her voice would come through her magic Cube on their mantel piece right before she walked through the door. But by his eleventh birthday, he'd been to enough funerals to imagine her absence in the house as her absence in the world. As they aged together, he saw death's inevitable march written on his own body; felt it in joints and eyes. When the bottom of his sister's ninth arrived, he was not surprised. He was also not ready.

When the daughters returned, Mozell climbed into the backseat, holding a cardboard box.

"So that's her?" Fletcher asked, still standing on the sidewalk.

"Yes. Beautiful blue and white urn inside here," Mozell said. "You wanna see?"

"No," Fletcher said, "just don't feel right."

"I don't like this idea of ashes either, Ourdaddy," Florida said, "but this is not about us."

"Like hell it ain't," Georgia said.

"Well, yeah, you right," Florida added, "but we might as well get with the program 'cause you can't argue with the dead."

"You know she never liked the backseat," Fletcher said, "made her carsick."

"All the more reason to get her home." Florida closed her door and turned the key. "So git in the car—please!"

They convened in Florida's small sitting room, just inside her front door; a sanctuary of French provincial furniture and silk flowers in oversize vases. Fletcher sat patiently on the love seat. His daughters kept him distracted, arranging Olga's mantelpiece placement by committee.

"Not like it matters where you put her," Mozell said, "it's only temporary."

"No it's not!" Florida said. "I decided to keep some of her ashes. That's why I had them put in this urn. Otherwise, they give them to you in a plastic ziplock bag in a cardboard box."

"Well that don't seem right!" Georgia said.

Olga ended up center stage with matching knickknack patterns repeating on each side: white pillar candle, Thomas Blackshear figurine, porcelain bouquet. The blue-and-white Chinese urn fell in beautifully with off-white furniture and blue glass accent pieces.

"OK." Florida dusted her hands as if she'd dug a grave. They all gathered around the mantel.

"It's perfect that we're having the memorial Thanksgiving week since that was her favorite holiday," Mozell said.

"Yeah," Georgia added, "there ain't nothing like a captive audience to drive your point home, and Auntie was calculating."

"She sure was!" Mozell said.

It was not her favorite holiday for reasons most might think. Every year, somewhere between peach cobbler/pecan pie and video games/football, Olga would start hitting hard with truths about the carnage native peoples suffered after history's forgery of a friendly meal between Pilgrims and Indians.

"And we'll do the same at the memorial," Florida said.

Fletcher sat quietly on the little couch, legs crossed, arms folded, gazing blankly at the floor.

"Auntie Olga always liked this little room, Florida said, and she gave me grief about not using it enough."

"Yeah," Fletcher said. "I've caught her napping on this funny little sofa many-a-time when the sun hit that spot."

They were all quiet, staring at the urn, as if trying to imagine beautiful Olga reduced to ashes.

"Auntie Olga don't want us being sad," Florida said, flipping through her Bible. "I'm gone read from the Book of Psalms, chapter thirty, verse eleven:

*"You have turned my mourning into joyful dancing. You have
taken away my clothes of mourning and clothed me with joy."*

"Well, big sister," Fletcher said, touching the urn, "sometimes this
is as close as it comes to fair warning. But don't worry, you kept your
house in order."

Mozell rubbed his back. "Yes indeed, she always said *Stay ready so
you don't have to get ready.*"

"No stranger to death, but new to dealing with urns," Georgia
said, "and I just have to add this: since Obama's midterms are in four
days, in a real way she's in this room with us, asking if y'all voted
early."

"I know that's right!" Mozell said, and they all agreed, volleying a
buoyant laugh around their small circle.

"Now we need to plan the scattering," Mozell said. "That was one
of the few things she left up to us."

Fletcher said, "Olga couldn't tolerate fishing, and never learned
how to swim, but even after her sight went bad, she still liked going
out in my boat, so Bo D came up with a plan to scatter on the Flint."

"Good idea," Florida said, "just a handful of us can go—and for
real though—did y'all vote yet?"

"Georgia. Omygoodness . . . of course we voted . . ."

" . . . how you gone even be asking us that . . ."

Her sisters carried on with levity and Florida sat down on the sofa,
suddenly wiping tears with a wadded-up tissue. Within seconds, her
shoulders shook as grief quietly overtook her. Fletcher sat next to
her. Mozell and Georgia brought a glass of water and a wet facecloth.

"I-I'm sooooo sorry, Ourdaddy," she whispered now, "please forgive me."

"For what?" Fletcher asked. She rocked back and drank water.

"I didn't mean to—I didn't mean to—" she moaned. "I messed
up so many things: putting Terrence out, and he almost died. He
almost died, Ourdaddy! That was my fault."

"Not your fault and he didn't die," Mozell said.

"And he'll be fine," Georgia added.

Florida continued to weep and rock. Then she spoke through quivering lips.

"Everything's changed. Mama and Auntie Olga sure would've known how to deal with all of this."

"But remember, Lil Sis," Mozell said, "they equipped us to deal with it, too."

"And everything sure has changed," Georgia said to Mozell, "it's been forever since you called us *Lil Sis*!"

"That's true." Florida wiped tears and almost smiled. "I miss them so much."

"Yeah, I know." Fletcher needed to move on. "But onethingaboutit, can't neither one of them stop you from doing exactly what you want to now."

"But Lord knows," Florida said, "that ain't always smooth sailing. It's like Auntie said when Mama died: *death is easy, it's the living that's hard.*"

37

Death sets up its own pecking order, based on many things, starting with proximity. How closely were you related and how close by
do you live? These determine how quickly a niece, nephew, or cousin
drops everything and packs a car or books a flight. Family members
never seem to agree on who should come for what, and how often.
Elders think mainly in terms of miles, quick to grant pardon if a flight
of more than two hours is required—*Well, you can't come for all of
'em*—while younger generations are more apt to lay blame—*She got
plenty money to go on cruises every year, so hellyeah, she ought to be here.*

Bo D avoided funerals. There was always some mess. Especially
if there's money involved. There's good reason folks say, *Death and
a dollar make you wanna holler.* Auntie Olga even had a good saying for that: *Blood is thicker than water and will drown you twice as
fast.* His mom and aunt chose the Saturday after Thanksgiving for the
memorial, since many folks would be in town anyway. Bo D could
recite his aunt's annual Indians and Pilgrims speech verbatim. He had
to be there to help his mom. He came up with an idea to do something smaller and more special for his favorite aunt. Early Sunday

morning, the immediate family would go out in Fletcher's boat to scatter ashes. Then, joined by a few more family members, they'd attend 11:00 service at New Hope Baptist Church, not far from Fletcher's place on Sumac Road. This was their family's original place of worship and the famous grounds where his great-grandfather Purvis became enamored with Alpha one Easter Sunday. Bo D had heard the Brunswick stew story many times from Olga, who often took him and a group of cousins to New Hope when they were younger. They suffered through the long services because afterward the reward was cardboard boxes brimming with cakes, pies, and mouth-watering meats and side dishes. Olga never liked mega churches, said the spirit had less ground to cover in small country churches, so the experience was more intense: a reasonable amount of pews, no carpet, and a single piano accompanied the small choir. Otherwise, church shoes tapped a bare wood floor, the only percussion needed for old-time long-meter hymns.

Brisk fall nights often brought a dreary sunrise like the one Bo D saw through wavy glass windows, lying on his back, pumping iron. Loblolly's workout cottage was part of their sober living program and had become his regular haunt. Exercise helped him manage what his doctors called protracted symptoms. Nurse Reynolds' translation: *emotional stuff and cravings leftover from detox.*

Bo D's peach seed monkey rested on his sweaty clavicle well as he pushed and puffed, his chest heaving.

His trainer helped rest the barbell, and Bo D looked past the explosive Afro and the man's upside-down face, at wooden rafters and knotty pine walls, then back out at clouds.

The trainer clapped his hands. "OK, one more rep!"

Lifting, Bo D expelled air in a long, controlled exhale, then refilled from lungs to core thinking of Auntie Olga still taking care of him. The week after she died, he and Indicca sat side by side in the lawyer's office.

The trainer counted. Bo D pushed through.

Olga left strict instructions about everything.

The trainer urged him on.

She left her house to Bo D and Indicca with a list of conditions that he must meet to Indicca's satisfaction for his inheritance to go through. Top of the list was rehab and staying sober. He was two weeks into Loblolly's ninety-day sober living program.

"Good job, man!" They slapped five. "See you tomorrow."

⁂

Sober living days were a loop of cabin chores, meals, group sessions, and exercise. All made tolerable by an online theater tech course. Bo D still struggled with insomnia, his usual antsiness, and even reverted to detox chills when he overexerted. Since Olga's death he had struggled to feel any forward motion. Counting days had helped him believe he was not going backward.

A network of fire roads and hiking trails connected Loblolly's rehab ranch with a cluster of sober living cottages. Bo D jogged from his cottage to his favorite dock bench overlooking Large Pond; it was one of his sacred spots for watching sunsets deepen with color, a dashing backdrop for tall pyramidal cypress crowns draped in Spanish moss. Their inflated trunks reflected in glassy, steel-blue water, like girls in prom dresses ready to dance. He caught his breath, sipping water, and tuned in to a bobwhite quail before calling Siman; he was not sure he'd know what to say.

"Hey, Bo D!" Siman's voice was deep and melodic; maybe he was a singer, like his mama. "Nice to finally talk to you."

"Yeah, Unc, it's about time, right?"

"Thanks for that picture you texted. Beautiful family. I look forward to meeting Indicca and little Bright Tarshieka. That's quite a name."

"We all call her Cricket, but yeah, she likes telling people her whole name. She also tells people she's sixteen so—I'm warning you."

"So you holding up OK since your auntie Olga's passing?"

"She's your aunt, too, you know."

"Yes, indeed she is. I have to get used to that good fortune! Was looking forward to meeting her."

"At least you met on Skype. She worked so hard to connect you with the family, a shame she can't be here to reap that reward."

"Same is true for all the work she put in to keep Obama in the White House."

"Yeah. Auntie was a force."

Looking out over calming water, Bo D waded inside a silence that ordinarily would have him bouncing his leg and counting. But this quiet opened out, and he jumped in, seeing a path to talking about rehab.

"—and speaking of Auntie, I made a promise to her that I'd come clean with you."

"OK." Another gaping hole of silence. Another chance to jump.

"I finished six weeks in rehab and coming up on four weeks of sober living, so it's all good."

"Congratulations, man! Two major milestones."

"Yeah, well, that's not a thing to lead with, know what I mean."

"Sure, I do—and now you have reason to celebrate," Siman said. "Whatever you're doing is working well for you."

"That's all thanks to Auntie Olga." He wasn't sure why he was telling this. "It's like, even though she was losing her sight, she could see how bad things were with me long before I could. I didn't see it until it was right up on me in the car that night. For a while I couldn't remember details—and I have no idea why I'm spilling all of this to you."

"Please, feel free if it helps. I don't mind at all."

"OK," Bo D said, surprised that it did seem to help. "I had scored some oxy from a new source and drove out to a big tree out past G-pop's. Been going there since I was little. I crushed and snorted and seconds later I threw up and then saw a black tunnel, closing in. I know this sounds like a cliché movie scene, but I actually saw white light and felt my body rising up. And that's all I remember."

They both let silence hang between them.

"I hate that Auntie saw me at my weakest."

"Or, you could look at this another way: she saw you find the strength to pick yourself up."

As their call ended, Bo D watched a bald eagle in the distance land atop one of the prom dress cypress trees. He tucked his phone in his pocket. He was ready to meet his shiny new uncle with this new brand of conversation.

38

~

A golden pink twilight sky, tinged with lavender, made a solemn backdrop for distant trees and those hugging the church grounds. Naked oaks and evergreens, fully dressed, stood like sentinels— one crying meekly, the other boldly, as a melancholy crowd flowed through the doors of Greater Goshen Baptist Church.

Travelers from near and far tightened coats and scarves against bracing fall air. A mix of families, academicians, students, and lifelong friends gathered to comfort each other and pay respects to Olga Delzina Dukes. Accolades and condolences came from around the country as well as Canada, Europe, Africa, Asia, and of course, Amsterdam. All these years both sides of her family knew how phenomenal Olga was, and now they saw firsthand how many other people knew.

With Cricket's head resting on his shoulder, Fletcher stepped out onto the lawn, greeting folks with his free hand. He paused, seeing the potent sunset through a stand of pine trees, remembering how much Olga loved sun; whether it was a patch radiating in her house or garden or the sunny side of the street, she sought warmth even more as blindness took hold. He saw right through his sister; she was using cremation to force them back into life by forgoing death's usual duties: no body to prepare, no casket or outfit or shoes to choose or gravesite to visit and tend to. Her ploy overachieved. They were left with too much time to wring empty hands and look for reasons to put one foot in front of the other.

Florida chose her church for the memorial. All three sisters came with their families: Fletcher saw no reason to point out that Olga was not a fan of Greater Goshen, with its puffed-up sanctuary, acres of red carpet, giant flat screens, video cameras, drum cages, coliseum raked pews, and theatrical lighting. In his sister's words, "Why no windows or skylights to let celestial rays shine through? It's like a casino up in here; where God is the jackpot."

On the other hand, Olga would be satisfied at seeing how pleased Florida was looking over the huge fellowship hall where folks from all walks of her life huddled family style over Brunswick stew, ribs, and fried chicken.

White-gloved ushers herded guests out to the lawn, where they milled about before returning to their cars. Empty-handed grief rested on all of them. Women clutched purses and men gripped obituaries, rolled up like diplomas.

Cricket had fallen asleep, so Fletcher handed her off to Indicca and spotted Bo D, chatting with Altovise. As she listened, she rubbed the nape of her neck, and Fletcher longed to worry the stone that lived there, like a peach seed in his pocket, rub away the grief she was storing for their dear, dear Olga. If only the oils from his touch could replenish.

Altovise moved on to a small covey of people she knew from the Movement, including women who had been incarcerated in the Larson Brig with her. Fletcher moved closer but remained on the outskirts of splintering conversations.

"... in the '30s and '40s ... whites didn't want negroes leaving sharecropping ... falsified documents, trumped-up accusations, beatings, killings for anybody trying. .."

"... and that prison what used to be on Newton Road? ... torturing and murdering Black men for sport ..."

"... King said he made our Movement demands too vague ... needed to zero in on specifics ... he took that knowledge on to Birmingham ..."

"... yeah, he also said we were left very depressed and in despair ..."

"... not true! ... we was strong before he came and kept going strong after he left ..."

Ursula approached Altovise and Fletcher shifted slightly to a new periphery as the two women spoke about how much Olga would love to be there, visiting with people she had not heard from or seen in decades.

"We handle death in America in a strange way," Altovise said, adding, "even though we have a saying: *give me my flowers while I can yet smell them*. Still, people will not visit you for years and then travel miles for your funeral."

"Yes, this is true," Ursula said. "My *grootvader* Levie is old and not well and even he wanted to come." She leaned in to whisper, "You know he and Dr. Dukes were very much in love when she lived in Amsterdam."

"I do know," Altovise said. "Olga and I talked quite a lot about your grandfather and her Amsterdam days."

Ursula said, "And now my father said no, *grootvader's* heart is too weak for travel. Why, why, why did he not come when they were both younger—or—at least when Dr. Dukes was alive? This I never can understand. Two people who loved each other as they did should be together always."

Levie Kroon was ninety-two years old. His wife died over thirty years ago. Olga invited him a few times to visit her in Albany, but he never came and never invited her back to Amsterdam.

Altovise said, "There's so much about life, death, and love that we will never understand."

Altovise returned to her covey, and Fletcher walked quickly to tap Ursula's shoulder.

"Ah! Mr. Fletcher." She stopped. "I was about to look for you." She placed her hand on his shoulder. "We are all going to miss her so."

"That's for sure, and the family sure appreciates all you've done for her these past two years."

"I received much more than I could ever give."

"Never intended to take so long, and now is probably not the time but, I didn't know what to do with this." Fletcher took the DNA vial from his jacket pocket.

"Ah! This would please Dr. Dukes. I see you found time to spit!" They both laughed as she pulled a shocking green envelope from her bag.

"She asked that I give you this."

"What is it?"

"Something of great importance."

They paused in silence, not rehearsed in speaking without Olga as their common denominator.

"I will keep you updated on your DNA results," Ursula said, referring to the vial and excusing herself.

Fletcher walked on, looking at the envelope. Olga had scribbled his name on the front in a shaky, yet elegant, cursive. This, and Ursula talking about her grandfather, took him into his deep sadness for his sister's unending plights with love, forever tainted by a scourge their family took great pains to hide.

Two years before Fletcher was born, when she was sixteen, Olga was hired to help prepare for a huge party at a former plantation where one of her sisters worked. Olga had been too impatient to wait for a ride home from her employer. Against her sister's orders, she chose to walk a mile into town to catch a bus. Along that road, a local white man and his son abducted her. Olga struggled against the son's hand on her neck, forcing her face into the pickup truck seat as a liquor bottle rolled around at her feet.

The sun had not yet set when they reached a modest farmhouse where the two men lived. The drunkard father ordered his son to watch. When the repulsive bull finished and collapsed beside her, ordering his son to take his turn, Olga vomited. With sand in her eyes, hair, and mouth, she pretended to pass out. The son accused his father of killing her and this prompted a heated argument between them that allowed her to escape. She made it to the main road and, by some miracle, into the safety of a Black couple driving by.

The rapist owned a hardware store downtown, so she and the family agonized over seeing him and his son around, cloaked in white privilege, knowing that neither would serve a day in jail for their crimes. Five years later, her move to Montréal helped ease a pain that could never be fully erased.

Fletcher tucked the envelope in his breast pocket, drifted toward his daughters, and they formed a circle around him. A few feet away Altovise caught his eye and waved as she held up a matching bright green envelope.

꙳

"Is that your fantasy date?" Fletcher said to Altovise the following week as she stood at his back door.

She held up *GQ* magazine with a cover shot of Denzel in a fancy suit.

"Please." She smirked, walking into the kitchen. "This is *your* New Year's Eve outfit." With a sweeping hand she said, "I like the whole package from the tie to the shoes."

"I just bet you do!" He laughed.

"I'm serious, Fletcher. This Tom Ford suit cost four grand, but trust me—we can put together this same look for a fraction of that."

"That may be—but there's only one way you'll get me in that lavender shirt," he said, "and if Olga was here, she'd back me up."

"Are you sure about that?"

"One hundred percent," Fletcher said. "I have no doubt that she opted for cremation to keep from ending up in a lavender shirt!"

"You know what?" Altovise shared the laugh. "You may just be right about that!"

Though they often took opposites sides, for the sake of flirty banter, Fletcher and Altovise agreed that Olga would be pleased that they were staying in the process of life.

He agreed to drive to Atlanta for a weekend shopping spree, anxious to get Altovise's 650i out for a long stretch. The plan included two nights at the Buckhead Ritz and jazz at the High Museum. Fletcher agreed to pay for their own shopping sprees and split the tab equally on everything else, even though it was a little too modern and obliging in his opinion. At the same time, on his fixed income, there was no way he could afford to keep up with Altovise's lifestyle.

Her convertible took to the road like a shark cutting through water; solid, smooth, hugging corners. With the top down, windows and windbreaker up, and heat blowing on their feet, Fletcher felt sharp and new in crisp November air.

He was pleasantly surprised that Altovise opted for a six-speed manual. When did she learn to shift? When women buy cars, there's too much emotion in the choice. Luckily, Maletha left it up to him. He always bought practical, domestic. Over the years, his Fairlane watched many a Dodge/Chrysler come and go for Maletha. None of this was to say he had no appreciation for what the Germans had done with their 6 Series.

He slid his hand over to caress her knee, and Altovise entwined fingers. Like a cat, she nestled into butter-soft leather, pulling a soulful Pura Fé from phone, to large screen, to speakers, surrounding them with quiet moments, peaceful music.

"Here we are again," Altovise said, pushing a button to recline, "with the motor running."

Fletcher replied with a smile, hands now back at ten and two.

They had decided to discuss Olga's bold final gesture en route. She lifted two bright green envelopes from the middle console.

"Mind if I compare these?"

"Not at all."

She turned his over. "You haven't even opened yours."

"Be my guest."

"O-kaay—"

As Fletcher zipped cautiously through Oakfield and Warwick on Highway 300, she compared the letters side by side.

"Identical," she said. "Should I read it aloud?"

"No, I'm good."

Fletcher needed his focus, so at his insistence, they postponed their letter talk until they returned home. That discussion would ruin his enjoyment of the incredible machine between him and the road ahead: I-75 North. A route he knew well, but he and the 650 were only in courtship phase, according to Bo D, who shared his research with Fletcher at Olga's repast: *Lucky you, G-pop! Listen to this dating profile: 4500 pounds of Deep Sea Blue magic, 400 horses, 4.4 V8, zero to 60 in 4.9 seconds. Dang! Take me with you—Please! I'll squeeze into the backseat—you won't even know I'm there!*

Fletcher shifted down to ease through the south Georgia drawl, where 300 flows into I-75 below Macon. If this stretch had a profile, it would be *curvaceous and luscious, an abundance of trees.* And what a shame: being forced to succumb to small town speed traps. Wasn't the ultimate driving machine designed for something called an *autobomb* where you go as fast as the car can handle? In a few miles, this mid-Georgia calm would give way to defensive/offensive schizophrenia as Atlanta 75 turned beastly.

High Museum jazz set the stage for an intimate evening. The next day Altovise tracked down a perfect Tom Ford knockoff: double-breasted, midnight-blue pinstripe, and paired his skinny bronze tie from high school with a black shirt. She topped this off with a surprise gift: jade tiepin and cufflinks, carved to look like a totem. Later, sitting outside her dressing room at Phipps Plaza Nordstrom as she modeled floor-length gold dresses, Fletcher had no complaints.

each generation
is a ship at risk but for what we know
and freely give
master rudder
and anchor
guiding Purvis Dukes
the first name to survive the predator's story
followed by many sons and daughters

39

~

"If you can't find a wench yourself in your travels, then I'll find one for you," Calhoun snarled a week after Malik's twentieth birthday. The pirogue business took him and his team up and down the Sea Island coast doing what he had loved most back home in Podor. Daneejo overseers watched their whole process, making this a vengeful freedom. His range of loneliness was curtailed as his friendships deepened and his language widened. He and his cabinmates no longer slept on boxes. In their new woodshop, they built tall oak bedframes to protect them from "blood-sucking spiders." He hid his money in a wooden box in the wall behind his bed. He had spent two years immersed in Horace's Lowcountry brogue and Crayfish's Bayou Creole. This drew from him a mash-up with a sound and cadence that surprised him as he emerged from his silence. All of this was helped by his growing role in expanding the Rise up and down the coast.

At home, elders had chosen Nbey, but neither the hearts of civil men nor the eyes of Allah would condone a union arranged by feral daneejos.

In late December, Malik, Horace, and Crayfish traveled to a plantation on Dewees Island to build two pirogues. The owner was at first glance a jolly, generous man named Thompson, who treated his captives with more respect than Malik was used to.

"Don't let them buckruh fool oonuh," Horace told Malik. "Jack-asses and mules look alike."

As dusk fell on their first day, a kitchen helper brought baskets of food to their cabin.

"Y'all hongry?" she asked, spreading a worn flour sack cloth over dusty floorboards. With a rhythm Malik did not know, she kneaded and folded the daneejo English and Sea Island Creole into a medley all her own.

"Ebele Okoro is my name." She stood with hands on hips. "Cook say welcome y'all with these biscuits an fried redfish an trout heads. Her make the best!"

"T'engky, t'engky, ma'am!" Crayfish sang, taking a seat on bare pine planks.

"Beg pardon, miss, that boy ain't have no mannus," Horace said, turning to Ebele. "Him from backwater." Then, putting palm to chest, "Horace is my name. An them be Crayfish and Malik. We happy to have yo fish heads flavor we mout!"

"Obliged to meet y'all—now eat up!" Ebele curtsied slightly and left.

Malik basked in the incense of her rustling skirts, woody fragrances like the barks, flowers, and oils Yaaye formed into balls and burned in hot ashes to purify their hut.

In the coming days, Crayfish set up his usual connections with house servants and learned that Ebele was Igbo from Akwa Akpa in West Africa. To his surprise, Malik looked forward to sharing a smile with her over baskets of food. She was demure, had restraint and grit in one breath, like Nbey. On more than a few evenings, she and Malik found time to sit alone, talking.

He told her about Nbey and their children and she told him of her husband.

"Banjoko." Her eyes moistened, but her voice remained steady. "His name say *stay with me*. Fingers in we village pointed to me husband, say he stole four goats. Elders sell him away. He ain't done that. Had no call to. Us had two goats! That was plenty. And he ain't have chance—him and me lay chest-to-chest when that deed was done. But us ain't have power against traders and elders. Profit from Banjoko help we village, but me can't abide that help with our child growin inside me."

This real world with Ebele overlapped with thoughts of his lost world with Nbey. Malik had no language to translate his conflicted feelings. Ebele twisted and pulled at her fingers, and Malik longed to quiet her hands with his. But was this only because he was thinking of Nbey?

"To this day, us ain't know where Banjoko be," Ebele went on. "Who gon conjure a place this evil? With them-buckruh-them thinkin they god an actin like the devil? These two years me done search faces, and search faces looking for Banjoko.

"After him gone seventy-eight days, me walkin with two friends tween we villages. Two buckruhs rush up on us, flauntin they stank breath and guns. Us just walking. After good fishing in the Great Kwa."

Her voice dropped from shrill to frail as she told about their baby girl, born on board the ship, too weak to thrive, buried in the Atlantic.

ॐ

Looking out at fallow winter fields around Dewees Island, Malik thought back to running through Podor's millet field with Nbey before their wedding. And now, he also welcomed thoughts of Ebele. Each doleful story, each tear and smile, drew them closer and closer.

In his usual way, Crayfish worked with house captives, and Malik and Horace with those in the fields. By the time they finished building pirogues, they had expanded the Rise by two: Ebele and the house mistress' maid who could read and write. This was a double-edged sword bringing great value at tremendous risk as they built on plans for schooling.

Malik was beginning to feel blood and breath return to his body.

He was in no hurry to leave. He had not known how deep his sadness was until he allowed this kernel of desire to crack open, letting Ebele in, bit by bit.

He wanted to protect her because that was his wish for Nbey, and he knew her husband, wherever he was, wanted the same for her. He was not concerned about the daneejo's threat to find him a mate. If she would not have him, he could remain alone; an empty man who makes pirogues that were once again in demand; a man with purpose and plan.

Satisfied that his intentions toward her were honorable, Ebele told Malik she was bound by honor to tell him: "That day us got took, them two buckruh had they way with us right there among trees where us had romped and played since knee-high. Heap a time us gone to the Kwa to fish. Us baskets was full-up with all the ekpai us caught that day." For a moment, a proud smile tore through her pain. "Only one balm eased that shame—me family and Banjoko never know bout that."

Malik took her hand, kissing each finger, and held her as she cried.

Their courtship was slow and steady. "Like Brer' Cooter," Ebele said, "us might take a long time gettin there but when us *do* get there, us stay put."

On July 25 in 1812, facing the Atlantic, bare feet buried in sand, Malik and Ebele were married on Pawleys Island. He carved a special cup from a sweet gum branch, and as best they could, they held to Igbo and Fulani customs. Through their strong connections up and down the coast, Malik accepted two yards of indigo fabric from a friend on Ossabaw Island. From this, Ebele fashioned a *gele* (head tie) and another long section of rough osnaburg became her *iro*, tied around her waist and flowing to her ankles. An Igbo friend on Kiawah Island grew henna and painted an intricate floral design on Ebele's hands for good luck. Back in Akwa Akpa, she would luxuriate in no housework for two weeks as the henna faded. They were both allowed only the afternoon off. For Ebele there was to be no playful banter between families and friends, no dancing or florid colors. For

Malik, no three days of celebrating, no elders blessed their union with stories and prayers and the ancestral urn. In place of these, a traveling preacher reading from a well-worn buckruh Bible. Would this union be recognized in the eyes of Allah? In the eyes of Chukwu?

"Take your pick," Ebele said when Malik asked what would her bride price be, were he able to pay. "Alligator pepper, bitter kola, a bag of salt, rice, or sugar," she razzed, "you would need many bronze manila rings!"

Horace and Crayfish stood with Malik; Calhoun's cook, Berthenia, stood with Ebele. Bride and groom melded wedding traditions by sharing a drink. In the absence of Igbo palm wine, and Fulani cola, they drank blackberry juice from their sweet gum cup.

Horace presented a small basket covered with sun-bleached cotton.

"Go head on," he said, "thems for oonuh! Take that rag off!"

"Aye-aye!" Ebele said, "where oonuh get peaches?"

"Oldmixons in season." He smiled and handed them each a fruit. "Took near-about a year but me done come through." He rubbed his palms, stepping back to address Malik. "Me know oonuh still harboring yo mother seed." Malik rode a surge of joy, tapping his shirt pocket. "And oonuh here, in sand again—done git hitched with this pretty little bride, and fresh seeds still in these here peaches. That all mean something."

"Well go head on y'all, eat up!" Crayfish said and struck up a frisky tune on his harmonica.

All present kept time to the music as Malik sliced into each peach with his pocketknife. He and Ebele watched with wonder as the fuzzy halves came cleanly apart, revealing honey-colored jewels sunken in golden flesh.

"This a freestone." Horace spoke over music and clapping. "Just lift them seeds right out. Ain't hardly no need to suck them clean."

Ebele and Malik giggled like children as peachy-sweet juice ran between their fingers, down their arms, and was soaked up by sand.

Impulsively, bride and groom pranced down to wade freely in the water.

40

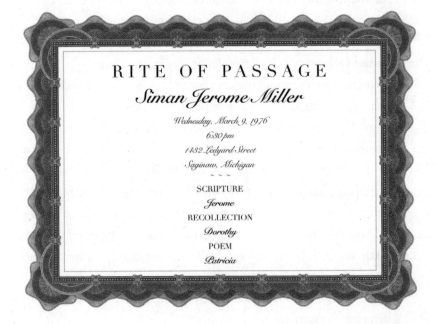

RITE OF PASSAGE
Siman Jerome Miller

Wednesday, March 9, 1976
6:30 pm
1432 Ledyard Street
Saginaw, Michigan

~ ~ ~

SCRIPTURE
Jerome
RECOLLECTION
Dorothy
POEM
Patricia

Siman turned thirteen midweek with school and work on both sides, so his rite of passage was abbreviated, as explained by Jerome. The following Saturday, they had a large family barbecue a few blocks down at McKinney Park. At Siman's insistence, their family of four never discussed his peach seed monkey outside of home.

Having no model to follow in designing the ceremony, his parents and Patricia turned to church and school for inspiration. Dressed in their Sunday best, they gathered in the living room.

"Siman," Jerome spoke in a stern, nervous voice, "we are assembled here today to celebrate your journey into manhood, and your connection to the mother of your birth. We do not know her name, nor have we seen her countenance, but her love for you lives undeniably, in this beautiful *talisman*." He held up the ring box. "That is a new, strange word for you—I can see by your face. Look it up after dinner, young man!

"I will read from the King James version of First Corinthians, chapter thirteen, verses eleven through thirteen.

> *When I was a child, I spake as a child, I understood as a child, I thought as a child: but when I became a man I put away childish things. ∼ For now we see through a glass, darkly; but then face to face: now I know in part; but then shall I know even as also I am known. ∼ And now abideth faith, hope, charity, these three; but the greatest of these is charity.*

"Dorothy, I pass this charge to you."

Dorothy stood, cradling the ring box with a crisp yellow handkerchief. "My dear son, Siman. On this day thirteen years ago we rejoiced at your passage into this world, and also at the privilege of being chosen, by your mother, to become your family. She gave us this monkey and charged us with guarding it until this day.

"Patricia, I pass this charge to you."

Patricia took the ring box and a folded sheet and walked slowly over to face Siman, beckoning him to stand.

"Baby Brother, well, this is the last time I can call you that, because you're not a little boy anymore, but don't be gettin a big head because—"

"Paaa-TRI-cia," Dorothy implored, "more solemn, please."

"Sorry, Mama." She and her brother stifled laughs, and she found her serious voice. "Young man! You're not a little brother anymore. You're thirteen and taller than me and I'm very proud of you. Makes me want to get out into that ring of life and fight for the things we believe in and want for each other that are good. And now, I'll read some lines from this poem by Rudyard Kipling:

> **If—**
> *If you can keep your head when all about you*
> *Are losing theirs and blaming it on you,*
> *If you can dream—and not make dreams your master;*
> *If you can think—and not make thoughts your aim;*
> *If you can talk with crowds and keep your virtue,*
> *Or walk with Kings—nor lose the common touch,*
> *If you can fill the unforgiving minute*
>   *With sixty seconds' worth of distance run,*
> *Yours is the earth and everything that's in it,*
>   *And—which is more—you'll be a Man, my son!*

"Siman, I end this charge with you."

She placed the monkey in his hand and hugged her brother. Dorothy followed, her handkerchief catching tears, and Jerome shook his son's hand. Siman tried shoving hands in pockets, but the ring box would not fit. He was at a loss for what to do, a problem quickly solved by Dorothy sending everyone off to wash up for dinner.

Siman held the peach seed monkey, imbued with his first mother's love. The woman who, since he turned six and learned he was adopted, had been an ever-present thought in his mind. He still did not know who she was, but on this day, touching what her hands had touched, she was transformed into matter. At the dinner table, he began asking questions and waiting for his new talisman to answer.

🙙

Her name was lyrical.

Her voice a song.

Siman clung to the moment, as he dreamed he would since the day of his rite of passage.

Even though for most of his life, his questions were unanswered, he still believed with a depth and breadth that matched his maturity at thirteen, at nineteen, at thirty—decade upon decade. And now, at forty-nine, his gap of uncertainty was closing.

Barefoot in his slouchiest sweats, he touched Altovise's number on his phone screen, looking calmly out at his view: *BEANS* bunny sign against a histrionic sky, golden windows reflected on water.

Altovise said, "I am so grateful to Bo D for orchestrating this phone call, and thank you for making time."

To hear his mother's voice speaking to him for the first time, he could see the astonishing soul he never doubted her to be.

"Trust me, there's not a single thing I'd rather be doing."

"I hope this will be our first of many, and it breaks my heart that you won't get to meet dear Olga."

"She worked so hard to make all of this happen," Siman said. "I'm heartbroken, too."

"Actually, I've been waiting to tell you about the month or so when she was incommunicado."

"She called it her *hiatus*. Would that be when *you* drove into town?" he asked.

"Yes. A very stormy time. Bo D and Fletcher were in the midst of a feud, and Olga and Fletcher were not yet convinced that my returning home was unrelated to your search for me."

"I can understand that."

"So could I."

Siman tried to imagine a call with Fletcher Dukes. What was their relationship like now that she was back? Would it be fair to ask her about him? Again, this called for granting grace.

"I thought I'd start by putting things into a historical context for you," Altovise said, "the hopeless teacher in me, I suppose."

"I think that's a great place to start."

He would think about Fletcher Dukes later. Now was the time

for singing. He would collect every note, every measure his mother offered, to rearrange in his mind until their meeting day. Feet up on the sofa, he relaxed, craving crunchy Cheetos as twilight shimmered. He imagined his mother in a lecture hall.

"Three years before you were born, the famous Greensboro Woolworth's sit-ins had spread nationwide. The South was a mess in the '60s, closer to post-Reconstruction than a solid, progressive future. Sad to say, not enough has changed in 2012."

"And then there's Obama!"

"Oh yes! Our beautiful president and first lady! None of us thought we'd live to see this day. And you were born into a change era for this country; we were carrying on a movement that began during enslavement and set the groundwork for such a miracle as Barack Obama to happen—but let me stop here, this is sounding like a lecture! I'll do my best to answer any questions you have."

"I'm interested in whatever you have to say." Siman wasn't sure what to call her.

"Let's see," she laughed, "I could tell you that I was the Monroe High FBLA Hula-Hoop Champion of 1960 to 1961!"

"And did you make it to the finals?" More laughs, and Siman stopped by the kitchen, poured a tonic with lime, and filled a bowl with Cheetos for his after-party.

"No, couldn't quite make the grade." She paused and her voice shifted in mood. "That young version of me was filled with angst and confusion, and you suffered the pain that naturally comes with feeling abandoned. My actions caused that pain, and for that I am truly sorry."

"I appreciate that, and I know you did what you thought best for us both, so it is enough for you to acknowledge, no need to apologize."

"I can understand why you might harbor strong feelings of resentment."

"Never. I resented a lot of things, even my stunning talisman for a while, for what he couldn't give me—but never you. I didn't know how to do that, because Dorothy and Jerome were very loving folk."

"That's beautiful." She hesitated. "I don't know if I'm deserving."

"Of course you are. The trauma of giving me up was compounded by the inconvenience of being Black—who was it said that?"

"That was James Weldon Johnson: *It's no disgrace to be black, but it's often very inconvenient.*"

"Right, that's the one—and you faced it all bravely."

"Siman. I appreciate what you're doing, but I've had to live with holding you in my arms, counting your perfect little fingers, your perfect little toes, tracing those pointy ears, and asking forgiveness for making the biggest mistake of my life."

"On the day I was born, you helped complete a family where none had existed. That was no mistake. That was a noble choice."

41

$\sim$

Bo D stood at the marble island in his mother's kitchen, waiting for his laptop to boot up. Although he didn't like that everybody was a little too surprised that his plan for the scattering worked well, thanks to him they now had a blueprint for how to do it, not that there would be another Dukes family cremation for a very long time. He felt good knowing that Auntie Olga's faith in him paid off.

His mother walked in from her poolside Weber, wearing heavy oven mitts, carrying a glass Pyrex sizzling with grilled meat loaf, Bo D's favorite since he and his parents lived in a small Jackson Heights apartment and she cooked out on their cramped second-floor balcony.

"OK, Ma, I got Skype ready to go," he said. "Auntie should be logging on any minute now."

Florida put the mitts aside. "I still can't believe this whole thing. Georgia will flip out."

Barely twenty-four hours had passed since he'd told his mother about their brother. She seemed more hurt that Auntie Olga confided in him over her, and was trying her best—for his sake he was sure—to hide her letdown with sarcasm. With all that was going through her mind, she didn't bother hiding the gin and tonic and cigarette she enjoyed while tending the grill. What could he say?

Olga advised Bo D to stage a conference call with both aunts, withholding information about Siman until they asked questions—that would show their readiness to receive answers. Florida switched directions, wanting to tell her twin first, so they could decide how to proceed with Mozell. Bo D held the laptop as his mother shook rice back and forth in a strainer under running water.

"Hey, sis," Georgia's voice crackled.

"Hey, where you?" Florida said. "We got a sketchy connection."

"At my office. What's up now?"

"Nothing much, just thought you'd like to know Ourdaddy has a *son*."

"This connection must be worse than you thought." Georgia chuckled.

"You heard right. Ourdaddy. Has. A son."

Bo D watched as torrential surprise washed all expression from his aunt's face. As his mother did so often, she then pinched her brow. Identical faces, even at forty-four, except for his mom's deeper worry lines. When he was a toddler Bo D called them both Ma-ma until Florida trained him to recognize her perfume.

"Hello?" Florida said, turning to look at the screen.

"I'm still here," Georgia said. "So Number One Nephew, is this really a thing?"

Bo D swerved the screen to face him.

"Yep, Auntie. Started well over a year ago: Uncle Siman's sister found Auntie Olga's blog, they started emailing, that lead to Skyping, and next thing I knew she was trusting me with secret family stuff about Uncle Siman."

"You say *Uncle Siman* like you've had practice," Georgia said. "I'm sure you're psyched. You been wishing for an uncle since forever."

"Word!" Bo D said, quickly looking from his mother to his aunt.

"But you know: can't nobody take the place of my beautiful aunties!" That was true, and felt like the right thing to say.

"What's his full name?" Georgia asked.

"Siman Miller," Bo D answered.

"And I suppose it's obvious who the mother is?"

"Now you know that's Altovise Benson." Florida turned to Bo D. "Tell her about them letters."

Bo D explained how things ratcheted up after the memorial with the delivery of two bright green envelopes.

"Did you actually read this letter?"

"Yep," they answered in unison.

"Did Auntie Olga sign it?"

"Yep. Totally legit, Auntie." Bo D had thought he would miss being Family Keeper of Secrets, but now he wanted everybody to know—what good was this gift of trust if it was a secret?

"How old is he?" Georgia asked.

"Forty-nine," Bo D said.

"Three years older than Mozell—and where does he live?"

"Saginaw, Michigan."

Florida cut in, "And he'll be here the day after Christmas."

"What?" Georgia cried. "That's in two weeks!"

"You heard me," Florida said.

"Let me get this straight: Auntie Olga's been dead six weeks and dropping bombs from the grave?"

"You mean from the urn on my mantelpiece." Florida dug through vegetables in the crisper drawer. "But—yeah—exactly."

Rather than wait for more questions, Bo D explained the story from bumper to bumper with one interruption from his mother:

"You forgot that part about how she wouldn't marry him."

"I think it's cool how they found each other again," Bo D said, summing up and aiming the screen at his mother. He tried to imagine a scenario where this family finally met Siman.

"It is what it is," Georgia said, "and better we find out now than at Ourdaddy's funeral."

"Is *that* all you got to say?" Florida said, chopping up cabbage.

"Well hell, Florida. All was said and done before any of us were even a glint: we have a brother three years older than Mozell, so Mama and Ourdaddy weren't even together yet."

No one spoke. Georgia recovered quickly and moved on. "So. What does Ourdaddy have to say about all this?"

"Nothing!" Florida furiously tossed cabbage in the colander. "He's just been acting like he saw a ghost, same way he was when the long-lost girlfriend rode into town."

"Give him time," Georgia said, "he's even more in shock than we are. Can you imagine? He's finally getting the son he always wanted and one thing's for sure: no use arguing with the past."

"He been calling us out of our names long enough," Florida said.

"I know that's right!" Georgia agreed.

Bo D didn't understand their laughter. Was this how they hid their dislike? He had to know.

"So, y'all don't hate being called *son*?"

"'Hate' is a strong word," Georgia was even-keeled, "as I said, it *is* what it *is*, Number One."

"And, Terrence, you and I know better than anybody: there're a lot worse things he could be doing—and not doing—as our father."

"True that, Ma. True that."

"Oh-Kaay!" Georgia trumpeted, "Tag. I'm it. I'll call Mozell."

❦

Bo D joined his mother at the counter, spreading a napkin in his lap. He felt a little bad about deciding to enjoy the serenity of her gin and nicotine buzz right along with her meat loaf.

"Thanks, Terrence. I appreciate you handling that Skype. Mozell will probably pitch a fit when Georgia tells her."

"Auntie Georgia sure took it in stride."

"That's the analytical accountant for you."

Facing two more months of sober living, Bo D looked at his mother without vindictiveness. They all wanted to see her sober, but without Auntie Olga, who was willing to walk through that fire?

"Shoot," Florida said, "this rice is crunchy!"

"Just a little," he said. It was pretty bad. His whole life he'd never known his mother to make crunchy rice.

"Measured the water wrong, I guess—"

"It's OK, Ma. You had a lot on your mind and there's a first time for everything."

"Oh hell no!" She rose. This called for order: scrape-rice-into-garbage-disposal-ON-OFF. "We can't be eating no crunchy rice up in here—I have some mashed potatoes I can throw in the microwave—"

Bo D took a big bite of meat loaf.

"Ma. You put your foot in this meat loaf. Again. Where you get this recipe? Never heard of nobody else making grilled meat loaf."

"I don't know. Just made it up."

"For real? That's dope, Ma. You ought to send it in to one of them cooking shows."

"Boy, hush and eat!"

He saw clearly what to do next. Auntie Olga had the right idea: he would arrange a conference call with just him and his aunts to start walking through the wildfire called Florida.

﹩

Such icons as Oscar Micheaux, Carman Newsome, and Hattie McDaniel stared out from movie posters blanketing Eusi Theater's lobby walls. Floor-to-ceiling tarps cordoned off the renovation area as Bo D treaded through, dodging young recruits. Their loud chatter rose above buzzing saws, drills, and pounding hammers as they moved wardrobe, props, and set parts to various locations in the building and parking lot. Bo D was officially on payroll as makerspace coordinator and was close to finishing the tech director apprenticeship.

He bounced upstairs to meet Tyrone in their makeshift head-quarters: the old balcony, now stripped of seats, with computers, office machines, and files on folding tables.

Greeting Tyrone, Bo D felt a surge of nervousness, not sure if he was ready for his first crew meeting.

"Before we go," Tyrone said, handing Bo D a large shopping bag, "you'll be wanting to open this!"

"What?!" Bo D grinned removing tissue paper.

"I know it has high Cricket-value but it's about time you reserve your camouflage backpack for family outings, don't you think?"

"Dog! This is dope!" Bo D lifted out a brown leather messenger bag.

"You'll demand much more respect with distressed leather."

"As if the laptop wasn't enough," Bo D said, "you going whole hog on me. Thank you."

Tyrone slapped his friend on the back. "Let's go! Our guys are waiting."

They passed rooms with dancers stretching and shuffling through playlists, actors running lines and blocking scenes, finally entering a large room where a dozen young men joked and chatted as they arranged a circle of chairs.

Tyrone called for order and Bo D was happy to be away from Loblolly for a few hours, but as he looked around the circle of slouch and swagger, it seemed the ranch's group therapy had followed him—except this time, everybody was Black.

"First want to welcome y'all!" Tyrone said, and then gestured toward Bo D. "This is my brother from another mother, Terrence Fowler."

"And y'all can call me Bo D."

"A little later he'll be pitching our tech/makerspace division, but first, we getting ready to break some ice."

Tyrone rubbed palms together. "So! From *your* perspective, what needs fixing in Albany, G-A?"

No one replied.

"C'mon now," Bo D urged, not sure what emboldened him. "I bet ya'll have plenty complaints and ideas when nobody's asking. Now we're asking."

"Shiiit—ev'ry-thang broke," said a young man whose slumped posture was amplified by the waist of his jeans hitting around midthigh.

"Thanks, Davian, say more," Tyrone said, adjusting his recorder.

"Have to go to clubs in Atlanta for fun, too many drugs, pawnshops, and liquor stores in the Black community. That's four broke things right there. And I'm just getting started."

"Just because there's liquor stores and all that," Jahrel added, "don't mean you got to go up in there. To have freedom in one place you got to exercise restraint somewhere else. I feel like we bring a-lotta this stuff on ourselves, for example: Obama back for his second term and we still got Black people saying *What he doing for me?* instead of thinkin' what we can do together for the whole world, because regardless of race on Judgment Day? . . . it's gone be over for all of us."

"Don't fool yourself, man," Davian said. "Every day is Judgment Day for the Black man. You talking about restraint and I'm lookin for justice."

This idea rippled, sparking cross talk.

"OK-OK," Tyrone said. "Let's hear from some of our more thoughtful brothers."

The talkative young men shifted in their chairs, looking around. Finally, Christoph spoke up.

"Older people always axing why we younger guys do this and that, 'cause when they was coming up there was plenty to do. I know things was bad back then, but I feel like neighborhoods was more structured and people could find good jobs—but now? Justice is still on holiday right now in 2012."

"Damn right!" a voice yelled out, followed by more babel.

"Hold up, ya'll." Bo D moved to the center, pivoting, with all eyes on him. "Bringing up justice reminds me of a story my auntie Olga always told about Sis Goose. Y'all wanna hear it?"

Bo D felt old in their presence, watching his offer fall to the floor.

"Yeah, man," Christoph said, "tell your story."

Bo D slipped his great-aunt on like a warm sweater, starting the story as she always did:

"Well—they tell me Sis Goose was sailin' on the lake one day, and Brer Fox was hidin' in the high grass. Sis Goose came too close to the shore and Brer Fox snatched her up. *I got-you now*, he said, *an I'm gon wring yo neck an pick yo bones.* Sis Goose said, *We'll just see about that, 'cause I got jes' as much right to sail on this lake as you got to hide in the grass.* So they took the matter to the court. And when they got there, the judge was a fox. Both the lawyers was foxes, all the jurymen was foxes, too. And they tried Sis Goose, convicted her, and wrang her neck and picked her bones."

"Ooo—you could see that coming!" Davian hooted.

Bo D waited until the laughter subsided. "Goes to show: when all the folks in the court is foxes and you just a common goose, there ain't no justice."

"That's deep!" Jahrel called out.

"Paradox," Tyrone added, "looking for justice in the same place we lost it," and Bo D knew he was quoting Lysander Songtree.

"So what do we *do* about it?" asked Zevanté, who had been sitting quietly.

"That's obvious," Christoph said. "We have to work to change the systems that keep perpetrating foxes over everybody else!"

"I wants to start with me a *good J-O-B*," said Davian, "'cause it take a lotta bills to make it rain!" This was met with boisterous agreement.

"I like your goal, Davian," Bo D said, "but your motive needs work."

Tyrone reeled in the chaos and recognized Zevanté's raised hand.

Rocking back in his chair he said, "Y'all ain't never done no time. I'm on probation from juvie right now."

"How old are you, man?" Bo D asked.

"Fourteen and the onliest reason I'm here is 'cause them foxes made it mandatory. So, yeah. Y'all don't even know."

"Zevanté's right," Bo D said. "We who haven't done time are lucky. Like a wise man told me once, the difference between us and our brothers in jail is the thickness of the bars. By my own hand I have been imprisoned in my mind and soul, held hostage by drugs." He faced Zevanté. "So you and I may have more in common than you think." Bo D extended his hand. "You feel me?" Zevanté faced him sternly and shook his hand.

Bo D took back the floor to talk about tech and makerspace plans. There was genuine interest around the circle and lots of questions.

This led to a clamor of friendly banter as they stacked chairs until a collective "Shhh" swept through the room.

"Knock, knock." All heads turned as Altovise stepped in.

"Dr. Al!" Tyrone rushed over. "What a nice surprise!"

"Just came from props and thought I'd drop in on you."

"Listen up, crew!" Tyrone said. "This is the phenomenal woman I've been preaching about. Dr. Altovise Benson: international scholar, jazz and blues singer/songwriter/piano virtuoso, and member of the Muscogee Creek Nation. She's helping us take Eusi to the next level!" He led them in applause.

"No-no," Altovise said. "I applaud all of *you*, for seeing this dream through." She looked toward the door as Vada walked in.

"Mrs. Stanton?" Tyrone and Bo D said in harmony.

"Yes," Altovise said. "This is my dynamic sister, Vada Stanton."

"Wait a minute!" Tyrone said. "*Our* Mrs. Stanton from second grade is your sister?"

Tyrone announced, "If not for amazing teachers like this woman right here, Bo D and I might not have survived those foxes in the system Davian was talking about."

The bustle resumed as Tyrone and Bo D moved Vada and Altovise out into the hallway.

Vada placed herself between them, an arm around each. "You two!

It's a rare day that we get to witness former students out here paying it forward. I'm not surprised. Even at seven you both had big ideas and big mouths. I'm so proud you chose to run your mouths for good."

Bo D adjusted his backpack and new messenger bag, one on each shoulder, scarcely able to believe this was his life. He had taken to the streets in search of rock bottom. Veteran addicts told him it has nothing to do with how long you're out there, but rather how fast you fall.

Bo D thought back to rehab. He wrote a poem that he committed to memory and recited at their culminating ceremony:

Bitter Sacrament

When I was using
I called the drugs my highball
   a Holy Trinity
   Weed
      Pills
         Beer
But for real?
She was my love.
She courted me
   I courted her
And we married
   for better or for worse.
She became my Jesus & Mary.
I worshipped at her altar
Smoke
   Swallow
      Drink
         Chew
            Crush
              Snort
Process & Product
We evolved side by side.

I was raised in Sunday School & Church
Until I traded the pulpit of my mother for
My love's holy table.
Tasteless wafer and grape juice were lost
To the bitter sacrament of white powder.
New sacred vessels claimed me:
Pipe
   Bottle
      Pill Crusher
         Mortar & Pestle.

Love can destroy.
Love can rip and roil
   scrape like road rash
   glass and gravel
      your new skin.

But sometimes.
If you lucky.
If you let her
      Love can heal.

42

Deke's and Tonk's hunting overalls swished loudly as they walked around Altovise's car parked in Fletcher's driveway.

"A convertible with white interior? Now that's what I call living dangerously," Deke exclaimed as they rejoined Fletcher at their pickup trucks. A flurry of wagging tails took over until Tonk's whistle and hand signal sent three dogs galloping off toward the pond. The men approached Altovise sitting on the porch, sealing an envelope.

"Must be halftime in heaven," Deke continued, "'cause there's a angel down here taking a break."

His reference to her hit song was well-placed, and Altovise wasted no time retaliating. "And I'm sure coach wants to see you in the locker room 'cause you definitely need a talking-to."

"You done met your match now." Tonk laughed. "Take it like a man, Deke, take it like a man!"

"My pleasure, Miss Altovise." Deke rested his cap on his chest. "I got all your records and been waiting my whole life to say that to *somebody*!"

"Thank you." Altovise extended her hand. "All in good fun. But you gentlemen have me at a disadvantage, you know my name but I don't know yours."

"That's Silas," Fletcher interrupted, "and we call him Deke. And this sucker here is Friday. We call him Tonk."

"Friday is such a unique name," Altovise said. "I had an uncle named Friday."

"Yeah? Turns out I even like fish," Tonk said.

"Pardon me for barging in on y'all; had hoped to drop this in the box before you got back, but since we're all here, this is an invitation to my New Year's Eve party out at Cromartie Beach."

"Sound like fancy doings," Deke said.

"Dress-to-impress." She beamed, handing the invitation to Fletcher. "I'll get two more from my car."

She had tried in vain to discuss the letters in the two days since their shopping spree. His letter was in the punch bowl, still unread. The time had come to find middle ground in their Siman ordeal.

While the men continued unloading, Altovise returned and handed out invitations.

"I can take that for you," she said, walking toward Fletcher to receive a grocery bag. He was still not accustomed to seeing her in Maletha's yard.

"This isn't a good time," she said, "but maybe I could come by later so we can talk about Olga's letter?"

Fletcher had a freezer full of fish—didn't make sense to spend good money just to keep from cooking—but they agreed that she would return in two hours with Chinese carryout.

"You know, Fletcher, not dealing with those letters might postpone your arrival at the platform, but it won't keep this train from coming into the station."

Before leaving, she pecked him on the cheek and said, "You'll understand that reference after you read the letter."

Being in no mood for dressing quail, Fletcher divided his kill between Deke and Tonk, who left after a fair amount of taunting.

Fletcher freshened up and took his envelope and a cup of coffee to his chessboard. He stood the king up on the white side and sat down to read.

Fletcher,

I'll get right to the point: pending acceptance by at least one of you, all arrangements have been made for your son, Siman Miller, to come to Albany. Would that I could be at the airport when he flies in. That's not in the cards, but I have faith that you will make that a grand day. It is in your hands.

Your beautiful monkey has led Siman home, and the day you meet will be the beginning of your time as a family—— however the three of you decide that will look.

I leave it up to you to get in touch with Altovise with this news.

Then you both can reach out to Ursula and Bo D (yes, he knows) for flight details and such. Here's her email and cell: info@dutchfriedchicken.com 229-898-9875.

Bear in mind: This train may pull into the station without your consent. Please, baby brother: get on board.

With all my love ~

. . . and one last word from the Berbers,

"Your secret is your blood, when you shed it, you die."

She signed her full name; her once delicate, flowing script now crept along in quaky curves.

In eerie stillness Fletcher tapped a pawn lightly in his palm, imagining Olga calling any minute. This was followed by a tornado touching down and slamming him against a wall.

He read Olga's words again. She specifically said it was up to him to let Altovise know. And how long had Bo D been involved?

"Onethingaboutit," he said, returning the pawn to its square, "a whole lotta cloudy skies getting ready to be cleared."

He laid the black king on its side and looked at the wall clock. Two hours had flown by. Setting out placemats and flatware ate up the last few minutes before Altovise returned.

§.

"Smells pretty good." Altovise unpacked white carryout boxes and chopsticks. "I wasn't sure what to get, settled on moo shu pork, broccoli beef, and shrimp fried rice."

Fletcher did not bother to say all Chinese food tastes the same, because in spite of what they were going through, it didn't much matter what they were eating; he was still happy to have her sitting across from him. While she washed up in the bathroom, he set out glasses of sweet tea.

"So. You read your letter?" she asked as they sat down.

"I did."

He slipped his envelope from punch bowl to table.

"So why did you hold yours up at the service like you knew I'd know what it was? Did y'all talk about her sending these?"

"We did not. Seemed like Olga's modus operandi, so I took a chance."

"Did you know Bo D was involved?"

"Trust me, I knew nothing about any of this until Bo D spoke to me briefly at the memorial. And I have to say, Fletcher, I'm excited to meet our son."

Their plates were full. Altovise started in with chopsticks; Fletcher used a fork.

"You reckon he's excited, too?" he asked.

"I know he is."

"How you know?"

"He called me two days ago, after Bo D and I spoke about it at the memorial. He first suggested Skype, but I'm not ready for that."

"I see." Fletcher pushed broccoli around with his fork.

"Bo D also suggested that you and I do a conference call with Siman. I'm sure he was following Olga's orders, but I didn't think you were ready. Was I wrong?"

"You know I've never thought much of phones."

"Can never forget that!" She poured iced tea then jumped ahead. "Siman wants to come right after Christmas, thinking the holidays might ease pressure for everybody. What do you think?"

"As good a time as any, I guess." Fletcher chose to be neutral. This went against his habit of ripping out an emotion like fish guts, calculating risks, before moving on. His time on Sapelo had brought clarity to these latest revelations. Her being pregnant and unable to tell him proved one thing: she didn't love him. Otherwise she wouldn't have walked away and carried this alone all these years. And now he suffered yet another loss: having no input into the man Siman had become. More proof that fathers are largely insignificant. Mothers matter even when they give up their child. Siman came looking for *her* fifty years later.

He paused, unaware that his expression had given her reason to ask—

"Fletcher? What is it?"

"Not long ago you said you left because you couldn't get everything to line up." He looked straight at her. "But after you left town, I had things lined up pretty well."

"What do you mean?"

"It wasn't just that you had to go to college. You didn't want *me*. Situation was cut-and-dry."

"That's not true." She stopped eating and leaned toward him.

"Don't get me wrong." He lifted a palm. "Can't nobody blame you for that. Why wouldn't you leave? Sure wasn't worth staying for me and my pride."

"That's just not true, Fletcher." She sat back in her chair. "There were many more reasons to stay than there were to leave—my family, my home—and at first the choice was so hard. The fact that you were worth coming back for proves you were worth staying for."

"What you mean it was hard *at first*?"

How could there be more to this story? Fletcher tried to brace himself.

"After the brig and finding out I was pregnant, I was on the brink of changing my mind about leaving. While inside, a group of us made a pact not to let those white folks chase us from our home, since south Georgia was built on the backs of our bloodlines. I was looking into enrolling at Albany State. But—"

"But what?"

"You proved you didn't love yourself, so I knew you couldn't love me and our baby."

"Don't know how you could think that."

She exhaled. Her face was awash in more blindsided regret with no time for him to shore up. Her words were an effortless crawl. "What else could I think after seeing you with Tammy Sue Harold. In her shed."

Fletcher was stunned.

"My God, Fletcher." She pushed her plate away. "Remember so-called *reckless* eyeballing? Black men were lynched for far less."

She had seen them.

He flashed back to that morning she told him about Siman, when only one of them knew there was more story to tell, when she kept carrying this second layer of torment in order to spare him. And here it was, that plaster ceiling finally crashing down.

"Veesy. Look at me." She seemed more and more fragile, turning her head but keeping her eyes lowered. "Will you look at me, please?" He caressed her hand.

"Nothing happened in that shed," he said. "I know that's hard to believe after holding on all these years to what looked apparent"—he slowly shook his head—"but nothing—"

She raised a finger. "Fletcher, please don't. I appreciate you trying to take care of me, but there's nothing between us that I haven't seen in a daydream or a nightmare a million times already. Will you let me tell you what I *did* see?"

He sat back to listen.

That afternoon Altovise had walked along a narrow path past the garden shed. She was delivering a package to her auntie Mac, who was the Harolds' maid and had raised Tammy Sue and her brothers.

She heard a sound she couldn't decipher coming from the shed and peeked through one of several small, dingy windows out of concern. Through streaked light, the black-and-white houndstooth shirt stood out—she had given it to him their first Christmas together. Then she saw his face in dappled shadow and the side of Tammy Sue's blond head. Her muffled moans were like an alluring cat, with paws stroking his bare chest. Altovise clutched the package and quickly pushed away, eyes squeezed shut, wringing tears, black-and-white houndstooth repeating even after she opened her eyes.

"My heart was beating in my throat," she said, "and I looked around, glad that I didn't see anybody else. I was trying to get my face in order before knocking on that kitchen door, because my aunt could read me like a book. Before I could get there, Ann Harold's gold Cadillac pulled up."

Fletcher whispered, "So that was you talking with Ann Harold?"

"I complimented her hair, her dress, her shoes, trying to stall. But I had to leave before knowing if you got out. Also realizing you had nowhere to go."

Her smile was downcast, arms crossed in a self-hug. And he was stuck for a moment on album names, song titles, and lyrics. He knew them all. Intimately. He now knew the very song she wrote about this. She had laid out her life in songs. That's how she made it through alone all these years. She brought him back with what she said next.

"Fletcher. This was about more than you giving up on us. You *literally* risked your life! I figured you had to be serious about the girl to do that. But I couldn't understand. Still don't."

"I had messed up and lost you. So by the time I ended up in that shed, my life was already gone. Had nothing to lose. I'm so sorry. I was a fool. That girl meant nothing. Less than nothing. Little did I know she would end up costing me everything."

Altovise spoke in a cracked whisper, "All the way from Ann Arbor to Albany I wrestled with whether to bring this up. Seemed pointless after all this time. Until what you said just now. I can't have you continuing to think that I didn't love you."

"Not in our hands, I guess." He tried to grant himself a modicum of the grace he felt for her. "The past dictates what parts will come to light."

He knew this was far from true. Our past has no more power than our future, because choices are made in the present. Life is careless, like kudzu, engulfing all that stands in its path, forging ahead with an eye on one thing—its longing for itself.

A newborn divide stretched between them, keeping him from kissing her eyes to free tears she held back. Fresh regret gripped his back, filled his shoes, and made it hard to push up from the table and walk around to her.

Fletcher asked how could they be dealing with things that happened and never happened half a century ago—like teenagers?

She didn't hesitate. "Because to hate another person is bad enough, but to hate yourself is beyond poison."

"But you had no reason to hate yourself," he said, "then or now."

"I'm not talking about me."

Because she said this with as much love as he had ever felt from her when they were young, he took those words as a gift. They only had a short time to be self-indulged teenagers before joining the Movement. Later, as they faced danger together, she diverted the rage he so readily carried underneath his nonviolent protests. She was still the water to his fire.

They were not like teenagers, in a dead heat to see who could most rightfully feel hurt and betrayed. They had seen life and known life and were capable of feeling each other's torment and willing to work through it.

Altovise's strength to move north, have their baby, go to college, and build an amazing life was not present now as she leaned her head into her hand. Based on what she saw in the shed that day, she had acted accordingly. What other choice did she have? Her leaving drove him to drink. Years later his only path to sobriety was transformation—he reimagined Altovise as a model of contentment, flying off to meet her dream life; and he preserved that memory in the amber of their youth. That invention became his higher power. But to learn now that she had seen them—his addiction seemed like ruffle and lace compared to her decades of pain.

Her chin trembled, and he cupped her hand in his.

"We got to let all this go, Veesy."

Like a boulder against crashing tides, he guided her up from sitting, to standing, to walking out to the dock, triggering floodlights as they moved. He held her face, and their divide stretched out and across, finally dissolving in deep water.

"Thank you," he said. "Your stalling that day gave me time to realize I needed to walk out that shed with my head high. Tammy Sue wanted me to hide in an old pickup behind the shed until dark. I told her she was crazy. I can see how hard it is to believe nothing happened, but walking away was the only thing I did right that day. I didn't care if her mama saw me. Finding you was the only thing on my mind. It was a dark night and I walked all the way home. Called you but your mother wouldn't let me talk to you."

"She was only honoring my wishes."

"I understand that now, but at the time it was more proof that you didn't love me. Couldn't sleep a wink that night, but believe me, nothing happened in that shed."

"I only wanted you," he said, pulling her closer. And there he felt her shift. She shrank in his embrace, as if she'd crumble.

"Nothing happened." He kissed her forehead, his palm caressing her kitchen. He would rather have kept living his lie than face her truth. "And we got to let this go."

"I can't," she said, her voice strong but shaken. "I'm glad you walked away from that shed. You can call it selfish and stubborn, but I call it pride. And it's your silver spoon, Fletcher. Handed down from cargo holds, cotton fields, paddy wagons, and jail cells. That can't be bought."

With his arms around her waist, he felt her tremble. After all that had come to light, *this* would be her undoing? This! A houndstooth shirt, a white girl, and a musty shed where nothing happened. She was plain and simply broken, wounded and weary. She had carried so much for so long for so many that it was not surprising that she would break with only words. A Sentence. A boulder that upset the balance of her strength. She wasn't crying, and if this had been anybody else, Fletcher would see that as a bad sign, like an immune system too weak to mount a fever. But this was Altovise. He had only seen her cry once, sophomore year at her grandmother Arnela's funeral. He saw clearly now. This *was* Altovise crying; letting tears fall on the inside.

"Veesy, I'm right behind you. Never left."

With a pardoning stroke of her hand on his face, she pulled away. He stepped back as she leaned into the banister and spoke down into dark water.

"Olga talked a lot about people who hate you more when they can find nothing to hate. It was the opposite for me. For a long time I wanted to be angry at myself: for all I'd done, all I hadn't done. But I couldn't find any reason for this. I couldn't be angry for giving Siman a better chance because he deserved two parents who loved him. I could only speak for myself, and you had spoken loudly, according to what I thought I knew. So instead of being angrier, I showed myself more and more compassion. And that's how I built my life."

"Sure is a lot more than most folk do. But weren't you angry at me?"

"No. I was hurt. And confused. But not angry. Everyone has a right to their own choices, and in my mind, you had made yours."

Fletcher rapped hard on the banister. She tapped a gentle hand on his fist; *water to fire.*

"Fletcher, the action chose you," she said.

"And we can say the same for you."

"Maybe. But to learn that it was all based on misperception? Now when I look at you, all I see is what we could've had." She covered her mouth. "I can't let go of that!"

He spread ten fingers apart on the banister, across wood and water. "But, Veesy, with the time we have left, what else *can* you do?"

She was always there for others. But in *her* moment of greatest need—did she really believe she was alone? Alone with words. Alone with a weight no one should have to carry? He asked if she would spend the night, just sleep, so he could keep an eye on her.

"I can't."

"Then I'm driving you home. We'll get your car to you tomorrow."

Inside the Fairlane, she had no more words. Fletcher wanted to be there for her. But she wouldn't look at him. Before he could turn off the engine, she was out and walking fast to her front door, turning the key and disappearing. He gripped the steering wheel and blinked to clear his view, which had somehow become wavy with water.

43

~

Bo D and Fletcher stood side by side, holding empty boxes, staring into Olga's study. Sidney followed, moping and sniffing around. Like the dog, her things seemed to be waiting: porcelain teacup with dried residue, *Yes We Can '08* buttons, silver watch, her sunglass collection.

Bo D knelt to rub Sidney's ears.

"That's a goo' boy! Cricket is so excited to have you around all the time now!"

Bo D watched his grandfather, slowly walking, running his hand along Olga's desk, book spines, rattan chair, and knitted afghan. He seemed burdened by an extra sadness. Couldn't be easy, having your long-lost love walk back in and your sister be taken away.

"It's like a museum in here," Bo D said.

"Yeah," Fletcher said. "Y'all set aside the books you keeping?"

"Yes, sir. Indicca already put ours on the top shelves." Bo D pointed. "After The Twins pick out what they want, the rest go to the library, just like Auntie Olga wanted, for those bookcases you made."

"All right," Fletcher said, starting to load boxes.

In a stack of old magazines, Bo D found multiple copies of the same issue of *Science Woman*. He turned to a paper-clipped section. "Look at this, G-pop."

"I remember this article," Fletcher said.

"Wow." Bo D scanned the page. "Listen to this—"

. . . But in 1955, after the torture and murder of Emmett Till, I would return to my southwest Georgia home. I was thirty-one and understood much that I had not grasped when I left at twenty-one. For centuries, torture, death, and jail have been the hammer used to pound fear into oppressed people the world over. Georgia gave the world the chain-gang system, bringing mostly Black prisoners from behind bars out into public view, chained together, toiling roadside under watchful eyes of armed guards for whites to see how government was answering their demand for a better transportation system, and Blacks were reminded what could happen to them if they stepped out of line—"Bad boys make good roads."

For as long as there have been albatrosses and millstones, downtrodden masses have risen up. But what changed in the 1960s? I'll tell you what: as we unbent our backs to move against the hammer's threat, technology added lights and cameras to our action. For the first time, the world saw aggressions of war and human rights <u>*in real time*</u> *and could never turn away again.*

"Auntie was fierce."

"Yeah," Fletcher said, his voice unsteady. "That was Olga."

"Seems right to keep one of these here in her study?"

"Yep, and give the rest to the library and Civil Rights Museum."

Failing to make neither heads nor tails of his grandfather's solemn mood, Bo D stuck to the tasks at hand.

"So you good, G-pop? Ma said she needed me."

"Yep. Go on."

The house was too quiet. Even his mother, whose voice always carried upstairs and through walls, spoke softly in this house now.

Indicca stood in the breakfast room, following a list as she wrapped items in newspaper. Florida knelt and rummaged through a lower kitchen cabinet. She was wearing Olga's silver watch necklace.

"What you looking for, Ma?"

"Found it!" She presented the smallest of Olga's cast-iron skillets. "Remember this?"

"Who could forget?" Bo D said. "I can taste that cake right now."

Through four generations of making her caramel cake, Olga always started by "spilling" a dollop of batter in this skillet just as her mother had done. Their scratch cake never needed adjusting, and generation after generation of kids looked forward to warm slices of sample cake.

"You know how to make that cake, Ma?"

"Not like Auntie Olga." Florida held the skillet next to her heart. "Do y'all mind if I keep this?"

"Whatever you want, Mama Florida," Indicca said, taking a dish towel from the drawer. "I'll wrap it up and put it in your box."

Fletcher and Florida drove off in his pickup loaded with boxes and Sidney in his crate, leaving Indicca and Bo D alone. The final condition of Olga's will—Bo D staying sober—would have to be satisfied to Indicca's liking. Meanwhile, Bo D was pleased to have her and Cricket finish moving within the week.

Indicca took a shower and changed into a flowing magenta robe. She sat in their guest room right off the kitchen at an antique dresser set, applying lotion to her legs. Bo D walked in and out, removing file boxes from the closet, but was soon capsized by her legs draped in shiny fabric.

"So. You satisfied that I'm sober yet?" he asked. "How long is long enough?"

"Slow down, Mister! You still got about a month in sober living," she said, now scrolling through her playlist. "I'll know when I see it.

"Oooo! This my song!" She jumped up, swaying, to Jill Scott's opening.

Exposing more than legs, head bobbing, she sang, "... *woke up in the morning feeling fresh to death, I'm so blessed, yes, yes ... momma on my right side, daddy on my left ...*"

He joined her, pressing his body into her back, slipped the robe aside to kiss her bare shoulder, smooth and sweet with some kind of oil; her hair smelled like coconut. There was a time when he knew every one of her favorite songs, and could sing them with her. Not anymore.

"I got a stipulation of my own," he whispered under the lyrics.

"And what would that be?"

"You let me take you shopping for paint—fastest way to change a decor."

"Wait." She put her hands on her hips. "Did you just say paint? And decor?"

She turned to face him. "How you gone be looking at all this," she traced her curves with waving hands, "and be talking bout some paint and decor?"

"Hol up hol up! Time out!" Bo D said and they both laughed.

"First of all, you look a-mazing, babe!" He hadn't used this nickname in years, and it was a good sign that she was letting him. He kissed several spots on her face. "I just want to make this house special for you and Shieka."

She sat on the bed. He followed.

"I know you do," she said, "and we will. You'll see."

He fell back, staring at the ceiling. "I worry if I can ever provide for y'all like a want to. Just look at what my mom did, by herself at the brewery. Did you know she had me the same year she started there?"

"No, didn't know that."

"Auntie Mozell and Auntie Georgia went to college, and Ma wanted to make that good money right out of high school. But she had to work other jobs for three years 'til she turned drinking age. After that? She started out on the packaging floor, and between raises, promotions, overtime, and double time she worked real hard! And look where she is now—Senior Distributor Sales Executive!"

"Don't worry. We gone get there," Indicca said.

"You off to a good start," he turned to face her, tucked a tendril of hair behind her ear, "and I'm proud of you. Got your own salon."

She perked up. "Specializing in old-school press and curl!"

"You and Cricket deserve this house, even if I don't."

"Stop that, Bo D!" She shoved him. "We deserve to be here together. *That's* what Auntie Olga wanted."

"Yeah, you right," he said. "She told me once: *throw a lucky man in the Nile and he will come up with a fish in his mouth.*"

"That's a good one," Indicca said. "I always liked them Auntie Olga sayings."

"I'm that lucky man," he said, "she did so much for me; and now this house." His voice cracked and faded. "She keeps on doing for me—even when I was on the streets, when she could've died."

"But she didn't." Indicca faced him. "Bo D, you could've died, too. But God willed it and you didn't. That was your sick time. When we said grace every Sunday dinner while you was gone, Auntie Olga reminded us that sometimes people get sick—mind, body, or soul. Now you getting well, and that's what matters. Like the song said, we so blessed!"

"For real," he said, "and this right here gone be one dope Christmas!"

"I know, right?" Indicca's eyes twinkled. "All Cricket want for Christmas is a dog."

"—now she got Sidney!" they said together.

Bo D fell into her big brown eyes. She kissed him softly.

"Can we forget about paint and decor for now?"

"I'm down with that," he whispered.

"But—we got to get one thing straight right now."

"OK."

She slipped a condom from her robe pocket into his hand. "I'm serious. At least for now."

He pulled a string of four from his back pocket.

"I'm serious, too. And I told you, there's nobody else. Hasn't been for months."

She looked beautiful, standing her ground. He raised his arms, and she pulled the T-shirt over his head. He lifted her, and with her legs wrapped around his waist, eased back onto the bed.

"Welcome back," she whispered.

"Welcome home," he said.

Months ago, on Spruce Cabin's back porch, Bo D had dreamed of kissing her, deeply. He did that now, released from his usual highball fluster. Bed became water, and they were a belly-whopping boat, salty and unmoored. Their bodies returned to each other and they took time; song after song her playlist mingled with their moves until they both gave in to exploding pleasure and washed ashore.

Their bodies sank into a lingering space, with time to take a nap before sober house rules beckoned him. With his hand in the small of her back, he flipped them over, her back against the bed, kissing sweet, cooling sweat on Indicca's face.

She turned on her side, pulling his hands around her to nestle like spoons.

Her voice was sleepy, almost a prayerful lilt. "What was it like anyway—out on the streets?"

"Everything."

"Everything?"

"Yeah. Gritty and smooth. Fragrant and rank. Light-dark. Heavy and featherweight.

"I liked early mornings best. I'm talking three to five A.M., quiet. Even barking dogs were still sleep, no people stirring, no traffic. If it was snow there would be no footprints yet. When you out in it like that, you can see the untouched newness of a day, feel how each one is like no other."

"That was God's hand, keeping you safe for us."

"Hey." He shifted focus, whispering and tucking covers around her. "Uh?"

"We should take Shieka to get a Christmas tree soon. A huge one!"

"Huh-uh—now go to sleep, boy—"

44

~

Siman tucked a pair of socks into itself to make a bundle, a trick learned from his mother, when she first packed him off to Boy Scout camp.

During these hours before a flight, the ten years since Jerome's and Dorothy's deaths felt like yesterday. Every move made as Patricia helped pack—rows of socks, crisply pressed khakis, jeans, and custom shirts—validated their bond as brother and sister, an attempt to bring order to the chaos in their forever broken hearts.

"Bo D said people dress pretty chill except for church or clubbing, so warm layers and my heavy sport coat should handle December weather in southwest Georgia."

Patricia rolled in a suitcase carrying a dozen gift-wrapped Saginaw hoodies, compliments of her and Thatcher. She tried again to convince Siman to shop for his New Year's Eve suit once he gets there.

"It'll be fun!" she said. "You can go to the Albany Mall, or whatever it's called, with your new nephew!"

"Guys don't shop like women, and I have only four days before her party." He had not meant to be snippy.

Patricia sat quietly, as if she could see their familiar heavy mood. Siman first witnessed this intensity in Patricia's hospital room moments after Trinity's birth and at their parents' wake. Identical energy level each time, but for a single detail: one brought remarkable joy, the other unfathomable grief.

"I'm sorry," Siman said. "It'll be good to have a mission the first day or so. Maybe I'll finally see why you like shopping so much."

"Either that or you'll never go to a mall again!" They both managed to laugh.

Patricia picked up the ring box. "You didn't tell anybody it broke yet, right?"

"Didn't see the point, at first—"

"Meaning you have no idea *how* to tell them." She chuckled.

"Right—figured they'll find out soon enough—but ended up telling Bo D, and he's got a plan."

"A plan, huh?"

"Yeah, told me, *Don't worry, Unc, I got your back*. I'm sure they'll all want to see my peach seed monkey as soon as I get there, so we'll get this out of the way first thing."

"Can't wait to get the scoop on that!" She slipped the ring box into his shirt pocket. "So don't forget to pack your exalted talisman. And have a good time, baby brother," she said before exiting. "You deserve this."

"You deserve just as much. We'll work on you next."

Siman never had trouble sleeping, but he tossed and turned all night, finally rising an hour before his alarm, his heart racing from a dream:

> *Inside an enormous, unfamiliar house, black-and-white chessboard squares cover walls, floors, and ceilings that twist and curve at strange angles into oblivion. He is alone against this backdrop, morphing between boy and man—moving giant chess pieces around. He moves fretfully in and out of rooms until he*

is suddenly in a car driving up a steep hill with his eyes closed,
trying frantically to pry them open.

He had arrived at a state of calm when he met Thatcher downstairs for his ride to the airport.

❧

Thirty minutes from Atlanta to Albany: Siman wiped sweaty palms
on his pant legs. From his computer bag he pulled a photo labeled
MY 87TH BIRTHDAY showing Fletcher and Olga standing outside a
restaurant; he's in a dark chocolate suit, she in layers of silk and velvet
muted earth tones. In her photo, Altovise stands next to a podium
looking stately in PhD regalia, as if she had just delivered a keynote.
Siman tucked both photos away and with one final deep breath, prepared for landing.

A patchwork of farmland below was dressed in somber winter
colors mixed with evergreen. Siman rolled his shoulders and tapped
his shirt pocket again. Who would be waiting? Both of them? Other
family?

With an overly perky intercom voice, their flight attendant went
through rote quips and brought to mind his grandfather Wilson
mimicking that accent: *That naa-sal twaang was one more good rea-*
son to leave the South. Both families, Wilson and Miller, severed from
their southern roots in the late 1940s. Until now Siman had struggled with not knowing his adopted roots as he mourned his absent
biological past.

Wheels touched down placing Siman fully at the mercy of Time.
Seat belts clicked, and he focused on his loafers until stepping onto
the metal staircase into chilly Georgia air.

Was he ready? They were all meeting one new person, but he was
walking into two massive families that had already opened their arms
to him. At least he hoped so. He did not know how to embrace them
and wished he had forced Patricia to come. She would have been

a good balance—old family meeting new. He had not yet decided what to call his parents. Olga's advice: *You can never go wrong with Mr. Fletcher and Ms. Altovise, until otherwise inspired.*

With no more time to think, he and the other passengers flowed across the tarmac and into the building. He saw two Black women waving, a young Black man shifting from foot to foot standing next to an older man with his hands in his pockets. Time pushed him forward to Altovise, who said, "Hello, Siman," as she opened her arms and he walked into a hug. "Welcome home."

She was taller than he'd imagined and smelled like a vintage talcy perfume, but not in an old-lady-with-blue-hair kind of way, and she was even more of what he dreamed her to be: refined and beautiful. As much as her voice had been like a record on the phone, this was the live performance.

"Thank you, thank you," he said. "It's truly good to be here."

"This is my sister—your aunt—Vada."

"Siman, Siman," Vada declared. "We're a hugging family, so come on over here!"

Altovise stepped aside, making way for Vada to sweep her hand theatrically. "—And this is Fletcher."

Their tag-team introductions seemed rehearsed, but Siman could see that Fletcher was holding back, not from him, no doubt, but from electricity flying off of the mother and aunt. He and Bo D had discussed the recent gap between his parents, and Siman was seeing it firsthand.

"It's good to meet you, Mr. Fletcher." Compressed between two palms was a lifetime of curiosity and doubt. Fletcher was also taller than he seemed in the photo.

"Likewise—welcome to the birthplace of Ray Charles."

"And I bring you greetings from the birthplace of Stevie, Serena, and Venus!" They had both lingered, making the handshake more like a brief embrace.

"And Bo D!" Siman said. "Feels like I just saw you yesterday."

"Hey, Unc! Welcome home." Bo D sank into the hug like a child.

"You looking good for almost half a century," Fletcher added.

"I come from good stock," Siman turned slightly, "and at last I can thank Ms. Altovise for my cheekbones and you for these Vulcan ears!"

After chatting nervously about checked bags and sunny, frosty weather, Siman fumbled with his shirt pocket. He and Bo D exchanged a quick glance: their plan.

"So, G-pop," Bo D said, "remember when I was little how upset I'd get whenever a monkey broke, no matter who it belonged to or how it broke? Well, now Unc here knows exactly what that feels like."

Siman passed the box around their small circle to a collective lament.

"C'mon over here, Fletcher," Vada motioned, but he didn't move closer as Bo D passed Altovise the ring box.

She cupped her hand over her mouth. "Look at that—diamond eyes and all—in spite of the break, he's as perfect as ever—"

Taking his turn, box in hand, Fletcher carefully lifted the monkey, squinting. Altovise handed him reading glasses from her purse.

"Your work held up nicely," Siman said.

"Been a long time," Fletcher said, "didn't think I'd ever see this one again." They watched intently as he turned the large piece between his fingers. "Easier with a magnifying glass, but you see this?" Siman moved closer. "Long groove passing through his right eye? I remember that."

Siman laughed. "I always said the monkey was a pirate and got that scar in a fight, but my sister, Patricia, said it looked like a teardrop, but a perpetually sad little monkey never worked for me."

"The diamonds are still so brilliant," Altovise said.

"Yeah." Fletcher moved the monkey into a stream of sunlight beaming through the glassy waiting area roof. "Still got a nice sheen. How'd you manage that?"

"Olive oil, canola, whatever I had," Siman said.

"A good rub between some pecan slices works, too," Fletcher said, "but onethingaboutit, you kept him nice and clean."

From what Olga had told him, Siman did not expect Fletcher to be so talkative.

"And as for that break," Fletcher added, handing the monkey to Siman, "it's nice and clean. I can fix it."

"Really?" Siman said. "That's good news. He's lived in this box all these years, and at my birthday in March, I decided to show him to my niece and nephew, who got a little too excited. Just a fluke accident."

Fletcher said, "I've carved plenty that broke right at the end. Just think how many broke through all these years the Dukeses been in the monkey business."

"So true," Altovise said.

"I had intended to give this back to you," Siman said to Altovise, "seemed right somehow."

"No-no-no!" Altovise said. "Fletcher will fix him up like new and then you must keep him."

She handed him an envelope. "And this is also for you." Her hand trembled.

Siman opened the card to a cascade of one-dollar bills down to the floor. "Whoa! What is all this?"

"A dollar for every year," Altovise said, joining the others in picking up money. "Happy Belated×49 Birthday!"

"Siman, this is an old tradition in the Benson family," Vada added. "I always told our parents I couldn't wait to turn a hundred!"

"Thank you—this is a tradition I could get used to." Siman granted himself permission to relax and moved on to his next rehearsed scene.

"You know, my mom, Dorothy, could never recall the phrase connected to the monkey." He gestured toward Altovise. "So many times over the years she apologized for losing your note card."

"*This will keep the monkey off your back*—" Altovise timidly recited.

"Pardon me?" Siman said.

"That's what I wrote in the note card: *This will keep the monkey off your back*—but I forgot the rest." Altovise turned. "Fletcher?"

"*—because being a man is more than a notion*," Fletcher added.

"I'll write it again for you," Altovise said.

"You can write it in that birthday card!" Vada chirped.

"Thanks," Siman said, and they moved through a tunnel of silence a train could pass through.

Altovise clasped her hands. "So—there'll be plenty of time for home-cooked meals, but I thought we'd go to my favorite seafood place—you like fish, Siman?"

"Love it!"

"Then let's get your bags and hit the road!"

As they walked a few feet to baggage claim, Altovise walked on one side of Siman, Vada on the other, hooking her arm into his. "So much to tell you about. Your maternal great-grandmother was Muscogee Creek. Her name was Onawa Crow."

"Beautiful name," Siman said, thinking he should cup his hand over hers. In time he would have to get used to hugs and pokes and loving punches; they came so naturally to his new family.

"Onawa means *wide awake*," Altovise added. "Granmama was born with a veil over her face, meaning her eyes were open to many things."

Bo D accepted his Saginaw hoodie before returning to Loblolly. Altovise insisted that Siman ride with Fletcher. Siman had heard about the mint condition Fairlane; Olga divulged that he was conceived in this very backseat. Maybe he and Fletcher would reach a point where they could joke about this father-to-son, when small talk would not be as difficult as now. He highly doubted it.

They enjoyed a catfish, crab, and shrimp dinner, and Siman had enough gin and tonic to feel lighthearted, learning about Fletcher's sobriety after the fact. As they drove to Cromartie Beach, he made unnecessary apologies until Fletcher stopped him.

"Haven't had a drink in over thirty years," Fletcher said, "glad to know you don't share that particular trait."

They arrived at Altovise's in time for the annual Yuletide Parade of Boats on Cromartie Lake. From her dock kitchen under propane heaters, drinking tea and spiked coffee, they watched a long procession of vessels and Jet Skis decked out with Christmas lights.

Vada received the second hoodie, and Siman silently thanked Patricia for sending him off with a suitcase filled with identical gifts—even though he would have far more cousins than hoodies on both sides of the family.

They rearranged Adirondack chairs in a circle and Siman brought out more gifts. A mesmerized Altovise received her sterling silver box, the size of two decks of cards, etched with an intricate peach tree branch and flower design. Nestled behind a door, inlaid with glass, was a velvet bed, fitted to the diamond-eyed monkey.

Siman fingered the box. "I commissioned a local artist to make this, and of course the plan was to return our little guy to you, where he'll fit perfectly."

"Siman—this is stunning! So unique." Altovise lifted the box. "Look, Fletcher."

"Never seen anything like it." He cupped her hand with his. Witnessing this, Siman had not considered how he could be a light, however small, to shine on the path that led them back to each other.

"And for you, Mr. Fletcher—I have this." He presented a large felt bag.

Fletcher pulled out a wooden box with a chessboard top and ran his hand across the surface, asking, "Is this pecan?"

"Yes, sir, you know your wood—spalted pecan mixed with curly maple—another Saginaw area artist; I've bought her work for years."

"Must be something special in that drawer," Vada said, pointing.

They all exclaimed when Fletcher pulled open the drawer, revealing the Pullman Porter chess pieces, each nestled in a cutout carved to its shape.

"Let me guess who told you I play chess," Fletcher said.

"Yep. Bo D was that little birdie," Siman said.

"Well onethingaboutit, your artist sure outdid herself with this, and you going above and beyond giving it to me. 'Preciate it.

"Do you play?" Fletcher asked.

"I do indeed," Siman said. "We'll have to get a little tournament going!"

"I don't know, Fletcher," Vada touched his shoulder, "you might want to rethink that. I heard that the man who plays himself at chess has a sucker for an opponent!"

Siman was grateful for the giddiness to ease tension.

"You know I'm just playing with you, brother-in-law," Vada said, "but can we talk about these queen and king outfits?" She lifted the Black couple and studied them closely.

"Yes, Miss Thing is working that tam and fur stole!" Altovise added.

"Oh. Mygoodness!" Vada said, handing over the queen. "Al. You need your reading glasses for this."

Altovise picked a pair from a nearby bowl and zoomed in.

"Stop!" she whooped, bringing the king and queen together in her palm. "This couple is passing!"

"Hell yeah!" said Vada. "How else could Black folks travel first class on trains back then."

The king's and queen's skin was painted the color of sugar cookie dough; their noses and lips had a hint of fullness, evidence of melanin in their blood. Such details go unnoticed by those blind to the meaning of "passing for white."

"That was the artist's brilliant idea," Siman said, handing the king to Fletcher, "and, of course, my white friends never notice."

"Onethingaboutit," Fletcher said, "that's a detail you can't usually slip past Black folks—not even in chess pieces."

"You can say that again!" Altovise and Vada said in chorus, slapping five as they all laughed.

To close, all hands helped clean up. Siman was spared the pressure of deciding where to spend his first week: Fletcher assigned him to Altovise.

He would not look back at forty-nine years gone, but forward, only as far as his next hour, his next day. He and his parents were each a prayer that time had thrown to the other.

45

Five days later, while his mother was in her room on a call, a winter storm pounded Cromartie Lake. Siman could scarcely believe all that had happened in the two years since he had sat in his condo with snow instead of rain falling, having no idea that all of this lay ahead.

He stood next to a meditation cushion facing a small shrine in Altovise's library. Her new gift box sat next to a smudge stick and a silver bracelet inlaid with turquoise and etched with breath scroll medicine knots matching those on her wrists. This symbol repeated on a beaded medicine bag, a silver medallion, and a pendant. These were surrounded by postcards: Grand Canyon; Joshua Tree, California; Nanyuki, Kenya; and Etowah Mounds in northwest Georgia. A neatly penned, framed note at the back of the shrine read: *Breathing in, I come home; breathing out, I let go.*

Her much-awaited New Year's Eve party would be in four days. Siman was still moving past his angst. He organized a Skype call earlier in the week to introduce Altovise to Patricia and family. Patricia was happy to mention that she helped collect all six albums and invited

Altovise to come meet the family and sign them. That helped him feel more and more comfortable with his parents and his new families. Mounting friction between his parents was fervidly discussed, on both sides. He wanted to help in some way but, other than Bo D, he didn't know who he could turn to as an ally.

Later, mother and son buzzed around her kitchen, enveloped in wood rafters, cabinets, and slate floors. Siman served up salad and lentil soup, Altovise made fry bread, and Vada's plump German chocolate cake stood waiting.

They sat down, napkins in laps, and both took a silent moment of blessing.

"So you meditate," Siman said.

"I do. Came to it by a less traditional route. You had two amazing great-grandmothers who helped raise me: Arnela was an African Methodist Episcopal minister, and Onawa was a Muscogee Creek healer. They were good friends who loved talking about their similarities. At our house we believed in God Our Father and we trusted the healing power of sage, cedar, and sweetgrass."

"Wow."

"And then, there was Anderson Stone, who couldn't have been more conspicuous hanging around A&T and Bennett's campuses in 1963: white, hippie, trust fund pothead from Connecticut, preaching yoga and meditation as training for nonviolent activism. He lived in his VW van filled with flyers, pamphlets—and other *paraphernalia*."

"Sounds like quite a character."

"That's for sure! He was our age, dropped out of Yale, and devoted himself to civil rights, and of course, he had the means. My friends and I were all for inner calm over lynchings and bombings, so we embraced Anderson's meditation practices, which I melded with grandmother wisdoms and still use to this day. My main defense against the ringing in my ears."

"Oooo. That's rough. The result of years singing in bands?"

"Yep—I suffer from that and a relentless case of jukehead. At nearly any given moment you can ask me, *What song?* and I'll tell you a hit from one of six decades playing in my head."

"Ah! My high school band teacher called that an earworm!"

"Then you're aware of its seriousness."

"I am." Siman followed her laughter, pleased with the ease of their conversation.

"What was your instrument?"

"Trombone. Lucky for my family, that only lasted one year."

Siman thought back to years trying to imagine how his mother's laugh would sound. From puberty through college, he vacillated between ecstasy and despair at the idea of finding her.

Pounding rain and wind on Lake Cromartie had not let up. Fry bread and lentil soup brought Siman back to the moment.

"I hope you don't suffer from jukehead," Altovise said.

"No, I don't, but I wish I had inherited your musical talent."

"Music and math have a lot in common," she said.

"I had the math, but just didn't have the trombone X factor. But I've practiced yoga for years, and rowing is my meditation."

"Pisces is a water sign, so of course you live right on the river."

"It's a lifesaver. My brother-in-law, Thatcher, rows with me. Sometimes we join other groups, but mostly just the two of us. He's a solid guy."

"I look forward to meeting your family someday."

"And they share that sentiment!"

They finished their meal, easing through a few beats of silence that neither rushed to fill.

"Hummm-uh!" Siman said. "Let me just say, this was my first time having fry bread, and it's delicious!"

"So glad you like it, but you ain't seen nothing yet! Wait 'til you taste your aunt Vada's pound cake!"

Stories poured easily from Altovise. Siman had spent a few afternoons in Putney with Fletcher and was becoming accustomed to acres of quiet and many hours playing chess. His father's sad solo game was replaced by the Pullman Porter set. Fletcher told stories only when prompted, but Siman was equally at home with Altovise's breezy nature, weaving tales like arias in whatever order they presented themselves.

As they cleaned up, Altovise ignored her vibrating phone on the counter. She set out cake and tea and Siman prepared to hear about her Larson Brig days.

"While I was incarcerated, and for a long time after, freedom songs joined top hits as my soundtrack to life."

"You remember any songs?"

"Let's see—'Duke of Earl,' 'You Beat Me to the Punch,' and, of course, 'Hit the Road Jack,' was at the top of the charts—and—was exactly my prayer for those white bigots."

Night bloomed, and all around the property, mesmerizing rain shimmied in floodlight beams. They moved upstairs to her movie room and lit a fire. Four buckskin recliners faced the wooden entertainment center built to house a large screen.

Altovise wrapped her shoulders in a Muscogee quilt.

"That was the hottest, most intense summer I'd ever seen. And—I discovered I was pregnant with you while incarcerated."

King and Abernathy returned to Albany in early July 1962 for the verdict from their December arrests, prepared to face *jail, no bail*, as many others did, prompting more mass meetings and demonstrations. On July 30, Fletcher and Altovise joined a protest in Albany against the downtown theater.

"Since Reverend King's nonviolent tactics were heavily influenced by Gandhi, Albany's police chief, Pritchett, studied both to plan his own, by ordering his police to be nonviolent. Well. He lost control that day. I don't remember what prompted those cops to turn on us."

"Mr. Fletcher told me a group of white teen boys threw rocks at police from the sidelines and police naturally thought it was protesters and things escalated."

"I vaguely recall that," Altovise said, "at any rate, as always, Fletcher marched right behind me. He stepped in to protect me when one of them grabbed me around my rib cage. Fletcher held my hand until another cop zapped his wrist with a cattle prod." Her lips trembled into a smile and she rubbed her wrist, near the medicine knot tattoo. "He still has the scar right there, and you've seen the one above his eye. He says that's a billy club and cattle prod's job: to help you remember."

This memory overtook her, and Siman wondered if he had any right to the consequences of this privilege? Had he pushed too hard? His mother gathered strength, her long legs and arms swaddled in a patchwork of colors. She looked safe. Still, he was concerned.

"Are you OK?" he asked.

"I'm fine." She inhaled deeply and rose to put another log on the fire. "And I want you to know all of this, Siman. It's part of who you are." She smiled, settled back in, and went on.

"In the end, two dozen of us were packed into a paddy wagon meant to hold twelve to fifteen. We had no idea where we were going—also Pritchett's strategy: keep Albany jails empty. Luckily, we all knew each other because each of us either provided a lap, or sat on one."

"I can only imagine how frightening that was," Siman said.

"We were concerned, of course, but also at peace; living the struggle between good and evil. In SNCC trainings, our leaders, Charles Sherrod and Cordell Reagon, had us practice how to face beatings and possible death head-on—to feed good even in the presence of bad. I can hear Sherrod's easy-paced voice still. He said this so many times: *You must be ready to face danger—every day—face some kind of violence—every day—in the guerilla-style life you are choosing to live.* So as always on my desk in my room, I had left my will, which included a letter to my parents. A love letter, really."

"And how old were you, again?"

"Eighteen."

"Hard to imagine," Siman said. "My biggest struggle at eighteen was deciding between Carleton and Howard."

"Mothers and fathers want nothing more," she said and continued. "After about a twenty-minute paddy wagon ride, we filed out and huddled in front of a squat, dilapidated building that could've been in any one of the little towns around here. Chiseled in block letters across the top of the stained white brick: LARSON COUNTY BRIG."

"Is it still there?"

"Still there, a Civil War remnant. An 1860s prison. I'll take you there if you'd like."

"I would like."

"Dripping with sweat, we walked into a dingy fifteen-by-thirty-foot cell. I was carrying nothing, wearing a pair of denim pedal pushers, a light yellow seersucker blouse, a new pair of navy-blue Keds and socks, always white socks. As was standard practice, I had three pairs of clean underwear padding my bra."

The drab cell was flooded with sunlight coming through several barred windows with jagged, broken-out glass and no screens.

Altovise had sat on the cold concrete floor, facing a window, and leaned against the wall, exhausted and hungry. The one toilet was clogged with feces, and their only source of water—hot water—was a constantly running showerhead in a stall cluttered with cardboard and used as a toilet. She held her breath each time she washed her hands. Gagging, she needed clean hands to cover her mouth against the stench of urine, feces, sweat, and monthly blood. Her wrists still carried a faint smell of Estée Lauder Youth Dew. Just before leaving home to protest, she had rubbed on a few drops. The aroma brought images of Fletcher.

The next morning, her back still pressed against a wall, legs stretched out before her, sunlight flooded in. Altovise felt heavy and jittery from lack of sleep. In the corner where the floor and wall met, she used a shard of glass to scratch a line.

To avoid broken-down bunk beds with skimpy, grungy mattresses, the young women spent tortured nights on cold concrete—or pieces of filthy cardboard—never finding comfort, sitting up for a while, then rocking or pacing.

Over the weeks, her cohorts came and went—to other jails or back home—as their count rose to forty-two. Guards pushed meals of fatty sausages, stale bread, and undercooked hamburgers. Nights and days crept by; unrelenting hours; taking turns at the windows, shaking off heat, tedium, and stench, fighting mosquitoes, red bugs, roaches, and rats, in addition to their fears and horrid thoughts.

Altovise never slept through a night, only dozed when her body and mind had no choice. Slowly, as their whereabouts become known, family and friends delivered messages and dropped off packages through the windows. After two weeks, her mother and father came, with fresh clothes, candy bars, books, and toiletries—which were useless with no working sinks, showers, or toilets. Like all families, they were working on getting releases. Midway through, Fletcher came, and Altovise refused to see him; she told her friends to make him promise not to come back.

"None of us had a mirror, so I didn't know how bad I looked. I just knew I didn't want him seeing me like that."

Inside the brig, she held back tears, bolsterd by a spectrum of musical legacies: from Muscogee Creek hymns to Mahalia Jackson's "In the Upper Room." Music carried her into calm.

"Only a month before," Altovise said, "I had begun studying improvisation, and that helped keep me in the present moment. I cherished and moved to the music in my head—stirring, placating, at times maddening—music, and we all sang and rewrote freedom songs, to fit our struggle."

> *Ain't gon' let nobody*
> *Turn me 'round,*
> *Turn me 'round,*
> *Turn me 'round.*
> *Ain't gon' let this jail cell*
>   *Turn me 'round.*

Reeking of cigarette smoke and body odors, rotating guards disparaged all aspects of the Movement. Altovise expected to see them pass a bottle—to numb themselves against the indignities of their job, but they seemed to be high on hatred.

"So awful," Siman said, "and how long were you in?"

"My last day I counted thirty-two lines on the floor."

"Did they ever bring charges?"

"No. On our way home after my release, my mother said: *Y'all brig girls made news already, all the way up to Atlanta—lost in jail for that long.* I explained that we were not lost. Or stolen. We were wrongfully incarcerated, like so many other people working in the Movement. Many of us resented people claiming that we did any more than so many others."

"And why were you finally released?"

"Somehow, we came to the attention of Danny Lyon, who was the SNCC photographer. A young man drove him onto the property one day in a hooptie, and he took pictures through those broken windows. SNCC passed them on to a congressman, who entered them into the Congressional Record. That's how we were finally released."

"The power of photo journalism," Siman said.

"Yes."

"This must've been pure torture for Fletcher Dukes?" Siman felt the need to guard his father's place in these stories.

Altovise fixed her eyes on the floor, as if her next line was plastered there.

"Fletcher was a wreck." She rubbed palms, as if in prayer. "He came to my house the day of my release and my parents turned him away, told him I had been through too much and to please let me rest. He left letters on my porch swing for a week, but I couldn't bring myself to see him. I wasn't angry at him, but he was at the center of my world of anger, so he got all that fallout."

Siman had learned from Bo D, and confirmed by Olga, that there was a time when Fletcher would have laid down his life for Altovise. What was it that stood in her way?

Parents and children have necessary secrets. Siman could feel those sections of his mother's story galloping toward them. He understood now that it was not for him to make a place for her to talk about any of that, but instead to help them all move on as a family despite the past. Together they paused, leapt over those chasms, and continued.

Altovise stood to stretch her arms and legs. "I felt fortified, electrified when I left for that protest—the way we were back then, ready to make change happen. But after the brig I was done. I wasn't showing yet but my family knew because I had the spits—excess salivation—and that's a long story for another time. I rarely left the house—kept my curtains drawn, slept a lot. My family didn't know what to do." She sat back down, wrapping the blanket tighter around her shoulders. "And then one really hot night, I was sitting out in our porch swing when Fletcher came by with that ring box holding our beautiful little talisman, as you call it, which I love, by the way—really says it all."

"Thanks to my dad, Jerome. He introduced me to that word at my rite of passage."

She studied her hands. "Almost funny to think about it now, but I was never without my plastic cup spittoon. Fletcher didn't even notice it on the windowsill. I was sucking on a lemon and had to swallow all that saliva while he was there so he wouldn't suspect anything."

Here they met another chasm and jumped over it in unison.

"Of course, we couldn't see it at the time," Altovise said, "through our veil of teen invincibility—but the one thing uniting us during our protest years was that we were so young. The Movement and our passage into adulthood met at a juncture"—she brought her index fingers together—"and that juncture morphed and caused a series of big bangs—unique to each of us."

"I can see how such a detonation could land you in a place very far from Georgia—say Michigan, for example."

"Right. Right—or—as was the case for your father, push you deeper into the land that is your home."

"Putney, Georgia."

"Exactly."

"It seemed Fletcher and I were destined to land in separate places." She sat back and chuckled. "And here's a wild double entendre: you were conceived during our big bang! Literally!"

Siman dropped his head, grateful for a light moment. His shoulders shook as they laughed.

"Olga called it a manic time, and it was. And through it all, Fletcher was doing what he always did: protecting me. I suffered a lot of humiliation but—except for that last march—no cop or guard laid a hand on me. I knew many others who were not so lucky. So, for him to willingly stand between me and possible death—I thought I had learned to live with survivor's guilt, on top of my not telling him about you after all he had sacrificed. But when I faced him that day baling hay from his truck, it was clear I wasn't ready to have that wound reopened and salt poured in."

"Little did you know I was headed your way with more salt."

"Siman." Her face remained tender, her voice soothing. "You were my one and only pregnancy. And of course you know that in 1963 abortion was illegal in all fifty states. I've always supported a woman's right to choose even though it was never a choice I personally considered." She leaned toward him. "So you're not salt. You are liniment for my aching soul."

Was it words such as these that had him falling so deeply into his mother's comfortable presence? Corners tucked, pillows fluffed, like a well-made bed.

Altovise buried her face in colorful patchwork folds. Siman waited in silence as she wept. Were they tears she had kept even from her pillow? Was bearing witness to her release his right, his privilege? He did not know, but he was grateful to be there to catch her, honored that she trusted him enough to let go, and leap.

Siman was unsure of what to say but aware that silence was also their creation, and necessary.

46

~

"Sweeeeet!" Bo D sang, screen door easing shut behind him. "Never thought I'd see the day—G-pop got the Galaxy!"

"Ain't that what you told me to get?" Fletcher sat at his kitchen table with Siman, bemoaning the absence of an owner's manual in the box.

"And onethingaboutit," Fletcher added, "when I was coming up, we didn't have no online-social-this-and-that, no phones with cameras everywhere—so even though we did our share of craziness, couldn't nobody prove nothing."

Bo D and Siman laughed.

"Nice phone, that's for sure," Siman said, "and Mr. Fletcher here is a quick study. Go ahead, send him a text."

Fletcher typed slowly, then bumped fists with Siman.

> FD: you ready to carve a monkey?

"Now you just showing out!" Bo D exclaimed, typing.

> BD: I been ready!!!

Three men with coffee mugs, followed by a dog, walked to the woodshop.

"Pond turned out real good, G-pop," Bo D said.

"Yeah—before long we'll be fryin 'em up."

"How many fish did you put in there?" Siman asked.

"Six hundred pounds. Mostly channel cats," Fletcher said.

Siman whistled. "Six hundred pounds of catfish and I've never even been fishing."

"You spend all that time rowing on the Saginaw River and never took a pole?" Fletcher asked.

"Nobody in the family fished."

"Can't say that now!" Bo D said.

A smell of fresh sawn wood incubated them. Siman commented on five slingshots mounted on the workbench wall.

Bo D perched on a tall stool, listening quietly. He pulled his tally notebook from his back pocket, not sure why he still carried it, since he had not counted days since Auntie Olga died. He sifted through pages of haystacks marking his street days, as his grandfather told slingshot stories.

"This is dogwood," Fletcher explained. "First thing I ever whittled. Made it the year my mama died. My daddy taught me to whittle to *shave off grief*, he said. And this one is from a plum tree, so you know I got a butt-whipping for messing with a fruit-bearing tree. This here is sourwood and that's maple; got in trouble for killing a stray cat, even though my brother Clifford did it. He was caught with my slingshot, so we both paid. We sucked the bones of many-a squirrel, but when it came to killing just 'cause you could, Mama and Daddy drew the line."

"What did you use for bands?" Siman asked.

"Old truck or tractor inner tube if we could get our hands on it. This was around 1949 to 1950. We had left sharecropping years before, but we still had to scrimp and save to get anywhere, so we used whatever we could find—so long as we didn't have to spend no money."

Bo D stuffed his notebook into his backpack. He was riddled

with envy. How is it that he had never heard these slingshot stories? Was it because he'd never asked? His uncle Siman was able to see the family with freshness: outside looking in, where every little thing is new and different. Maybe he deserved that right, since he spent his whole life severed from his roots.

"Bo D," Fletcher said, "you bring the pouch?"

"You in for a treat, Unc," Bo D said, pulling a pouch from a backpack pocket. Inside was his great-grandfather Purvis' peach seed monkey. "This the oldest one in the family: a hundred and fifteen years old."

Bo D rested the monkey on the workbench.

"And this one is mine," Fletcher said, adding to Bo D's display.

"Look at that," Siman said. "This makes four monkeys I've seen, including mine; same carving style and yet remarkably unique. Wish I could say I've imagined this moment many times," he said, "but even the fact that I'm standing here is far from my wildest imaginings."

Bo D and Siman sat like children around a campfire as Fletcher began.

"This is about forty years late, Siman, but it's a true story." Fletcher took on the usual formality. "This came to me directly from my daddy, Purvis Dukes. He was a farmer who fathered twenty-one children. After his first wife, Clara, died, he married my mama, Alpha. Olga was the youngest of the first set, and I'm the youngest of the second set. Got plenty nieces and nephews older than me. That's why they call me the 'baby uncle.' And now I'm the last one living of twenty-one. Our father never knew much about his family. Between slavery and the Civil War, a lot got destroyed or lost. But by some miracle, the story of my great-uncle, Isakiah Dukes, my grandfather's brother, made it through. We don't know who in the family started this monkey business or how far back it goes, but it's always been a father-to-son deal. My daddy learned to carve from Uncle Isakiah and ended up having fourteen boys and plenty monkeys to carve. We usually give the monkeys when boys turn thirteen, but I was only twelve when I got mine. Daddy must've known to give it to me early because he died in his sleep ten days later. That tore me up, 'cause Mama had already died, and he never got around to teaching me to carve a monkey. When I was sixteen, I spent a summer working in the steel mills in Philadelphia with my nephew Frederick Douglas Dukes, we called him Freddy D. He wasn't but five years older than me. Freddy D taught me to carve the monkey. Now my job is to teach both of y'all."

Siman said, "I sure do appreciate this. It's far more than I ever hoped for."

"This is a good time for me to show you this." Fletcher pulled a bulky old photo album from a shelf. Its dark brown leather was cracked and chipped and a yellow Post-it note stuck to the front read *Show to Siman*.

"Oh, that's Auntie Olga's peach seed monkey album!" Bo D exclaimed, as he felt that jealousy toward his uncle rise higher in him.

"Wow," Siman said, "this is her handwriting?"

"Yeah," Fletcher said, "found this in her library when we cleaned up. She was the only one in the family who took pictures of our monkeys, going back to that first camera she bought."

"I know all about it from her blog!" Siman carefully opened the album, his eyes marveling at each photo.

"I keep that here at the house, you can look through it later."

"Yes, sir," Siman said. "I sure will. Thank you."

What Bo D felt was pure and simple and surprised him. His grandfather had not organized this carving lesson for him. He had done it for Siman. Bo D was ready to sink into anger around this when he recalled that it had been *his* choice not to learn to carve a monkey. For years his grandfather pestered him and even tried shaming him into learning. He'd finally given up when Bo D hit high school.

Rehab taught him to confront emotions on their own terms. So he faced his resentment nongrudgingly, not targeting Siman personally, but going after the causes of their vague and dismembered family story, a story that left them perpetually hungry for more. A story that now also belonged to Siman.

"All right." Fletcher lined up penknives, jackknives, and homemade awls. "Siman, you'll be here at the sanding table, and Bo D, over here at the workbench."

"If Olga were here, she would have a tape recording going, I'm sure," Siman said.

"You got that right," Bo D said, "and her old Polaroid plus her iPhone camera!"

"And have all of us spittin' into test tubes," Fletcher said.

Bo D and Siman shared a knowing smile. The secrets and details leading up to Siman's visit had become a bond between them.

Fletcher lifted a bowl brimming with peach stones as if they were a delicacy: "These are your heroes: nice plump shapes, dry, deep grooves, clean of pulp." He slid the next bowl out. "Then you have your practice seeds: second string, got flaws in the grooves, dull complexion, may be stringy with dried pulp. And last, we have rejects—I give these to the kids to play with."

"G-pop." Bo D's tone shifted. "I always wondered why it's got to be a monkey in the first place? Everybody knows white folks already think we monkeys, so why not carve something else?" He turned to Siman. "What you think, Unc?"

"I hear what you saying, Bo D, and even though we'll never know how it all started, for me, this little monkey has always held a bit of the divine, and from my experience it's not for us to question or tamper with the divine."

"Never thought of it that way," Bo D said, pondering. "I like the way you put that. So did your sister have some bit of a different divine from her birth family?"

"No, not a physical talisman like our monkey. And that made it hard for me at times, because she was always so supportive of me. We both want the same for her."

Fletcher's hands stopped carving. "So, even though she didn't have something like our monkey, she still knew being grown was more than a notion."

"Ex-aactly!" Siman sang. "Our parents were very devout people. Our dad, Jerome, was about as close to the pulpit as possible without being a preacher, always quoting scripture. My favorite story was from my adoption day when the nurse gave them Altovise's envelope with the card and monkey. Dad told my mom, Dorothy, that the monkey was like Moses' tar basket and they were pulling me from the Nile."

Bo D watched his grandfather smile and nod. This was new: being in the company of Dukes men using so many words to talk about actual feelings! Not just barbershop banter. Deeper. Real.

"Seems like they made it hard for y'all to feel abandoned or unwanted," Bo D said.

"They did. Of course, when we were younger, we managed to, despite all their efforts. There was even a time when I was sure I knew better than they did what was best for them!"

"Oh yeah," Bo D concurred, "I been there!"

"I was sure they would be hurt by me searching for my birth family."

"What changed your mind?" Fletcher asked.

"A combination: my niece Trinity's birth in 2000 and my parents' deaths three years later."

"Did you have cousins and stuff to help you through that?" Bo D asked.

"Pat and I were grown—forty-three and forty. We had each other, and she also had her husband, Thatcher. Family on both sides are mostly still in the South, so our little family unit had always been an island unto itself, and they always saw my peach seed monkey as a miracle to be shared with my sister."

"I played ball with a dude who was adopted," Bo D said, "and his parents told him and his sister they were special because they were chosen. Did your parents tell y'all that?"

"No," Siman said. "In fact, that's a common myth, which can be a burden for adoptees because it's close to saying adoption is a loss for which you are supposed to be grateful."

"Never thought of it that way," Fletcher said. "Good point."

Siman said, "So Bo D, that's the long way of saying don't let anybody mess with what you know to be divine."

"Mighty right," Fletcher said, "and onethingaboutit, we ain't never been, and never will be, monkeys just 'cause some white man think it."

Bo D and Siman exchanged satisfied glances before choosing knives.

Fletcher worked his old jackknife, turning a plump seed deftly as he talked. Both students started by carving a simple peach seed basket, first using rejects to get a feel for the hardness and degree of delicacy and control needed, then moving on to practice seeds.

"Keep your knife nice and sharp and it won't take as much force as you think," Fletcher said, gently scraping. "You got to show authority over that seed, but sometimes you hold back or you'll go too far—or hurt yourself."

"So, Unc," Bo D said, "did you ever try to carve a monkey?"

"No, never did," Siman said. "My dad and I worked with wood quite a bit though—we made a tree house and go-carts, stuff like that, but we could never imagine how to even start a monkey from a peach seed."

Fletcher paused, observing. "You got good knife grip—firm but gentle."

"You know, G-pop," Bo D chimed in, "I did some research, and technically, this is a peach *pit*, not a seed. The *seed* is that little smooth white thing *inside* the pit." He rattled two seeds in his hand like dice.

"Yeah, you right." Fletcher tilted his head to peer through the reading glasses. "But just keep carving and you'll get there, then I'll show you how to grind that part out. He blew dust from his hand. "And onethingaboutit, in the Dukes family we've always called them seeds. We not about to change that now."

"So," Bo D said, still slicing, "I already got me a plan for the monkey I'm gone make."

"Yeah? What's that?"

"In about ten years, I'm giving it to Cricket."

"Breaking with tradition again, huh?" Siman said.

"Or better still—starting a new tradition." Bo D carefully studied his grandfather's face. "What you think about that, G-pop?"

Fletcher closed his jackknife and smiled. "I think in no time at all Cricket will be carving circles around all y'all."

"I have no doubt!" Bo D said. "But we'll have to modify that catchphrase."

"Your granmama Maletha did that a long time ago," Fletcher said, choosing to give credit where it was most due.

"What had the catchphrase been?" Siman asked.

"We always said 'being a man is more than a notion.' But Maletha changed it to: *Being grown is more than a notion.*"

"I like that!" Bo D said.

"It's perfect," Siman said, "and I'd like to give mine to Patricia, if that's all right. Wasn't for her pigheadedness, I never would've found y'all."

"Sound good to me," Fletcher said.

"So who gets yours, G-Pop?"

"Well, seem like a certain singer I know is down a monkey, so—"

"Yeah! I hear you," Bo D said. "That's dope, G-pop!"

Siman agreed. "Seems only fitting. Now her new sterling box will finally have an occupant."

Fletcher coached as his students worked diligently on their baskets. After a while, they took a break. Fletcher moved on to repairing Siman's broken monkey. The two younger men, ginger beers in hand, took a pondside break with Rockhudson, tail wagging.

"So," Siman said, "what do you think is behind their lovers' quarrel?"

"No clue," Bo D said. "I just know they put brakes on after they went to Atlanta right after Auntie's memorial."

"Is it worth trying to talk with him about it?"

"De-finitely not!" Bo D shook his head briskly. "That will go one of two ways, depending on his mood: either he'll tell us he's got it covered, or he'll invite us to stay out of grown folks' business."

"I see," Siman conceded. "It's like that!"

"Yep. Sure wish Auntie Olga was here. She was the only one who could really handle G-pop."

Siman and Bo D laughed and talked. Rockhudson barked as they skipped stones across polished, glassy water. Bo D looked out over pond-forest-chickens-pecan trees. Without its counterparts, each piece had a void; together they completed him. And there was plenty to share with Siman.

~

our silence among you is simple
this is how you and we are written
marks on paper
can never be enough

but
these will do
for now

~

47

~

"This be a good plot," Ebele said, scooping up a handful of rich, loamy soil. "Plenty sun, and us can erect a fence to ward off critters."

Malik agreed, standing two rows over. Adjacent to the garden plot was the site Calhoun designated for them to build their cabin, shaded by three sweet gum trees. They would plant collards, okra, field peas, squashes, peanuts, onions, sweet potatoes, and gourds. Ebele laid out plans for keeping four goats and a flock of chickens.

Malik used his wages to build their cabin and convinced Calhoun to cover workshop costs for his growing pirogue business. He negotiated their rice field tasks down from a quarter to an eighth acre, and he, Horace, and Crayfish combined efforts to get all work done as quickly in the day as possible to focus on boat building. Even-trade transaction papers were drawn up: an eleven-year-old girl was traded to train with Thompson's cook in exchange for Ebele switching her service from Dewees Island to Calhoun's kitchen, and her name to "Abbey."

Building their twenty-five-by-twenty-five-foot cabin, with shutters and four glass windows, would take longer than most because

Malik used *tabby*, a mixture of lime, sand, water, and oyster shells. Meanwhile, Malik continued to bunk with Horace and Crayfish, and Berthenia temporarily folded Ebele into her large family.

One Saturday after tasks, husband and wife sat in the shade shucking peanuts.

Malik held up his dusty fist, lightly clinched.

Ebele watched with a quizzical look as he placed a peach seed into her hand.

"Oonuh been hushin this secret these many months." She cocked her head. "This yo mother seed Horace talk of? From Yaaye?"

"No, she know nothing of it." He smiled. "But it has her blessing."

With a deep breath he told her of a comforting dream that had come with fretful sleep during his horrid weeks crossing the Atlantic:

> *He is a boy, sitting next to Yaaye as she carves a monkey on a new pirogue. He shows her the strange seed and she pinches it between her fingers like a jewel. "Eh!" She smiles. "Do you see a monkey hiding in this stone?" She traces with her finger. "He sits just so, his head is here, the tail curls this way—"*
>
> *"Yes, Yaaye! I see it!"*

After waking, in spite of the stench and misery around him, Malik's waistcloth stowaway became much more than a worry stone. From the moment he stepped on the peach seed in the sand, a hope was born that he still harbored: he would someday build boats again, and use one to escape.

"So? What you waitin on?" Ebele asked. "Yaaye say little monkry trapped." She handed back the seed, leaning into his shoulder. "Set he free!"

He leaned back, smiling at Yaaye's essence shining through Ebele.

Through trial and error, willing his swollen fingers to scale down from gouge to rat tail file, Malik turned small blocks of pinewood into tiny statues of monkeys, elands, elephants, and cheetahs, using Yaaye's special recipe to paint black spots. Charmed by what she called *yea-bigs*, Ebele kept them in a circle on their eating table and told Malik someday these would make good play toys for their babies.

Based on his Yaaye's sideboard monkeys, Malik roughed out peach seed designs and began training himself to carve. He thought of his collection of smooth sticks and river-hardened wood found over years and years along the Senegal. Had his two children-who-will-never-know-their-Baaba found his sack tucked away with carving tools?

He had only three seeds, but given a wider choice, he would look for plumbness, deep groves, pleasant lines, and caverns that satisfied his need for order. He learned these basic elements from his father, who learned from his, going back to the first hands to carve their ancestral urn.

Carving in between rice field and pirogue hours, he finished what would be the first of many peach seed monkeys.

"This beautiful, Malik!" Ebele said, admiring their new charm. "Which seed you carve?"

"The mother seed. Practiced on my wedding seed. Saving yours for future."

"This be good!" Ebele said, cradling and gently stroking the monkey in her palm, "good for true!"

Hickory and maple trees were ablaze all over Charleston. Malik and Ebele harvested sweet potatoes, pumpkins, and collards from their garden, and moved into their new cabin. Horace gave them two buckets of paint made from indigo, buttermilk, and lime that many coastal Blacks used to cover cabin and porch ceilings. Over and over Malik had held on to a failing faith in his pirogue to deliver him from capture. He was not inclined to imbue sky-blue paint with the power to keep away evil spirits. As a boy, he heard elders often say, *Trust in Allah, but tie down your pirogue first*. He knew that if he and his family were to be saved, it would be by Allah guiding their own hands.

But Ebele insisted on the paint. "Us gone show them haints the way up and out through the sky!"

They performed private libations to declare their home sacred, evoke ancestors, and give credence to their homenames. Into a small sandy hole dug several yards from their cabin, Ebele said, "There will be no Sawney, no Abbey, inside we walls or we hearts. Us cast you out!" In turn, husband and wife spat and kicked sand into the tiny pit.

When pecan harvest ended, she surprised Malik with news: their baby would be born in August.

"When baby come," Ebele said, lifting the peach seed monkey from its center spot in the circle of yea-bigs, "let this *monkry* be them first blessin." She drew palm circles on her chest. "That way us keep all us peoples settin right on we heart."

On August 23, 1816, a strong, shrill cry found Malik at his post on the porch and brought thoughts of Nbey and their children. He could not hold back tears. He could only pray that he had been wiped from their memory as he stepped into his new child's life.

Berthenia had assisted Ebele's midwife. Standing broad-hipped and steady, a foot holding his cabin door open, she said to Malik, "Come on in! See yo sweetnin gal-chile!"

Their cabin ceiling radiated bright, sky-blue light, and Malik treaded lightly on blades of sunrise jutting across floorboards. Sweat shimmered on Ebele's umber skin.

From a tiny pouch Ebele stitched from flour sack remnants, Malik plucked the little monkey: nature chiseled hard, crisp grooves along its spine, but Malik's hands—like so many to follow—shaped neck and head, hollowed out arms and tail. He dropped dots of Yaaye's soot and egg paint into the tiny eye sockets.

Malik whispered a prayer to Allah, then softly kissed Ebele and their beautiful baby girl. She was his heart, beating on the outside.

"I would call she Akunna," Ebele said, fatigue unable to dull her smile, "in Igbo this say *father's wealth*."

"We make it so," Malik said, holding the monkey gently against Akunna's tiny heart, her clear sweet eyes locked on his face.

"I match your Igbo name with this story still told by our elders in Podor."

Akunna slept to the sound of her father's Pulaar, like music, whisperings of the three Fulani brothers, Pullo, Bambado, and Labbo, ending as the elders would: *I wasn't there but somebody was*—to which he guided Ebele to respond—*and passed it on to me*.

Though Malik and Ebele would pray for more, Akunna would be their only child. A week after her birth, word came from Calhoun that their beautiful daughter had been listed on his papers as "Kitty Calhoun." This called for more digging, spitting, and sand-kicking.

Akunna Okoro Welé grew fast from suckling to knee baby, already showing signs of Ebele's fire and grit balanced with her father's even temper. Holding Akunna and thinking of his children in Podor, Malik fused his plan to escape by boat, with a single-minded mission to save enough wages to buy freedom for himself, Akunna, and Ebele. He expanded the headquarters on Calhoun's plantation, training others to build. On occasion, he still traveled the string of islands managing boat-building shops and continuing Rise activity with successes and far, far too many failures. Their pirogue business was naturally under constant scrutiny, every move monitored by an overseer, so they kept Rise activities clear and free of waterways, focusing instead on helping new arrivals adjust, and pointing captives to the houses of free Blacks on solid land. When Malik was away, Horace and Crayfish watched over his family, warning Malik against placing too much faith in a promise from Calhoun—freedom papers were more often used to wield rather than surrender power.

Malik and Ebele built new traditions with Akunna; they mixed Pulaar and Igbo to invent their own patois and told stories of the

Fulani and the Igbo. Ebele was not lettered but she insisted that Malik teach Akunna all that he knew. Although she condoned Akunna's request, Malik would not allow his daughter to help fell and hollow out trees for building pirogues. This was men's work.

By her eleventh birthday, Akunna was taller than her mother and helping paint boat designs. She had a talent for making her grandmother's paints. She wore her peach seed monkey as an earring, or strung it into beads worn as a necklace. Due to her constant fear of their girl losing or breaking her charm, Ebele made a new pouch from scraps of leather, wrapping the monkey in cotton bolls. Akunna wore this gris-gris as a necklace for luck and protection.

"She a careful girl," Ebele said, "don't mean her little monkry can't be thiefed or broke. But if oonuh learn she to carve a monkry—that hers from now on."

A short time later, as Akunna helped Malik paint a sideboard, he said to her, "Sometime you sit and stare into the distance, same like me as a boy. My Baaba say: *if you old enough for idleness, you old enough for work.*"

"Baaba—I am good worker." Akunna scraped soot from burned wood as her father stirred the egg yolk and honey. "And strong, too!"

"True? Show me." Malik squeezed her small arm. "Eh-eh! Us daughter *is* strong! Can be your mother speak right. Time done come to learn oonuh our pirogue trade."

"Baaba! This been me dream!"

"How well us know."

"And—oonuh will learn me to carve the monkry?"

"Reckon us gone make both them dreams come true."

Akunna turned fifteen in 1831, with beauty and grace that brought her parents joy and anguish in equal measure. Too often they witnessed daughters of their friends come of age only to fall into gazes and hands of demon daneejos. They kept Akunna busy and away from the main house as much as possible. She was skilled at all aspects of the pirogue business, patient and adept in training others. For this, Malik was proud and grateful, but he cherished even more that she had perfected the art of carving peach seed monkeys. Peaches were as rare as ever, but Akunna had her own connections and managed an ample supply of seeds by trading yea-bigs she and her father carved together.

Once at the close of day, as they packed away tools, she sang to Malik, "Aint me tell oonuh, Baaba? This gal-child be more than meet the eye!"

"True-true. Oonuh work from dayclean to first dark," Malik said, "never been one to flash about, chasin fun—but time gone show: fun got a place, too."

"Baaba. Me got plenty time down this life-road for flash about. Us have good work. Oonuh the one say we boats can't make theyself."

Malik smiled, and they walked home to Ebele's dinner of biscuits, grits, and fried mullet.

Calhoun made more and more demands on Malik's time, often barking about how much work was required for freedom papers. Malik now saw the wisdom in his friends' warning. What was to stop the infidel from changing their agreed price once Malik and Ebele had saved enough? He sensed that this demon of a man held resentment toward him, but how could such a thing be true of a man who had been free all his life?

"Aint got to make no sense," Horace said, "buckruhs got power to haul off and do what so ever they want, just 'cause them can. One thing God done teach a dark man: evil answer to nobody."

Malik learned a new level of evil when the unthinkable came to pass a few months later. The three partners had just begun hollowing out a cypress log. Malik did not speak, coming down with all his might with the hatchet.

"Horace," Crayfish asked, "is you done heard right? Could be they tuck Akunna to work a buckruh fête over to Kiawah Island—or some such."

"Oh I done heard him all right," Horace said, "'cause Calhoun intent on that, so I come tell Malik. That how them high buckruhs do."

That how them buckruhs do—echoed in Malik's head—he came down hard with his hatchet—*devil daneejo traded us precious daughter for two young boys because*—*That how them do*—he felt blood and breath slipping away, like a goat to slaughter—*spineless coward*—*That how them do*—

Akunna had been called away from painting a sideboard, told that her mother needed her in Calhoun's kitchen, and was never seen again.

Three weeks passed, an eternity to Ebele and Malik, who did not give up—he would work and save and find her. His hatchet came down again.

"What place he say?" Malik asked Horace through burning eyes, hatchet resting now. "*What* them call this place where they tuck our Akunna?" He spat these words through clenched teeth.

Horace grimaced. "Aint say no name but them is mention a river. Can't recolleck that name right off. For all us know, she ain't been tuck far."

"But when you ain't know for sure where," Crayfish added, "that's plenty far."

Malik returned to his hatchet blows. Where there be a river, there be boats and a path to freedom.

Calhoun possessed a cunning evil. Malik knew that he must guard his mock freedom to come and go in order to keep strengthening the Rise and find out word of Akunna. These things hinged on a thriving pirogue business. Like creeks and backwater feeding a river and flowing to the sea, all were necessary to his plan.

Horace snapped his fingers and laid a steady hand on his friend's back. "Done thought up that name. It be Sapelo River."

Malik knew rivers. The Senegal and the Doué cradle his precious home. The Cooper and Ashley were innocent waters forced on him by infidels. Now this Sapelo River would someday lead to their beloved Akunna.

48

~

Talk of Altovise's New Year's Eve party had been buzzing around town for weeks, and Bo D had his Mach 1 detailed for the occasion. As he walked around to open the door for Indicca, he checked but saw no sign of the royal blue Chevy C10. He had to admit, the pickup was Anthony's best work yet. His grandfather had been driving the truck around for a couple of weeks, turning heads wherever he went. He was still waiting for a reply to a text sent an hour ago and hoped this most recent lovers' quarrel would not leave him home watching TV with Rockhudson. Indicca stepped out with tiny silver pleats clinging to her curves and showing off her cheerleader legs. She'd dressed him in a black tux with velvet Nehru collar. His jacket had metallic flecks that only revealed themselves in the right light, up close, a perfect backdrop for his peach seed monkey on a new chunky chain.

"Extreme prom," he whispered as they passed the foyer mirror.

"You know it!" she replied, pressing her shoulder into him.

Outdoor and indoor rooms overflowed with guests, who took to heart Altovise's gold-silver-bronze theme; this was to be a night of glitter and glam. Downstairs was transformed into a bedazzled night-club—a festive bar and dance floor surrounded by round tables with white tablecloths and candles. Her grand piano marked center stage and Altovise was stopping traffic in gold sequins, wafting from room to room. Indicca pecked Bo D's cheek before whisking away with two cousins. Perfect timing. His immediate task was straight ahead: his aunts talking with Siman, silver dresses meeting gold velvet jacket.

"Bingo!" Bo D whispered, giving himself points for scoring on Siman's tuxedo, brocade bow tie; all a perfect complement to his peach seed monkey. None of it was lost on the aunts. They were both husband-free at the moment, their men off mingling with some other crowd in the house.

Judging by the way they were caressing Siman's velvet jacket, either they had already had too much champagne or were genuinely interested in getting to know their brother. Bo D couldn't make that claim for his mother yet. She stood back, a lone silver dress sidelined. But he was on a mission, deployed by Olga Dukes, to lead his mother *down the road to acceptance.*

"Here's to Siman!" Mozell said, raising her glass. "It's about time you showed up, since Ourdaddy been calling all of us by your name since day one!"

Bo D moved closer, hoping he wouldn't have to intervene.

"I know that's right," Georgia said, "*how you doin SON . . . What you got there, SON . . .*"

"*And, SON, come go with me to the store . . .*" Mozell added.

This topic haunted Bo D so he was more than relieved to see it was all in good fun. Still, to save himself, and his mother, he joined her on the sidelines, and they slipped away.

§.

A young, hip Gladys Knight tribute band had folks rocking and waving hands with their version of "Midnight Train to Georgia." This helped Siman fall freely into the mercury of his two sisters; girl group minus one—quicksand in silver dresses. No footing, no handles, no up or down. Clearly, Bo D delivering Florida would take time. Siman was eager for their tales of growing up with Fletcher and Maletha because, yes, he was interested in knowing about the woman who should've been Altovise. Gin and tonic helped, but mostly Mozell and Georgia's quickness to accept him gave enough grounding to stand—and flourish!—in their midst. He'd have a colorful report on his next call with Patricia.

He looked around for his parents; no statuesque gold dress in the vicinity, and Fletcher had yet to make an entrance.

Bo D had shared his deployment, and Siman had one of his own. But he needed help. Which sister was most approachable to be his ally? His natural choice was Georgia; with her CPA brain, they had numbers in common. And half a twin was a good start, so Siman drifted toward Georgia, who was now sitting.

"Mind if I join you?"

"Not at all, Big Bro! What's on your mind?"

He pulled up a chair. "Been thinking about the tension between my parental units."

She chuckled. "Is that what you've decided to call them?"

"For lack of more endearing terms." He laughed, too. "But I'm looking to help bridge the gap. Any ideas?"

Georgia studied the question. To Siman, her identical twin face felt like a practice run for actually having a conversation with Florida.

"That's a tall order," she said. "All this merriment can't disguise the tension in every corner of this big ol' house. But. For all intents and purposes, as their one and only common denominator, you're the best bet for bridging that gap."

"You got kids?" he asked.

"Yep, my husband and I have two girls. You?"

"No. But I have a niece and nephew who feel like mine."

"Believe me," Georgia said, "I know that parents and children have secrets they don't even *want* to know about each other."

"For real–for real!" Siman said.

"Altovise is cool. She came by the table right after we got here to chat with us since we only met in passing at Auntie Olga's memorial. And we're working on Florida—but the truth is, how well does any-one really know anyone else? Life's not like reading a novel, where we get to bounce around from head to head!"

Siman would've given a lot to be inside her head at that moment, to know what all the sisters honestly thought about him. Then again, maybe not.

"You make a good point," he said.

"Conundrum for sure," Georgia said, "'cause you want to help bring them back together without getting all up in their Kool-Aid." She sipped champagne.

"You just have to trust your gut, have faith that you'll know what to do." Her face brightened, and she pointed slowly toward the front door. "And speak of the devil—you will get your chance."

Siman turned as Fletcher walked in and headed straight for them.

"Ourdaddy!" Georgia walked toward him. "Look at this, y'all! Ourdaddy bringin' it!"

"Oooo Mr. Fletcher Dukes!" Mozell razzed, "What you gone wear Sunday?"

Siman moved in to bump shoulders as Fletcher swam in their pool of adoration.

"So," Georgia said, "I'll just be the one to come out and say it. We know you been worried, but we met your Altovise and we like her, I mean—how could we not like a woman that can get *you* fitting into all this glitz and glamour!"

"Goodness, Georgia," Mozell chided, "could you be any less discreet?"

"That's all right," Fletcher said, "this *was* all her doing—in cahoots with Denzel Washington."

"Well, you look fantastic and this is for you," Mozell said, putting a flute of sparkling cider in her father's hand.

"Thanks, son," he said, looking around.

Siman and his sisters volleyed a knowing smirk. Fletcher set down his glass and struck a serious note.

"Where's your sister?"

"I know where she is," Georgia said. "Be right back."

"You looking mighty sharp, Siman!" Fletcher said as Mozell looked on. "Always have liked bow ties, but they don't like me—looks like you found a two-for-one."

"Yep." Siman adjusted his tie. "Butterfly and arrow edge. I have Bo D to thank, he took me to the mall. And after I talked him out of a full-on bling jacket—and vest—I bought everything he picked for me."

"My nephew did good!" Mozell jumped in. "But I don't know, Siman, I'm thinking you should've looked to Ourdaddy for wardrobe advice. He is sharp as a mosquito's peter!"

"Wup!" She touched Siman's shoulder. "Beg pardon, Big Bro, I guess I don't know you well enough for that kinda talk."

"It's all good." Siman laughed with the group to cover up any signs of blushing.

The Gladys band finished with "If I Were Your Woman," and in between bands, DJ house music switched to jazz.

Georgia finally returned, arm linked with her twin's.

Siman noticed a shift in temperature. His father seemed nervous, as if he was preparing to make a speech, so Siman stepped off to the side. Fletcher motioned for him to step back into their circle.

Fletcher addressed his daughters. "While I got all three of y'all in one place, I can take care of some business that took a wrong turn."

He handed out three small tan suede pouches from his breast pocket, each with a name tag, scribbled in his chicken scratch.

Fletcher's voice was thin. Siman wondered if his sisters could pinpoint exactly which *daddyvoice* this was. Then again, maybe they were hearing this timbre for the first time, too.

Fletcher went on. "I should've listened to Olga and your mama telling me for years and years to change the tradition."

The daughters were speechless. Cells of their silence floated on soft jazz music and their father's sudden pageantry and remorse. In this void, isolated and fragile, three bubbles hovered momentarily. Then, as cells are fated to do, they migrated until they joined with their brother's tension to form a new body: a mass of collective hush.

"These been in Mama's jewelry box all these years," Florida said, breaking the silence.

Siman studied Georgia's face.

"That's right," Fletcher said.

"Oh. Oh. Oh." Georgia sat her flute down to cradle the little monkey. "And *now* you give us these precious monkeys? Now? At the rusty ages of forty-four and," she turned to her older sister, "how old are you, Mozell?"

"Forty-six."

"Well, if you don't want it, give back." Fletcher held out his hand.

"Oh that's rich, Ourdaddy," Georgia said, shaking her head. "Rich indeed."

"It's not that we don't want them, Ourdaddy," Mozell stepped in, "you know we've wanted them our whole lives."

"Just put yourself in our shoes." Georgia came back in. "First of all, finding out after all these years that you *did* break your boy club tradition for somebody outside the family—but you couldn't break for your own daughters!"

"I was eighteen," Fletcher said, "and didn't know my ass from a hole in the ground."

"But one would think you would have figured out which end was up by the time we were thirteen. Boy, it's a good thing Mama never knew about a monkey with diamond eyes."

"Hold up now, Georgia," Mozell said. "You 'bout to cross a line."

Siman felt like a nosy neighbor who'd walked in on a family feud.

"Let me finish, let me finish," Georgia added. "Like you just said, Ourdaddy, think about how hard Mama and Auntie fought to have us included in your rite of passage. But not even they talked to *us* about what *we* were feeling at the time."

"Actually," Mozell said, "I talked to Mama about that."

Georgia cocked her head. "Oh you did?!"

"Yes, I did. When I turned thirteen. She told me that everything she, Auntie Olga, and other women on both sides did with us and for us was like a *perpetual rite of passage*."

"Perpetual rite-of-passage, huh?" Georgia said.

Siman wished he could rescue his father, but he also knew silence was his best tactic. Clearly, there was no place for testosterone in this discussion.

"Yeah," Mozell said. "I remembered it because that's where I learned the word 'perpetual.'"

"So why didn't they package this alleged perpetual rite-of-passage like the men did with the boys?"

"That I don't know." Mozell was snappish.

Florida walked silently away.

"Now where you goin'?" Georgia called after her.

Her twin threw up a palm and kept walking.

"So typical," Georgia shouted, "walk away when the gittin' gets good."

"Onethingaboutit," Fletcher said, "better late than never." He chugged the apple cider. "And seem like all y'all need to switch to cider." He placed his flute on the table and excused himself.

Siman registered Georgia's cynical smirk as she examined her peach seed monkey.

"Welcome to the family," she said. They clinked glasses. "Sorry for this crash course."

"That's champagne talking," Mozell cut in, "you so focused on this physical thing, you forgetting your manners and your place. Don't nobody need to be out here trying to cut Ourdaddy off at the knees this late in the game—and especially not in front of his son."

"Oh my God, Mozell! The patriarchy is strong!" Georgia relented.

"Georgia. Stop that shit!" Mozell whispered loudly. "That man showed up every fucking day of our lives." She turned to Siman, saying more calmly, "When they were starting out, Mama and Ourdaddy held up the poverty line with two hands, while building the roof over our heads and putting food on the table with the other two." She turned back to Georgia, "So you cut him some slack!"

Georgia rubbed the peach seed monkey between the fingers of her free hand. Siman kept eyes downcast.

"All this?" Georgia added, taking a step back, "is exactly why I moved to Tucson. Pays to keep family at a manageable distance."

"You preaching to the choir," Mozell said, and gave her sister a motherly squeeze. "This shit is complicated. Fix yourself, baby sister, and apologize to Ourdaddy."

Mozell rejoined the New Year's revelry, leaving Siman and his new ally. What could he say?

They were all justified in their feelings, and Maletha was right to focus on raising girls to be strong women. From what he had learned from Fletcher, and felt throughout their house, Maletha had modeled her own fight instinct. Not unlike Altovise.

Ironically, he had come by his monkey through his parents' secret wrench in the tradition, a singularity that epitomized his sisters' revolt. And all these years, he had a talisman and tradition apart from his birth family, while his sisters had an excess of family, no talisman, and a tradition they couldn't yet recognize.

He had already figured Patricia's summation: blood relations just don't get that family is a gift you don't rip open with a knife.

Siman was surprised at how Georgia turned on a dime.

"Glad that's over," she said. "Let's get back to *your* mission. Sounds like much more fun!"

"Are you sure you're OK to help me—I mean, after what just—"

"That's water under the bridge." She polished off her glass. "Man! This stuff is good! Wait. Is this champagne, champagne? 'Cause I feel like your mother would be pouring the real deal—don't you?"

"Yep." He couldn't help but laugh. "I have to agree with you there."

"OK. Look at Ourdaddy." Georgia pointed. "He's trying to be cool, but you know he's looking for that gold dress."

"Clearly," Siman shifted gears to keep up, "and how am I supposed to get those two in the same room?"

"Don't you worry." She patted his shoulder. "That's where your sisters can help." She took out her phone. "Give me your number."

❦

Fletcher had arrived over an hour late and hardly recognized Altovise's house or his reflection when he slipped past her foyer mirror. He had come close to leaving Tom Ford's knock-off hanging in his closet next to his funeral suit, and watching westerns with Rock, but he couldn't turn his back on his plan to deliver the monkeys. Now he wished he had opted for *Gunsmoke* and *Bonanza*. He expected such rage from Florida, but—even though he shook it off and stomped it down—having it come from Georgia had thrown him off. She never could hold her liquor. At first, he was surprised to see Siman with his sisters, and then pleased, figuring it would help ease his fatherly nerves. But within seconds he was wishing he could help the poor man escape. Now he looked across at Georgia and her brother, heads together, thick as thieves, and gave up on figuring any of it out.

He ordered another cider and moved room to room like a man all dressed up with no place to go. He was glad to see Bo D with Indicca, looking spiffy and hanging on to each other. Tyrone with a boyfriend made his stomach a little queasy. He felt a familiar tinge of sadness, knowing Olga would have delivered a Berber saying to quell his bias.

With his first order of business behind him, he moved into the festivities with caution, until he finally spotted his number two goal, straight ahead at two o'clock: gold dress.

Across the room, Altovise and Vada talked with their brother, Thaddeus, who sat at a table with Deke and Tonk. Fletcher made his way over to test the waters.

"Son-of-a-gun." Thaddeus pivoted in his wheelchair. "If it ain't

Duke Dukes himself! I ain't seen you in a hundred years, and Al's so stingy with the light, can't hardly see you now." Thaddeus extended his hand. "Put it here, young man!"

"You looking good, Thaddeus!" Their palms met in a soul shake.

"I don't know 'bout all that." Thaddeus slapped his knee. "As you can see, my get up and go, done got up and went. But I'm still here. And I have a toast—"

They all raised glasses. "To my baby sister! The illustrious Altovise—and—my new nephew Siman," he scanned the room, "wherever he is: just enough for one, not enough for two, I'll drink this, and hand the glass back to you!"

Over roars of laughter Altovise shook her head in playful disapproval. "Thaddeus Benson, you still ain't no count!"

She turned to Fletcher and dropped a quiet, friendly, "I'm glad you came."

"I'm glad I came, too."

"I saw the girls and Siman making over you." She smiled but kept her distance. "Didn't I tell you that suit would be a hit?"

If she only knew.

She floated away, glitter in motion. Is that why he voted that she go backless? His reward every time she walked away?

A showcase of Eusi Arts musicians continued; from soul, R&B to jazz, pop, American Indian fusion, and hip-hop. Since Georgia apologized and moved on from her ambush, Fletcher loosened his tie and danced a few times with his out-of-town daughters. Then he sat with them, enjoying a plate of food. He wondered about Florida's whereabouts but didn't want to sour the moment.

Then Mozell launched right in. "Florida's situation is escalating. How do we nip this thing in the bud?"

"I knew we were headed for problems when she wouldn't ride with us," Georgia said, "because she wanted to drop by Greater Goshen and hear the first Watch Night sermon. So I don't know where and when she tanked up but—"

"She drunk?" Fletcher asked.

"Very," the daughters agreed.

"—an accident waiting to happen," Mozell added.

Fletcher knew that was a bad sign, because Florida was good at controlling her liquor.

"I'll go talk to her," Fletcher said.

"Definitely not," Georgia said. "Florida ain't no teenager and this is not for you to worry about. We will handle her."

"Right," Mozell said, "you should focus on Siman. I think he headed for the library."

"C'mon, Ourdaddy." Georgia looked at her phone and stood. "Let's all go up there for a change of scenery."

The library was empty except for Siman and Altovise. Fletcher paused before entering; Mozell and Georgia claimed points of a triangle. He knew an intervention when he saw one.

"Ourdaddy," Georgia said, "just keep an open mind; go on in. We'll be downstairs."

"I promise this won't take long," Siman said to Fletcher, walking closer. "Please come on in."

Fletcher took a seat at a small chess table, looking across the spacious room at Altovise. He felt a rush of every daydream he'd had about her in that dress since he first saw her in it. As hard as it was, he wanted to keep giving her space and time.

"Whew. Little more nervous than expected." Siman stood in front of the fireplace. "But there's no time like the present 'cause none of us is getting any younger!"

All three laughed, and Fletcher asked Altovise, "You OK with all this?"

"I think so." She folded then unfolded her arms. "We'll see."

"OK, well." Siman gestured alternately between Fletcher and Altovise. "Not being a parent myself, I can only speak from one side of this, but one thing I've been hearing a lot since I got here is that parents and offspring have necessary secrets. And I want to guard that for us. It's normal, and I want normal. But also, after forty-nine years of not getting what we want, I want us to have our cake and eat it, too, as much as that is possible. We're together here against some pretty insane odds—from the point of view of us mere mortals, that is." He ran the monkey charm along its chain. "Of course, from our little talisman's point of view, our finding each other was just business as usual."

Fletcher smiled and caught Altovise's eye. They had not been alone together in nearly a month. He missed her and was too engulfed in their silent glances and subtle gestures to see that Siman was paving a road.

Siman went on. "I'm guessing some well-seasoned secrets have created this gap between you, and after this much time, I couldn't imagine there wouldn't be. You don't have to say a word. I'm just hoping we can close this gap right here," he drew an imaginary capsule between his parents, "and if I can be a light, to shine on your path back to each other, then please—let me be that."

Unclear on what had changed for Altovise, Fletcher was surprised by what came next.

"That's beautiful, Siman," Altovise said, "and we both appreciate how hard this was for you—and your sisters, bless them—and I hope you know that this gap, as you're calling it, has nothing to do with you. We're both thrilled that you're here."

"She's right, son," Fletcher said.

Siman was glad his sisters had not heard that.

Altovise stood. "You should also know that Fletcher and I have no hard feelings toward each other, that's not what this is. You hit the nail on the head: after this much time, how can there not be some rough waters to cross? But—I have no doubt that we'll get to solid ground."

She crossed over to join hands with Siman and motioned for Fletcher to join them. "Thanks for this, Siman—and now—we've got a new year to ring in!"

An hour before midnight, Fletcher and Siman were playing chess in the library. The room was now alive with men talking trash, drinking, slapping dominos and checkers. Fletcher noticed one of Altovise's set designers walk in.

"Mr. Dukes, I've been sent to usher you to your private table."

"Oooooo," Siman exclaimed.

Within minutes, Fletcher sat alone at a table for two near the stage. On Altovise's piano sat a giant hourglass, lit from within. It would run out of sand at exactly midnight as nets attached to ceiling hooks released a shimmery backdrop of bronze, gold, and silver streamers.

An indigo spotlight burgeoned, bringing an instant hush, then faded to rose gold, following Altovise as she returned to her piano, composed. Her slow, lilting voice, grounded in Nina and Odetta, spread through silence as she sang her ballad "More Than a Notion." After two or three measures she brought in keys soon followed by bass, sax, and drums, siphoning power from beneath her feet each time she dipped down for a note, then turned and slid upward. Thrilled, Fletcher looked out at the audience, each soul joining him, floating inside Altovise's voice, never losing trust in a solid landing. His feet kept time as the crowd erupted in applause.

A quickened pace kept people dancing to favorite covers and climaxed with Altovise's Grammy-winning "Shake 'Til You Knock the Blue Do' Down."

A standing ovation brought on a reprieve. After a second ovation, she talked over applause, whoops, and whistles.

"Thank you! Thank you, everybody . . . thank you . . . not much more we can say—thank you—y'all sit down! Sit down now!

"We only have a few minutes left on this hourglass and there's one more song I have to do."

Altovise followed her bass player and drummer who harmonized the opening chorus.

> *I can't stop loving you*
> *I made up my mind*

Older folks swooned, hands waving high. Fletcher held her gaze, exposed and rooted in memory. This had been their song in high school; they turned up the radio volume every time; first ones on the dance floor whenever it played.

Last notes floated out to more cheers, and Altovise bowed toward Fletcher, who was smiling and applauding.

"OK, y'all, we're almost there!" Altovise said. "Servers are coming around with champagne and sparkling cider so we can get 2013 rung in!"

"Here you go, Ourdaddy." Georgia appeared and handed him a flute of cider. "Looks like it's all gold," she snickered, "I mean all good?!"

"All good." Fletcher raised his glass. "What about Florida? Is she with y'all?"

"Yeah, we got her. Don't you worry."

The band launched into "Auld Lang Syne," waving hands to invite guests to join in; and then a chorus-loud din filled the room as neon numbers appeared inside the hourglass, counting down: "Ten-Nine-Eight . . ."

At midnight, Fletcher wanted to step up on the stage and kiss Altovise in a storm of confetti and balloons, but he waited for her to make the first move. She stepped down and pecked him on the lips. She wasn't ready for more, but that didn't stop him from fast-forwarding to liquid gold pooling at her feet as soon as all these people went home.

As the final band set up, Altovise took off her shoes and rested, talking with a group of Eusi board members. He was headed her way when he saw Georgia and Mozell rushing toward the kitchen and joined them.

Florida pointed a shaky finger at Bo D, who was standing between her and Siman.

"What you think?" she slurred.

"Ma, don't do this," Bo D said.

Fletcher ordered Bo D to leave and take Siman with him.

"That's enough, Florida," Mozell said, grabbing her sister's arm.

"Naw, naw—" Florida leaned on Mozell, pointing toward Siman's back.

Georgia took her other arm. "Let's go."

"Damn," Florida sneered. "All y'all act like his shit don't stink."

Fletcher followed his daughters out onto the sunporch, a small room drenched in evergreens and tiny white lights.

"Naw, le-leave me alone," Florida insisted, tearing up. "I-I'm not through." She tried jerking her hand away.

"Yes you are, baby. You are so through." Mozell was firm. "Shut your mouth, sweetheart, and sit down right here."

Florida sat in a rocking chair looking out on Cromartie Lake.

Mozell handed her a glass of water. "Drink. All of it."

Florida obeyed and Georgia handed her a face cloth. Fletcher raised his chin toward the door and Georgia and Mozell left. Florida turned toward Fletcher, her voice watery with regret, mascara running.

"Ourdaddy, I'm sorry for mistreating your lady friend. And Mama is turning over in her grave at how I been acting like a fool about your son."

"I'm the one that's sorry," Fletcher said, "you been taking care of me since your Mama died, and I been turning my back on you for just as long."

Florida took deep breaths, burying her face in the wet cloth. She leaned toward him, like a child.

Fletcher rested his forearms on his knees. "Look here. You know in this family we don't deal in fractions—no half-this and half-that. Siman is y'all's brother. Period. And we have to deal with it."

"I know. And his mother is perfect for you. Mama would like her."

"You think so?"

"Yep. I do." She slowly rocked back and nearly chirped. "And you know what else?"

"What." Fletcher sat back, too.

"Remember what *you* told *me* that first night Bo D was at the hospital—how God already forgave me and I need to forgive myself?"

"Yeah. You still need to do that."

She poked him. "Well—you need to practice what you preach."

"Is that right?"

"That's right." Now she had an impish smile, teetering between euphoria and weariness. "I been noticing you—walking round like *you* did something wrong—but Siman don't need to forgive you. You didn't even know he existed so you ain't done nothing wrong. And God know that, too."

Fletcher twirled his totem cuff link. He was an imposter again. All that glamour came crashing down. He removed his bronze tie and dropped it in his pocket. Once again, Olga had words to fit this scenario. Right before he had Bo D's junk cars and truck towed, she'd told him: *We're all out here fighting for one thing or another. Show your teeth when you're favored to win; show your belly to concede your loss; and show your hands when you're ready to work things out.*

Florida looked out at the lake and fell silent.

"Come on," he said, opening his palm. "I'm taking you home."

She stood and took his hand. "I'll forgive me if you forgive you."

"Deal."

He steadied her as they walked silently, then closed his Chevy truck's passenger door, and she nestled in. He took out his cell phone, thinking about a gold sequined dress.

He looked back at Florida. She was not nodding off, as he had expected. She held up her peach seed monkey, turning it in the warm dome light, smiling.

He typed a text.

FD: leave the light on

Be right back.

The reply was immediate.

> AB: with the motor
> running?

Upon his river of regret, Fletcher set a boat to sail. Her name was Forgiveness.

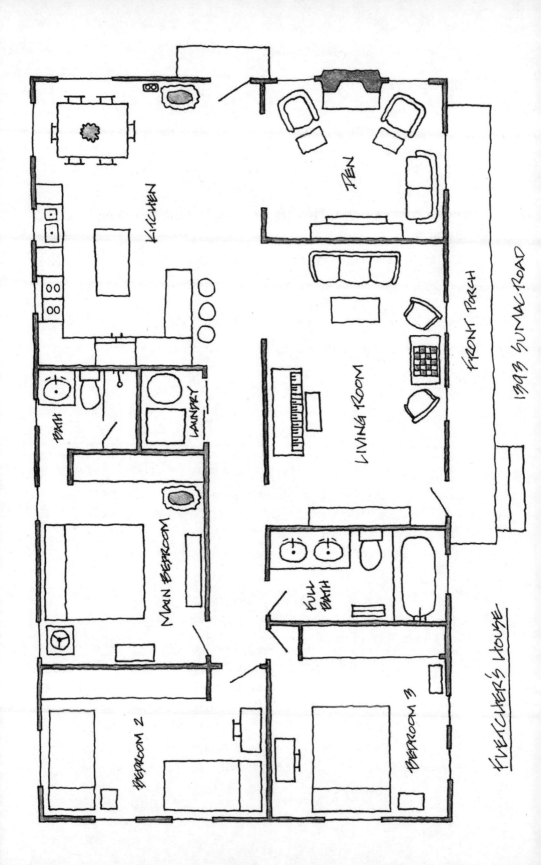

Acknowledgments

In one way or another, many people helped bring this book out into the world. While it is not possible to list each and every soul, I've done my level best to include those who deserve special mention. For all events, omens, harbingers, and connections along the fourteen-year journey it took to get this story between covers, I am humbled and grateful.

To my family for their respect and support: Robert Michael Roehrick, my husband and first discerning reader/editor, for also providing expert graphic design help to this day. Miranda Irene Jones Roehrick, our daughter, diligent reader and muse, the original "Cricket" and her late Granmama's namesake, who grew to maturity alongside this story.

Steve Ross, my agent. Across miles and through a pandemic, serendipity ordained that we would work together. Your astute edits truly did "dress the manuscript in its Sunday best" for the marketplace.

Retha Powers, my editor, the longitude and latitude of this book, who elevated the story while remaining true to my world-building voice and mission.

Amy Einhorn, Sarah Crichton, and the entire team at my publisher, Henry Holt & Co., especially *The Peach Seed* team working in front of and behind the scenes. I feel honored and respected as an artist: Hannah Campbell, Ally Demeter, Judi Gaelick, Meryl Sussman Levavi, Shelly Perron, Jason Reigal, Lulu Schmieta, Alyssa Weinberg, Natalia Ruiz, Carolyn O'Keefe, and Laura Flavin.

A. J. Verdelle, a master in the art of literary revision, who believed in and helped guide this work from its earliest days. Hedgebrook Women Writers' Retreat, Headlands Center for the Arts, Barbara Kingsolver and PEN/Bellwether Prize for Socially Engaged Fiction, Resora at Cypress Pond, the Leesburg Stockade Stolen Girls, PureSaginaw.com, Celeste Di Iorio, Pura Fé, SNCC Digital Gateway, Saginaw Rowing Club, Dakar Eats, Crmvet.org, Point Reyes National Seashore, Homeward Bound of Marin, Book Passage bookstore, Left Coast Writers, Paula Farmer of Silent Water Productions, Cynthia Ladd-Viti for being a confidante and personal stylist along this journey, Mark Batson and Sealhenry Samuel for their inspiring lyrics ("... time threw a prayer to me" from "Love's Divine"), *Poets & Writers*, Thierry Kehou, Lauren Cerand, *Elle*, LibraryCall, *Shelf Awareness*.

A host of friends and authors from the 2011 Student Nonviolent Coordinating Committee (SNCC) Fiftieth Anniversary: Carolyn DeLoatch, Rutha Harris, Dr. Rachel Henry, Annette Jones, the late Charles Jones, Jayne Kelley, the late Charles Sherrod, Shirley Sherrod, Russia Sherrod, Bernice Johnson Reagon, Dennis Roberts, Penny Patch, Erma Wilburn, Curtis Williams, Deloris Spears, Carol Barner Seay. Peter de Lissovoy, *The Great Pool Jump*; Danny Lyon, *Memories of the Southern Civil Rights Movement*; Lee Formwalt,

Looking Back, Moving Forward: The Southwest Georgia Freedom Struggle, 1814–2014; Mary Royal Jenkins, *Open Dem Cells: A Pictorial History of the Albany Movement.*

Research consultations: Ambakisye-Okang Dukuzumurenyi, PhD; American Federation for the Blind; Sam Odawo; Betsy Watkins; Dan Roberts; Julius and the late Cornelia Bailey; Caesar and Nancy Banks; Chris R. Calladine; Alisa Clancy; Bill Merriman, Sapelo Island Ferry, Darien, Georgia; Dr. Hamé Watt; *Woodcarving Illustrated* forum: Whittlin' John and Big John; the late Richard "Dick" Dietrich for his website Carving Peach Pits.

Family and friends for inspiration, support and research: Alphonso-Gibbs Family, Robin Alderson, Alphonso-Gibbs family, Derek Anderson, Dan Babior, Kathryn Barcos, Wyna Barron, Tavi Black, Holly Blake, Nancy Boutilier, Bernice Bowen-Montgomery, Francine Caldwell, Sara Campos, Corine Carter Cato, Christa Champion and Mary Craig, Gloria Chapman, Nancy Culhane, Dr. Dervin Cunningham, Lashon Daley, Flora Devine, Johnny Mack Devine, the late Malcolm Devine, Wyndolyn Edwards, Kathleen Emory, Betsy Fasbinder, Tom and Diane Ferlatte, Tura Franzen, Andreas Freund, Tatjana Freund, the late Kim Gagnon and our Mother-Daughter Book Club, Angie Garner, Doreen Gounard, Constance Hale, Mrs. Rubye Hampton: my first English teacher, Fannie Hayes, LeShawn Holcomb, Judith Eloise Hooper, the late Howard "Doc" Hughes, Ethel Johnson, Mildred and Ditanya Jones, Michael H. Jones: for details of his time among the tires, Dr. Robert Jones, Kenneth Jones, Ann and Joselyn Jordan, Reverend Van Jordan, Ben Kirkland, Lisa Law, Karen Lindquist, Karen Lynch, John MacLeod, Marilyn Mackel, Suzanne McIntosh, Cheryl McLaughlin, Saundra McLester, Bill Meyer, Joe Niesyn, Lauren Norton, Tom Okie, Cherilyn Parsons, Paula Pilecki, Maurice Pollard, Camille Pressley, Lucy Puls, Shimi Rahim, the late James "Jaime" Redford, Pam Redmond, the late Barbara Roehrick, Charles Roehrick, the late Greg Roehrick, Deborah Santana, Natasha Singh, Bill Socolov, Dottie Stone, Derrick Stovall, John Trout, Nicola Viti, Leslie Wardle, Angela Washington, Marion Weinreb, Roland Williams, and Pamela Winfrey.

Book trailer cast and crew: Author and friend Annie Spiegelman, D'Adonis Moquette, Alex Ajayi, Cynthia Ladd-Viti, Brahna Stone, Yoel Iskindir, De'Meir Calmese, Bennie Lewis, Chidinma Ukoha Kalu, Keonte Turner, Symil Austen, Doonie Love, Kavin Chan, Christian Smith, Tehan Davis, Joel Tejada, Tate Weathers, Will Fallet, Claire Austen, Taylor Lambert of Aura Casting, and Richie Blasco.

For hosting writing respites and private readings: Erv and Juanita Scott, Reverend Clifford and Mary Alice Jones Browner, Kip and Sara Howard, Don and Lyn Klein, Catherine Bacon and Ed Krayer, and Vivian Poole.

Deep gratitude for each faithful *Peach Seed Monkey* and Anita Gail Jones blog follower through the years and around the globe.

Eternal thanks for generations of devoted activists who served and continue to serve in southwest Georgia's continuing struggles for human rights and equality. May more of their untold stories find a lighted path.

About the Author

Anita Gail Jones is a visual artist and writer born and raised in Albany, Georgia. She is a Hedgebrook alumna and was a 2018–19 affiliate artist at the Headlands Center for the Arts. *The Peach Seed*, her debut, was selected as a 2021 top ten finalist for the PEN/Bellwether Prize for Socially Engaged Fiction.